REBEL BLADE

"Fuck you," Siyon growled, leaning harder against his own need, pulling with the weight of a city. "I'm Siyon Velo, and we know about me and the impossible."

We knew. Izmirlian knew. As though the thought was a summoning, the faintest whisper of a voice came into Siyon's mind. *Are you buying the city with your life?*

He was trying *not* to, but he would, if he had to. If it came to that. If there was no other way.

By Davinia Evans

The Burnished City

Notorious Sorcerer
Shadow Baron
Rebel Blade

REBEL BLADE

The Burnished City: Book Three

DAVINIA EVANS

orbit-books.co.uk

ORBIT

First published in Great Britain in 2024 by Orbit

13 5 7 9 10 8 6 4 2

Copyright © 2024 by Davinia Evans

Excerpt from *The Last Hour Between Worlds* by Melissa Caruso
Copyright © 2024 by Melissa Caruso

Map by Sámhlaoch Swords

The moral right of the author has been asserted.

A CIP catalogue record for this book
is available from the British Library.

ISBN 978-0-356-51871-8

Printed and bound in Great Britain by
Clays Ltd, Elcograf, S.p.A.

Papers used by Orbit are from well-managed forests
and other responsible sources.

Orbit
An imprint of
Little, Brown Book Group
Carmelite House
50 Victoria Embankment
London EC4Y 0DZ

An Hachette UK Company
www.hachette.co.uk

orbit-books.co.uk

For Sam (born to live la vida bravi)

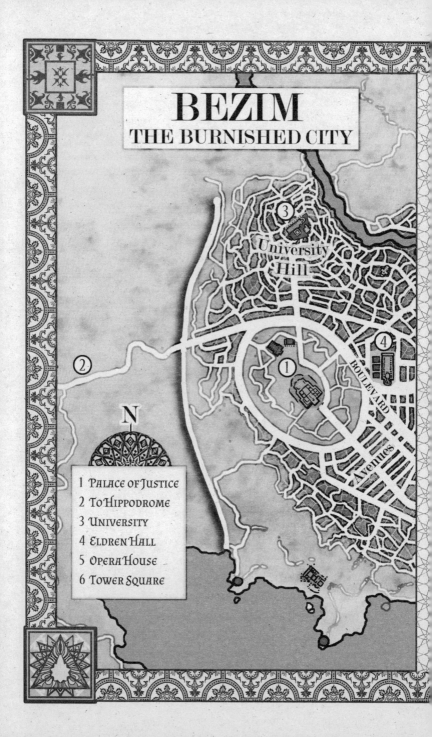

BEZIM
THE BURNISHED CITY

University Hill

N

1 PALACE OF JUSTICE
2 TO HIPPODROME
3 UNIVERSITY
4 ELDREN HALL
5 OPERA HOUSE
6 TOWER SQUARE

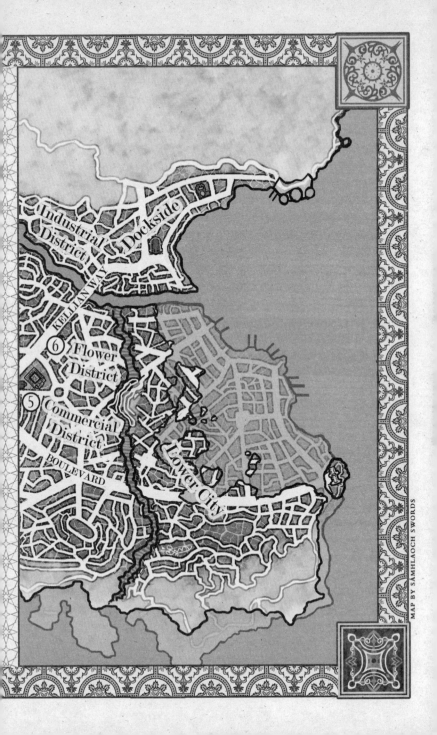

MAP BY SAMHLAOCH SWORDS

CHAPTER 1

Down by the hotmarket, there were bloodgulls competing with the mud-spattered alleycanal kids for discards and charity (and brazen theft). Siyon perched on a nearby arcade, feet braced wide in the gutter so his skewer of still-sizzling squid wouldn't drip on his boots (though they'd seen worse recently). One of the gulls landed on a nearby girder, cocking a hopeful eye his way.

Not close enough for him to lay hands on, of course. But close enough for him to be sure. It gleamed, to Siyon's stranger sight. And its legs and feet were definitely *red*. Red like the blood spilled in the gruesome murder of Papa Badrosani by the Bitch Queen's underlings, twenty-odd years ago. The blood a flock of gulls had landed in, shrieking and flapping and driving the murderers away until Mama and her sons had come to retrieve the body. The gulls had been stained by Papa's rage and vengeance.

Or so said the alleytales. Siyon would have sworn the Badrosani had spread them to enhance their own power. But this wasn't the only story currently popping out of the nooks and crannies of Bezim's long history and many strange beliefs. And if Siyon didn't stamp and hiss, this *story* was going to steal the last of his lunch.

"Hey!" one of the kids called, from down on the street, all mud spatter and sharp eyes. "Grab the gull. The gutter alchemists pay good money for 'em; we'll split."

1

Too late. The gull took off with a frantic swipe of white wings, clawing its way over the skeletal remainder of the arcade's crumpled dome.

The kid spat a curse that would have had Siyon's ears boxed at that age, but there were no grown-ups in sight to be bothered with these children. Except, possibly, the gutter alchemists or other lower city folk they delivered to.

"Here." The kid squinted up at Siyon. "Do I know you?"

"That's what your mum asked," Siyon shot back, but he was already pushing up from the gutter.

Because a kid who was willing to risk the rage and parasites of a lower city gull for the profit would *definitely* sell out the Sorcerer Velo. If not to the Council (bit high to reach) or to the inquisitors (because even down here, they had standards) then probably to Mama Badrosani. The cruel and callous queen of the lower city and all its scrambling poverties was making no secret of wanting to get her heavy-ringed hands on him.

Just to talk, she'd suggested, in a message carefully filtered through Redick, sergeant of the Awl Quarter bravi. Like Siyon was going to believe that. He'd lived down here for years, between fleeing Dock-side and scraping a place in the Little Bracken bravi. He'd learned his first scraps of alchemy down here, from practitioners who patched up the bruises, cuts, and broken limbs of those who'd *talked* with the Badrosani. And if Siyon had learned one thing from the events of Salt Night, months ago...

Well, if he'd learned *one* thing, it was the extent of how badly he could fuck things up. Waking a dragon who trashed a quarter of the upper city, including the Palace of Justice itself, was a new low, even for him, but Siyon wasn't going to make the mistake of thinking he'd found something he couldn't top.

But he'd *also* learned that he truly, desperately, utterly didn't want to get anywhere near the barons. Probably none of the others were actually a centuries-old and stretched-to-insanity manifestation of a promise to the last Power of the Mundane... but why risk it?

As Siyon leapt to his feet, the kid shouted an alert, and another urchin popped up behind the rooftop gazebo—far closer than Siyon had realised. Panic sparked in his heels, and he scrambled in the other direction, up and over the peak of the next roof.

When he glanced back, there was far more distance than there should have been between him and the kid, staring agape. Between them, burning bronze footprints slowly faded from the roof tiles.

Fuck, it had happened again.

Siyon gritted his teeth, tugged at his satchel strap—slung across his body to be secure when he had to run—and kept going. He swung down inside the gutted arcade through a gap in the roof, and then out a window to cross a shallow, muddy canal on a scavenged plank bridge. On rooftops and makeshift paths and cutting through buildings, Siyon worked down toward the sludgy, sinking, tilting buildings by the water, where the bay had bitten hard into the fallen city.

The kids hadn't followed, but he still took a circuitous route home. Mama Badrosani was watching, after all. Not to mention the bloodgulls. Alleytales said they reported straight to her; that's how she knew everything that went on in the lower city. Siyon didn't think she needed that, when every runner and thug and dodgy trader in the entire place was in hock to her one way or another.

He still kept a cautious eye on the pale winter sky.

Blame that—and half his mind still chewing on bloodgulls and other manifestations of magic—for Siyon not noticing the voices *before* he swung in through the once-second-storey window they used as their main entrance.

In the dim and dank interior, where the floor was warped by the damp that also crept in darkening waves up the walls, two people turned to look at him. Mayar had that sharp look on their face, like they might launch straight into insisting Siyon practice meditating, or moving a cup with his mind.

Like that had worked *at all* since he'd first woken up after Salt Night.

The other person was a fish from the school of every man Siyon had grown up around in Dockside—hair trimmed short to avoid getting tangled in rigging and nets; rough clothes faded to grey by salt and wind and washing; mud medallion on a short leather thong at his neck. Impossible to guess his age. The sea took very little time to beat everyone into the same hard-worn mien.

"And here he is now," Mayar said.

"No." Siyon considered climbing right back out the window again. But this was his home. Or at least his temporary squat in a totally decrepit building no one else wanted. "Whatever you think I can do for you: No."

The *other* reason he'd prefer if no one knew where to find him: so people would stop asking him to fix every single problem they had. With *magic*.

The Dockside sailor squared his shoulders, like he was setting himself to haul in the nets. "Fine. I'll ask the mudwitches."

"Wait." Mayar stepped between them. "Both of you, wait. Velo—" And Siyon didn't like using that name in front of a Dockside man, but it wasn't like there was any secret to his provenance. "This good captain wants protections placed on his boat. A whaling vessel, he says. One particularly at risk from the monsters of the deep."

Siyon wanted to scoff at the superstitions of sailors, who'd traded tall tales of those very monsters when he'd been small and gullible enough to listen wide-eyed. Stories of tentacled monstrosities, or long and scaled worms, or just massive fuck-off fish. Now he was older, and taller, and knew the world.

Knew he might have made those monsters real.

Mayar had warned him, that the wisdom of the Khanates suggested it might be good that Mother Sa slumbered. That there had been wonders, but also monsters, in her world. Too bad Siyon had woken her, good and proper.

"You seen the dragon out there?" Siyon shot over Mayar's shoulder, not quite as flippant as he sounded.

"Not yet," the whaling captain replied.

"The mudwitches of Dockside can't help you with that," Mayar continued, as though neither of them had spoken. "They are limited to the mud and the people thereof. But Master Velo has access to far greater resources." They fixed Siyon with a look. "And why would he have them, if not to use them?"

Siyon ground his teeth, and didn't repeat any of the things he'd said the last time they'd had this argument. That using the resources was how he got into this mess. That he still had no idea what he was doing. That the city was skittish enough about him without him prancing around adding extra bait to the bucket.

But mostly because he was starting to wonder if the answer to why he had these powers was just that he'd been the only one. That he wasn't the *best* choice, or even a *good* one. That this was all a desperate mistake.

"Also," Mayar added quietly to Siyon, "we need the money."

Unfortunately true. They didn't pay rent, but food wasn't cheap down here, if you wanted anything other than questionable fish. Siyon certainly wasn't claiming his stipend from the Council any longer.

Siyon sagged against the water-warped sill of the window he still hadn't quite finished climbing through. "Fine."

The captain had brought his boat over to the Awl Quarter docks— for the ease of Master Velo, he said, with an emphasis that suggested he knew why Siyon might be avoiding his clan. The boat was called *Bessie*; he didn't offer his own name on the muddy slog around the bay.

Once this area had been the beating heart of Bezim, bustling with the trade of the most prestigious docks. Now it was old tenements with their lower floors soaked through and washed away, and fruit bats roosting in the mangroves that burst up through the old shopping arcades. The only sign of old glory was a fringe along the riverbank, where the Awl Quarter made their safehouse in the old ferry terminal.

Amid their elaborately carved gondolas bumping at the pier, the whaling boat stood out like an osprey among gulls. She wasn't a pretty thing, but she was solid, and well maintained, and had vicious-looking harpoons mounted fore and aft. Worth protecting. If Siyon could figure out how.

It wasn't that he didn't have power. He could barely sleep for it, sloshing and surging around him, tugging at every part of him like an urgent toddler. It came zipping out when he least expected it—like it had earlier, on the roof with the urchins.

5

But using it consciously had so far eluded Siyon entirely.

Mayar pestered him constantly to practice—pushing a cup, or lighting a candle, or wringing a little damp out of their walls. This wasn't a cup, or even a building no one cared about. This was some- one's livelihood. Someone's *boat*. It mattered.

With a sigh, Siyon reached for the knotted rope hanging down the side and walked his way up the hull and over the rail.

When he blinked—long and deliberately and reaching out into the plane around him—the boat (*Bessie*, named and cared-for and known) was already humming with bronze energy. A thing made from wood and hemp and tar and nails by human hands, human inge- nuity, human effort. Shaped by tasks and ritual, by hauling together, by mutual and reinforced purpose. She was a shared talisman, a ward against the deep, as much as a tool of work.

Bessie absolutely oozed Mundane power. She glittered and gleamed, singing in the sunlight.

Was this how she looked to the monsters as well? Was this what drew them? Out in the deep ocean, far from the brazen blaring of Bezim, was a boat like this a beacon?

If Siyon *added* to that—if he reinforced her hull, strengthened her masts, charmed her bowsprit—would that just make things worse?

Voices intruded from aft, where Mayar was asking about the oper- ation of the boat, with all the curiosity of someone who had never even *seen* the ocean until they came to Bezim last year. Siyon tried to tune them out, tried to keep his mind on the tenuous ideas he was plucking out of thin air.

When he reached out to the power around him, thick and bur- nished, it slipped and slithered like a live eel. But Siyon gripped it tighter, until its twisting stirred up *other* energies. A faint breath of Aethyreal potential. A murky memory of the Abyss. A bright burn of Empyreal affinity.

They didn't stain and streak all over his vision now, *except* in these echoes. Siyon had woken the Mundane, and nudged aside the incur- sion of other planes. He'd managed to fix *something*. Right?

Not the time to worry about it, when he needed to concentrate on those echoes. On teasing them out, gathering them up, and using *them* to ward the ship. With one hand still knuckles-deep in the bronze Mundane, Siyon used his other hand to loop Aethyreal energy around *Bessie*'s masts, whispering of the wind, of discovery just over the horizon, of the mysteries of the sea. He smeared the sweltering ooze of the Abyss as far as he could reach down the side of the boat, letting it seep into the hull with its affinity for salt and thick, tarry certainty. He dusted the harpoons with Empyreal potential, gleaming with the swift strike of righteousness.

And when he let the magic drop, stepping back with satisfaction, Siyon found himself staggering, falling to the deck on knees and aching hands. Lungs heaving, eyes blurring, thoughts sluggish in his head.

It shouldn't be this hard, surely. He should be free, and flying, and lifted up. He should go with the thick Mundane energy as it left his grasp, let it pull him down, down, down…

"Hey." A hand on his shoulder, Mayar's face behind the sparks dancing in Siyon's vision. "You done?"

Siyon blinked in the winter sunshine, dizzy and disoriented. He felt like he'd stumbled back from a cliff's edge. He'd done it—he'd used energy consciously.

But what had *that* been?

Anahid woke to early afternoon sun slanting into the bedroom that had once been Geryss Hanlun's, and then Siyon's, and now hers. The bustle of well-heeled commerce rose from the street below, a far cry from leafy Avenue hush.

This time half a year ago, Anahid would have been up for hours in the house she'd shared with Nihath, managing her correspondence and preparing to make and receive calls. At least no one expected her to host guests any longer, not since news of her divorce had sizzled around the gossip circuit. Which was just as well, because Anahid—or rather Lady Sable—had only gone to bed after the dawn bell called an end to trading hours in the Flower district.

A district that had more than enough complication to occupy all of Anahid's time. She was already turning over all the tangled little problems as she pulled on a plain dress—the only sort she wore, these days, with no one about to help her into a fancier gown.

Well, no one who knew what they were doing. Though Anahid smiled to see a breakfast tray waiting on her dresser, with tea kept warm by the charms in the pitcher's gilded etching, and a bowl of fresh—

"Mandarins?" Anahid asked, as she came down the spiral stairs into the main room, peeling the fruit eagerly. "Already in the market this early?"

A low, rasping laugh preceded Laxmi into the room. She was honestly no less confronting fallen than she had been in full demon manifest. Now she was a challenge not of scaled skin, hooves, and horns, but of flashing yellow eyes, ink-black curls tumbling over a shoulder, and dangerous curves barely covered by a loosely tied short robe.

More confronting, perhaps, so dangerously human. So reachable. Anahid found herself wondering, not for the first time, whether Enkin Danelani might have another change of heart, if he saw Laxmi like this. Or perhaps he'd preferred her not as a person, but as a threat made strange flesh.

It was none of her business, of course.

Laxmi sauntered over to swipe a segment from Anahid's peeled fruit. "They're local. And the merchant claimed there are firebees nesting in his orchard, helping the ripening."

"But firebees are..." Anahid didn't finish it. Didn't say *a myth*.

Not when there *was* a naga in the Flower district, regularly harassing those who'd won big at the tables until they bought her a cone of candied walnuts. Not when all the lottery wheels were now encased in a fine filigree cage of silver charmed against the myriad luck-modifiers that every second alley alchemist was selling. Not when three different Houses had been dealing with infestations of pixie skinks, who liked to lick the residue of excitement off the soft furnishings.

Firebees—said to carry the warmth of spring in their drowsy buzz and faint golden glow—weren't any more wondrous than a dozen other things Anahid had seen in Bezim since Salt Night.

"Don't see why he'd lie about it." Laxmi shrugged. "Most of the other shoppers visibly flinched at the news."

Anahid wasn't surprised. She had to brace herself to eat a segment, though the mandarin tasted bright and tangy. It seemed unnatural; it *was* unnatural. Except that nature had become a strange and wondrous thing itself. It made people nervous. And being nervous, Anahid had learned, was also a little bit exciting. "Did you order a box for the House as well?" she asked.

Laxmi smirked. "Nura was with me at the market."

Anahid scoffed. "Do *either* of you ever sleep?" She crammed two more chunks of mandarin into her mouth and found her street shoes, where she'd kicked them under a couch last night.

"About as much as you do," Laxmi said pointedly. "Going down to the House already?"

Anahid whisked a headscarf off its waiting hook. "Qorja has new Flowers to interview. We're still two short." They'd lost four, since Salt Night—one injured and two leaving the city to return to homes that might have been boring but were far safer than the city now seemed. One had been poached by another House.

A Zinedani House. A House not owned by an azata meddling beyond her concerns. The woman who wouldn't bow to the Zinedani. The harpy who'd brought them down entirely.

Well, no, that had been Laxmi. The actual harpy, painting the walls with the blood of a dozen Zinedani thugs who'd assumed they had the upper hand. All Anahid had done was murder Stepan and nearly be strangled to death by Garabed, before Qorja had smashed a mirror over his head.

The memory turned her cold, the bright taste of mandarin turning to thick blood on her tongue and curdling in her stomach. Anahid forced herself to loosen her grip on the headscarf, before she tore the delicately beaded fabric.

Laxmi frowned at her hands. "Why do you still even bother with those things?"

Anahid swallowed hard, forcing the fruit pulp down. "In the hopes that I can make it until after Zagiri's Ball before I bring the

9

whole family into disrepute." Despite her carelessness before Salt Night, the scandalous news of her position—an azata managing a Flowerhouse—had not yet escaped into society. To keep it that way, Anahid would haul on a hood and veil, let alone the simple scarf she'd worn her entire adult life already. She flipped it over her hair and snapped, "Are you coming?"

Laxmi came, of course. Three months since that night in the Badrosani theatre. Almost as long since Laxmi had walked, entirely human, into Sable House. And she hadn't let Anahid down once in all that time.

She was solid at Anahid's shoulder, a shadow and a shield both. Reassuring enough that Anahid didn't flinch at the clatters and bangs from the building sites they walked past. There were plenty of them, after Salt Night. These days, it seemed more of the Laders' Guild could be found in the upper city, working laborer's shifts, than down in Dockside. Just as well the trade voyages had already sailed.

In the District, repairs were long finished, with only one House having been substantially damaged, and it having taken the opportunity to rename itself the Dragon's Lair, complete with a new glittering statue out front. But the normality was a fiction; little remained as it had been before Salt Night. Not with Midnight vanished and his organisation splintering into squabbling gangs. Not with the Zinedani baron and his heir both dead. Garabed's daughter—Marel Sakrani, who'd married into a lower-tier azatani family—had taken things in hand, but business had been substantially disrupted.

Or so Anahid had heard. She could hardly *ask*. Drop in for tea, introduce herself as the reason for Marel's inheritance, offer her assistance. The very idea was appalling.

Zagiri would probably do it.

As though reading her mind, Laxmi said, "Lejman heard word the second daughter was back from the New Republic. Came in on the ship that arrived the other day."

That would have been the first one to sail after reports of Salt Night had reached the far side of the Carmine Sea. Ruzanna Zinedani—the daughter who'd married a trader—now back to assist her sister.

10

Anahid said firmly: "It's none of my business."

Laxmi snorted. "Maybe now they'll take *their* business in hand. Stop everyone skittering around like crab-legged imps." She directed that at a runner edging past, who *did* scuttle around them in a manner unfortunately similar to a crustacean.

In the yard of Sable House, Qorja and Nura were in furious, hushed conference. The stage mistress oversaw the Flowers and all aspects of their business, and Anahid's former housekeeper had now stepped into a new role as provisioner of the House. Anahid knew few more capable women, so it was alarming when they looked perturbed.

"We've lost more Flowers?" Anahid guessed. The roster was already stretched.

Nura shook her head briskly, though Qorja's face tilted farther toward unease. "We may," she said quietly, barely audible over the wagon unloading at the kitchen door. "If word gets out that we can no longer source sureties."

The bottom dropped out of Anahid's stomach.

She barely heard Laxmi asking, "Sureties? What are those?"

"Essential tools for maintaining the intimate health of the Flowers," Nura explained politely and—by Laxmi's deepening frown—entirely opaquely.

"Contraceptives," Anahid summarised.

Qorja wrinkled up her nose. "And protection against diseases, parasites, and—these days—potential curses."

"What's happened?" Anahid demanded. "I thought our supplier wasn't involved in any of the new gangs."

"Maybe that was the problem. We've heard our usual provider was included in the last purge." Qorja paused delicately before saying, "Perhaps if we got the inquisitors involved—"

"No," Anahid interrupted, too abrupt. But her involvement with Inquisitor Xhanari had been a mistake she had no interest in revisiting. At least he'd stopped sending innocuous messages.

"A purge," Laxmi repeated. "A Midnight purge?"

Except there was no Midnight any longer. Strange and inexplicable as he'd been, he'd held his tangled web of a barony together. Now parts of it were pulling in all directions, tearing apart like a wreck on a rock. But Anahid needed to shift this topic before—

"You have to step in."

Before they got to this again. Anahid sighed and didn't look at Laxmi. She knew what she'd see; that set to her jaw, that burn in her eyes, that *determination*. "It's not my business," she insisted.

But Laxmi had never been easy to ignore. "It bloody is. This mess has taken out your provider of—whatevers. How much closer does it need to get before you'll *do something*?"

Nura looked hurriedly down at her ledger, flipping through the pages, and Qorja developed a fascination with the bed of one of her perfectly manicured fingernails. Neither of them wanted to be involved in this. *Anahid* didn't want to be involved in this.

"Painting the walls in blood won't find us a provider," she stated through gritted teeth, glaring at Laxmi; she immediately received a glare in return. "Violence can't bring back the dead."

"Nor can hiding," Laxmi spat.

Anahid wasn't *hiding*. She was being *sensible*.

Before she could say that, Laxmi stalked away, grabbing one of the unloaded barrels and hefting it onto her shoulder to carry into the House.

Anahid ground her teeth, bailing the boat of her anger, until she could say evenly: "Where were we?"

Nura cleared her throat. "I can't confirm that our provider has been purged. But nor can I find her anywhere. I haven't heard from her in four days, and a delivery was due yesterday. I hunted down her workshop and found some other alchemist in there."

This was the real problem. *Her* problem. Let the barons and those who would be one worry about jostling for position and resources. All Anahid wanted was to run her House in peace. That was all she'd ever wanted.

"Don't we have another alchemist on retainer?" Anahid asked. "That Lyraec fellow who got snooty over the tampered lock?"

Nura's mouth tightened slightly. "I made inquiry with him. He was...quite put out at the suggestion that he might sully his reputation with such things."

12

That sort of attitude—entirely common among alchemical practitioners of the upper city—was why Midnight's alchemical workshops had cornered the Flower district trade in the first place.

Anahid sighed and tilted her head back, scanning the sky as though there would be answers writ there. Along the top of Sable House, the star jasmine was crawling with pixie skinks, the little winged lizards nibbling at the tight-furled flowers.

Magic was alive in Bezim now. Sorcery was no longer a crime. There were more practitioners than ever, setting up in shops and stalls and trading door-to-door. But contraceptives were not an area where you wanted to trust in just anyone. It was right there, in the common District name for them: sureties.

You needed to be *sure*.

"How long until the situation becomes dire?" Anahid asked.

Nura exchanged a look with Qorja. "At current rostering, we can still cover the next ten days."

But Qorja had already made mention of the problems that could arise if the Flowers found out. It was fair enough. They deserved safety and certainty. She needed to get it for them.

"Shake down every lead we have on a new provider," Anahid instructed firmly. "Chase every option. This is our top priority. If we haven't found something in the next three days…" She drew a breath. "I'll go and see Nihath, and ask him to recommend someone."

Qorja nodded and hurried out of the yard.

But Nura caught at Anahid's sleeve, in a way she never would have as housekeeper. "Mistress," she said, which was almost the same. "That will be an azatani practitioner."

Anahid inclined her head. "Or one closely affiliated with the azatani, yes."

Those were the circles her former husband associated with. The Summer Club, where a good quarter of azatani society dined and gossiped.

Anahid would have to tell one of them what she needed. And why. If she did *that*, there was little chance it would remain secret.

Nura folded her hands firmly. "I will find someone," she vowed.

The Eldren Hall was sweating light, the golden stone almost glowing from within, powered by a small fortune in alchemical charms and the astounding self-importance of the azatani. Sparkling motes danced along the facade and twined around the four narrow towers. The stained-glass frontage burned against the gathering dusk, lending extra drama to the depictions of the higher beings of each plane. The angel's sword and wings were appropriately flaming, the djinn's eyes flashed, and the incubus was wreathed in malevolently glowing seaweed.

Among them was the noble portrait of an azatan, staring boldly into the future and clutching a sextant and scroll—symbols of rationality conquering wilderness. As she glared up at him, Zagiri told herself she was almost certainly not the only young woman grinding her teeth as she climbed these stairs, stewing over her parents. They were all climbing in a sparkling stream, proudly presented in pristine new gowns for the first official rehearsal of the Harbour Master's Ball.

Probably none of the other sponsors were angry for quite the same reason.

"Father," she tried again, keeping her voice low and her frothy skirts carefully out from beneath her feet, "of course I'm aware of what we've lost in the leadership of Syrah Danelani—"

Even if there was a terrible part of her that was faintly relieved. The prefect's censure for what Zagiri had done to achieve her sorcery reform had died as well on Salt Night. Azata Markani had been injured too, sufficiently that rumour said she was retiring from public life. All things considered, Zagiri would still rather have Danelani's hand on the helm of the city in these turbulent waters. *She'd* not flinch from the chance presented to them.

"Of course she is," Zagiri's mother chimed in at her other elbow. "She *worked* with the woman for months. Oh!" Kemella squeezed Zagiri's elbow again, beaming. "I'm so proud of you. My little gull, all grown up! Your first rehearsal!"

Which Zagiri appreciated, but it wasn't really helping right now.

She turned back to Usal, but her father just patted her net-gloved hand. "Your mother's right, petal. This is a very important time for you, the start of your adult life, and it only happens once. You're busy enough with this, and your bravi things. There will be other chances to get involved in politics later, if that's what you want to do."

"Not like this one!" Zagiri objected, loud enough that a younger girl in front of them glanced curiously over her shoulder before her mother nudged her back into propriety. Zagiri lowered her tone. "Not like a new Council commencement, Father. *That's* when we could bring a proposal for alteration to the entire membership in a—"

But they were out of time, cresting the staircase, where Azata Malkasani waited in the portico, beaming in welcome.

"Who is this that comes to the heart of society?" asked the woman who'd been pestering Zagiri to sign up as a sponsor for three years now.

But this was all part of the ritual, as carefully choreographed as any of the dances they would be taught to perform in the rehearsals to come. Zagiri made her courtesy, as her parents stood by—ostensibly letting her speak for herself, in actuality beaming right back at Malkasani. "One who would join that society," Zagiri responded, as she'd been taught. "And lend her hands to keep its sails in trim."

At least she was trying. All she wanted was to make Bezim better. For everyone, not just the azatani, but that would be better for them too. If they'd just listen to her. If they'd just *pay attention*.

This was how she started: by participating in the Harbour Master's Ball as a sponsor, making her presentation, and being addressed as *azata*.

In the foyer of the Hall—all red velvet and gilt edging—her mother embraced her with care for her froth of a dress, and her father gave her a proud nod. And then they went off with the other parents to the upper balconies, to congratulate one another on the maturity of their offspring and the elegance of their expensive dresses.

Those dresses—swaths of billowing skirts in the colours of seafoam and clouds and the bubbles of djinnwine—clustered at the bottom of the stairs, a tight puff of young women in the daunting space

15

of the ballroom floor. They looked like a soft landing. Zagiri wasn't fooled as she descended alone.

Surely every young azatani woman felt herself observed as she came down these stairs, but Zagiri knew it wasn't her imagination. Heads turned her way, then tilted together in low-voiced discussion. Not everyone bothered to whisper. Halfway down the stairs, Zagiri clearly heard someone say: "—in league with the Sorcerer."

She jerked her chin up a little and understood anew why Anahid's had so often been at this angle. Let them talk. Zagiri *had* helped Siyon, and she'd do it again. She didn't regret any of it.

Supporting Siyon was the least of the things this crowd would turn their backs on her for. They all probably thought she hadn't deserved that prestigious clerkship with Syrah Danelani. They'd have been horrified to hear she'd been tangled up with the Laders' Guild uprising. They'd tear the dress off her and cast her out in the streets if they knew she'd used all of it for a wild and destructive—but *effective*—plan to drag the Council into doing the right thing, at least as far as the sorcery laws went.

She intended to do worse. Or better, depending on where you were standing. But first, she had to make it through this whole business. She needed to be recognised as grown-up azatani if she wanted to achieve anything.

If she had to do it alone, then so be it.

Zagiri cut across the ballroom, the cluster of other sponsors parting easily for her, until she could pause for a moment next to one of the pillars along the side of the ballroom.

Not *hiding*. Just taking a moment.

From the other side of the pillar, a low voice said, "I say we tip firewater into the punch."

Zagiri felt like smiling for the first time since she'd set out with her parents on the promenade to the Eldren Hall. She wasn't entirely alone in this business after all.

She tilted around the pillar until she could see Yeva Bardha properly. The young woman looked almost regal, with her golden hair braided in a crown and a haughty tilt to her head that reminded Zagiri

16

of Yeva's mother, the ambassador from the North. The impression was only strengthened by the differences between Yeva's white skirts— stark and falling clean to the floor, with a gold-embroidered bodice over the top—and the traditional, wispy gowns of all the others.

But any regality was dispelled by the way Yeva leaned one shoulder casually against the pillar, dangling a little metal flask from her hand.

There were a lot of reasons Zagiri shouldn't be pleased to see her, but she had to fight against a smile as she said, "What, you think this lot would be better if they were drunk?"

Yeva cast a sidelong look at the fluttering crowd of sponsors. There were a little over two dozen of them this year, cooing about the details of one another's dresses and playing at who could be more modest and reassuring.

Zagiri should be more generous. They were probably all nervous enough about this whole business—the most important of azatani rituals—and that was without the uncertainty that still lingered in the city from Salt Night. The destruction, the deaths, the ongoing magic.

Zagiri *would* be more generous, if they weren't all excluding her, turning away, and shooting her looks over their shoulders.

"I think this lot would be better if *I* were drunk," Yeva countered, and held the little flask out toward Zagiri.

"I don't trust you," Zagiri reminded her. Reminded herself. Yeva had used Zagiri, taken the alchemical devices she'd arranged, and been part of a plan to blow up the Swanneck Bridge. A plan that had failed, and that Zagiri had had to clean up after.

Yeva jiggled the flask at her. "We're in this together, though."

They had been officially registered as co-sponsors for the event, partnering up to guide some naive little debutante through her first Ball. Zagiri wasn't sure Yeva was a wise thing to expose any young society girl to, but here they were.

They were all going to have to make the best of it.

Zagiri accepted the flask but used it to point at Yeva. "No tipping this into *anything*. Malkasani would bar us from the Ball entirely."

"This would be bad?" Yeva lifted a lazy eyebrow.

"I need this," Zagiri reminded her. It was all very well for

Yeva—daughter of the ambassador, only really participating to show her mother's commitment to good relations, or perhaps in a doomed attempt to keep her out of the sort of trouble she preferred to dive into headfirst. But Zagiri was azatani. Whatever future she wanted to build for herself in Bezim—be it marriage or politics or trade—it started with being accepted into azatani society.

And if Azata Malkasani decided she was unsuitable for society, she'd have to wait another year. Everything Zagiri wanted to achieve—everything she could *be*—hinged on this set of rituals.

"That's ridiculous." Yeva snatched her flask back and took a sulky swig. "*This* is ridiculous," she added, gesturing to the fluttering flock of other sponsors. "They're wearing enough wealth to feed half the lower city for a week, you know."

This was just a rehearsal, though admittedly the first one, a special event in its own right. The Ball itself would be bigger, grander, gaudier…worse.

Zagiri sighed. "This is the azatani. This is how we define ourselves."

"Definitions change," Yeva declared, chin up and mouth thin with belligerence.

Zagiri allowed herself that smile, though it was a thin and sharp and bitter thing now. "Not for us. Not like that. Not that fast." And she should know. She felt like she'd been beating herself against this one for years now.

"They do," Yeva countered, taking another thoughtful sip from her flask before she added, "if you get their attention properly."

A chill skittered down Zagiri's spine. She took a quick step around the pillar, as though she could physically block Yeva from attacking the rest of the girls. "You promised," she said, voice lower now, but tighter in her throat. "No more gullshit like the Swanneck."

Yeva straightened off the pillar, taller than Zagiri now. "I did not. I said I would talk with you before blowing anything up." She pulled a face. "Stop glaring at me. There's nothing I *can* do. The laders are all too busy with gainful employment." And didn't she sound sulky about it.

"Good," Zagiri said firmly. "Because I have things in progress that I don't want you messing up."

Yeva snorted. "What, your little bravi workgang? Helping out with the Palace ruins? You think looking all well-behaved is going to get you what you want?"

Not if she couldn't even make her *father* pay attention. But Zagiri lifted her chin. "It's only one part of my plan. You'll see. This is our chance."

It *was*. She was going to grab it.

But first, she had to become a proper azata.

Zagiri glanced over her shoulder, at the fluttering butterflies ready to enter society, and held out her hand for Yeva's flask after all. It was, as she'd suspected, Northern firewater, clear and cold and sharp as a lightning strike. Zagiri hissed through the burn of it and tucked the flask into her own sash. Being tied to Yeva would be a liability if the girl got drunk and belligerent.

"Now, come on," she ordered. "If we're doing this, we need to actually *speak* with the others."

Yeva pulled a face, but she came along as Zagiri tugged her away from the pillar.

Toward the daunting wall of froth and suspicion and gossip. Toward Zagiri's future.

She wasn't letting it get away.

CHAPTER 2

The lower city squat wasn't the worst place Siyon had ever lived. Of course, when he'd first hauled himself out of the river after fleeing Dockside, he'd camped out in some truly appalling places. At least all the external walls were sound on this building, even if the lowest floor was sunk in the mud. There was only that one place where a room had collapsed down to the floor below; Siyon, Mayar, and Daruj just went around it.

When they were there. Daruj still kipped in the Bracken bunks a fair amount, or at least he stayed *somewhere* in the upper city, and occasionally came back smug and smelling of a perfume so fancy, Siyon couldn't even begin to name its properties. Mayar kept even odder hours than Siyon did, between bravi business and their own. Quite often, it was just Siyon alone, with the scrabble of gull feet from above, and the knock of the water against the walls as the tide drove little wavelets down the alleycanals between the tilting buildings.

Him, the noise of the lower city, and the journals of Izmirlian Hisarani.

Balian had sent them down to him, after Salt Night. After he'd been revealed as *Balian Hisarani* and had helped Siyon achieve his goals anyway. *I think you deserve to have them*, he'd written. These remnants of Izmirlian, left behind like footprints in wet sand.

Almost as elegant and eloquent as the man himself had been. They were impeccably bound in tooled leather covers and made of better-quality paper than Siyon had even known existed. The pages were smooth as sin and covered in the even lines of Izmirlian's familiar whiplash scrawl.

He'd not written nearly as much as the famous Kolah Negedi, but he'd had a good crack at it, and been nearly as curious about the world. Izmirlian had read voraciously and spoken to a wider variety of people than Siyon would have expected from an azatan. He'd scribbled down all his notes and questions and ideas.

And then he'd gone out into the world and found out what no one could tell him. *Did* the beaches of the far eastern Storm Coast have sand as red as blood? (Yes, it turned out, but caused by ore deposits in the headlands above, rather than any mythical massacre.) Were there really crabs the size of coconuts that climbed trees? (Probably yes, though Izmirlian had only seen them dead in the markets of the Far Khanates, and only had the merchants' word about the tree climbing. But they'd apparently been delicious.)

He'd known, and seen, and done so much. It made Siyon's life—Power and all—feel small and shuttered.

At the very least, Siyon needed to go out and find his own answers to all the questions that needled at him right now. What was happening with this sloshing abundance of Mundane energy? What had he felt the other day, on the whaling boat, when the energy pulled him down?

What was the Power of the Mundane *for*?

Siyon sighed, slung his satchel across his body, and went out into the late afternoon.

The muddy bridges and dim arcades of the lower city were waking up as the afternoon shadow of the Scarp stretched deeper over all of them. Those with respectable jobs were starting to trickle back down the Scarp at the end of their days; those with more shadowy professions were rising to begin theirs.

Siyon slipped his way through the crowds in the market, where fresh fish hauled over from Dockside was touted alongside the slightly battered leftovers from the upper city fruit market, opposite silks and velvets skimmed from incoming ships, and trinkets straight-up stolen from the upper city. Above them fluttered the baron pennants advertising other, even less-legal wares and services, available if you knew how to ask for what the colours and patterns offered.

And then there were the alchemists.

Years ago, when Siyon first started learning the trade, he'd had to skulk down alleyways, knock on rune-scratched doors, risk rickety staircases just to track down a practitioner who could barely raise a spark with a fistful of firesand.

Now there was a whole corner of the market crammed with stalls touting extraplanar goods and alchemical effects. They spilled out of the market proper and lined a twisting alleyway that curled along the base of the Scarp. Siyon didn't recognise a single one of them, shouting their promises, waving their glittering sleeves. This one offered intoxications and delights beyond the reach of rakia, that one promised beauty and charm with a swipe of an unguent. Disappear into the shadows, climb like a spider, change her mind...

When Siyon went past that one, he tried to reach out through the Mundane and hook one of the stall legs, bring the whole thing crashing down. But all he managed was ruffling the edge of the grubby purple cloth draped over it.

They all had something like that. A purple drapery, or fringing on their sleeves, or ribbons festooning their stall posts. A new sort of pennant.

"The Sorcerer's own recipe!" someone shouted, farther down the shadowed alley. "Gleaned from his secret notebooks."

Siyon snorted and laid a hand on his satchel. He *had* secret notebooks, but they were more likely to contain bitching about the academic pretensions of some historic azatan than anything like a *recipe*. And they weren't exactly *his*.

Behind him, someone else shouted, "*Fuck* the Sorcerer." There was a cheer, and general good-natured jostling, and someone muttering about *bloody monsters*.

None of them knew him. *He* wasn't wearing purple; the coat was wedged in a particularly drafty gap in a wall in their squat, finally making itself useful. But Siyon still turned away, hunching his shoulders. His eye snagged on a hefty man leaning in the lee of a stall, one crossed forearm displaying a tattooed *B* made of curving daggers. A Badrosani thug, keeping an eye on trade. Keeping a cut flowing to his mistress.

The guy caught Siyon looking, and his permanent frown deepened just a little.

Time for Siyon to be elsewhere.

He ducked down a different alleyway, blocked by the rubble of a collapsed building that Siyon climbed like a staircase, up and away from the market. He ducked in a window, down a corridor, hopped from a creaking balcony to the roof across the way.

He had to shoo away a pixie skink before he hunkered down in the lee of the crumbling chimney. According to Daruj, above the Scarp they were delicate creatures with sparkling wings. This one was grimed and tattered, and it hissed at him as it slunk away.

Siyon pulled out a notebook—his, filled with scratchings far less elegant than Izmirlian's—and the stub of a pencil. Note the pixie skinks—and now that he thought about it, he'd never seen any down near the squat. Coincidence? Maybe he should map their territory. Maybe they were clustered up here like the alley alchemists, with their bold claims and wilder results.

A gap between buildings showed him a sliver of the market. Even as Siyon wrote, someone sent up a shower of bright sparks, leaving deep green Abyssal eddies in the flow of energy.

And it was a *flow*. Like not seeing a river until a thrown pebble sent the surface into ripples, suddenly Siyon could trace the power oozing thick and bronze all around them. It was *everywhere* now, rising up from the ground like a sea mist, far thicker and more urgent than it had been before Salt Night.

Siyon absently tangled his pencil hand in the energy around him, twisting it into a knot that only he could see. The burnished ball of power hung for a moment where he'd left it and then started to tilt away, like a little paper boat caught in the current of a river pouring past Siyon, flowing down toward the mud and the sea, like it was rushing out of…

He swivelled to squint at the looming bulk of the Scarp. A chain of golden lanterns followed the switchback path up its face, leaving the rest shadowed and secret.

But Siyon knew some of what was in there. Tunnels and caverns and things better left undisturbed.

"Nope," he said aloud. "Absolutely not. Not going back in there."

It wasn't so much that he was afraid—though surely he had reason, having woken a fucking *dragon* last time. But now that he looked, properly and with the right combination of his senses, the power was *boiling* down from the cliff face. It should be audible, a low and steady roar, like the water churning through the river chasm, gushing out into the tidal pool of the harbour.

Just as ready to pull him under, drag him down, drown him forever.

Was *this* what he'd felt, hooked into him after he'd worked on *Bessie* the boat? Just looking at the energy surging out of the Scarp, Siyon could feel the tug of it, nibbling at his toes, whispering at the edge of his awareness. Like some opera-story siren, promising secrets, promising pleasure, promising everything would be better if he just came down off that rock and—

"Fancy seeing you here," a hearty voice declared as boots hit the rooftop next to Siyon's elbow.

Siyon startled, slipped on the worn roof tiles, juggled his notebook in one hand while he grabbed for the chimney with the other.

Above him, a figure planted hands on leather-clad hips and snorted in derision. "Graceful."

"Go fuck yourself," Siyon suggested, still a little breathless. He'd teetered on the edge of something far higher than a rooftop there, just for a moment. He had to force his fingers to unbend from the chimney's brickwork. "What do you want, Redick?"

The sergeant of the Awl Quarter bravi sprawled on the roof next to Siyon with his fancy fringed Lyraec sash and his braided-and-beaded hair. His teeth glinted gold as he grimaced and rubbed at his knee. "Getting too old for this."

Weren't they all? "Hand your sabre in. Walk away."

Redick pulled a surprisingly prissy face. "Hand to whom? Now if *you'd* joined the Quarter like you should have, I could make *you* sergeant after me."

Any guilt Siyon had felt about following Daruj into Bracken, rather than joining the tribe who'd helped fish him out of the river in the first place, was long gone. "Yeah, that'd make you popular right now."

That cry was still ringing in his ears. *Fuck the Sorcerer.* Not unusual, since Salt Night, but it always stung. He'd not expected the city to love him, not when he'd flattened a quarter of it, dragged a monster from its depths, sent magic in all its uncomfortable glory sizzling down the streets.

But he'd hoped for a little more lower city support.

Redick blew dismissive air between his lips. "That's mostly Badrosani gullshit. Mama's heart is broken that you never visit." He shrugged, far too casual to actually be so. "She's leaning again, trying to get her mitts on you."

A chill slunk into Siyon's gut. Far too late, he looked surreptitiously around the rooftop; had Redick come alone, or with enough blades to take him in? The lower city was Badrosani territory, and that meant even the Awl Quarter needed to play nice sometimes.

Redick cuffed Siyon's ear. "Don't be insulting," the bravi snapped. "I turn on you, you'll never see us coming. I'm trying to warn you, twerp. You've kept out of her reach until now. Don't get stupid."

Getting out of Badrosani reach had been one of the reasons he *hadn't* joined the Awl Quarter. Even then, young and heedless as he'd been, Siyon had scraped up enough alchemical tricks for the Badrosani street crews to take an interest. They didn't produce like Midnight, but petty alchemists could come in handy.

Don't get tangled up with the barons. Advice he could only wish he'd stuck with.

"Where else can I go?" Siyon meant to sound resigned; it came out plaintive. "They say worse things about me in the upper city, and the inquisitors are leaning harder than Badrosani. You think I'd fare any better with Aghut?"

Not to mention all the other reasons he'd prefer to avoid Dockside.

"All I'm hearing," Redick said thoughtfully, scratching at his beard, "is what other people want from you. What are *you* doing?"

"Fuck off," Siyon retorted, because it was better than saying that he didn't know. That he had no ideas. That he was terrified to move at all, lest he break anything else.

Redick levered himself up off the tiles, dusting down his leathers. "Much as I'd love to stay here with you swearing at me all evening, nothing bites if you don't bait the hook. Oh..." He hesitated, ostentatiously casual. "You see the Star Whisper much?"

Took Siyon a moment to remember that was Zagiri's bladename. "I won't carry either your challenge or your love notes."

Redick looked alarmed. "No, I'm not— It's this workgang she's organised. Stealing three of my blades every other night. I just want to know how long it's going to go on for."

Siyon shrugged. "So ask."

"And look like I'm trying to get out of our commitment?" Redick struck a pose, one hand on the sparkling hilt of his sabre. "The Quarter sticks to its word. You tell her *that*, if you see her. And tell the Diviner Prince from me that he's a dandy show-off disgrace."

That made Siyon grin, despite everything. "Tell him yourself, unless you fear his blade."

But Redick was already off, running quick and quiet and surefooted, for all his talk of age. As the silence settled behind him, Siyon's mirth slid off his face.

What *was* he doing? Staying in place? Doing nothing? Letting his fear get the better of him?

He didn't know what he *could* do. He didn't know enough. Izmirlian had shown him, in his journals, how to solve that problem: Go and find the answers.

Siyon could still feel the energy beating at his back, pumping out of the Scarp behind him. As though whatever was at the root of all this could be found in there.

The one place he *really* didn't want to revisit.

The place he was going to have to go.

The three bravi from the Bower's Scythe were singing a fishersong as they worked, though they were hauling stone rather than nets. They had good voices—the Bowerboys favoured performers and creators—and the remnant of the curved staircase gave a nice resonance to the song.

Zagiri couldn't stop to enjoy it. She was just grateful that at least *they* were all doing what they were supposed to.

Forming a workgang from the bravi tribes had seemed like such a good idea. The hastily appointed committee for unfucking the city after Salt Night—or the Interim Rectification Board, to give it the proper title—had declared they wanted around-the-clock work on the Palace site. Which meant there was this midnight-to-dawn-bell shift, the sort of time that sensible people were asleep.

No one would ever describe the bravi as *sensible*.

The site supervisor—a harried middle-aged woman who'd been promoted from within the Harbour Master's office—had nearly burst into relieved tears when Zagiri came to her to offer a bravi workgang for the time slot. Talking the tribes into loaning her three each of their blades every second night . . . well, that had been a lot more work, and she'd spent most of a week scrambling between the safehouses, wheedling and negotiating. If she never again had to make the leap to the Observatory, out at the tip of the lower city, that would be absolutely fine with her.

Not that a month of work seemed to have had a great deal of impact on the ruin of the Palace. If anything, it seemed to have gotten *worse* since Salt Night. (And when she thought that, Zagiri could just imagine the sharp, bitter bark of Siyon's laughter. Of course, he'd say. That's what things *do*.)

She'd seen it on Salt Night, when the dragon had shattered and scattered it. She'd seen Siyon climb out of the cavernous depths beneath and try to bind the dragon anew. She'd attempted to help with the injured—and the dead—in the aftermath.

A working group of Summer Club alchemists had spent weeks

stabilising the parkland. They'd been mostly successful. What was left of the Palace had slumped down into a natural amphitheatre around the blown-open core of it. The crumpled dome still sat off amid the trees, on its side and half full of rainwater. Some of the trees were still tilted; a couple had fallen over entirely. One near the Palace was still growing vigorously, but every new leaf that unfurled was a vibrant, impossible pink.

No one was talking too strongly about the impossible in Bezim this winter. Not with pixie skinks and firebees and old carved charms glowing anew. Not when the university entrance examinations had been postponed until the faculty could prevent the ghosts from helping the candidates cheat. Not when every traveller who came through the western city gates had a new story about the dragon, sighted in silhouette or carrying off someone's cattle. None of the bravi had so far reported the seventh runner shadowing their steps on the tiles yet, but Zagiri wondered if that was just a matter of time.

"Giri!" someone called from the former front steps of the palace; a lean figure, waving arms, lifting hands to his mouth. A Bracken whistle cut across the space, travelling sharper and clearer than words ever could. *Raid incoming.*

Shit. They were here already.

Zagiri clambered and slithered her way down the remnants of the grand staircase and crunched across the ruined mosaic to where Daruj waited.

"Bunch of Avenue types," he reported.

"I know," Zagiri said, trying to beat the stone dust off her leathers. "The Board's inspecting."

Daruj's eyes widened, a little like panic. Another time it would amuse her: the Diviner Prince, most feared blade of the city, undone by a little bureaucracy. "Is this a problem?"

"No, it's an opportunity." Zagiri peered out into the midnight parkland, at a line of sparkling lights approaching. "Find the Bleeders and make sure they're on task, will you? And try to keep Mayar from doing anything crazy."

Some nights, Mayar did something with hands and song and

strange symbols chalked on the walls, and the stones they were clearing weighed half of what they usually did. *Other* nights, Mayar spent half a bell staring at a tree root and muttering about energy flows. Zagiri didn't want the inspecting councillors asking questions about the odd Khanate practitioner when they could be listening to her answers about...

Zagiri peered more closely at the approaching inspection team. "Fuck," she muttered. "*Go.* Get everything in line."

She shoved Daruj and hurried down the steps, trying not to grind her teeth.

Because the first azatan in the line was Avarair fucking Hisarani. He looked grim, striding along fast enough to almost outpace the clerk holding the lantern.

Zagiri's heel skidded on rubble and she nearly went over. *Fuck.*

The clerk was Balian Hisarani. The youngest brother, the sneaky one. The one who'd lied to them all about who he was, even as he cozied up to Siyon.

Even as he cozied up to *her.* Zagiri had let him. She'd have let him do more. She'd *liked* him.

The utter *snake.* He'd suggested he was still on Siyon's side, had continued helping them. But look who he was helping now, scurrying at his brother's elbow, holding his lantern, carrying his notes. Blood won out, especially in the Avenues.

Zagiri pointedly looked past the Hisaranis. There were two more Council types in the procession, each with a clerk at their shoulders. Either of them might prove more reasonable, more interested in the actual good of the city and its people. It wouldn't be difficult. If Avarair had had his way, Siyon would have been locked up, and who knows what would have happened. Maybe the dragon would have built up so much pressure, it exploded the *entire* city. Zagiri didn't know how these things worked. But neither did Avarair, and he'd shown no signs of letting that stop him trying to knock Siyon down at every opportunity.

She pulled a smile forcibly onto her face, the polite and genial expression Anahid had made her work on in the mirror. "Good evening," she called to the approaching group. "Or I suppose it might be good morning, by now."

One of them—the older azata, who wasn't still in her evening finery—smiled back, which Zagiri chose to take as a good sign. The younger azata—perhaps five years older than Anahid, sparkling with beadwork, looking like she was keen to get back to whatever party she'd left to be here—turned to Avarair and said, "Can we get on with this?"

Reluctantly, Zagiri turned to Avarair—and the satisfied tilt to his mouth that said he knew how much she disliked this. "Miss Savani," he said, and was she imagining the emphasis he placed on that address?

The Harbour Master's Ball couldn't come fast enough.

"Azatan Hisarani," she replied, and then turned away from him again, to smile at the other two, holding out a hand to shake and getting in before he could perform introductions. It was petty, and she enjoyed it. "Hello, I'm Zagiri Savani."

"Ah," said the glittering azata, like she'd stumbled over interesting gossip. "We miss your sister Anahid so; do give her my regards. But *you* are the one who clerked for Syrah, aren't you? The one who was tangled up with the Sorcerer."

She gave it that slant everyone was using these days. As though Siyon were some charlatan who'd infiltrated society and pretended to have better manners than he had. As though he'd been a passing fancy of fashion who everyone now swore they'd never really liked.

Before Zagiri could say something she'd probably regret, the older azata stepped forward and shook her hand. "Buni Filosani," she said simply, and nodded past Zagiri. "Let's get on. I'm keen to see what you have underway here."

Anahid had given Zagiri a long and often tedious list of people to impress, or avoid, or be careful when addressing. It was difficult to remember all of them, but Buni Filosani...that name had come with a wistful little sigh from her sister, and additional notes. Anahid had been at a luncheon with the woman, at Azata Parsola's, when she received word that Zagiri had fallen off the Clock Tower and been caught by Siyon.

She'd also mentioned, just tossed in as well, that the woman would likely be running for prefect, now that Syrah Danelani was dead.

This was a greater opportunity than Zagiri had anticipated. If she could get the next prefect on her side, that would make a *lot* of things easier.

"I am very happy to answer any questions you may have," Zagiri declared, pulling up that smile again; it came a little more easily this time. "However, I can't take you any closer than this staging point. It's against the site guidelines."

Avarair looked sour. "We *wrote* the site guidelines."

The younger azata sniffed. "I'm not going anywhere near all that dust. Avair, why are we here?"

Between the shortened name and the touch of a whine to her question, Zagiri rather thought Azata Nameless was here because Avarair had asked her to be. She wished briefly for Anahid, with her keen eye for details. But Zagiri suspected that Filosani had wanted to inspect, and Avarair didn't want Zagiri having a chance to speak with her alone.

Filosani strode forward, to the edge of the safety barrier, and Avarair hurried after her. In his wake, Balian was suddenly at Zagiri's side, saying quietly, "Filosani ran as a freeblade in her youth."

Zagiri glared at him. "I don't need your help," she hissed.

Except, damn him, that might be useful. If Filosani knew bravi ways, had some sympathy to the joys and spirit of running the tiles, Zagiri could use that.

When Zagiri joined the Board members at the safety barrier, they could see five bravi—looked like the three Bleeders, and the two Haruspex blades who weren't Mayar—taking sledgehammers to a half-fallen wall in chanting unison.

"Good to see the bravi actually working," Avarair commented.

"It's our city too," Zagiri pointed out. As she'd said to the sergeants, when putting this workgang together in the first place. It was their city too, and if they showed that to the azatani, if they set hands to the rope and hauled as one, then when the next crews were picked, that would be remembered.

Zagiri hoped.

"Their city too," the other azata said, and gave Zagiri a bright look. "After all, you won't be one of them for much longer, will you? Aren't you on the sponsor lists for this season's Ball? You'll have to hand back your sabre."

Zagiri kept her smile by force of will. "Indeed. I'll no longer carry a blade, but I'll always be a part of my tribe. Being bravi is a commitment. We have a reputation as heedless, but we fight for our city as furiously as we fight one another."

Avarair turned to her with a supercilious expression that she longed to smack right off his face.

But Azata Filosani spoke first. "It's still a feat, bringing the tribes to work together. It's like the spirit of Grand Bracken awoken." She seemed pleased about this, smiling out at the works.

"Don't let any of them hear you say that," Zagiri said quickly. "I had to convince the sergeants this wasn't a Little Bracken plot to regain our lost grandeur."

Filosani's smile seemed genuine as she turned to Zagiri. "Was it a real thing, then? I always thought Grand Bracken was simply a myth. A story we told about ourselves. Once upon a time, we all fought together."

Before Zagiri could answer, a voice behind her said: "There's nothing simple about myths, or stories we tell about ourselves."

Filosani inclined her head. "Well put, Za Hisarani," she said, even as Zagiri shot Balian a glare. "We've heard many accounts, in the course of our rectification work, about the bravi involvement in maintaining what safety and order was possible on Salt Night. I must say, it's heartening to see this civic spirit continuing. Please pass my thanks to the sergeants and the workers themselves."

This was almost perfect. Zagiri was unlikely to have a better opportunity, though she might wish for a chance to speak with Filosani without all these other ears listening in. But here they were, and she said: "I've often thought it a missed opportunity that there's no greater way for the bravi—or indeed the other engaged citizens of Bezim outside the azatani—to assist with the governance of the city."

The younger azata frowned. "Slinging stones around is hardly *governing*."

"Quite," Avarair agreed smoothly. "We are all working to build—and rebuild—Bezim according to our strengths."

But Zagiri didn't give a small silver fish for either of them. *Filosani* was all that mattered. "What an interesting notion," she said with a little smile. "I do hope someone will raise it at the commencement of the next Council."

Just what Zagiri had been telling her father: that this was an opportunity. Because when a new Council was sworn in—as one would be, when the recess was over, and new members chosen from the azatani families—there could be suggestions made to alter the standard rules of assembly.

As long as one of those new members—an azatani councillor—proposed the alteration. A councillor like Zagiri's father, for the Savani family.

With Filosani on board, it would *work*. If Zagiri could get her father to agree to make the proposal.

She had to *make* him agree.

CHAPTER 3

There was a section of one of Izmirlian's notebooks—and it had taken Siyon a while to work this out—where he was having an affair with an opera singer. It wasn't visible through any journalled confessions, or even a glut of overwrought poetry. Rather, the previous speculations on the geography of the coastline north of the city gave way to investigation into the historical antecedents of opera tales, and then pages of diagrams of the machinery used to stage the finale of *A Simple Maid*, where the scullery girl is shot out of a Khanate firework launcher but thankfully caught by an angel. (Even Siyon knew this one; he'd gone along to laugh at the alchemy and had to put up with Daruj falling loudly in love with Gayane Saliu, in her first starring role.)

From the detail and interest in the workings, Siyon was almost certain Izmirlian had been sleeping with the angel. The fascination showed on the page, through learning everything about how the work was performed.

At the bottom of a page, before the journal turned to the investigation of ancient Lyraec trading routes through the Khanates, a single line read: *Let not love of the artist obscure the art.*

If Izmirlian had still been here, what would he have observed about alchemy? What could he tell Siyon about his own business, gathered with his furious consideration, his keen eyes and keener mind?

Or would Siyon have been dismissed with a single line as well, not worth half the time Siyon was spending poring over these journals in turn?

Izmir never met anyone he loved more than his own wild dreams. Avarair Hisarani had told him that, spat it in his face.

The author of these journals *had* wild dreams. He had brilliant dreams. He had a mind as sharp as a knife and yet as tight-coiled and intricate as well-braided rope. Siyon was just the idiot who'd fallen into being the Power, and made a mess of everything. If Izmirlian *had* been here, he'd have done a far better job. And he'd likely have left Siyon far behind.

"Hey," Daruj said from the doorway.

Siyon flinched hard enough to set his hammock rocking. He slammed the journal shut, wedging it between his knees, as if he could shove away his thoughts as well.

Daruj lifted a dubious eyebrow, but all he said was, "I thought you were going out?"

"I am." Siyon had been, and then he'd opened one of Izmirlian's journals to just check something. Or get a little bit of comfort.

Or because he didn't want to go. Not back into the tunnels behind the Scarp, beneath the city. Not into that surging maelstrom of Mundane energy, eager to carry him away. Freed along with the dragon, both escaping in a wild rush that Siyon couldn't control. The consequences of the last time he'd pushed ahead without understanding. He *didn't* want to go wading back in. What if he made it worse?

He was still clutching Izmirlian's journal, the leather cover rich and supple under his fingers.

Ridiculous to suppose he could extrapolate anything about Izmirlian, what he might or might not have done. Perhaps equally ridiculous to still be clinging to him now, in this lesser paper-and-ink form. A weakness. A wallowing. Siyon had hoped that he might one day follow after Izmirlian, take that journey of discovery as well. He'd promised. But he was supposed to finish here first.

He didn't even know where to start.

Daruj was frowning at him now, one forearm propped against the warped doorframe. "You all right?" he demanded.

"No," Siyon admitted, and smiled. Tried to. It felt pretty flat on his face. "But I wouldn't know what to do with myself if I was, right?"

Daruj frowned, and when had he developed those lines beside his mouth? Both of them had lived hard, burning brightly in a city that loved the light. "Come up with me," he said. "Have a drink, see people, walk the streets. The city's not dead, and neither are you."

"Come up?" Siyon repeated. "*You* told me the sorts of things they're saying about me up there." All his fault; dangerous and unstable; that he'd *meant* to do this, all along, in league with violent elements.

"They say the same things down here!" Daruj objected.

"No one down here is going to turn me in to the inqs," Siyon pointed out.

Daruj crossed his arms. "Back before Salt Night, you were palling around with the inqs. They aren't going to poison you now. Sorcery isn't even a crime!"

They'd think of something. But Siyon knew this argument; they'd had it before. There didn't seem to be much point in having it again. "Enjoy your night," he said, and tipped out of his hammock to start getting his own things.

When he looked again, Daruj had gone. It was fine. Siyon had his own business to be about.

The tunnels were hardly a secret down here; they couldn't be when the openings were visible, and every child was looking for a secret or an escape. When Siyon had been younger and sticking his nose into every corner—as opposed to now, when he only had time to poke at the really big messes—it had been known that one particular complex of caverns, stretching back from beneath the rubble of a collapsed mansion, was a warren of Midnight's activities.

So he certainly wasn't going *that* way. Whatever had become of it since Salt Night and Midnight's disappearance, Siyon didn't want to get involved. He had enough on his chipped plate without dealing with some jumped-up lieutenant, or a territory war between factions, or some other baron muscling in, or any of the *other* things Anahid regularly muttered about when she came down to hide with him for half a bell.

Besides, when he went past the little square that had once been the front courtyard of the fallen mansion, a storyteller had set up and was entertaining a rapt audience with wild declarations and a handful of cheap squibs as magical effects. His limp and tattered hat was more a deep wine than purple, but the intention was clear. Siyon could do without hearing further embroidery of either his exploits or his fuckups. Back before Salt Night, there'd been talk that someone was writing an opera about him; probably a relief that would never see the light of day now.

It wasn't difficult to find another entrance. He could *feel* them, this close, as places where the energy pulsed particularly brightly. Where the riptide pull of the power was stronger. Where the siren song soared higher.

And he was going *in there*. Clearly he hadn't learned anything about not doing the blatantly stupid thing.

Think of it like wading, not like sinking into the river. Siyon shoved the power down, mentally. Kept it below his knees. It couldn't wash him away. He was sturdier. He was larger. He wouldn't succumb. But it was a fight, pushing uphill and wriggling his way through a crack and into darkness.

When the stone folded around him, the clamour of power dropped away to a murmur. As though the cliff stretching above him, the whole bluff upon which the city was built, wrapped him up like the softest, warmest gullfeather quilt, protecting him from having to get up and face the day.

Siyon blinked, swaying on his feet at the sudden absence of something pressing against him from all sides, and tipped forward into an unintentional step. It came so easily, with nothing to push against, and he took two more before he thought about it, continuing deeper into the cave. Relief made his skin tingle. Or maybe *that* was the Mundane power, not really gone, but waiting. Full to the brim.

He kept moving, and nothing leapt out or pulled him down. His vision swam more bronze and burnished with his eyes closed than open. It was dark in here, he realised—entirely so, as though no daylight could fit through the crack that had admitted Siyon himself. But his surroundings were still entirely clear.

The least of the impossibilities of his life, right now.

With each step, the ruckus of the world above fell away behind him, and a deeper and stranger awareness of the Mundane *below* unfurled. A labyrinth curled through the earth, tunnels pulsing like veins, knotted like cobwebs, crossed and tightening like the warp and weft of the world. Nestled in its centre, like the sun in the sky or a pearl in an oyster, was the empty, beating heart of the dragon's former lair.

Like the warm body in the bed, urging you to roll this way. Siyon gave in, and rolled.

He walked, probably. Along the tunnels, not through the walls. It was difficult to be absolutely certain. His head swam with the glow of power. His ears rang gently, like the memory of a bell. He could feel a breeze upon his face, cool to the point of cutting, fresh in his nose with the promise of snow.

(What did snow smell like? He'd never even seen it, save the sprinkling of glitter used at the opera.)

Siyon spread his wings and tilted into the wind—

(spread his arms, fingertips grazing the stone walls on either side)

—letting it lift him up as he turned toward the mountains rearing up on the horizon, rank upon rank of them like the little humans who had once gathered to oppose them, to push them out of the *civilised* places, and into the wild.

As though that were not where she would rather be.

Here, with the sun spilling golden and thick as honey over the rolling hills beneath her, glinting off the twining rivers even as it did from the spines of her wings.

The only tragedy was being here alone. But her side still smarted, as did her heart. She had been pushed away quite enough, and she—

Siyon stubbed his toe on rock, staggered and nearly fell in sudden uncomprehending dizziness, one hand clutched against his ribs where...

Where he had never been shot with a ballista bolt. Not *him*.

He blinked, and again harder, until his vision was clear of black specks and whirling burnished sparks. Until he was *him*, sure of it, alone in the dark.

Not quite alone. There were noises ahead. The shuffle of feet on stone, a faint cough, insinuating whispers.

There was *light* ahead, faint and flickering and real.

Siyon edged along the tunnel, shuffling his feet against the uncertain ground. The light grew, though it was still dim, barely a lantern or three against the weight of the entire bluff above them.

The tunnel wall fell away from Siyon's fingertips, and the cavern opened in front of him.

He knew this place—had seen the massive tear in the ceiling made, had seen those stalactites fall, had seen those gouges dug in the floor by the dragon's claws as she'd gathered herself to push up and out.

He blinked again, and the past faded into the present—ranks of narrow camp beds set up in the shattered remains of the dragon's stone encasing, barely illuminated by lanterns hanging from the remaining stalagmites.

Every bed was occupied—some two dozen of them, perhaps. A body each, some sleeping, some just lying there staring at the ceiling. Some sitting up and eating blankly from wooden bowls. One or two sat with attention fixed on the dark gash where the dragon had torn her way out into the free sky.

As Siyon muttered, "Shit," all of them turned to look at *him*.

He didn't quite recognise them. He didn't quite *not*. Every single person had the same eyes, deep and liquid black.

Midnight's eyes.

Not Midnight's face—the people were all sorts, big and small, foreigners and locals and everything in between, male and female and beyond Siyon's ability to tell at a glance. But they all had those eyes, and they'd all recently shaved their hair down to stubble. There was... something. In their faces. In their bearing.

They *weren't* Midnight. But they also weren't entirely *not* Midnight.

The nearest one, sitting up on her camp bed, reached out a hand toward Siyon. "The power," she croaked.

More hands stretched out to him. Bodies shuffled, edging toward him.

Siyon legged it.

Back the way he'd come, with a clamour rising behind him—skittering, unsteady steps, and a clatter as something got overturned. They were *chasing him*, and Siyon didn't bother looking back, or wondering why. He just ran, up the slope, and around the corner—

Straight into another black-clad figure, who grabbed him even as she went over backward with an audible "Oof!"

They both went down, hard on the tunnel's stone floor, but she was twisting as they did. She slammed Siyon's shoulder into the floor and the scars the griffin had left on his back prickled strangely as she loomed up over him. Her hood fell back—and fuck, her head was shaved down to a russet fuzz, just like the mob in the cavern—even as she brandished—

Was that a *dowsing rod*?

Her eyes widened—and they were *her* eyes, a murky grey—and she hesitated. "You're not one of them."

Siyon jabbed at her side and heaved her off, scrambling to his feet. He looked back in panic—she was wearing black, she had Midnight's *mark* on the back of her hand, she was already regaining her balance and glaring at him—and sprinted into a darkness that closed around him, sure as stone.

She shouted after him: "There's no escape! You made sure of that!"

But Siyon didn't stop—not to listen, not to ask what in the Abyss she was talking about, not to think.

Not until he saw daylight, his breath scraping raw at the back of his throat and the blood thundering in his head.

He burst out into the middle of a crowd, scattering children with indignant squawks, leaving the storyteller shouting in his wake: "Fleeing the demons! The Sorcerer is in league with them, you know. He has a harpy, bound to his every whim—"

Siyon shoved through the crowd and kept running.

There's no escape. You made sure of that.

He hadn't found any answers. Only more questions.

"I'm sorry I couldn't be there," Anahid said again, topping up Zagiri's teaglass from a pitcher with warming charms etched into the gold decoration. Many teahouses were getting them now, showing off the new alchemical assistances that were flourishing in Bezim. Nura had found charmed barrels that would keep their contents cool, liqueurs that changed colour as they were poured, a coaster that would continually stir any glass set upon it.

There were alchemists doing all sorts of things, now that they could.

Just like that, Anahid's mind skittered away from their table at this quiet teahouse, away from her sister's social and political concerns, circling anew—and interminably—the problem of Sable House's provision of sureties.

Three days, she'd said. Nura had made inquiries through all her connections in the staff of Avenue townhouses, whose residents had their own demands for quality and discretion. Qorja had struck up not-exactly-idle conversation with Flowers in nearly every House of the District. Even Laxmi had interrogated the sorts of hard men who might be shaking down practitioners in the struggles between splintered fragments of Midnight's organisation.

None of their efforts had yielded any firm results, and it was the third day now. Anahid was going to have to ask Nihath for aid. Was going to have to reveal herself to the azatani practitioners. Was going to bring everything crashing down, not just on *her* head, but on Zagiri too.

"Well," Zagiri said, with an overly careless shrug. "You could hardly help it."

Anahid blinked and forced herself back to their actual conversation. What had she said? That she was sorry she hadn't been at Zagiri's first Ball rehearsal. "There were *many* things I could have done to help it," she noted, turning her glass on its coaster. "Beginning with not winning the House in the first place."

Zagiri snorted—in a manner entirely unbecoming a young azata, but they were hardly anywhere she might be seen by society. That was the entire reason that Anahid had chosen this teahouse, well out of the fashionable way.

That, and it was close to the District. She still felt exposed, strangely vulnerable without the weight of Laxmi at her shoulder. Which was ridiculous. She *wasn't* running her business on the promise of violence.

But one barony was vacant, and another in a mess. The uncertainty set a stone in her stomach and her eyes to scanning the street, as though some threat might wait among the respectable shoppers. People passed down the street, and lingered chatting on the corners, and lurked in the alleyway just across the street, watching the teahouse.

Anahid froze, a chill sweeping up her spine and wiping out the sound of Zagiri's voice. There *was* someone over there, dressed in black a little too dusty and ragged for this part of the upper city. Whoever it was, they weren't hiding their interest in this teahouse.

"Oh, did I tell you?" Zagiri leaned forward over the table. "I met Buni Filosani. She asked me to pass on her regards."

That pulled Anahid's attention back to the table. "To *me*?" Of course the woman—polished and polite and politically minded—remembered the names and relations of *everyone*. But while Anahid's deepest scandals yet remained a secret, there were plenty of other reasons to whisper about her. Her divorce from Nihath, for instance. Or her connection with the Sorcerer.

Anahid didn't regret any of it, save in the ways it made Zagiri's entrance to society more difficult. But now Azata Filosani was sending her regards, and Zagiri looked very pleased.

"She was quite positive about people other than azatani having a say in governing the city," Zagiri said, though her smile was fleeting. "She hopes someone will raise it at commencement."

"Your hope as well," Anahid noted, taking a sip of her tea.

Frustration twisted Zagiri's mouth. "Except Father won't *listen*. The next prefect of the city—"

"Possibly," Anahid corrected. "Filosani won't stand unopposed while Azatan Rowyani draws breath." Rowyani was the leader of the Pragmatic faction, concerned only with wringing azatani profit from the city.

"Fishguts to Rowyani," Zagiri muttered, like a reflex, and returned to her primary point: "But my own *father* won't take any heed. Tells me I've had a difficult year and the Ball is an important undertaking."

"Neither of which is untrue," Anahid said on a sigh.

"The Ball is descending a staircase and making inane conversation," Zagiri snapped, immediately wincing. "It's more than that. I know it is. It's my entrance into society as an adult. It's my declaration that I belong—that I *choose* to belong. That's why I'm *doing it*."

In the slump of Zagiri's spine against her chair, Anahid saw an echo of her own frustrations from years ago, as she'd done this herself—three times, in increasing desperation that it wouldn't matter how proper she was, how well she performed the role of azata...that no one would ever want to marry her.

And look how *that* had turned out.

"You needn't do it this year," Anahid suggested gently.

She got a glare for her trouble. "I wish I'd done it years ago," Zagiri returned heatedly. "I wish I was *already* an azata. I could speak formally in the family gatherings. Father might listen to me. And I wouldn't have to stand being draped with all sorts of wispy fabric while I could be doing something *useful*."

None of this was getting them anywhere, and if Zagiri grew any more frustrated, she might slide right off her chair and under the table, which would draw attention even here. "You can have my proxy in the family gathering, of course." Anahid could hardly attend herself; she'd be busy at Sable House. "But perhaps you should find someone else to propose your alteration at commencement. You made a good connection with Palokani last year. Perhaps start there."

Zagiri wrinkled her nose. "And have to explain, over and over, why my own father couldn't be brought to support it? How *can* I expect to convince anyone, if I can't convince my own family?" She sat up straight again—thank the Powers—and lay her hands firmly on the table. "No. It's got to come from the Savanis. I just have to make sure of it."

Once, Anahid might have shrugged and carried on, but the past year had taught her to listen more closely to her sister's planning. "What does that mean?"

"I'm going to convince him." If determination counted for anything, Zagiri would do it too. But she added, "Or I told Yeva I'd take the family Council seat, and it was a *joke*, I know I *can't*. But what if…"

"You don't want to be a councillor," Anahid pointed out. They'd discussed this before. But then again, Zagiri had come a long way since then. "You did well at your clerkship, though."

The face Zagiri pulled was a complicated twist of frustration and reluctance and possibly regret. "*You* don't want to be a baron," Zagiri flung back at her. "But what if it ends up being the only way to achieve what you actually want?"

"No." The word leapt from her lips, and Anahid busied her fingers with straightening her glass and plate and little pastry fork. "No," she repeated, more calmly. "There will always be another way. There will always be a *better* way. I'm not cut out for that sort of thing. I'm not interested."

That sort of thing led to blood on her hands, a man dead at her feet, all her fault, *her* actions, her choices.

Her victory. Her whole body singing with the thrill even as it twisted sick in her stomach.

What if she *was* cut out for that sort of thing?

She refused. It was too awful.

Zagiri sighed. "A better way. I'm *trying*. And I need to get going, or I won't have time to dress for promenade." The roll of her eyes made it clear that Zagiri's opinion of the ostentatious parading of the azatani hadn't changed, but she was still doing it. She was making the effort.

Her sister was growing up.

But Anahid's strange, wistful satisfaction froze in her chest as Zagiri left the teahouse—walking straight past that watcher, still lurking in the alleyway.

The watcher who lifted a hand and gave a little wave to Anahid.

Panic fluttered briefly at Anahid's ribs. But she could hardly make a run for the District, and she refused to be always hiding behind Laxmi's implied threat. So Anahid settled her account, wrapped her shawl around her shoulders against the faint winter chill on the breeze, and marched straight across the street.

Leaning against the corner of the building, the watcher waited with apparently endless patience, and a faint smile. A woman, Anahid thought, as she grew near enough to make a guess, with a shapeless laborer's hat hiding any sign of hair, and a battered black coat covering arms that Anahid suspected would show the marks of allegiance to Midnight.

The woman tilted a little, not quite a bow, and murmured, "Lady Sable."

"Are you selling or threatening?" Anahid asked. There seemed little point in being coy about things.

"Are those my choices?" The woman's smile was crooked, revealing a chipped tooth and lifting her red-tinged eyebrows. She had warm brown skin with a dusting of freckles across her cheeks. When she tipped the hat back a little, it revealed hair barely long enough to show its dark russet colour.

She didn't seem as tightly wound, or posturing, as the others of Midnight's former underlings Anahid had encountered. "If you have a more complicated deal to propose, you'd have taken it to the Zinedani," Anahid pointed out.

The woman shrugged one shoulder. "The Zees don't have what I want."

Anahid didn't know what *that* meant, and she wasn't interested in learning. "I'm not getting involved," she said starkly.

The woman snorted. "Sister, there's blood in the water and surf on the rocks; you really think clutching to an oar's going to help you?"

Better than using that oar to start a fight with the circling sharks. But all Anahid said was, "Good day."

She turned back downhill, toward the District.

A laugh, and a skipping hush of boots on cobblestones, and then the woman fell in beside her. "All right," she said, with a little hop in her step to keep pace; she was a head shorter than Anahid. "Have it your way. Yes, I'm former Midnight. Yes, I'm running my own crew these days. No, I don't want to get involved in the baronial fighting, not out here, not in the District. And you aren't in that fight. We could do good trade; I have quality products."

"You and every other former lieutenant of Midnight," Anahid snapped. And none of them could be trusted to deliver what Sable House needed, when they needed it. Ink and ashes, Anahid was going to have to ruin herself, but what other possibility was there?

The woman coughed a laugh. "You ain't talked to any lieutenants of Midnight, za. None of them are talking, not sensibly."

Anahid slowed her pace. "What?"

"Folks you're talking to might be claiming it." The woman shrugged. "Ain't no one to put 'em in their place anymore. Every lieutenant Midnight had went completely moonstruck within a week of Salt Night. *That's* why it's all such a mess."

It might have sounded ridiculous, if Anahid hadn't met Midnight—more than one of him, stepping out of thin air, summoned by Siyon's strange and disappearing token. Further strangeness didn't seem outlandish. Anahid stopped altogether, considering this woman anew. "Why are you telling me all this?"

"Because you have an association with the Sorcerer," the woman said, easy as anything. "And I need to see him. So I'm willing to cut a deal. Whatever you need, sure as eggs, and you tell the Sorcerer I'm sane and serious."

They *did* need their sureties, quite desperately. But Anahid wouldn't sell Siyon for it. "He's his own man. And he doesn't like barons. Especially not Midnight."

The woman smirked. "He probably likes us even less right now. But I think we can help each other. Just tell him I want to see him. Same place as last time."

That hardly made any sense. But just passing a message seemed harmless enough. And it might *save* her. Keep her secrets for at least a little longer. "Who do I say is asking?"

"Call me Peylek." She gave a little bow, flaring out her coat. "I'll let your people know how they can place orders. Looking forward to doing business with you."

She peeled away down a side street, disappearing quickly into the shadows, and leaving Anahid still uncertain. She mistrusted seren-dipity. She feared hidden traps. *What if it ends up being the only way?* she heard again. *You don't want to be a baron.*

Peylek was right; clinging to an oar wasn't going to be enough. But Anahid *had* attended the Harbour Master's Ball three times. She could dance as delicately as anyone.

She *would* find a way through this.

CHAPTER 4

Zagiri followed her father along the upstairs hall, fists bunched in her skirt as she fought the urge to shake him.

"Father," she tried, for the fourth time, "you keep saying that the Council should be building Bezim, making something for the future, not simply maintaining the past, and here we are—"

"Zagiri." He stopped to face her, and the sharpness of her name—not *petal*, not *little gull*, but her actual name—stopped her cold. He frowned at her. "You are about to become an azata, but this is the petulant insistence of a child."

Zagiri's fists clenched tighter; she swallowed hard against a wail that would not help at all.

But the family gathering to confirm the Savani councillor and policies was *tonight*. Downstairs, cousins and uncles were being ushered into the spacious back parlour.

Zagiri was out of time, and Usal Savani still wouldn't listen.

Her father turned back to the hall mirror, straightening the councillor chain and its Savani seal around his shoulders. He'd carried it for as long as she could remember. He was respected. If she couldn't convince him of the need for reform, of the benefits of change, then how could she expect anyone else to listen to her?

It *had* to be the Savani councillor who stood at commencement and proposed widening the membership of the Council to non-azatani candidates.

Zagiri took a deep breath and relaxed her grip on her gown. "You are treating me as a child," she said as evenly as Anahid would have. "Instead of a family member with a proposal that is in the interests of this family and the city as a whole. Bezim will be made stronger if its betterment is the work of everyone, not just the azatani. And *we* will be made stronger if we have the vision and the voice to push forward and not cower in the past."

She thought she'd done that quite well, all things considered.

But her father sighed heavily and set a hand on her shoulder. "Little gull, I know you mean well. You see all the things that could be done, and want to do them *now*. But you must understand..." He shook his head. "The death of the prefect and our fellow azatani is not an *opportunity*. We could have been among them, had your mother not been unwell on Salt Night. Now is the time to reflect on our blessings and show our commitment to Bezim."

Zagiri opened her mouth, words flooding her tongue—she *was* committed to Bezim and what it could become; and did he think the azatani were the only ones so committed; and what did he think Syrah herself would have wanted—but he lifted a hand, swift and stern.

"No." Usal Savani sighed. "No, petal. Come to the gathering if you wish. But this will not be a part of our determination for the new council."

He started down the stairs.

Leaving Zagiri clenching her fists again, with frustration clamping like a scream upon her throat.

Downstairs in the golden parlour, the rest of the family were waiting—old Uncle Adel and his annoying son Gildon; the cousins who shared the vote and the petty trading concerns of the now-dead aunt for whom Zagiri had been named; the head of the third-tier branch of the family who they only saw on these occasions and who didn't, technically, have a say in proceedings.

They were all waiting to confirm the Savani position for the new council—to name Usal the councillor again, and endorse the matters of concern to the family. One of which *should* be a proposal to widen the membership of the Council beyond the azatani.

For a moment, Zagiri considered not going downstairs at all. She could change into her leathers, swing out of her bedroom window, run the tiles wild and heedless beside her Bracken blademates until this tight itch crawling in her veins had been swept away. That was what she would have done this time last year.

She was trying to make other choices now. Better choices. Choices that *mattered*, and that used what she had to make more and better options for everyone.

Zagiri squared her shoulders and marched after her father. She just managed to slide into the parlour as Gildon was closing the door.

He glared at her and said loudly, "Is Zagiri supposed to be here? She's not even of age yet."

"I'm presenting *this year*," Zagiri snarled, elbowing him in his badly patterned longvest—and relishing his grunt—as she ducked past him. "*And* I'm carrying Anahid's proxy."

The room was mild chaos, with the cousins exclaiming over each other's dresses, and the third-tier family head repeating himself louder and louder in an effort to suck up to old Uncle Adel, who was sometimes deaf, or confused, or both.

Usal lifted his voice over the din with the ease of long practice. "Everyone please take a seat, and we'll get this done. Then everyone can get along to your proper evening plans."

The cousins perched on a sofa like a trio of twittery birds, all wide eyes and primly tucked ankles. "Why are we even here, Uncle Usal?" the paler cousin whined. "Didn't we confirm you as our councillor just last winter? We don't have to do it every year, do we?"

Gildon rolled his eyes, obviously and obnoxiously, as he leaned forward to answer. "If you'd been paying *any* attention, Ilya, you'd have heard that the Council's resolution of recess after Salt Night required all families to confirm their membership anew, regardless of their internal candidate schedules or whether they suffered any disruption from casualties incurred."

"It's so sad," the littlest cousin breathed, her big eyes shining with tears, or perhaps wistfulness. "The prefect, and all her guests, just the entire party...gone." A little overdramatic—Markani hadn't been the only guest injured rather than killed outright—but still worthy of her heartfelt sigh.

Father cleared his throat. "Yes, well. Young Gildon is correct. And so here we are. If there are no further questions, we can—"

Zagiri shot to her feet, grabbing her last chance. "Will the Savanis be making any proposals to the Council's resumed session?"

Even as her father sighed, pressing a long-suffering finger to his brow, cousin Gildon frowned at her. "What does *that* mean? What sort of proposals?"

He didn't matter. He'd never support anything Zagiri wanted, just *because* Zagiri wanted it. He'd hated her since she pushed him into a pond when they were both small children. He'd deserved it then; he still deserved it now.

Zagiri glanced over the cousins—who were all watching her agog—and the third-tier family head—who was scarcely less so— and back to her father, whose mouth pursed as it always had when she'd come before him to admit to breaking something in a fit of exuberance. Ink and ashes, she *wasn't* a child any longer, and this was not some childish whim. It was the fate and future of their city. She wouldn't back down over a frown.

"I wish to place on the family priorities a proposal that the renewed Council open membership more widely."

"Petal," her father sighed, closing his eyes in a gentle wince.

"You can't just—" Gildon started, probably about to say something that would make her want to punch him.

He was saved by the third-tier family head—of all people—tilting forward from his self-effacing corner and clearing his throat. "More widely?" he repeated.

Oh, he was hoping she meant that the lower tiers might get their own representation, rather than relying on their higher-tier families. "More widely," she confirmed, "than merely azatani voices. There is more to this city than us. It is time we recognised that."

Gildon lifted his chin in a way he probably thought made him look important, but actually only drew attention to the unfortunate jut of his nose. "Or what?" he demanded. When Zagiri frowned at him, he sniffed. "You say you want..." He fluttered his fingers dismissively. "To waste the family influence on this wild notion. What will you do, if you don't get your way? Challenge us all?"

His lips twisted into a supercilious smirk. There was never a pond when you needed one. "How do you think the azatani *got* this city in the first place?" she snapped. "They *challenged* the Last Duke. And they won." She turned away from his scoffing; he didn't matter. "Father? Please. This is important."

But if there was regret in her father's eyes, it did not soften the steely set of his mouth. "We have spoken already about this, and you have my answer. Your cousin has the right of it, you cannot mount public challenge and expect—"

"No." Zagiri took half a step forward—but what *was* she going to do? She *couldn't* challenge them, not for this. But she needed her father on board, respected and speaking for her family. She couldn't *force* the Savani representative to bring the matter to Council.

Unless...

Unless she *was* the Savani representative.

Zagiri had told Yeva Bardha, one wild night crouched on her roof, that she planned to take the family Council seat. She'd known, even as she said it, that it was a ridiculous ambition. One day, perhaps. One day in not too many years, even, because her father did keep sighing over his breakfast and speaking wistfully of retirement, and the only other option was Gildon, who was awful and pompous and hated by the cousins.

But she needed this *now*.

"I do challenge," she said, half breathless with what she was doing, scared like she'd never been, even the first time she'd leapt from a roof. She had to clear her throat to get the words out. "I nominate Zagiri Savani as Savani family councillor."

The sudden flash of hurt in her father's eyes cut like a sabre strike. But he'd *made* her do this. Why hadn't he just *listened*? Maybe now, at least, he'd take her seriously.

"Can she do that?" the cousins hissed to each other.

"No, she can't," Gildon told them loudly, also up on his feet. He turned on Zagiri, actually planting his hands on his hips. "You're not even of age," he repeated.

"Actually," Uncle Adel said, his voice creaky as an attic staircase. He raised a wavering finger. "Actually, there are no requirements of age nor wealth nor significance on councillors, only upon those nominating."

Gildon pointed in triumph. "Then you can't—"

"On behalf of Anahid Savani," Zagiri said over him, flashing a tight smile, "I nominate Zagiri Savani as our councillor."

Surely her sister would understand and forgive her. Even if their father's face had gone stiff and cold. He was no longer looking at Zagiri.

The cousins goggled at her. "*Why* would you want to do that?" the pale cousin gasped.

"Because we have a chance now." Zagiri tried to marshal all the arguments her father had dismissed, like threading beads with trembling fingers. "The city has come together in the past half year like never before. We have *all* been injured, and pulled together to make Bezim anew. Now is the chance to make from our disasters a new opportunity to be stronger together."

Gildon snorted, very rudely. "Fanciful."

"There is interest in this," Zagiri snapped at him. "Serious political interest, that would ally us with strong families and make us a part of their rise. But someone must take the risk now." She wished her father would look at her. "I can't let this chance pass without doing everything I can."

"Oh," said the littlest cousin, and looked at her tall sister.

Who nodded. "We support Zagiri."

A vote on her side. But with the first terrifying moment past, and a chance to actually think, Zagiri realised how utterly impossible this was. She didn't even have a vote of her own, and obviously Gildon would *never* support her. Her father would be returned easily. At least she'd had a chance to raise the matter in the family gathering. Perhaps that, or the cousins' interest, might convince her father that this was worth more attention, and he might—

"I nominate Gildon Savani."

Zagiri blinked at her awful, smug cousin.

Who looked even more superior as he continued: "And I carry also the proxy of my brother, Telmut. So that's one for me and one for her. Father? I believe you have the casting vote."

The elderly Adel blinked under the sudden attention. "Oh. I say. Er. What?"

Zagiri's chest felt tight. Uncle Adel had *always* supported Father, happily ceding control of the family to his much-younger brother, far more interested and able.

Gildon kept talking. "The nominations for Savani councillor, Father. It's Uncle Usal, or the daughter he can't control, or me, your son."

"Oh, you?" Adel smiled faintly, and patted the arm of his chair. "Proud of you, of course. Yes. I support my boy." He looked around the gathering, blinking now at their stunned expressions. "Who's got the vote?"

Gildon turned a triumphant look on Zagiri's father and held out a demanding hand. It was him—with the votes of himself, and his brother, and his father. Because Zagiri had split the rest of the vote.

It was all her fault.

Zagiri had to watch as her father lifted the heavy chain, and the Savani seal, from his shoulders. "Gildon Savani is confirmed as councillor." His voice rang as hollow as Zagiri felt.

"Thanks," Gildon declared, slick as a gull in mud, and draped the chain around his neck. "It's for the best, really. We can't be foolish about our future. Good night, everyone. Come along, Father."

He did at least help his father out, the old man leaning heavily on his arm and sounding confused about what had just happened. The third-tier head hesitated a moment, casting a wild and harried look at Usal, before scurrying out as well, calling after Gildon. The cousins crept away like nervous alleycats, but as they went past, the smallest whispered to Zagiri, "I like your idea."

For what *that* was worth.

The door swung shut. Zagiri swallowed hard. "Father, I'm sorry," she started.

But she wasn't surprised when he said only, "Get out."

She wanted to beg. To throw herself at his feet and wail that this had all been a terrible mistake.

He still hadn't looked at her. She couldn't blame him; she didn't deserve his regard.

She'd done this. She'd ruined it all.

"Very effective," agreed one of the Sable House Flowers—a young man with a glorious spill of silken black hair that was possibly the source of his stage name, the Waterfall. He gestured with a languid wrist around the little group. "I'm sure we've all tested it in the ways we prefer. And may I just add that it's quite..." His hesitation was far more coquettish than coy. "Quite invigorating."

Laughter from the rest of the Flowers, and more when one of them noticed Anahid's blush. "Effective is excellent," she said firmly. What she *cared* about was whether the sureties and other aides provided by Peylek's people were suitable. The *invigoration* of the Waterfall—who was now smirking at her—was entirely beside the point. Anahid tried to pull this gathering back to business. "Everyone is satisfied with the new provisions?"

As the Flowers nodded, Anahid sighed in relief that *this* snarl in her nets was untangled. Peylek had provided a substantial shipment, which would last them half the season if they were careful. The pressure was lifted, and Anahid could keep her secrets a little longer.

If only all the House business would smooth itself out so well. Customer numbers were still low across the District, and with so many former Midnight people lurking about, it seemed there must be trouble sooner or later. Anahid braced herself when Lejman ducked past the heavy curtain in her office doorway, but what he said was: "There's a visitor, mistress. He would prefer not to come up."

Anahid thought she understood when she saw who was waiting in the private dining room. "Master Attabel. What an unexpected pleasure to welcome you to—"

She stopped as Attabel's sparkling blue-painted nails sliced through her sentence. "I am not attending your House, Lady Sable, rife with pleasures though I am sure it is."

A clandestine visit, then, not one for his own pleasure. A visit that, perhaps, he didn't want getting back to the Zinedani, who owned the Siren's Cove, the House he managed.

Anahid wasn't sure she wanted him here at all, in those circumstances. She'd meant what she'd said to Peylek; she wasn't getting involved in baron business. Anahid laid a hand on the back of a chair, but neither took it nor offered it to her guest. "I shan't trouble you with impertinent offers of refreshments, then," she said, and lifted an expectant eyebrow. He could say whatever he had to say, and leave.

He gave a coy little smile. "I am merely checking on my neighbour, in these trying times. We are all tossed on the same seas, are we not? The reduced patrons, and the pinch in the purses of the city. The disruptions to supply of so many useful things. The frankly unsettling presence of idle thugs roaming the streets." He shook his head, dark hair shimmering with gold powder. "We all wonder how you are managing, over here by yourself."

A chill prickled at Anahid's skin. Was this the first suggestion that the Zinedani daughters wanted Sable House back as much as their father had? "I manage," she replied curtly.

"You do," Attabel replied, smiling warmly. "Your little boat stays afloat so well. A firm hand on the tiller is something many of us are interested in."

Oh no, it was *worse*. For the Siren's Cove was already *under* the strong hand of the Zinedanis. "Things will improve with time," Anahid blurted, almost tripping over the words. Her breath caught in her throat, thick with the remembered scent of blood. "You'll excuse me, please. I must open the House."

Attabel seemed to take no offense, sweeping genially away again like a stately peacock. Anahid had to take a moment or three in the private dining room, gripping the back of the chair as she dragged her body under control. Even that faint suggestion that she might step up into the space Garabed Zinedani once occupied set panic banging against her ribs.

She wasn't getting involved. She just wanted to run her House.

And run it did, more smoothly than many nights in the last little while, with the Flowers happy and the customers—fewer though they might be—merrily spending. The evening progressed, and Anahid put Attabel's visit firmly behind her. She'd been clear; he wouldn't try again.

Shortly after the Merry bell rang, Nura caught Anahid's elbow in a hallway, to say quietly, "You may wish to come to your office as soon as possible, mistress."

Alarming enough by itself, from Nura. More so when she'd give no further details, merely glancing pointedly around them. Anahid hurried to extract herself and rushed up the stairs, brushing aside the heavy curtain that had been pulled tight across her office doorway to find—

Zagiri, bouncing to her feet from where she'd been perched nervously on the chaise. "I didn't know where else to go," she said. Nearly wailed. She was *wringing her hands*? There was nothing so obvious as tears on her face, but she was pale as overmilked coffee.

"What's happened?" Anahid pulled the curtain firmly closed behind her. Nura was right: No one could know that Zagiri was *here*. It would cause a terrible scandal, especially with her Ball so close.

"I—" Zagiri gulped, and then she launched herself at Anahid, clinging as she hadn't since she was ten and declared herself *not a baby any longer*.

Anahid wrapped arms around her and held on tight, as she'd longed to any number of times since then. The beads on Zagiri's evening dress—an elegant and sophisticated one, an *azata's* dress— pressed against Anahid's palms, as Zagiri panted half-desperate breaths against Anahid's black costume tabard.

A cheer rose from outside, half a dozen raucous voices, but Anahid's attention was pulled back as Zagiri admitted: "I fucked up. Ana, I've ruined everything."

"I'm sure you haven't," Anahid replied, purely by reflex. "You can't have released another dragon."

She'd never let Siyon hear her say it.

Zagiri hiccuped, almost more sob than laugh, but close enough to start them moving. Anahid settled her back on the couch, glad to see that Nura had left not just tea, but also a flagon of rakia. They each had a little of both, and Anahid coaxed the whole story out of Zagiri, of just what had happened at the family meeting that Anahid had missed this evening.

Truth be told, *fucking up* about covered it. "Cousin Gildon," Anahid repeated. As family councillor? He wasn't even as old as Anahid.

"I know." Zagiri sighed, tilting her empty rakia glass. "It's a disaster."

"It's … not good." Anahid pinched the bridge of her nose. Not least because Gildon's brother, who'd ceded his proxy, was away because he was head of the Savani trading interests. This put both trading and politics in the hands of that branch of the family.

It was still, next to everything that had befallen the city this year, hardly a problem at all. But it ruined all of Zagiri's plans. In more ways than one.

"I can't go home," Zagiri said in a very small voice. "Not when I'm the reason Father has lost everything."

"It's not everything," Anahid pointed out. "He's still head of the family."

But that meant very little, if neither the family's trade nor the family's politics were his responsibility.

"I can't ask him to let me stay there." Zagiri shook her head. "He's right to be angry with me. I'm angry with him too. Why couldn't he just *listen*?" She tilted back against the chaise, eyes shining alarmingly. "If only I were already an azata. If only I could speak for myself."

But here they were, and *if only* filled no sails. Anahid could only solve one small, simple corner. "You can stay with me, of course. For tonight, at least. And perhaps tomorrow, things will look different." When Zagiri looked askance around the office, Anahid added, "Not here. I'll take you back to the apartment."

"You've—" Zagiri tapped a finger at Anahid's cheek, fingernail clicking against the beaded widow's mask. "You've work to do. Just give me the key and I'll sort myself out."

Anahid shook her head. "Laxmi has insisted on strict security. Charms and all."

Her paranoia had been borne out. It wasn't only the inquisitors who were eager to get hold of Siyon, or anything else he might have left behind. Some of the others—splinters of Midnight's organisation, or other rogue practitioners, or Anahid hardly knew who—had been quite assiduous in attempting to force the gate or find a way around.

"It's a quiet night," Anahid continued. Hadn't she just been thinking that things were working well, before Zagiri had arrived? She could take half a bell off, to get her sister settled back at the apartment. "Come on, I'll just let the others know."

Qorja produced a cloak from the Flowers' communal wardrobe to give Zagiri some discretion, and a little sophisticated mystery. Just as they were getting it properly draped, a heavy tread coming up the back stairs turned out to be Laxmi.

She was dressed in her showy House armour, her belligerent version of livery, with far more buckles and chains than were strictly necessary. Her full lower lip was oozing a sluggish trickle of blood from a split.

Something tugged at Anahid's stomach; probably irritation. "What have *you* been doing?"

Laxmi's grin widened, and she swiped at her bloodied lip with her tongue. "Entertaining and earning. Isn't that what we do here?"

Anahid remembered, now, the cheer she'd heard from the yard earlier. "You *can't* stage fights in the courtyard. We've been over this! We don't have the permits for it, and what if the children see?"

"They can come run the bets." Laxmi leaned forward, reaching past Anahid to tilt up the hood on Zagiri's cloak with a finger. "Hello there, little imp."

Anahid shook her head to clear it—from the uneasy memories evoked by Laxmi's scent of blood and sweat—and said, "Zagiri will be staying with us tonight."

Laxmi just shrugged nonchalantly. "The more the merrier. You should get me the permits. For a proper fighting pit."

"No," Anahid said, like she was telling a cat to get off the table; it felt just as futile. "I'll be back by the midnight bell; try not to break any more laws before then. Come on, Zagiri."

They went out the back gate, through the yard still marked up with a chalk circle, empty boxes and barrels hauled around it as seating. There were dark spots of blood on the paving. Anahid didn't want to look more closely.

The Flower district was in full swing around them, though it was far more quiet than it had been when Anahid first took over Sable House. Troubles in Bezim usually saw the District bustling with those seeking distraction, but the events of Salt Night—earthquake or dragon or otherwise—had left buildings knocked down, businesses destroyed, families in need of homes. There was less coin free for ready spending, and those who had found new employment in clearing and rebuilding were working so hard they lacked the time and energy for gaiety.

The District was hungry, and those denizens of the baronies who'd lost their leadership on Salt Night prowled its fringes, hungriest of all.

But Zagiri scarcely seemed to notice the glitter or the glowers as Anahid steered her quickly through the District; she really *was* upset. They were out of the gates, walking alongside the fragrant hedges, before she spoke. "Maybe you should let Laxmi run a fighting pit." When Anahid shot a stern glance into the shadow beneath Zagiri's hood, those cloaked shoulders shrugged. "She's a fallen demon. She's going to start fights anyway. She might as well be doing it for fun and profit, rather than seriously."

It was a good point, and Anahid didn't know why she was so troubled by it. Surely Laxmi didn't *have* to. Perhaps violence was in her nature, but she didn't have to be ruled by it, did she?

And yet, surely Sable House could use the lure of a different sort of entertainment, with new patrons and the income from their attentions. Anahid had a sinking feeling that she would indeed be instructing Nura to acquire the relevant permits.

"I need to solve *someone's* problems," Zagiri sighed. "How am I supposed to host my first entertainment from your apartment?"

Anahid had lost track of the progress of Zagiri's preparations for the Harbour Master's Ball. "Don't worry about that now," she insisted. "After a good night's rest, things won't seem so dire, and I'm sure you and Father can resolve matters. Mother won't want to leave your first hostess event to the Bardhas, I'm sure."

A little sniff from beneath the cloak's hood. "I suppose I could just tag along at Yeva's, couldn't I? If it comes to that."

"It won't," Anahid said firmly. "But you'll certainly want to plan your apology in advance. *This* is your chance to really impress your new maturity upon Father, and I'm sure he will…"

They'd turned the last corner, off Glass and into the laneway, where there was an obstruction outside the entrance to the apartment—once Siyon's, now Anahid and Laxmi's. The lantern hanging above the grate illuminated two stacked trunks, heavy and hefty but charmed, Anahid knew, to be far easier to carry than they should be. The Savani family had at least a dozen of them, for carrying personal belongings on trade voyages.

A card on top of the stack read only *Zagiri Savani.*

Anahid's footsteps dragged to a halt, her sister's beside her.

Her sister's belongings, delivered here to Anahid, in the family trunks.

Zagiri pushed back the hood of her cloak, the better to look pointedly at Anahid. "Still think this can be resolved?"

There was nothing Anahid could say.

The easternmost point of Bezim had always been the Observatory, a glory of golden stone and copper dome, a gleaming trophy of the city's investigation into all the wonders of the world. Then, it had jutted boldly out into the Carmine Sea, atop the farthest point of the city's proud headland.

It had come down in the world—literally—since the Sundering. Now the Observatory was home to Bower's Scythe bravi, rather than telescopes or alchemical equipment, and wallowed on a low lump of island reachable only by daring leap, or Awl Quarter gondola.

The parkland that had once encircled the Observatory was still there, though what had once been the favoured promenade location for the azatani was now a playground for the lower city, a jumbled space of patchy grass and gone-wild shrubbery. Where it sloped down into the water, a little mucky beach had accrued, jagged with old shards of brick washed up from farther along the sunken coast.

Patches of pavers had been spread with threadbare rugs upon which couples were canoodling, or little groups of friends toasting with dented pewter mugs of salty low beer. There were more blood-gulls, undeniably red-legged, chasing and snapping in the half-hearted waves that pawed at the beach. Up toward the ridge, a trio of rangy teens were desultorily duelling, or at least poking at one another with rust-spotted sabres, probably waiting to tag along with the Bower's Scythe for the evening. And shortly after Siyon arrived, a parade of kids came tumbling out of a gap in a wall, dragging a bundle of rags and ratty paper and splintered bits of wood. Something they'd built, from the pride with which they carried it.

There weren't any Badrosani thugs, however, not that Siyon could pick at a casual glance. He'd be naive to think Mama wouldn't hear of anything he did here, especially if he drew attention to himself, but at least no one would grab him on standing orders. Probably.

So many people who wanted a piece of the Sorcerer. So many people leaning on him. Sometimes it felt like the whole city's weight upon him, demanding he *fix* what he'd done. And most of the time, Siyon felt far lesser than almost anyone else he knew. Never as driven as Daruj, not as bold as Zagiri. Anahid was more canny, Mayar far more intuitive, and Izmirlian, of course, had been much smarter.

Siyon had only made it this far with the help of all of them and more. But now *he* was the Power of the Mundane. The only one who could see the energy flowing and sparking, oozing down here to bleed slowly into the sea, pooling at the base of the barrier Siyon had drawn around the city.

It had seemed like a good idea at the time. It had seemed *essential*, to building up the Mundane and evening out the flow of energy—and beings—between the planes. But everything *else* Siyon had done was a problem, or so it seemed.

Down here, at the point of the city, the barrier looked close enough to touch, sweeping down and around the headland like a shimmering bronze curtain, somewhere out past the line of low water. Difficult to tell how far out, as it disappeared into something like heat haze over the water. Or maybe that was the thickness of the power pooling at its base, like rags shoved against a door to stop the cold draft beneath it, or like the spawn-foam that frothed up on the beaches in spring.

Was it supposed to do that? How would Siyon know? Who could he ask?

Siyon gnawed at his thumbnail, tasting salt and the seagrass he'd helped Mayar string up to dry at the squat this morning. Was it his imagination, that sensation of energy sloshing around him, like rakia in a glass? Was it *bad*? Why was all this scratching at him like an impatient cat?

There's no escape, that woman had shouted at Siyon, deep beneath the Scarp, as he fled those...those awful empty shells of Midnight. *You made sure of that*. It still rang in his ears.

It made him wonder, and he couldn't even say why. Except that they were down there, where the power seemed to be rising. Except it flowed out here, and didn't seem to have anywhere to *go*.

Siyon reached out—not with his hands, but with those other senses, in the way he'd once stretched out toward the other planes, but now could only manage within the Mundane—toward the shimmering nothing of the barrier. For a moment, he thought it really was nothing, not there at all even like this, but then...

Then, the faintest sensation of pressure. Like brushing your knuckles against the flank of a fish, just a little yielding. But if you pressed harder, it was firm. The city boundary held against his touch.

Maybe that was good. There were monsters out there, after all. Enough of them that Siyon was being paid to ward whaling boats. You could hear stories about more than just the dragon, down in the markets.

Shouting started behind him, spiked with frustrated anger; when Siyon whirled around, it was just the kids, now pushing and shouting over their tangled bundle of blackened rags and sticks.

It was a kite, Siyon realised, looking at the spread of fine cords that some weaver was going to be irate about losing. It would have been a good day for it, with a nice stiff breeze off the bay, but the kite itself was hefty and complicated, too easily tangled when none of the kids could hold it far enough aloft.

Before he really thought about it, Siyon stepped forward.

None of the kids were older than ten, but three of them jumped between Siyon and the kite, like it was bounty to be protected from his depredations.

Siyon lifted his hands. "I'll hold it up while you get it ready."

After a hard-edged moment of suspicious glares, one of them—a girl with straight black hair who couldn't have been older than seven—said, "All right. But you fuck it up, we fuck you up, get?"

Siyon got.

It was hardly less of a mess in his hands, long and sinuous and threatening to come apart or tip out of his grip at any moment. It had been patched together out of scraps of dark fabric, offcuts of tin, strips of charcoal-blackened canvas. There was something like a head twisted out of wire at one end. Maybe the whole thing was a massive bird?

"Ready?" the black-haired girl snapped, and Siyon stopped puzzling and lifted his aching arms.

Five kids smoothly took up the long cords, and on the girl's mark, they started running. Siyon lifted the body of the kite, with its dangling parts—wings and tail?—fluttering, and the breeze came in just *so* and lifted it out of his grip.

Had that been him? Had his wish brought the wind? There was too much power pooled down here for him to tell if it had moved.

As the kite climbed the breeze, and its body gained the structure it had always been intended to have, Siyon stopped thinking about all of that.

It was a dragon. It was *the* dragon, rising again as she'd risen over the city on Salt Night. The scrappy edges fluttered in the wind, her wings tilted and creaked, and a cheer rose from the kids that rang strangely in Siyon's ears.

He fell into it, the shape of her in the sky and the shock echoing in his veins.

Tumbling through endless blue, skidding in clouds, wheeling above empty hills rolling gently away beneath—

No, wait, they weren't empty.

Little blocks clustered in the valley that Siyon realised faintly—as though from a long distance, as though he had to reach through a veil for the memories—were buildings. A settlement. A town, even. Specks shifting and racing over the nearby hills. People, tiny and easy to overlook.

Easy but unwise to overlook. Siyon's ribs still ached where the human toy had bit into it—

(Not him, that hadn't happened to *him*.)

—and she had no wish to experience it again. She thought she remembered humans as friendly, bringing her tribute, lighting beacons to guide her path across the night sky. So much had changed; this was barely the world she remembered at all.

She'd slept so long. Her world was gone. Her humans were gone. Her Power was gone.

(Somewhere, far away, someone shouted, "Hey!")

She was alone. There was nowhere safe to land, not where people were. And yet she could not fly forever.

("*Hey!* Hey, mister!")

Siyon blinked. *Siyon*, not the dragon. He was here. He was... somewhere, scrambling at the tenuous border of mist and certainty, where his eyes didn't work, and his other senses couldn't be relied upon.

A whiff of sandalwood turned his head, sent him yearning after...

("I don't care if he helped us with the kite; I say we go through his pockets.")

Something tugging at him.

Reflex flared to life.

Siyon forced his eyes open, world spinning and blurring in his vision even as he grabbed the hand dipping into his coat. There was a yelp, and a scrabble of heels on dusty stone, and he still couldn't *see* anything, not until he blinked furiously once, twice, thrice.

The sky tipped the right way up, framed by two scruffy kids, both shouting, one beating at the other, who was beating at *Siyon*, and Siyon had an almost crushing grip on his skinny little wrist. He let go, and the kid went tumbling over backward, up on his feet in half a moment and racing away, shouting at the top of his lungs.

The other kid—the black-haired little girl—gave Siyon a sidelong look. "You're fucking *weird*, mister," she declared.

Siyon opened his mouth, and had nearly remembered how words worked when the dragon—or at least, the kite—flew over them again, and he flinched.

The girl rolled her eyes. "It's a *kite*. You helped *launch* it."

Propping up on one elbow, Siyon tracked the black shadow across the sky. Other people in the park were watching it too, with a hand shading their eyes and various expressions—bitterness on one, but mostly amusement or even something like pride.

"Did you see her?" Siyon's voice was barely a rasp, but the girl was still crouched at his side.

"The dragon's a her?" She shrugged. "I guess you'd know. Nah, I was keeping coin-toss tally in a den on Salt Night. Felt a shake, thought it was just some building come down. First I knew 'bout anything someone come bursting in shouting about the Zinedani bled out at Mama's." She snorted. "No one talking 'bout the dragon until later. Now it's all they talk about."

Siyon still felt lost in fog. He should get up. It felt like all he could do just to lie here without holding on. "It is?"

"Tales from all over," the girl insisted. "Off the ships and in the markets. It—she's—flown off now, but she'll be back, right? She'll come back to set us free. Won't she?"

A genuine question. This undernourished lower city urchin, with charcoal smeared on her cheek from the kite she'd made, was seriously asking him whether the dragon who'd destroyed part of the upper city was going to come back to the city and *set us free*?

"How would I know?" he managed.

He remembered too late. *I guess you'd know*, she'd said, with a little shrug.

"Because you're him, right?" she said, just as careless. "The Sorcerer or whatever."

Or whatever. That flip of her wrist, like it hardly mattered. Like no one was cursing his name or holding him responsible. Like no one cared.

Maybe she didn't. What did a few walking myths matter to a lower city street brat? It was just one more thing you couldn't control.

"You're going to help, right?" she continued, entirely unbothered when he just stared at her. "You're going to help set us free."

The whole world leaning on him. Looking to him. Fix it. Set them free.

And Siyon had no idea how.

CHAPTER 5

Zagiri was supposed to have hosted her first reception from her family home, receiving azatas—and their daughters, nieces, cousins—with her mother standing at her elbow in proud and silent support.

Instead, she was in the front hall of the Bardha townhouse, answering delicate but still nosy questions as to the change in circumstances.

"It is not quite what I always expected," Zagiri told the young Azata Kurlani, with the placid smile she'd practiced, "but when I think of what disruptions others have suffered this season, it hardly seems a sacrifice at all."

Which Zagiri had been hoping, when she crafted that answer with Anahid, would start steering thoughts in the direction of what *all* of Bezim had endured.

But Kurlani laid a hand over hers and said earnestly, "Salt Night was a tragedy, but young people like you are the azatani's strength."

She moved on, to greet Madame Bardha, and Zagiri swallowed down her annoyance so she wouldn't snap at the next guest.

Yeva—first in the receiving line, of course, because she was the full and proper hostess of this gathering—leaned her shoulder against Zagiri's and whispered, "Just imply that we're useless foreigners unable to follow your superior azatani niceties without you."

Zagiri jabbed an elbow into her side, but Yeva was already swaying away to take the next hand, make her bright sunshine pleasantries. She was sharpening her Northern accent, pristine in her white skirts and embroidered bodice. With her golden hair braided with gleaming pearls, she looked like something out of an opera.

Truth be told, the Bardhas likely *would* have made a mess of this reception—and all the fiddly little details of procedure and etiquette—without Anahid assisting. Yeva's mother, Ksaia, had tried to include Anahid on the receiving line, but Zagiri's sister seemed to think that if she kept a low enough profile, no one would ask why they never saw her out and about.

At least she was here, somewhere in the back parlour, mingling with the guests. At least *some* of Zagiri's family hadn't turned its back on her. Knowing she deserved it didn't stop the sting.

There was no way to make it right. So she smiled, and pressed hands in greeting, and made all the polite responses that a perfect aspiring azata should. Maybe her parents would hear, and know she was trying.

Or maybe some *other* councillor would hear, and remember it when Zagiri came begging for another champion for her proposed reform.

She refused to give in. She refused to let this helpless panic tie her in knots. *Fuck* cousin Gildon; he didn't get to ruin everything.

With the receiving line finished, the party commenced in earnest. The spacious back parlour of the Bardha townhouse looked out over a little courtyard garden. The trees had mostly lost their leaves, bare branches clawing at the bright winter sky, but there were also glossy-leaved shrubs with bright red berries, and clumps of the snowdust flowers that had been popping up all over Bezim. They were described in poignant detail in a beloved opera aria, pushing up between cracks in the pavers, offering hope of spring in the despair of winter—but Zagiri had never actually *seen* them until this year.

Not that Zagiri could see any of the garden out the windows for the heated press of gossiping bodies in the parlour itself. The noise hit them like a wall, and Zagiri hesitated in the doorway.

"I told you," Yeva murmured at her shoulder, "we don't have to do this."

Zagiri swallowed. "I need to make them listen."

Yeva snorted. "Then you need to get their attention."

She said it with pointed weight. Like they'd done before, she meant. Like setting off alchemical flares in the industrial district, and getting sorcery struck from the register of criminal acts on the back of it.

She wasn't doing that again, tempting as it might be. Yeva and her revolutionary cronies in the Laders' Guild had proven themselves too unpredictable.

"Stop it," Zagiri muttered, striding into the room.

As the hostess—or one of them, at least—Zagiri had a favourable wind for steering conversations to her own endeavours and plans. Such as her bravi workgang, pulling together with the azatani for the betterment of the city. Such as her interest in all of Bezim's citizens. Such as—

"Your colourful history with the Sorcerer himself," Azata Prishtani gushed, nudging Zagiri as though they were sharing confidences on a walk through the parklands, and not part of an avid group. "Tell me true, did he really kidnap you?"

"What?" Zagiri said, far too sharply. "No. Why would he—?"

"I heard," another azata said, tilting forward importantly over her saucer of djinnwine, "that he is living in the tunnels and caverns beneath the city, and could appear just *anywhere* at *any time*."

Her voice—and the shiver that passed around the little group—seemed rather more thrilled than terrified.

Another azata placed one net-gloved hand over the heavily beaded bodice of her dress. "I hardly feel safe," she declared. "He's so *very* unpredictable. What might he get into his head to do next?"

A firm murmur of agreement swept the group. "It would be different," Prishtani said, still holding on to Zagiri's elbow, "if he were one of us, you know. If we *understood* him. But who knows what these lower city types really think!"

"He's from Dockside, actually." Zagiri disengaged her arm from Prishtani like escaping from a duel, and walked away without another word.

How was she supposed to steer *this*?

And yet, if *she* didn't, who else would ever challenge the idea that only the azatani cared about Bezim? That only they deserved to be in charge?

Zagiri went to pour herself a glass of winter punch—which she *hated*, so stickily sweet—to have something to do that wasn't snarling at fatuous gossip. When Anahid suddenly appeared at her elbow, she nearly tipped it down her dress instead. "*There* you are," Zagiri gasped in relief, setting down the little cup. "Where have you—what's wrong?"

Because a proper look at Anahid's face showed it pale, and pinched tight. As close as Zagiri had ever seen her sister to a panic in public.

"Did you invite Tahera Danelani?" Anahid asked, voice urgent.

As well it might be. Tahera Danelani, who had taught her to play carrick, and refused to go down to the District with her, and then...well, Zagiri didn't know how it had all fallen apart, and Anahid deflected any questions about it, but Zagiri didn't need details to know whose side she was on.

Of *course* she hadn't invited Tahera, but Anahid was shaking her head. "It doesn't matter. She's here. I should leave. It's better."

She was already drawing back, as Zagiri gripped her skirt to stop herself reaching out. Did she *have* to go? Anahid knew so much more about society than Zagiri did. But she was also so nervous right now, and what if Tahera *did* make a scene?

Anahid clasped Zagiri's hand. Her smile tilted painfully. "I'm sorry, Giri. I wanted to be here. I'm so proud of you. You're all grown up."

Zagiri *felt* like a child out of her depth; she smiled back. "Thank you."

But it had been a moment too long. As Anahid turned toward the little side door that would have let her slip out quietly, a gap cleared in the press, and there was an azata in a gown with a wide-draped New Republic neckline.

Tahera Danelani spread her arms and said, loud enough to carry, "Anahid, what a charming surprise, it's been too long."

She was smiling, but her teeth were sharp as a shark's. In front of Zagiri, Anahid stiffened, her grip tightening on Zagiri's fingers—but she could hardly flee now. It would be a scandal all of its own.

Conversations lagged all around, as heads turned to see what was happening. Tahera stepped forward, closing the distance in a show of discretion. Her voice still carried when she tilted her head and asked: "Or am I calling you by the wrong name? Do you prefer to be known as Lady Sable these days?"

Anahid squeezed so hard at Zagiri's hand that she winced. Or maybe that was from the blow of Tahera's words. The gasps and indrawn breaths of shock hissed across the parlour like a wave receding down the sand.

It was the sound of the respectability of the Savanis draining away.

They could save this. Surely they could. "How dare you?" Zagiri snapped, lifting her chin. She wanted to slap the woman, but *that* wouldn't help. "You come to *my* reception and suggest that my sister is—I don't even know what!"

It wasn't going to be enough. She could see it in the avid eyes turned their way, the hurried whispers, the astonished but eager expressions. Clearly some of the women present had heard of Lady Sable, the supposedly azatani manager of a House. Zagiri could see the puzzle being put together, this piece alongside all the evenings that Anahid had been absent from Avenue entertainments, and her recent divorce from Nihath...

Anahid stepped away, pulling her hand from Zagiri's. Her chin was up, her spine straight as a mast. "I'm sorry, Zagiri," she said— quite clearly. Not *just* to Zagiri, but to their audience as well. "I should have told you. I—I'll go."

She was lying again, Zagiri's sister who'd faced down the inquisitors, who'd faced down the barons, who'd not flinched at any of that. She was turning tail, and taking all the blame onto herself.

And with all of Zagiri's plans in the balance—the last fragments of her chance to influence the Council riding on her respectability— there was nothing Zagiri could do but stand there silently and watch Anahid run away.

The crowd closed up behind her fleeing sister with eager whispers, azatas assuring one another that they'd *known* something was amiss. Probably suggesting that this was what came of associating with the Sorcerer. Not what *we* do. Not proper azatani behaviour at all.

Zagiri wanted to scream. She wanted to smash every single punch goblet laid out on the refreshment table. She wanted to tell them all just what she thought of their petty, selfish, narrow-minded concerns.

She couldn't. She *couldn't*, not if she wanted to change any of it.

She glared at Tahera, who had one hand over her mouth in a patently false display of dismay at the trouble she'd caused. "I am so very sorry," she said, and the smirk she was hiding was audible in her words.

And Zagiri had no choice but to say, "I am astonished. But I hope you'll still stay for some refreshment."

Tahera tilted her head in a very proper nod. "Thank you, Miss Savani. What a perfect hostess you are. I would be delighted."

She was instantly surrounded, of course. In barely a moment, she was the calm centre of a storm of avid curiosity.

No one was watching Zagiri as she turned furiously away. All they cared about was the gossip. All they did was peck and scratch at one another. All they wanted was to be sure that *they* were the top of the heap.

Yeva was on the other side of the refreshment table, one sardonic eyebrow lifted. "I say we poison the bitch," she muttered as she reached for the punch. "Just a little."

Zagiri drew a breath that did nothing to still the anger that simmered inside her, like a samovar ready to overflow.

"I say," she stated, quiet but heated, "we make them listen."

Yeva's hand paused on the ladle. "You mean..."

Zagiri smiled, tight and vicious. It felt *good*, to be saying this, to be doing this. Better than all the delicate dancing. "Yes. The Ball. Tell me what you have in mind."

Anahid fled the Bardha townhouse with little thought to where she was going beyond *away*. Away from those wide and eager eyes. Away from the questions that had hissed and slithered in her wake.

Has she sold herself? Has she become a baron? Has she killed someone?

They'd been given the shell of a most delicious scandal; they were all salivating to get at the tender meat inside.

So Anahid ran, before Zagiri could do anything stupid like stand with her. Like tell them all to go to the Abyss. Like ruin her own life.

The way Anahid had ruined hers.

No, she wouldn't think of it like that. She had *made* her life. She had taken the mast and crossbeam of herself, and hung canvas of her own choosing, and if it had not been smooth sailing—if there were parts she wished she had done differently—it was still *hers*. Leaping out on a journey she'd never even dreamed she might undertake.

No one else would see it that way. The scandal would spread like oil on water; it would cling to every part of society by the end of this evening's promenade.

Anahid's feet slowed, beaded slippers whispering. She'd been unconsciously heading for the apartment, but if she went *there*, she'd just end up in another argument with Laxmi, who didn't understand why Anahid hadn't turned her back on azatani society already. So few people who *did* understand Anahid—herself included, sometimes.

And just like that, where she should go instead seemed obvious. Where else but to the one person—the first person—to really see her?

Halfway down the Scarp descent, as Anahid turned a switchback bend into the rising afternoon sea breeze, her fuming despair sharpened into a sudden urge to feel that wind tug at her hair. She had scant respectability left to lose, and might well be safer in the lower city *not* being azatani. She yanked at the pins holding her headscarf in place, feeling those binding her hair slipping free as well. When she shook her head, mahogany-dark curls slithered down over her shoulders. The wind tugged at her hair, pulling loose curls across her face, catching on her bitter smile.

In the low market at the bottom of the descent, Anahid found a stall willing to trade her headscarf—embroidered with beads and golden thread—for what she wanted instead.

The stallholder looked almost as startled about her demand as Siyon did when he opened the door to her. "Your..." He waved a hand around his own head.

"Fuck it," Anahid stated, and thrust her newly bartered flagon of rakia into his ribs, where he grabbed it by reflex. He was still gaping as she brushed past him, into the frankly *decrepit* building. It struck her anew every time she visited.

Siyon recovered enough to shove the door closed—with considerable effort, as it stuck on both the warped floor and the warped frame. He held up the flagon and looked at it suspiciously. "Tell me you weren't drinking this on the way down the Scarp."

That twitched Anahid's smile toward genuine. "No, but I might have had a little between the low market and here. Just checking that it was worth the price I paid."

"Probably wise." Siyon waved the flagon toward the rickety staircase lurking in one dim corner. "After you."

The upper floor was slightly less water damaged, but not much more salubrious. Anahid looked skeptically at the battered tin cup Siyon pulled down from a high shelf, but when he sloshed it half full of rakia, and lifted his own toward her, she drank readily enough.

The rakia wasn't worth even a third of what her headscarf had cost, but something about the rending burn in her throat was immensely satisfying.

"Ink and ashes." Siyon winced. "What happened, that warrants doing *this* to yourself?"

Anahid set down her cup grimly. "Tahera Danelani called me *Lady Sable* in front of approximately a third of the womenfolk of the first tier of azatani families."

She knew just who'd been there; she'd constructed the invitation list herself, balancing respectability, society of Zagiri's age, and those with political influence. Azatas with connections. To whom they were no doubt relaying the thrilling news now.

Word would reach their family. Word would reach all the councillors. Word would reach *Malkasani*, coordinator of the Ball and matriarch of polite society. Hopefully she'd saved Zagiri from too much damage, but Anahid winced anew at the thought of that woman—who'd always beamed at her with such *pride*, who'd introduced her to so many others, who'd been so supportive through Anahid's three presentation Balls—now cutting her dead.

But she would. Of course she would. They *all* would.

There could be no other choice.

"Shit," Siyon said succinctly, and refilled their glasses. He lifted his own, and added: "Here's to fucking up egregiously."

They drank, and Siyon winced again—even more so. But he grabbed the flagon, and jerked his chin. "Come on. If we're doing this, let's at least do it in some fresh air."

There were only another two floors to the building, for which Anahid thanked angels and mercies. They clambered up the skeletal remnants of one flight of stairs, and then climbed a knotted rope. Zagiri could probably have whisked up it in a moment, but Anahid only managed with Siyon's somewhat indecorous assistance.

By the time both of them made it onto the slippery tiled roof of the building, Anahid was breathless and sore and dishevelled. But also laughing helplessly.

"How," she demanded, still breathing hard as she flopped down beside Siyon on the peak of the roof, "am I going to get *down* again?"

"Down's easy." Siyon waved the hand that wasn't busy pouring rakia again. "Just don't fall through the floor."

Something about that—or perhaps the adventures, the company, probably the rakia—made Anahid laugh even harder.

She'd needed this. She'd come to find just this.

The air was very fresh up here, blowing brisk off the water, grey and choppy among the shadows of fallen buildings beneath. The view was quite breathtaking, over the two mangrove-fringed blocks between.

"Why now?" Siyon mused.

"What?" Anahid sipped at her cup—not that this rakia particularly rewarded the restraint.

"Why is Tahera only exposing you now?" Siyon frowned thoughtfully out to sea. "You were worried about word getting out back before Salt Night. But there's been nothing. Until now."

A good question. Perhaps Tahera had only just learned Anahid's secret herself. She'd stopped attending the District over her gambling debts, or at least so Anahid had gathered, during their period of friendly acquaintance. How *had* she learned, then? Not that it mattered. Wishing wouldn't put a fish back on the line.

She saw again the keen sparkle in Tahera's eye as she cut away every shred of Anahid's respectability. She'd *enjoyed* it. Like laying down a winning hand.

"She did it now," Anahid said, considering her rakia, "because it was the absolute worst possible moment, for me *and* for Zagiri. That's the part I regret the most."

Siyon looked at her. "She hates you that much?"

"I—" Anahid hesitated to talk about it at all; she would never regret what had happened, not when it might have won Siyon his life, but it wasn't something of which she was proud. "I threatened her. I needed something from her, and so I cut her certainty out from under her. But it made me *always* a threat to her. Unless I was brought low." She flourished her hand, in demonstration: *Like this*.

From the face he was pulling, it was difficult for Siyon to comprehend. Possibly, Anahid realised, he had never had enough certainty for its loss to be a viable threat. That could be freedom, of a sort. A tragedy, in another light.

"What did you need from her?" Siyon asked.

Anahid just shook her head, downing the rest of her rakia. She wasn't telling him that she'd done it for *him*—for his life, for his chance to save Enkin, and perhaps all the rest of them as well. Siyon carried far too much guilt already that was not his fault. It had been *her* choice. Her blade to wield.

It had taken her too long to learn that the cut was always deeper than you intended.

He shrugged and offered her the flagon again. "So what now? The worst has happened, and you're still here."

"Was that the worst?" Anahid tilted her head, letting the sea breeze tug at her curls. An illusion of freedom. "What if it isn't? What if…" She trailed off, as all her worries stirred beneath the warm blanket of liquor. What if the splinters of Midnight's organisation started fighting in the streets in some second baron war? What if the District came apart beneath the Zinedani daughters' careless and inexperienced hands? What if everything Anahid had killed to keep was washed away in a rising tide of chaos?

She took a shaky breath and clutched at her battered tin cup, lest her fingers tremble.

Siyon sighed beside her. "I know what you mean. What if I fuck up even worse? What if that was only the *beginning* of the catastrophe? What if everything I do breaks rather than mends?"

Anahid leaned over and plucked his cup out of his hand, even as he squawked. "No more of *that* for you," she declared. "It's clouding your judgment. Of *course* you'll find a way forward."

"What if there isn't one?" he interjected.

He was missing the point. "When has there *ever* been one?" Anahid demanded, and fixed him with a look when he opened his mouth. "No, shut up. You came to my house having already done the impossible. You dumped the boy no one else could find into my bathtub. You turned everything everyone knew upside down. You will find a way that isn't there, because you're *you*."

"The Sorcerer Velo," he said, with a bitter twist to his mouth that had nothing to do with the rakia.

"No." Anahid grabbed his wrist. Tried to find the words that would make him understand, swimming in the whirlpool of her thoughts.

One corner of his mouth ticked up. "You're drunk."

"And you're," she said, seizing the thought as it went past. "You're *Siyon Velo*. I came down here to see *you*. Because you make things possible. You open doors I didn't even realise were there." She gave a little laugh. "You've never needed doors, when you could crash through a wall instead. You became the Sorcerer, yes. Like you became bravi. Like you became the boy who left Dockside and everything it had tried to force him to be. It's not *magic*, Siyon. Or if it is, it was yours long before you carved anything into my parlour floor. You can become whatever you need to be next."

Silence stretched between them; a gull called.

"Thanks," Siyon said, and a corner of his mouth twitched. "You will too."

Anahid sighed and felt herself deflate. She wanted to hold on to her anger a little longer. But the problem with good advice was that people tended to turn it back on you.

"I suppose I will," she allowed. "What else can either of us do? The boat's sprung a leak, and wishes aren't buckets for bailing."

The sun slipped down behind the Scarp, and the shadows dragged long over both of them. Zagiri's reception would be finishing soon. Anahid would never know how it went; not until after the Ball, at least. Zagiri would have to keep her distance. Anahid would stay at Sable House, and leave the apartment to her.

"Hey," she said, suddenly remembering, and turning to poke at Siyon's ribs. He batted at her hand, shuffling away with a little squeak, and Anahid ignored all of it. "Have you spoken with Peylek?" He just blinked at her, and Anahid added, "I sent a runner."

"Oh, that really was from you." Siyon raised his hands defensively. "I get all sorts of nonsense, from people wanting all sorts of things. Who in the Abyss is Peylek anyway?"

Anahid frowned at him. "She said you'd met her. Said you could find her in the same place." His eyes narrowed a little, possibly in wariness. "She's about Zagiri's height, grey eyes, shaved-down hair I think is dark red—"

"No," Siyon declared, pointing at Anahid like she was trying to borrow money from him at the carrick table. "No, nope, absolutely— Wait, how do *you* know her?"

"She's providing me with sureties for the House." Anahid pushed hair out of her face, which blew back again almost immediately. "Or at least, her people are. An actual functional remnant of Midnight's organisation. She seems...oh, what was the phrase she wanted me to tell you? Sane and serious. She said she thought you could help each other."

Siyon looked...she wasn't sure. Almost angry, but not with her. He grimaced into the wind, and muttered something that sounded like, "There's no escape."

"Look," Anahid said, "I only promised to carry the message, you don't have to—"

"No," Siyon interrupted, and flashed a tight and rueful smile. "No, I think I actually do. Little as I want to. Like you said. Finding a way. Finding a bucket to start bailing." His smile broadened a little. "I will, if you will."

Anahid found she could smile in return, without bitterness. "All right."

After Anahid had gone, Siyon sat on the roof with the remnants of her visit: half a flagon of excruciating rakia and her lingering words.

You're you. *You can become whatever you need to be next.*

When she said it, he almost believed it.

What he needed to be. Or just what he *needed*. What, perhaps, this Peylek person, not-quite shadow of Midnight, needed. She thought they could help each other.

He was going to have to go back and see her. He needed to know more. He needed...like Izmirlian had done in his journals. To start connecting the edges of the things he knew, finding the questions that would bridge the gaps.

Siyon settled his notebook on his knee and flipped to a new page, squinting out into the harbour. Easier without the rakia smearing his thoughts, but Anahid had seemed like she needed it.

The late afternoon sky was absolutely, definitely blue, but also—when he let his eyes drift out of focus—sheened with bronze. He could feel the pump of Mundane energy out of the Scarp behind him, like an enormous, distant heartbeat. Once, he'd thought that was the heartbeat of the slumbering dragon, but it was still there, bigger than ever. The heartbeat of the world, perhaps.

A steady, soporific rhythm. It could lull him, if he let it. Pull him down and swallow him whole—Siyon dug his fingers into the roof tiles beneath him, felt the grime push up beneath the nails, and the reality of it dragged air back into his chest.

Blinking away thick burnished dazzle, Siyon forced his eyes to focus on what was actually there. The harbour stretched out past the shadowed and sunken remnants of the lower city. Dockside skulked beyond it, shadowed and hazed in smoke from the industrial district. A bell rang from the upper city.

His city. His heart. His world. Siyon let it steady him, and—

Out in the middle of the harbour, where the water was too deep for mooring poles, a sudden agitation of bubbles boiled up, like the sea had turned into a samovar.

"What the—" Siyon leaned forward, squinting against the bronze shimmer of the city's boundary. What was happening?

He fell over backward as a ship launched itself *out* of the water.

Not actually a ship, of course. As Siyon flailed to keep his balance, his notebook skittering away down the roof tiles, the shape shook off water and rose higher. That wasn't a prow, it was a massive, blunt, scaled nose; those weren't masts and rigging but rather enormous, seaweed-dripping, multipronged antlers.

It *wasn't* a ship. It was some sort of terrifying horned sea dragon that probably *ate* ships.

Where had it come from? What was it *doing here*?

It boiled up out of the sea, writhing and dripping, wreathed in a burnished glow. A monster—a *Mundane* monster. Surely Siyon's boundary around the city wouldn't keep it out when it belonged to this plane as deeply as any human who walked through the city gate.

Siyon had to do something. There wasn't anyone else who could. His fault. His responsibility.

He let go of the roof and slid. His heels hit the gutter and he pushed off, leaping across to the next roof, where he staggered into a run. A long time since he'd run the lower city tiles, cracked and slippery, but he remembered how to do it: keep moving, don't think, don't slow down.

Siyon glanced out at the harbour as he skidded down the slope of a pitched roof. There was more of the monster visible now, a long serpentine neck rising out of the water. Taller than the Eldren Hall, and at the top the massive head shook, sending out spray and seaweed like a little storm. The water boiled around it; another bulge of scaled body looped out of the water.

Dizzy and distracted, Siyon was right on the edge of the next alleycanal when he realised it was too far to jump, but he couldn't stop.

His boot hit the gutter, and Siyon *pushed*, feeling a brief and desperate fizz of power. He hurtled across the distance, arms flailing, and came down *hard* on the far roof—too hard; his knees gave, and he barely managed to duck into a roll that left him splayed on his back on lichenous tiles, gasping at the sunset-streaked sky.

From down in the harbour, the monster screamed. It rattled the tiles beneath Siyon and scraped across his ears. He wanted to curl up in a ball, wrap himself up, just *hide*—

The screech stopped, and Siyon dragged air back into his panicked lungs. He'd flinched onto his side in the grip of that fear, almost tipping off the edge of the roof. He took the hint, grabbed the old downpipe—as sturdy as anything could be down here—and slid to the ground. If he fell over now, he'd only get muddy.

Siyon fought against the fleeing crowds—*far* more sensible—all the way down to the waterfront, where the old quay was still slick from the high tide. *Now* what? From here, the monster loomed over the harbour, rearing up to reveal a muscled front pair of limbs. The webbed toes had massive steel-grey talons, which flared and swiped at the air.

Air that flared in shimmering bronze and rang like a bell in Siyon's mind.

Maybe the city boundary *did* work after all.

The monster screamed again, and Siyon's mind went blank. He found himself on his hands and knees, seawater soaking into his trousers.

"Velo!"

Siyon sat back on his heels, shaking muck off his hands. A figure topped with ridiculous feathers waved from the next dock, outside the Ferry Terminal. Redick cupped hands around his mouth. "Velo! Need a boat?"

Yes, he did. But he wouldn't have called the river-ferry gondolas of the Awl Quarter the sort of boat you'd want to take up against *that*.

There wasn't much choice. Siyon needed to do *something*. The barrier might be holding, but the monster wasn't leaving. It thrashed about, working its way south, and the waves grew wilder against the quay. Out in the harbour, ships tilted and strained at their moorings.

He had to make it *leave*. Somehow.

"Sure!" Siyon shouted back, and could've sworn that Redick *grinned*. Mad bastard.

At least they were readying a *big* gondola, crewed by a full six Awl Quarter bravi—not their heftiest bruisers, but blades who clambered around like the bobbing vessel was a sturdy roof. Siyon sat where he was told and tried to come up with a plan. Could he extend the barrier somehow? Take a handful of mud and name it part of Bezim and push the monster out to sea that way? Surely that would just move the problem farther out, probably blocking the harbour entrance, and if the fishing fleet couldn't get out they'd all starve sooner or later.

The monster reared up again, scrabbling at the burnished barrier like a dog digging a hole.

What if Siyon just...whacked its nose?

Could it be that simple? Not *easy*, rowing up to a massive monster and *smacking it on the nose*, but would it go away if they poked it enough? The *dragon* had gone, with a ballista bolt in its side (and Siyon felt a phantom twinge in his own ribs). Maybe...maybe they *could*?

Siyon had no better ideas, so he hefted a spare oar as they pushed off from the quay. From the Dockside wharves, sharp-nosed ship's boats were also heading out, trailed by a few fishing craft. One shape looked familiar: *Bessie*, the whaling boat he'd charmed. Her big harpoon launchers were cocked and loaded.

The Awl Quarter found their rhythm, struggling against the wash from the monster. The bigger Dockside boats cut through the waves, surging forward. *Bessie* swung out wide, as though giving their prey a respectful distance, and another whaler wheeled around the other side. As the boats flanked the monster, little figures on deck went rushing to the machinery at fore and aft, aiming the bright points of the harpoons at the sea monster.

They fired in rapid succession, from *Bessie* and then the other boat. One harpoon went high, clattering in the antlers, and one shrieked across the scales of the monster's head. But one sharp metal bolt tore through the webbing on a raised foot before spearing into the monster's neck, just below the jaw, and the last thudded in solidly two feet below that.

The monster flinched, and Siyon was already crouching, slamming his hands over his ears...which didn't help at all. The screech scythed through him, carrying bright red pain and vehement white rage. By the time Siyon shook the whirling sparks from his vision, the monster was crashing down into the sea. The splash swamped one of the whalers, leaving it listing in the water.

The monster reared up, black blood streaked down its neck. It threw itself against the barrier, again and again. Not daunted by the pain, but driven into a frenzy.

Siyon needed a new plan.

The Awl Quarter kept rowing, chanting as they hauled together, fighting against the waves. The boat tipped and swayed beneath Siyon, but the world was steady around him. The plane, the Mundane, all that energy. All *his* energy.

Not just his. The monster's every scale gleamed bronze, to Siyon's sight. Not just a creature of the Mundane, but one of power as well. Like the bloodgulls, or the pixie skinks. It had risen along with the magic, a child of Mother Sa.

Energy was bubbling up from beneath Bezim, a new-flowing fountain, ready to drink. Was the sea monster thirsting for more?

If Siyon somehow delivered what it craved, would it leave?

Siyon twisted around, to where Redick wrestled with the tiller. "How close can you get me?"

Redick grinned, glinting gold. "How close would you like to be?"

Madmen, the lot of them, even for bravi. "Stay a length or two back. But approach from this side." The safe side. The barrier side.

Redick hauled on the rudder, and the bravi hauled on the oars.

Siyon started pulling in Mundane power. Easy enough, when he wasn't trying to do anything physical with it. He'd practiced, back before Salt Night, weaving the city's energy into a snug blanket to tuck the magic of the Mundane in for a deep sleep. *That* had all backfired, but *this* still worked.

Even easier, now, with the Mundane awake and roiling all around him.

Siyon coaxed power in a steady stream, coiling it around his arm, settling into rhythm. Like winding a rope, passing it across his palm, and around his elbow, and back again. Loop after loop, as the boat crashed through the waves, past the troubled whaler and her bailing crew, and into the waters nearer the monster.

The sea was all froth here, the monster's body churning in the deep. The thing was massive, taller than the clock tower, and who knew how much more of it there was below the waterline. What *was* it? Where had it come from?

Now was no time for curiosity.

Izmirlian would disagree. He'd say it was always time for curiosity, and for a moment, Siyon could almost hear it, in his crisp Avenue accent, with that faint undertone of amusement.

He hefted his armfuls of power, knotted and coiled like rope. Bracing himself in the tossing little boat, Siyon cast out his line.

He could never have thrown a real rope that far, not all the way up to the monster's snakelike head. But this wasn't real, and *he* controlled the energy of the Mundane; it went where he told it. Up, and up, and up, until it looped around the monster's head.

Siyon pulled, gently at first, and the monster's head twitched down toward him. Then it tilted farther, massive eyes of ice-pale blue swivelling down to look at him.

"Oh *shit*," someone gulped beside Siyon.

The rope of Siyon's energy flared bright against the monster's blue-black scales for a moment, and then it went fuzzy. Clinging to the side of that enormous body, the magic oozed into the cracks between scales in a final flash of bronze.

Absorbed. Gone. Like water between Siyon's fingers.

The monster gave a little shimmy, like a fish frisking across the top of the waves. Like it had just tasted something utterly delicious. It tilted down farther, eyes bright, a massive greenish tongue flickering out as it chased the rope of power back down...

Hunting for more.

Siyon bunched power together in his hands—no time for finesse, only for vehement hope—and hurled it wildly. Past the monster, beyond the barrier, out to sea.

The monster whipped about, chasing the power, leaping after it as the bundle of Siyon's energy skipped across the waves.

Oh no, *waves*.

The wall of water pushed up by the tight whirl of the monster's body crashed into the little Awl Quarter boat, and flipped it like a leaf in a gutter.

Siyon hit the surface of the sea with a smack, arms flailing, boots dragging him down. Panic closed over his head—back in that sack, back in his childhood, back in the knowledge that he was going to *die*—until a hand closed around his wrist and hauled him upward.

Redick dragged Siyon half over the upturned boat. The other bravi were laid out along the hull like someone's catch. "That," Redick declared, laughing through the seawater streaming out of his beard, "was utter madness. You should've been one of us, Velo!"

The others were laughing as well, waving to the other boats, who were circling closer to come to their aid. The crew members on the spray-lashed decks were cheering and waving back, lifting victorious fists. Cheering for *him*. Because the monster was gone.

But Siyon didn't feel at all like cheering. None of them realised.

The monster was gone, but if *one* of them had come thirsting after power, there *would* be more of them.

This was just the beginning.

CHAPTER 6

Cliffside wasn't new to Zagiri, but she knew it in the middle of the night, with her sabre at her hip and her blademates running at her heels. The Bleeding Dawn had their safehouse out here, in a half-tumbledown mansion perched right on the edge of the cliff. Dramatic, and not entirely sensible, just like everything else to do with that pack of show-offs.

In daylight, everything looked different, with all the mysterious shadows of street lanterns and the silvered moon revealed as everyday. Just an alleyway hung with washing. Just a staircase crawling around the exterior of an old azatani mansion now turned into apartments. Just a once-grand fountain now cracked and tilting, the statue on top looking more a drunken lout than anyone's illustrious ancestor.

Back before the Sundering, the first tier of azatani families had dominated this ridge with their magnificent houses and walled gardens. Most of that had fallen into the lower city—or the sea—when the city cracked. What was left was far too close for comfort to that loss; the mansions that remained had been abandoned, or carved up for apartments and street-level shops, or bestowed as gifts. That was how the Bleeders had wound up with the safehouse, and Zagiri had heard that Gayane Saliu lived up here as well.

"You're gawking like a tourist," Yeva said over her shoulder. "I thought *I* was the foreigner."

Zagiri hurried to catch up with her at the corner; the building was wreathed in ivy still covered in leaves despite the winter chill, except those leaves were a deep purplish green, and seemed to reach out as she passed. Just one more oddity in a city now full of them.

"Perhaps if you told me what we were doing here—" Zagiri started.

"I *did* tell you," Yeva interrupted.

"—or *who* exactly we're meeting," Zagiri continued, "I might not—"

She stopped hurriedly again, grabbing Yeva's elbow, and pulling her back into the shadow of the eldritch ivy. Leaf tips and tendrils caressed Zagiri's neck, and she ignored it entirely in favour of clamping a hand over Yeva's mouth and hissing, "Xhanari."

Behind the smothering hand, Yeva made a noise like a little owl.

Zagiri tilted out around the ivy-shaggy corner and peered along the street. There he was, coming down a flight of stairs beside one of the buildings. Vartan Xhanari looked almost as he had back in Anahid's parlour, where he'd burst in, shot Izmirlian, tried to arrest them all, and eventually been browbeaten into leaving in frustration and defeat. Outrageous that he'd done all that and was *still* an inquisitor, but there he was, in his crisp grey uniform. Anahid had mentioned that he'd been demoted, and that he'd apologised, both of which seemed fairly paltry consequences.

Yeva grabbed Zagiri's littlest finger and peeled the hand from her mouth, just enough to whisper, "Who?"

"An inquisitor," Zagiri explained at a normal volume. Xhanari had turned the other way, heading up the street, toward the old hippodrome. A lot of the Council functions were operating out of there, as the only space in the city that could hold so many people. Except perhaps the Eldren Hall, which obviously couldn't be spared in Ball season, or the opera house, which could *never* be spared.

"You know many inquisitors?" Yeva shoved Zagiri away with an elbow in her ribs.

"Just this one," Zagiri answered, brushing at the ivy that clung determinedly to Yeva's sleeve. It settled back against the wall with a disappointed rustle. "And he'd have known me. Probably." She hadn't been *that* important, during summer's chaos, and what reason would Xhanari have had to mark her since? But better safe than sorry.

Especially when they were out here to meet someone about disrupting the Harbour Master's Ball.

"He's already here," Yeva said as they finally hurried into the teahouse. It was a cramped affair, in a new building wedged between two former mansions, but only a quarter of the tables were taken. Yeva pulled Zagiri around a pamphlet-papered pillar to reveal a table in the far corner with a pitcher of tea already in front of a tall, hulking man.

A *familiar* tall, hulking man, who lurched to his feet so quickly that his chair knocked back into the wall. "Her?" he snapped.

"What?" Zagiri snapped right back, digging in her heels. "*Him* again?"

"Zin," Yeva said, like she was scolding a cat from whom she didn't really expect better behaviour.

And Zin—who'd grown a short and red-tinged beard since Zagiri last saw him, behind a barricade across the Kellian Way on Salt Night—hissed at her just like a cat.

"I'm not working with him," Zagiri told Yeva quietly but firmly. "He's irresponsible and he doesn't care who gets hurt."

"Fuck you, za," Zin growled. "Helped you on Salt Night, didn't I?"

And he had, he and all his Laders' Guild revolutionaries. They'd stepped away from their barricades and other plans, and they'd pulled together with the bravi and the Flower district crews. Kept some people safe. Kept some buildings standing. Kept a little bit of order.

Zagiri still didn't like this. The attack on the industrial district had been successful, allowing her to push through her sorcery reform, but with too many loose ends. Stray alchemical devices had been repurposed to try to blow up the Swanneck bridge, which Zagiri wouldn't have taken so personally if *she* hadn't had to go dangling over the side by her ankles to pry the bloody things off.

But Zin had blamed someone else for that. "Is the Knife involved in this as well?" Zagiri demanded.

Yeva planted fists on her hips. "Talk a little louder! People on the other side of the street don't know what we're planning yet."

Chagrin flashed over Zin's face, something familiar in the expression; he subsided back into his chair. Zagiri grimaced but also grabbed another chair and perched on a corner of it. Yeva took the third, the three of them cozy around the table.

"I told you," Yeva said quietly as she reached for the pitcher to pour tea. "The laders are all off the boil. Done with revolution and too busy earning. There's no will for change in this city right now, save us three here. So if you want to do something, this is your only chance."

Zin sneered across the table. "Got some other little law you want to tweak?"

"Yes, as it happens," Zagiri snapped, then swallowed hard to keep her voice low. "I thought it might be fun to throw open membership of the Council to more than just the azatani. You know, let people actually have a say in the running of their city."

If she was hoping he might be impressed, she should have known better. Zin just snorted. "Need to blow up more than a little dance to make the azatani loosen their grip on control."

Zagiri shoved her glass aside on the sticky table so she could lean forward and glare at him. "Not that I'd expect a Dockside heavy to know any better, but the Ball isn't a *little dance*. It's a pivotal ritual of azatani society. It's part of what being azatani *means*. It's so important they won't even change it for the death of the prefect, or the dissolution of the Council. It's *more* important than those things. That's why attacking it will be so powerful." She sat back again, and realised she was still here. She hadn't left. "But we aren't blowing anything up, all right? I'm not doing this if anyone gets hurt."

Zin looked disgusted. "What, because it's such an *essential symbol*?"

"Because it's teenage girls," Zagiri shot back.

"Teenage brats," Yeva muttered into her tea, and shrugged at Zagiri's sharp look. "They are! You thought so too, when they were all talking about your sister."

Just the memory set Zagiri's teeth on edge, but this wasn't about revenge for Anahid. Or her annoyance that the azatani concern after that monster attack was for their *ships*, not for Siyon's victory. "They're just people. They haven't realised the world they know isn't the only way things can be, or that it isn't just as rosy for everyone else. And they won't have a chance to change their minds if they're dead. But if we *shake* them, break that certainty, make them look around…" Zagiri had to hope. This was their *chance*. They could make things better.

Zin looked sidelong at Yeva.

Who shrugged. "We don't have the stuff or the people to do something big anyway, so why not be strategic?"

Not exactly a ringing endorsement for Zagiri's point of view, but she'd take what she could get.

Zin still looked dubious, scratching at his bearded chin. "We've got more than you think." He tilted a hand in a market-haggling gesture—a bargain still not quite reached. "I'm talking to some people. Might have a backer. Someone who can get us proper goods, even better than what she rustled up." He jerked his chin at Zagiri.

She snorted. "You won't find an alchemist better than J—my friend," Zagiri corrected quickly, remembering that Jaleh hardly wanted her name advertised to inveterate revolutionaries. "But good. The better the quality of whatever devices we use, the more precise they'll be. We can do just what we want, when we want it." The possibilities were starting to come together in Zagiri's head now, like planning set pieces for a display bravi brawl. "We can scare them, drive them out, bring it down, and no one gets hurt."

Zin eyed her speculatively across the table. "Would've thought you could just hit up the Sorcerer. Aren't you his special little friend?"

She didn't like the way he said that. "Fuck off. And he's busy with his own business."

"What's new?" Zin sneered and shoved back his chair again, pushing up to his feet. "Fine, then. I'm in. She's in. Let's do this. You scope the ground. I'll get the goods. We'll make a plan."

Yeva beamed at Zagiri as Zin strode out of the teahouse. "You see? I knew this would work out well. And if I'd *told* you it was him, you wouldn't even have come."

"Yeah well," Zagiri said, lifting her glass of tea in a toast toward Yeva. "I think he stuck us with the bill for this, and I didn't bring any money."

As Yeva squawked, Zagiri sipped at the tea—the mint a little sad and tired—and felt a small thrill. Of taking a step forward. Of *doing* something.

She wished it had been anyone but Zin. Maybe not coming would have been the better option. The safer option. The quieter option. The option of a girl who kept her head down, became an azata, tried to be the daughter her parents would want to take back.

But Zagiri wasn't going to be that, if it meant turning her back on everything else. Not now. Not ever.

"Come out and have a drink with me," Laxmi said from the curtained doorway of the office. She was almost draped against the frame, hip cocked, the loose collar of her shirt gaping askew, showing collarbone and pale skin.

"What?" Anahid said absently, and dragged her attention away from the glint of Laxmi's grin, back to the ledger on her desk. "You've got your fighting pit, what more could you want to persuade out of me?"

Anahid had heard the early fights from her office window—the grunts, the wince-inducing thud of fists on flesh, the raucous encouragement and heckling of the crowd. And Laxmi almost oozed satisfaction. The ledger Anahid was reviewing, of the past week's takings, was also full of the fighting pit, with entry fees and betting commissions and increased earnings throughout the House. The crowds thus far were small, but cheerful, and willing to spend. The pit *was* a useful investment of House resources, however long Nura had spent up at the old hippodrome chasing the permits.

A hand covered the ledger page, newly split knuckles blocking Anahid's view of the figures. A red mark circled Laxmi's wrist, like someone had grabbed her there and tried to twist. Anahid didn't imagine that had gone very well for them.

She looked up, at Laxmi perched on the edge of the desk; Anahid could smell the House soap, but also a faint lingering tang of leather and sweat and blood.

"You haven't left the House in five days," Laxmi said.

Anahid hadn't. She'd come straight back from the lower city—her head cleared of the rakia fumes by both the climb and the terrifying sight of the sea monster that she'd witnessed from halfway up the Scarp—and ordered one of the disused attic rooms made up into a bedroom. It would be unbearable come summer, but it sufficed for now.

Laxmi tilted her head. "Zagiri thinks you're avoiding her."

"I *am* avoiding her." Anahid pulled her ledger out from beneath Laxmi's hand and snipped it shut. "And if she thought for half a moment, she'd be grateful for it. I'm a walking impediment to *any* of her ambitions for this season."

That earned her a snort. "You're a *hiding* impediment," Laxmi shot back.

Anahid locked the ledger into its drawer and tried not to sigh. Yes, she was hiding. She wished she didn't have to. She *wished* Tahera hadn't chosen *now*. "If you suggest I start a fight to clear my head—"

Laxmi leaned farther across the desk and grinned at Anahid. It was a remarkably infectious grin, even with so many reasons for Anahid *not* to smile in return. "Come out and have a drink with me," Laxmi repeated. "And if there are any fights in the offing, I certainly won't be wasting the chance on *you*." She waved a hand toward the curtain. "Everyone else can solve their own knotty problems, for once."

They could, too. Anahid had taken time and care in expanding and supporting the already capable staff of Sable House. She trusted them, even with the current District uncertainties.

And she wanted to say yes to Laxmi. To get out and form her own sense of those District troubles. Have a drink. All right.

"Just for a bell," she said. "And we don't leave the District."

Laxmi grinned and grabbed Anahid's hand; her heart gave an odd little leap, caught up in the fallen demon's excitement. "Of course not. Come on. Let's go before anything catches you."

Not quite so simple, of course. Anahid needed to inform *some-one*, but Nura said she'd tell the others, and just about shooed Anahid down the stairs. Laxmi reappeared, buckled back into her ridiculous armour, still scraped from her earlier stint in the fighting pit.

"I have to protect you from any fights, don't I?" She grinned in response to Anahid's frown and ran her hands down the buckles, over her hips. "Don't you like it?"

It was armour for the Flower district, functional but also highly suggestive, strapped to Laxmi's curves with abundant buckles.

Anahid *did* like it, actually. But she just sighed and said, "Fine."

Hurrying through the now-empty courtyard felt bizarrely like sneaking out surreptitiously, which wasn't something Anahid had ever done, even at Zagiri's age. She'd spent so much of her life doing just the right thing, with the right people, in the right way.

No longer, and here Anahid was, picking up her life from amid the consequences. She still didn't regret much of it. A murder, of course. There was always that to weigh her down.

But it couldn't quite compete with the tangle of Laxmi's fingers in hers, as they stuck together through the evening crowd, still thick despite the downturn in the District.

More people came in groups now, and fewer alone. They meandered less, going from place to place. Those who *did* loiter were more menacing—like a knot of figures in the scuffed dark colours of Midnight's former organisation in one corner of a square, or a trio of House-paid thugs watching them steadily from the entrance to the establishment across the way. A threat managed but not dealt with.

"Here," Laxmi said.

She steered them beneath a terrace arch festooned with flowering vines that read: *Blueflower Promise*. A smaller House, and not popular; Anahid was unlikely to be seen by anyone she knew, partly because the Blueflower offered quite specialised entertainments. Even as Anahid hesitated among the sparsely populated tables of the front terrace, a woman's rich laughter spilled from an open window. It was sharp, and faintly mocking, and Anahid was not sure about this at all.

Laxmi leaned close, words barely more than a breath. "Stay out

94

here. I'll let the manager know you're here, and bring us back something to drink." She exchanged a professional nod with the hefty Lyraec man beside the door on her way inside.

The terrace *was* pleasant, beneath the delicate scent of blueflower, and the distant stars beyond. Alchemical heaters kept the winter chill at bay, and the few occupied tables were engaged in their own quiet merriment. Anahid took a seat away from the House, looking out over the quiet square, where a statue was wreathed in the merry sparks of dancing fireflies. To the left lay another smaller House—the Saint of Sinners, fronted with tall and narrow stained glass windows not unlike the Eldren Hall—and to the right, an arcade of discreet little shops offering all sorts of useful, but not commonly discussed, trifles.

It was pleasant, to have a moment to herself. To just be—not Lady Sable, not Anahid Savani, but another anonymous woman in the District.

A low chuckle slunk around Anahid moments before Laxmi slid into the seat across the table. "That's the spirit," she murmured, sliding a low tumbler across the table.

The liquor was thick and pale, glimmering with faint sparks of red when Anahid raised it to the light. "Do I want to ask?"

"The bartender's calling it Empyreal Ichor." Laxmi smirked as she tilted her own glass. "It's been alchemically infused."

They were even drinking magic in Bezim now. How could Siyon think the people of the city hated him?

The first sip danced sharp and clean across Anahid's tongue, striking warmth in her stomach and bringing a faint gasp to her lips.

Laxmi winked across the table. "We'll try the Abyssal one next, shall we?" That might just have made Anahid laugh—she felt unbound in a way she hadn't in weeks—except that Laxmi followed up with: "You do need to talk to Zagiri sometime."

Anahid sighed, and drank deeply of her Empyreal Ichor. It burned down her throat, a little like guilt. "After the Ball," she insisted. "It's only a handful more weeks."

"Don't know that she'll wait that long." Laxmi squinted dubiously across the square, perhaps at the fireflies. "She's liable to come marching down here to confront you."

Anahid winced. Even the most desperate debutante wouldn't risk her as a sponsor, if Zagiri were discovered gadding about in the District. She'd be removed from the Ball, and probably Yeva along with her, and if Ksaia Bardha took it amiss, it might be a minor diplomatic incident as well as the scuppering of all Zagiri's plans.

"Try to dissuade her," she suggested, with a snort for Laxmi's innocent look. She knew well how stubborn Zagiri could be, especially about a bad idea, but Laxmi had the persistence of the Abyss. "Tie her down, if you must."

"Kinky." Laxmi smirked into her glass. "Sure you don't want to go inside?"

Anahid rolled her eyes, and didn't reward that with a response, instead lifting her drink.

And nearly tipped the whole thing down her front at a sharp crack. It echoed around the small square, and Anahid whipped around, just in time to see the head of the statue—now devoid of fireflies—come tumbling down into the square. A shadowed figure leapt down from the statue and threw another firecracker into the air.

Anahid shut her eyes against the flash of it, but it still painted her eyelids red and rang her ears with its overloud *crack*.

"Good people of the Blueflower Promise!" someone shouted. "Or should I say: people!"

When Anahid blinked her eyes open again, there were five of them, standing in a little wedge beyond the terrace archway, dressed in shades of shadow and midnight, and hooded, save the shaven-headed thug in the middle. He planted a hand on his hip, all the better to show off the Midnight circle on the back.

Peylek had told Anahid that none of Midnight's old lieutenants were able to wrangle anything, these days. Whoever this opportunist *had* been, he had his eye on power now.

And, it seemed, on the Blueflower Promise.

"You've had your warnings!" he shouted, past the huddled people on the terrace to the building behind them. "Last chance to do things the reasonable way."

The Lyraec muscle at the door glanced uncertainly back inside the House, as though hoping his manager might come through as requested. The Blueflower Promise was a smaller House, and these were lean times; he might be the only security on duty tonight.

No one was coming out of either the Saint of Sinners or the arcade. Not even to see what was afoot. Everyone had enough problems of their own.

Everyone but Laxmi, who rose with a creak of leather and buckles, and said, "Let me finish my fucking drink first, will you?" She downed the liquor in one hefty gulp, but kept the tumbler in her fist as she stepped away from the table.

"Who the fuck are you, then?" the aspiring baron snarled, and the thugs flanking him fanned out more. Like the Zinedani men had in the Badrosani theatre, coming to surround Anahid. Closing off escapes and giving one another room for the fight to come.

Laxmi laughed, a low and liquid chuckle.

Anahid barely heard it for the ringing in her ears. Shadows closed around her, like she was back in the Badrosani theatre. The memory of blood clawed at her throat, rising like a promise of violence, always more violence.

She should leap to her feet. She should tell them to stop. She should try to find another way out of this.

She was frozen, clutching her glass, barely aware of the Blueflower's Lyraec security man coming forward to stand with Laxmi.

"Come on, then." Laxmi's voice was so familiar, wreathed in glee, bodiless in the shadows, just claws and a promise. "I'm not going to let my Lady have her evening ruined."

A mutter reached Anahid's panicked ears. "That's the Harpy. I saw her take on three men in the pit up at Sable House."

Past Laxmi and the Lyraec bouncer, the leader of the Midnight splinter hesitated for a moment, then spat on the cobbles of the square. "We'll be back," he threatened, as his little group turned around.

"Bring more men," Laxmi called after him. "I like a little challenge."

Anahid dragged air into her aching ribs. She downed the rest of her alchemical liquor, letting it burn her into a moment of clarity. The chill in her bones couldn't be warmed even by the strength of Laxmi's feral grin as she swaggered back to the table.

"Is this why we were here?" Anahid demanded. She barely recognised her own voice, rough and ragged. It made Laxmi blink. "Did you just...use me as an excuse?"

Not going to let my Lady have her evening ruined.

Laxmi shrugged. "I heard rumours they were having a little trouble here. Why not help out?"

Anahid shook her ringing head. "You can't just... This isn't our House."

"So?" Laxmi squared off on the other side of the table. "It's a Zinedani House, and they aren't doing a thing about protecting it. Doesn't sound like they deserve it, to me."

"It's not that simple," Anahid whispered, laying a hand on her forehead. *A firm hand on the tiller*, Attabel had said. "I can't just—"

"Why not?" Laxmi leaned forward, over the table between them. At least she lowered her voice when she said: "Someone has to be baron of the District. If not them, why not you? You *care*, Anahid. You want better. You—"

"No!" Anahid choked out, pulling her hand away before Laxmi's reaching fingers could touch her. Her hand, that had been coated and sticky with the blood it had cost to get just her own tiny corner of the District. "I can't!" she gasped. And that wasn't quite right. She *could*, couldn't she? She *had*.

It had been awfully easy, in the moment. It had felt so good, to win.

"I won't," she clarified.

She lurched up from the table and staggered off the terrace, across the square, away from all this. Back to the House that was hers. That she had bought so dearly with lessons hard learned.

That was all she could trust herself to have.

CHAPTER 7

Siyon's notebook was gone, knocked off the roof when the monster attacked. All his observations gone as well, all the conclusions he'd been trying to scrape together.

Maybe he'd been looking at this all wrong. Monsters scratching at the city boundary, energy pooling within it, shells abandoned by Midnight lying in the darkness of the dragon's absence, reaching out to Siyon...

He needed to speak with this Peylek person more than ever. Needed to know what *she* knew. Needed all the help he could get. Or the next monster might destroy more than just his reputation—what was left of it—with the ship-owning elite of Bezim.

(More than that, of course, had been destroyed. Four ships broken, two Dockside warehouses flooded, one cargo of factory-made lace lost overboard during the monster's attack. Redick had been almost smug about how much trouble had been caused to others during a crisis *he'd* been instrumental in resolving.)

Time for a new approach. But Siyon didn't exactly have a ready stack of waiting notebooks in which to start over with new observations, new conclusions, new investigations.

Except that he sort of did. They weren't exactly *blank*, but Izmirlian wasn't using them right now, and some had a double handful of rich creamy pages still untouched in the back. His reluctance was just that clinging, that weakness, striking again. The journals were objects to be used, not relics to revere. They didn't even really smell like Izmirlian, not anymore, not with how many times Siyon had read through them, as though he could find any real substance of the aza-tan he'd known in here.

Still, he turned over to a blank page before he started writing, unable to bear the idea of his own scratchings next to Izmirlian's beautiful whiplash hand. He was trying to be pragmatic, here, but there were limits.

Siyon started with a careful summation of the sea monster—what he'd observed, what they'd tried, what had worked. Trying not to dwell on how enormous it had been, how fanged and clawed, how entirely uninterested in the business of men.

There will be more, he wrote at the end, *and I wish I knew what to do.*

Siyon snipped the notebook shut, tucked it into his satchel, and set out for the Scarp before he could lose his nerve entirely.

He went in through the collapsed mansion that had once been Midnight's, through the square where a storyteller had been entertaining a crowd with lurid tales of Siyon himself. Today, early enough that the entire square was sunlit, there was no one here but a passel of kids playing a game that involved one of them up on another's shoulders among the rest. The crowd shoved and bobbed, kids trying to jump up and touch the head of the piggybacked child, who squawked like a gull every time they missed her.

As Siyon was halfway across the square, one whacked her solidly in the ear and started shouting: "I got you, I got you! I get to be the sea monster next!"

Siyon stumbled and nearly fell flat. They had turned the monster, and Siyon's fight against it, into a *game*.

It was almost a relief to flee into the tunnels, though he'd barely taken three steps into darkness when the shadows shifted around him. Siyon stopped, then winced at the sudden flare of a lantern.

Peylek lifted it overhead with a hand marked for Midnight. Light spilled over her freckle-dusted brown skin and murky grey eyes. It struck a dark ruddy glint from the faint fuzz of hair over her scalp. "I knew you'd come back, sooner or later."

For a moment, Siyon wished he could just avoid all cryptic, smug, shadowy *anybodies*. But he was here for a reason, and it probably still applied. "Yeah well, let's skip the part where you give me a whack with a dowsing rod."

Her smile was flat in the dim light. "I thought you were one of them. The Midnight-shells."

Siyon supposed he had come pelting out of the darkness, from the direction of the dragon's former lair. "They try to escape a lot?"

"More than I'd like," she said, entirely steadily, which didn't really tell Siyon anything, since *at all* would be more than he'd like. "I wanted to flee myself. There is a hollow in this city now, for us. But we cannot—can you guess why?"

There's no escape. She'd shouted it after him. "My boundary," Siyon admitted. "It binds you too."

"Yours," she breathed, and reached out toward him.

Siyon twitched quickly out of her reach. He felt a little foolish when she waggled her fingers at him—look, not holding anything. But only a little foolish. Midnight had laid hands on him and dragged him down into the depths of the earth, into the heart of the Mundane, almost straight to the dragon's lair. Siyon wasn't assuming he knew what anyone was capable of.

Peylek's mouth twisted into something that wasn't quite a sneer. There was too much pain in it for that. Too much regret. "Yours," she repeated. "*You*. The Power. Centuries of refining ourselves into perfection, holding the plane as close to steady as possible, and you—" She prodded at his shoulder—and he *saw* her move, not like Midnight had vanished and reappeared, but she was faster than a darting fish. "You slouch around like there is some virtue in ignorance. My master bartered his humanity for just the *chance* of you."

She went to prod him again, but Siyon knocked her hand aside. "I'm not responsible for his choices!"

"Just your own!" she shot back, fire in those eyes. "And what have you done?"

This burn on his skin, disapproval and challenge equally scalding, felt faintly familiar. Like breaking up all over again with Jaleh Kurit, hearing the worst she thought of him, and knowing there was a seed of truth at the root of it. But knowing, also, that she was just as wrong as she was right. She *was*, and somehow, he would prove it.

"I've done the best I could." Siyon set his shoulders, stared her down. "None of this was precisely my idea, so frankly you can like it or lump it, I don't give a fuck. I did it, didn't I? I stood with the Powers and became one of them. I went with Midnight down to the cave. I'm not some almighty being, I'm not centuries of weird-ass cult-making gullshit, I'm just a guy, and I'm *trying*."

It sounded weak, even to his own ears. Trying? What good would that do? When the monsters came beating at the city walls, when the magic drowned them all, when everything that Siyon wasn't came back to haunt the *entire world*, what would it matter that he'd *tried*?

But Peylek tilted her chin and looked him over again—not quite mollified, but interested, in a way she hadn't been before now. "It's somewhere to start," she allowed.

Siyon snorted. "Wow, thanks." Now that the moment had passed, it was just the two of them, standing too close in the darkness. He hunted for something to say. There was plenty to ask about. "What does *refining ourselves into perfection* even mean?"

Her eyebrows twitched up a little. "You've seen what it means." Peylek gestured over her shoulder, deeper beneath the earth. "You beheld the aspects of Midnight, as he was. As they were. And, more recently, you encountered those of us who have been scoured hollow by the loss of that purpose."

It was the sort of esoteric blather that had always annoyed Siyon from the Summer Club alchemists, and hadn't been any less trouble-some from Midnight. But maybe he was getting used to it; this one made a horrible, eerie, haunting sort of sense. "You mean…those people in the dragon's cavern. They're…They *used* to be Midnight." Multiple Midnights, coming and going, each a shard of a bigger purpose.

Midnight was gone, finally given the peace of his promise and purpose fulfilled. But the shells were still here. Lying in the dark, staring at nothing, turning upon *him*.

Peylek's smile this time was soft and wistful. "No body lives forever. But duty survives, and it can be…carried. With the proper preparation." She laid a hand against her dusty black tunic, over her heart. "I was not so far along in the process. Not quite ready to take on our task. But I still feel…an absence. A possibility that will never be realised, like an eternal chill. That chamber retains the warmth of our duty, but not quite enough. Or perhaps we cannot touch it. And you, Master Velo…"

Her hand lifted briefly toward him, an echo of yearning fingers. It made Siyon flinch back again.

Her smile turned sad. "You are a conflagration. You are walking, burning power, like a fire leaping new from fresh fuel. You *burn*, and yet you are so very nearly the thing we all crave."

Well, that wasn't creepy at all.

Peylek sighed. "Will you come and help us? I think no one else can, except perhaps you."

Put like that, how could he say no?

As they walked deeper beneath the city, the power thickened around Siyon until there were no eddies or flow, just *magic*. They were down here, these discarded shells of Midnight, *marinating* in all this energy…What more could he do for them, if this wasn't enough?

Maybe it wasn't about the amount. A man wrecked at sea could die for lack of water, after all.

The cavern was still there, so enormous that the lanterns hanging among the stalactites couldn't reach the edges of it. They cast lonely pools of light in which the people who were once Midnight clustered like moths. So many of them, turning to face Siyon, shuffling to be nearer as Peylek led the way in among them. Siyon followed with trepidation, like a new blade entering the training ring, about to learn how much he doesn't know.

There were other people here, moving quietly among the Midnight-shells, soothing them with quiet words and gentle hands, settling them in a loose circle around Siyon.

"My people." Peylek nodded to them. "Or some of them. It's difficult, at the moment, to hold on to a little of what we had. A problem for a lot of people, in the city as it stands."

Siyon couldn't help a wince of guilt at that. So much of it his fault. Maybe he could set a little of it right, here and now.

He looked around the circle, and the Midnight-shells looked back. They were placid, but keen, like a waiting blade. They didn't quite look at him with the hunger the sea monster had shown, but it wasn't too dissimilar.

With the sea monster, the rope of power had just soaked in through its skin; Siyon could see it again in his memory, glowing in the faint cracks between scales. Down here, at the beating heart, Siyon barely had to think of it, and his palms were heavy with burnished power, overflowing in thick spills.

The circle rustled as all those black Midnight eyes fixed more keenly on his fingers.

Like this was something different, the power in his hands, rather than the power all around. Sharpened with his handling, made into something else by his intent. *So very nearly the thing we crave*, Peylek had said.

Siyon twisted his double handful of power into a quick knot and leaned forward to deposit it in the eagerly lifted hands of the nearest Midnight-shell. It flared between her fingers, and for a moment those black eyes became a warm brown.

But it faded, as the energy dripped away between her fingers, slipping back into the mass around them.

Not enough. Or not right.

A sigh gusted around the cavern; Siyon wasn't sure if it came from the shells, or the people tending them. He was too busy thinking, chasing his instinct and hoping it led him true.

He wished, fervently, that Izmirlian were here; to see more than Siyon could, to know more, to twine it all together and give Siyon certainty. But in his absence, he could only keep doing what he did best.

Trying. And making it up as he went.

Siyon twisted another knot of power out of the air; smaller this time, barely enough to clutch in one fist.

Scoured hollow, Peylek had said. And look at these people. They'd had the heart pulled out of them.

Siyon leaned forward, and gently pressed his fistful of power against the chest of the shell in front of him. She was so thin, wasting away, scoured in truth.

The energy slipped easily from his fingers, gone in a moment through her thin robe, her papery skin, her sharply defined ribs. But still visible, to Siyon's eyes, glowing bright within. It pulsed—once, twice—and each time it shimmered out through her body, along her bones, along her veins, flashing in her eyes.

The third time it pulsed, and then faded.

But when the light left her eyes, they were brown.

She blinked, and drew a great breath that stretched her ribs and arched her back. "Ah," she gasped, like she'd woken from a dream.

Peylek cried out as well, lunging past Siyon to grab at the woken-shell's elbows before she could tip herself over backward. The other attendants were watching, hands to faces, tears in eyes; one came hurrying forward to help the woken-shell carefully to her feet, tottering on legs too weakened to carry her weight unaided.

But she was awake. She could heal. There was a chance.

Peylek turned back to Siyon. "You did it. Thank you." Her words were fervent, and her eyes scarcely less so.

He *had* done it. He could do it again. He could wake them all. He could *fix* this.

And maybe more, as well. If he could do this, perhaps he could find a way to get the monsters the power they craved. Keep them away from the city. Keep them all safe.

To be perfectly honest, Zagiri had never liked the Eldren Hall that much.

Oh, it was pretty enough. The golden stone was the last from the old Lyraec diggings in the western hills. Four narrow towers boasted stained-glass mosaics of the beings of the four planes, from an angel with a flaming sword, through a weed-wreathed incubus and a lightning-eyed dervish of a djinn, to that confounded azatan and all the gullshit that supposedly made humans equal, if not superior, to the other planar beings. Clear-eyed reason, strict rationality, a head for business and sensible decisions.

Or at least what made the azatani superior to everyone else.

There was a dome too, soaring over a little gallery of columns that Zagiri couldn't see from down here on the steps. Apparently the best vantage of the building was from up on the crag overlooking the city, but whenever Zagiri was up there—at a rare bravi event—she had better things to be doing than looking down *here*.

Yeva sighed gustily beside her. "You think if we wait long enough they'll all forget what happened last week?"

Of course they wouldn't. Zagiri hadn't managed to steer a conversation anywhere near politics since Tahera had run Anahid out of her reception. The closest she'd come was Miss Filosani eagerly telling her that even her aunt Buni was asking about Anahid. No one was *ever* going to forget. Or let her get a word in edgewise in their breathless speculation masquerading as sympathy.

Zagiri hadn't so much as seen her sister since then. Laxmi told her that Anahid didn't blame her, but Zagiri wished desperately that things had turned out differently. For both of them.

"Hey." Yeva stepped in front of Zagiri, grabbing her chin. "They're paying attention to the wrong things, and we're going to wake them up. Right?"

Right. But to do *that*, Zagiri had to do *this*. She had to walk into the first proper rehearsal of the Ball and find a debutante to sponsor. Somehow, from under the cloud of all this scandal.

Zagiri had denied Anahid in front of everyone. She'd said nothing when all the gossips hissed around her. And she was standing next to Yeva, a walking opportunity to establish trade relations with the newly open North.

Still, knowing that anyone who approached them would be doing it in *spite* of Zagiri burned more than a little. Her family was as fine as any of them, her sister as canny as any of their bold trading scions, her commitment to this city and the duties of the azatani far stronger.

Zagiri glared up at the Eldren Hall and pictured it cracked and leaking smoke, the stained glass dark. A powerful symbol. One to wake them all from their unthinking slumber. One worth swallowing her pride today.

"All right," Zagiri said, gathering the froth of her skirts in one hand. "Let's go."

The ballroom was more crowded today, bustling with not only sponsors, but the white-clad debutantes and their escorts. They were all mingling, observing, negotiating; escorts were sometimes brothers or cousins pressed into long-suffering service, but more often looking among the sponsors, or one another, for a potential partnership. Many marriages and other alliances might be born from this crowd. Or opportunities lost.

They all stared as Zagiri and Yeva descended, looking with disdain, or consideration, or uneasy curiosity.

Fuck them all. They'd learn how petty and irrelevant their concerns were soon enough.

But Zagiri's furnace of determination faltered as the crowd drew away from her. It seemed everyone was already gathered in little groups of three—a girl, her escort, and her newly selected sponsor. Panic fluttered at Zagiri's ribs. What if there was no one left who'd stand with them?

They moved on through the ballroom together, people slipping away like water around a ship's prow. Anxiety knotted in Zagiri's chest. If they approached the wrong people, and had shoulders turned against them, others would notice. Enough disdain might overcome even the strength of Yeva's lure. Then they'd find no debutante, and lose their chance entirely. Malkasani would politely tell Zagiri to try again next year, and she'd spend another year being ignored as a child, while the Council commenced without any change to their configuration, and everything went on *just the same*.

Yeva's hand on her shoulder stopped Zagiri, tipping her dizzily around to face a frown. "Do you need to throw up? Or scream? There's a service corridor just over there; we could—"

"Miss Bardha and Miss Savani," someone interrupted, with a lively and surreal geniality. "How good to see you again."

It was only as Zagiri turned by reflex that she recognised that voice—its pleasant timbre, its cheerful cadence, its bland Avenue accent. She considered not responding at all. Was even this situation worth acknowledging *him*?

But Yeva was smiling. "Balian! What are you doing at this ridiculous parade?"

Balian Hisarani looked just as he had, inspecting the Palace ruins at his brother's shoulder. His hair had grown in the past few months, now long enough to fall a little over his forehead, and he wore a day-patterned longvest in gentle yellows and pinks. His slight society smile wasn't at all the one that made him handsome, yet still her stupid heart tipped into her stomach.

Enough of *that*.

The girl holding his elbow looked more a sibling to him than either Avarair or Izmirlian. Her expression was a little nervous as she looked at Balian, and Balian—damn him—looked at Zagiri, as he said, "May I present my cousin, Miss Lusal Hisarani?"

The sort of proper society introduction he'd purposely avoided ever making himself, when he'd wrapped himself in lies and let Zagiri swallow it all whole. Well, she'd drink poison and die choking before she let him hook her again with a little politeness and how good he looked in that longvest.

Lusal smiled brightly; her eyes, so similar to Balian's, lit up with delight as she offered her hand. "I've heard so much about you both!" The words almost spilled out, like water pouring from a jug. "You're so adventurous. So bold! I was saying to Balian, I think that's just what I need, I think I'd be ever so much braver about this whole business if I could stand next to such fearless young women—oh!" She pressed her net-gloved fingers over her mouth, as a faint blush stained her cheeks. "I am getting ahead of myself. Miss Bardha, Miss Savani, if you are not already engaged, I would be so very grateful for your guidance during my preparation for the Ball."

It was the formal invitation to sponsorship. A gentle tide of relief met Zagiri's simmering frustration. This was a *good* offer—indeed, there were few finer families than the Hisarani among this year's debuts. But it would mean spending all the preparation for the Ball in company with Balian.

"Of course!" Yeva declared, bright and cheerful, and then said, "What?" as Zagiri squeezed at her hand.

Zagiri could hardly say that it would be so much more difficult to enact their surreptitious plans with Zin under the keen eyes of Balian. She didn't want to admit her reluctance to parade, and dance, and speak, and spend time with him.

So she pulled up her polite society smile and added the formal acceptance: "It would be our honour to assist you in any way."

It started immediately: They all had to line up together to enter their names into Malkasani's gold-embellished ledger, Balian trying to catch her eye and Zagiri ignoring him. Eventually, he nudged Lusal into asking Yeva questions about the North, and sidled in next to Zagiri.

"I hope you've been well," he began, as though they really were just social acquaintances.

"Are you lying to her as well?" Zagiri tipped a nod toward young Lusal, whose face was bright with curiosity as Yeva talked about snow.

Something flitted across his face as he glanced at his cousin—something soft and fond that kicked Zagiri right in the stomach. Surely he'd never look at her like that. Not that she'd want him to. Snake.

A moment later, his face was back in that bland pleasantness that she now knew for a mask. "I said I was sorry about all that." When she just shrugged, shuffling forward in silence, he added, "*Siyon* doesn't hold a grudge, you know."

"*Master Velo*," Zagiri corrected with a sniff, "does not always know his own best interests, nor act in them." Balian opened his mouth, but Zagiri cut him off. "You *said* you were going to explain everything, and then you went scurrying back to work with your brother, helping him and that pack of Pragmatics who'd like to drag Siyon up the Scarp by his ear and bury him forever so we all forget about him."

Her tone was too sharp; Lusal glanced over her shoulder, and Zagiri flashed her a reassuring smile.

Balian sighed. "Better to know what they're doing, isn't it?"

Zagiri snorted quietly. "If only anything you said was believable."

"Zagiri," he said, drawing a little closer. He still smelled unfairly good, of paper and ink with a sharp touch of resin. "Distrust me if you will, I've earned it, but given your plans with the bravi workgang, you should know that there are forces moving and plans afoot—"

"The mural on this wall really is magnificent, isn't it?" she interrupted, pointedly lifting her chin to consider the artwork on the wall behind Malkasani's desk.

"Really?" Balian murmured, sounding amused. "You'd rather talk about Telmut Hisarani and the First Council?"

His ancestor, of course. His family had been in the thick of things right from the start. The first prefect of the city, and the leader of the delegation—certainly not a rebellion—that overthrew the Last Duke. The mural covered the entire back wall, punctuated by windows that continued the painted city's skyline in stained glass. At the far left, a grand gathering of azatani elected their leader—Telmut Hisarani, depicted with a frankly unnecessary amount of ornamentation in gold leaf.

"Looks like bloody Avair," Balian muttered, and Zagiri absolutely didn't smirk, not at all.

The painted azatani marched across the hall toward the Palace of Justice—then the Ducal Palace—in declaration of the independence of the city, and to insist the Last Duke take heed of their demands. At the far right came the part that had always been Zagiri's favourite—Telmut Hisarani and the Last Duke facing each other over crossed sabres.

Just a dramatisation of events, of course. What had really happened, the historians all agreed, was that the Duke had been seized—arrested, if you were being polite—and forcibly removed from office. The duel was a subsequent and fanciful addition, put in there so everyone could feel things had been more honourable and romantic.

It was a story Bezim liked to tell about itself. Zagiri had always quite liked it too. Until she realised things were rarely honourable and romantic, not when it came to politics. Those azatani—the first azatani council—had done what they needed to, to make the city the way they believed it should be.

Zagiri would too. Even if she had to put up with Balian Hisarani to achieve it.

They stepped forward and followed Malkasani's beaming directions to sign in the appropriate places, squashing both Zagiri's and Yeva's names into the space that usually only held one.

After Zagiri passed the gilded gullfeather quill to Balian, she tugged Yeva aside. "Say I need a moment; he'll think it's just pique. You said there was a service corridor somewhere?"

It felt like escape, and if her scuttling away into the discreet side corridor was hardly unmarked, all those nasty little gossips probably just thought she was hiding.

Behind that fanciful mural there was a whole servants' hall, with scullery and servery and a well-appointed kitchen. Cramped spiral staircases in the back corners gave access to the dome for cleaning and maintenance—or other purposes, like theirs. Zagiri crept up a few steps, but couldn't see any sign of locked gates or other obstructions.

There was also a wider staircase leading straight down, and Zagiri realised she'd seen no sign of storage space up here, nor access out to the rear, and surely there would be, for deliveries and such. *That* could be useful for their purposes as well.

But no sooner had she set her foot on the top step, peering down into the shadows, than a bright voice behind her said, "Are you doing something important?"

Zagiri spun around, grabbing at the stair's railing, and there was Lusal, her eyes wide with an avid interest. "I—no. I just needed..."

Lusal gave her a polite moment, to see if Zagiri was going to manage to think of something she needed back here, before she continued, just as brightly: "Because Malkasani wants us to practice the opening processional, but if you need more time, I can pretend to have a fit of nerves, so we can delay."

No one had ever looked less likely to suffer from nerves; Lusal nearly vibrated with eager curiosity as she stepped even closer to Zagiri.

"Is this," she whispered, her voice hissing off the hard surfaces of the corridor around them, "part of a secret adventure?"

Zagiri stared at her. At this girl, just starting her journey to being an azata, who looked thrilled to pieces at the idea of *a secret adventure*. Who'd been *eager* to meet Zagiri. Who'd said she'd heard so much about her—from *Balian*, surely—and thought she was bold, and fearless. She'd said it like those were *good* things.

Zagiri stared at Lusal Hisarani, and saw herself at that age, looking up at who Anahid was trying to be, and despairing at fitting herself into that shape. Not knowing there were other shapes she could be.

She laid a finger against her lips, and took Lusal's net-gloved hand in her own. "It's our secret, Miss Hisarani. You can't even tell Balian."

"Lusal, please," she said, actually bobbing a little on her toes. "Oh, how thrilling."

Zagiri, at this age, looking at Anahid. Lusal, here and now, looking at *her*.

And society out there, insisting there *were* no other shapes for an azata to be. That all deviations would be shunned.

Zagiri was going to show them they were wrong.

CHAPTER 8

The invitation Anahid received was merely a plain card with a handwritten message: *Will you take a turn in the gardens with a few fellow concerned citizens?*

It might have been entirely innocuous, if it hadn't been signed: *Attabel.*

The House manager who had come to see her, a busy two weeks ago. He'd spoken blandly in naval metaphors, of stormy seas and firm hands to steer. Terrifyingly, with its implications that he didn't consider the *Zinedani* hands to have that strength. That he might be looking for alternatives.

Anahid wanted no part in any of it. But she turned the card over between her fingers, and thought about concerned citizens, about what had happened at the Blueflower Promise, about the shadows lurking in the District.

She didn't know enough about what *was* happening. This seemed an innocuous enough way to find out more.

Anahid thought she'd just go briefly, quietly, informally. But Laxmi was waiting at the yard gate, buckled into her armour.

"I hardly need your assistance to walk in the gardens," Anahid said crisply.

"I hardly care what you think you need," Laxmi growled back.

That was almost more than they'd spoken in the past few days put together. Laxmi had made her view clear at the Blueflower; Anahid didn't share it. She *would* find another way.

She was not stepping back into the world of the barons.

The pleasure gardens were far from their best at this time of year, with half the leaves fallen and only the cold white flowers of winter in bloom. In balmier seasons, many in the District enjoyed days amid the greenery, but today the only people present were Attabel's *fellow concerned citizens*.

They numbered, it turned out, more than merely a few. A dozen and few, perhaps, clustering into the central gazebo for the scant protection its latticed walls gave against the chill wind off the harbour. The ruckus they made, all talking at once, echoed back off the curved cupola.

And they were all House managers, greater and smaller.

"What's she doing here?" one demanded at Anahid's entrance, hauling his stiffly embroidered robe tighter around himself. "*She's* not one of us."

Ink and ashes. They were all the managers of *Zinedani* Houses. Anahid's neck prickled.

Master Attabel rose from a little travelling stool and waved one hand; today his long nails were painted a glittering red that reminded Anahid unpleasantly of fresh-spilled blood. "She's here at my invitation."

"And mine." That was an older woman across the circle, who Anahid did not recognise at all. Steel streaked her dark hair at both temples, and the nod she delivered was stiff with age or pride or both. "I manage the Blueflower. I thank you for your intervention these few nights past, Lady Sable."

That hadn't been *her* intervention at all. Anahid shot a sharp glance over her shoulder, where Laxmi shrugged with blithe unconcern.

"You wade in for *them*," someone else shouted, "but what of the rest of us? We're all suffering these disruptions. I can't keep paying three times the usual security."

"And *we* will not subsidise *your* activities," another woman snapped—Anahid recognised this one, with her hair sculpted in spikes and the sleeves of her leather dress shaped to wings, as the manager of the newly renamed Dragon's Flight. A large House, a lucrative House, even with the repairs they'd had to complete after Salt Night.

"I don't understand," Anahid found herself saying before she'd really thought it through, and then they were all looking at her. She might as well ask. "Why are the Zinedani not providing security?"

For their Houses. For the District. For the stability and safety required for business to proceed smoothly and profitably for *all* of them.

"Damn good question," the Blueflower manager grumbled, folding her arms.

Attabel's smile was a little condescending. "You are not to know, of course," he said, as though about to suggest she not bother her pretty little head, "but the Zinedani daughters are...making changes to their priorities and arrangements. Not interested in maintaining their father's cronies. And as a result, they will no longer be providing certain services. Our rents have been reduced, but..." He spread his blood-tipped fingers and gave a delicate little shrug.

Anahid could still barely understand what she was hearing. The Zinedani were shedding muscle? No longer providing District security? "With the saved rent money, can you not hire those now looking for work?"

A manager she didn't know snorted. "Half the old Zee thugs are banding up with Midnight's crew and coming to stand over us."

A slender Northern lady waved a pale hand. "And now there are monsters in the harbour, disrupting trade further, raising the prices on imports...What next? The dragon back again? Some new magic fresh from the Abyss?"

"That's *hardly* the point," the Dragon's Flight manager snapped. "Unless you're suggesting we support the Sorcerer as a new baron."

A new baron. Anahid hadn't realised things were *quite* so bad. This meeting wasn't innocuous at all. As the argument raged, half of them waving arms and pointing at one another, she stood very still. As though if she didn't move, none of them would point at *her*.

She would not. There *must* be another way. But with panic hemming her in, Anahid couldn't think of one right now.

"Lady Sable?"

Anahid flinched—from the attention, from the name, from being too much a part of this.

But it was just a message runner, peering into the crowded gazebo, calling again, "Message for Lady Sable?"

Relief made Anahid's knees weak as she slipped out to the runner's side. "Yes?"

"Visitor for you at the gates, mistress," the runner reported briskly. "And I'm to add that if you're expecting someone you need to give them a card. New policy is we don't let anyone in without paperwork, see?"

Given Anahid's new awareness of the District's circumstances—its insecurity—that seemed a very sensible policy. "I wasn't expecting anyone."

The runner shrugged, already turning away.

Who could be visiting her? Not Zagiri, surely, even she wouldn't be that silly, but no one else could possibly want to speak with Anahid. Though she was only too pleased to flee this meeting, and all its uneasy connotations.

"You know," Laxmi started, from behind her.

"I don't want to hear it," Anahid snapped.

Laxmi's silence was pointed. She was sure she was right. Anahid wouldn't let her be.

The back gate of the District was more clogged than ever with handcarts and shouting delivery drivers, tangled up in a raucous mess.

Which made the scarved-and-gowned azata waiting quietly stick out like a pearl in sand, even from a distance.

"Shit," Anahid muttered. That wasn't Zagiri. Not with such an elegant carriage and a stately figure, waiting with endless patience. Anahid was wearing neither mask nor headscarf, but there seemed little point dithering about that, when someone had come to find her *here*. She braced herself and called briskly: "You have business with me, azata?"

She was still not ready for Azata Malkasani to turn around and beam at her. "Anahid, dearest, how good to see you again. I don't know about business, but I was rather hoping we could take tea."

Anahid gaped. She couldn't help it. Malkasani was beyond respectable. She organised the Harbour Master's Ball, setting the standard for propriety, and nudging all the young women of the Avenues into appropriate behaviour.

She couldn't *possibly* be here, visiting Anahid, in the Flower district.

Malkasani blinked at Anahid's stretching silence. "Oh, but perhaps you are busy? I'm sorry, I didn't know what sort of hours were kept in the District. I'm sure things are arranged quite differently here. Should I come back another time?"

"No, of course not," Anahid blurted. She couldn't send Malkasani away, when the woman was smiling at her, as though Anahid was still worth associating with. "Would you," she said, scarcely believing the words in her mouth, "care to come and take tea with me at Sable House?"

Malkasani's approval still struck a spark of pride in Anahid. "That would be lovely, thank you."

They walked through the District, in surreal silence and broad daylight, Azata Malkasani and the disgraced Anahid. Laxmi fell back to a respectful distance behind them, though Anahid could almost *hear* her grinning.

Malkasani looked around with obvious interest. "I've always wondered what it was like down here," she confided as they skirted the pleasure gardens, where the gazebo was still crowded with argument. "But I never had as much courage as you. Of course, I imagine it's far more exciting after dark."

"I thought you'd disapprove," Anahid said faintly. *Someone* had to raise it. When Malkasani glanced at her in apparent surprise, Anahid felt compelled to add, "You always said you thought I'd go far in azatani society."

"My dear, you certainly could have. All the skills you must have to keep one of these places running?" Malkasani gestured at the Houses they were passing. "I admit, I always hoped that one day I would pass responsibility for the Harbour Master's Ball into your capable hands. But this sort of thing isn't for everyone, and part of the endless joy of life is that it never quite turns out the way we expect."

Anahid was still reeling when they reached Sable House, and she felt almost shy as Malkasani admired the enormous black doors, and the window boxes of star jasmine. It was amusing to see the boistrous children of the House startled into quiet good behaviour by the presence of an azata—a *real* one, not just the mistress of the House—and when Anahid asked for tea to be brought upstairs, the kitchen girl actually gave a little bow.

By the time they were settled in Anahid's office, surrounded by her own tasteful furniture, and lulled by the ritual of pouring tea, offering pastries, taking the first sips, Anahid felt almost balanced.

And then Malkasani said, "This is so lovely, but I do have business, of course. I've been sent by other parties who couldn't come themselves. Well, I volunteered. Far better to speak down here, you see. The Council is so precariously balanced right now."

Anahid tried to swallow the sinking of her heart. Of course Malkasani hadn't come merely to see her. This was about something else. "The Council is in recess, isn't it?" she asked, and immediately knew it for a silly question.

Malkasani sighed. "Politics never sleeps, of course. Especially in trading season. I miss Syrah so dreadfully, and never more than when I hear that awful Matevon Rowyani is scurrying about looking busy."

Anahid knew *that* name. Azatan Rowyani was the leader of the faction of the azatani Council known as the Pragmatics; he'd been behind Avarair Hisarani's harassment of Siyon, before Salt Night. "This is about Siyon, then?"

Over the gilded rim of Malkasani's teaglass, her eyebrows went up. "Oh, him too," she added. "Certainly Rowyani is visiting *all* the families who lost shipping assets in that spot of bother in the harbour. And I do think Bezim should be less hasty in judging the worth of her unique assets. But Master Velo is too unpredictable and far afield to have a real impact on the forthcoming race for the prefecture."

Malkasani waved one hand, dismissing all the power and potential of the Power of the Mundane as irrelevant to something like politics. "No, my dear, I came to see *you* because what we really need is a new arrangement with the barons. Another war is the last thing anyone sensible wants, but Syrah's deal expired along with her, you see."

Anahid was staring again, she knew it, and it shouldn't be such a surprise. Of course it had. Syrah Danelani had owed her election to prefect to the whispered knowledge that she'd single-handedly resolved the baron wars with her timely but clandestine negotiation with the remaining barons, before and after the death of the Bitch Queen. The arrangement they'd forged had allowed the barons to operate largely untroubled, though within set bounds, for the past twenty years, and given the rest of society reassurance against further unpleasantness.

But now two of them, and Syrah herself, were gone. What happened next would be a key question. Buni Filosani—for that must be who had sent Malkasani here, to Anahid—needed a new arrangement if she was to present herself as Syrah Danelani's replacement.

"How did you know I could direct you to the most coherent remnants of Midnight's organisation?" Anahid asked.

Malkasani blinked at her, barely glancing up from selecting a pastry. "Oh, can you, dear? That would be delightful. But I'm here rather to get you involved."

The breath caught in Anahid's chest.

"It's all a bit of a mess, isn't it?" Malkasani continued absently, shifting a delicate little pastry roll to her plate. "And these new Zinedani women—well, I can't say I blame them for seizing the opportunities they always wanted; their father sounds like a terrible beast of a man, but it really is inconvenient for the rest of the city. Now is hardly the time to experiment, but when we heard *you* were down here, we thought the solution was clear. Anahid, I said, is just the sort of person you can trust to handle any situation."

She smiled again, warm and approving.

But Anahid had gone cold. "You want me to step up as baron of the District?"

Malkasani hadn't risen to the pinnacle of society by not being sensitive to the reactions of others. She set her pastry down again and said carefully, "Only if that wouldn't put you out too greatly. With everything in such turmoil, we need *someone* holding firm, you do see that."

Anahid had just come from a meeting of people made desperate by that. She felt laughter pushing up her throat, bitter and biting. Laxmi would have been *thrilled*. Everyone, it seemed, thought Anahid would make an excellent baron.

She probably would. Blood on her hands and the thrill of power in her veins. She *could* do it. She could be another Bitch Queen, and gather them *all* to her whims.

"I would prefer not to," Anahid heard herself say, as though at a distance. "The Zinedani are the rightful baron. You don't want further disruption when things are already so disordered." Malkasani frowned, and Anahid hurried to head her off. "I'll speak with them. A little guidance may be all that's necessary."

Malkasani's face brightened again. "Oh, would you, dear? That might be just the thing."

Just the thing. Anahid *guiding* the daughters of the man whose death she'd caused. The cousins of the man she'd killed. The women she'd been avoiding for all those reasons and more.

Who *needed* to pick up their duties, so Anahid wouldn't have to.

There was a tunnel beneath Bezim that ran right to the basement of the university library.

There were tunnels almost *everywhere*. Midnight could have got around *without* having been an eldritch oddity who could pop out of thin air. It was a warren of natural caverns and fissures (possibly relics of the dragon's slumber, or earlier flows of energy) and the additions dug by centuries of Midnight's various organisations. Passages and carved staircases ran between workshops, and barracks, and a larger complex complete with windows tucked away cunningly in the uneven face of the Scarp. The newly rewoken former shells of Midnight had been brought up out of the dragon cavern to convalesce there.

"We don't have control of the entire labyrinth," Peylek told Siyon brusquely, with a sharp curve to her mouth as she added: "Yet."

But the struggle among the remnants of Midnight's organisation wasn't Siyon's concern. He had enough on his plate already with Mundane energy, monsters, and the barrier he'd drawn around the city.

That was where the library came in.

Siyon was fizzing with questions, since waking Midnight's shells. He kept scribbling notes—on what he'd done there, on the monster in the harbour, on the similarities and differences. He'd had to push the energy into those he'd woken—past the barrier of their skin—but then again, the sea monster had absorbed energy Siyon had handled.

He couldn't push fistfuls of power through the city barrier for the rest of his life. That wouldn't be *enough*, surely. But he wasn't sure he could pull the barrier down. He'd made it with a map sketched on an old slab of the abandoned Lyraec fort up in the hills, and reinforced it on Salt Night with a wild surge of the city's power. Did he even *want* to destroy the barrier? It had kept the sea monster out, after all.

So many questions, and few firm answers. But Siyon knew where he could find a lot of knowledge, and tales, and tidbits. Kolah Negedi, after all, had written down *everything*, even if often to dismiss it as silly superstition. He knew where the notebooks were; had once been allowed to peruse them. *Now* he couldn't get close without a dozen inquisitors descending on him to enact the still-standing warrant for his arrest on grounds of making a big damn mess on Salt Night.

But what they didn't know couldn't hurt him, right?

Except that when Siyon shimmied his way out of the crack in the library basement, sneezed and snuffled his way through the century of dust coating the archives, and staggered up the cold stone staircase, there were people waiting for him.

Not inquisitors, but three women shouting at one another. Jaleh Kurit was never surprising where an argument was underway, but Siyon was startled to recognise Miss Plumm, who'd attended his interrupted and ultimately doomed entrance panel to the Summer Club. The last was Melis, a sharp-faced industrial alchemist he'd last seen fleeing the city in desperation during the wild uncertainty of the summer. So apparently she'd come back.

Jaleh hefted a leather-bound ledger covered in almost as much dust as currently coated Siyon. "If you think demonstrating the economic viability of the department won't be relevant to consideration of reinstatement, you are missing the realities of this city and its azatani administration." Her gaze found Siyon, frozen at the top of the stairs from the basement. "Oh, he's finally here."

"What are you doing here?" Siyon demanded.

"Waiting for you," Melis said, which wasn't reassuring; if *they* knew he was coming, so might others.

"Arguing about an application we haven't started writing to a body that doesn't exist right now," Miss Plumm grumbled, still glaring at Jaleh. After a moment, she added, "Yes, and waiting for you. We thought there might be something useful in the interdicted gallery for the reinstatement of alchemy as an academic discipline."

"How did you know that I—" Siyon started, and then blinked as all of that caught up with him. "You're trying to get alchemy back in the university?"

"Of course we are." Jaleh gave him that familiar look, like she was astonished she'd ever deigned to sleep with someone this thick. "Sorcery has been struck, alchemy is now entirely legal, but practitioners have no formal skills, which is an invitation to other prosecutions." She slapped the ledger she was holding in emphasis, raising a little cloud of dust.

"Not to mention making them unreliable for azatani employment," Melis added wryly. As a practitioner so employed—in an azatani-owned factory—she had a fairly pragmatic approach to the Art.

Siyon hadn't even considered it—hadn't had time, probably wouldn't have even if he did—but they were right, of course. They didn't need his consideration or his approval; Bezim had plenty of people with a stake in the state of alchemy, in its future, in its practice.

He was the Alchemist, but he was not the only one.

"Surprised Nihath isn't here as well," Siyon managed.

Miss Plumm waved toward the stained-glass dome of the library, beneath which the golden galleries ran. "He's already up there, poking around in the locked-away material with Master Unja."

Melis made a disgusted noise. "I *wish* you hadn't brought him too."

So did Siyon. Who *hadn't* heard that he was popping up to the university? Were the inquisitors just waiting for a shift change?

No time to waste, in any case. Siyon headed for the stairs, as the women fell in behind him, bickering about Master Unja. Apparently he'd interrupted Plumm and Jaleh speaking with Mayar about Siyon's intentions—so *that's* how the word had gotten out—and insisted on coming along to see the Negedi artifacts or he'd report them to the Summer Club stewards for not having signed in a visitor.

"As though Mayar couldn't be a member if they wished." Plumm sighed.

The gallery gate was open, and inside Nihath was paging through sheafs of notes from one of the shelves, glasses perched on the end of his nose. Another gentleman with oiled hair and a glittering longvest pointed at one of the folios spread open on the table; Siyon realised Master Unja had *also* been at his interrupted Summer Club entrance exam.

"And Negedi *states* it, quite categorically!" he declaimed.

"Negedi did the best he could with the information that was available to him at the time," Nihath murmured, not even looking up from his stack of notes, "but he could hardly be expected to—ah, Velo. How good to see you."

Astonishingly, he offered a hand for Siyon to shake. This time last year, Nihath Joddani wouldn't even let Siyon into the Summer Club when he made his contracted deliveries of material raided from the other planes. And he certainly wouldn't have been casually dismissing the carefully recorded observations of the great Kolah Negedi as *the best he could*.

Master Unja stiffly tugged imaginary wrinkles from the front of his longvest. "I," he announced, to no one in particular, "will take my leave. I cannot in good conscience remain with this…" His mouth pursed as he eyed Siyon.

"Criminal?" Siyon suggested brightly, baring his teeth. "Reprobate? Delinquent?"

No better than the plane-raiding provisioner who'd peddled his wares at the back door of the Summer Club. But even when that was all Siyon was, he'd still been a person.

"Hero and saviour of the city," Jaleh added, behind him.

Unja snapped his fingers at her. "Flashy and destructive violence in the middle of our city's mercantile and maritime thoroughfare is hardly *saving* anything!"

Melis snorted. "Fuck off if you're just going to repeat Avenue politics talking points."

He pointedly ignored that. "Nor is disrupting a tradition of alchemical practice that has persisted perfectly well for centuries before your rude interference." He marched stiffly past them, only pausing at the gate to add: "I am disappointed in all of you."

Siyon hardly knew how he felt. He hadn't expected Unja to be so vehement. He hadn't expected Jaleh—of all people—to support him. "Can we lock him in the basement?" he asked quietly. "Is he likely to go straight to the inquisitors?"

"Given usual student pranks, they're unlikely to heed him, even if he does," Miss Plumm muttered, already over next to Nihath, peering at the bundles of notes on the shelves.

"Can we lock him in the basement anyway?" Melis cast Siyon a sympathetic smile. "Best just get on with it, I think."

At least Unja had already brought out several folios of Negedi's notes, and the big black-leather coded index. Siyon pulled out his notebook—Izmirlian's repurposed journal—flipping it open as he rummaged for a pencil.

"I don't want to pry," Jaleh asked, which was a patent lie; she *always* wanted to dig into things. "But what *did* happen down in the harbour?"

Siyon snorted. "Did it look more complicated from the outside than—" He glanced at his notebook, open on the table next to Negedi's, and the rest of what he'd been saying evaporated from his mind.

There were the notes he'd written, scribbling after waking the shells of Midnight. His list of increasingly wild questions.

Beneath it, there were new lines of writing, in a heart-stoppingly familiar whiplash hand, the ink fresh and glittering black as the heart of the Abyss.

I'm wildly jealous that everyone else gets your impossibilities now, it read.

Below that, on a new line: *But not so jealous I don't want to help; tell me more.*

Siyon stared, heart caught in his throat. He flipped a few pages back, where Izmirlian had written, years ago, about the view from the sea cliffs of a famous historical shipwreck.

The handwriting was exactly the same.

When he turned back, the impossible words were still there, glistening as though newly inked. Siyon touched a trembling finger to them, but they didn't smudge or stain.

Your impossibilities, he read again. A whole new sort of impossible.

"Are you listening at all?" Jaleh demanded, right beside him.

Siyon yelped and flinched, grabbing for his notebook and sending it spinning sideways into one of Negedi's folios.

Jaleh whisked it quickly away, fingertips checking for damage on the Negedi book; when Siyon snatched his notebook back from her, she frowned at him, which was only strange in that it seemed to be both indignation at his manners, and…concern? "We just want to know what's going on," she said. "In case we can be of assistance."

Tell me more, Siyon read on the page again, the words still there. He steeled himself and turned the notebook around. "Can you read this? The black text."

"Of course I can." She shoved the page away. "A far more legible hand than *yours*. Siyon, this is our city too, and if there are going to be monsters popping up out of the sea, I think we can all—"

"Probably not just the sea," Siyon interrupted, forcing himself to close the notebook and set it aside. Jaleh had seen the words as well. They were *really there*. But he needed to concentrate; she was right, that they deserved to know what was going on. Or as much as *he* knew, at least. "I think…everything's waking up. Monsters, other things." Mother Sa, woken and returned to the world. "It all needs magic."

Miss Plumm sighed. "*Magic*," she repeated.

"Power," Melis countered. "Energy. Vibrations. Numinous fucking potential or whatever twaddle's coming out of the Summer Club these days after the third round of brandy."

"Rude." Plumm sniffed. "But accurate."

Jaleh still stared at Siyon, arms folded across her chest. "And we have the magic here. Your whole business at Salt Night was about bringing it forth, wasn't it? Stabilising planar interaction by stimulating the Mundane." Her frown deepened. "But regardless of where a fountain spouts, sooner or later the entire bowl is inundated. Given time, energy will flow out from here to the entire plane."

Siyon wished it were that easy. "It's not, though. Flowing. Leaking a little, maybe. But it's mostly trapped behind the city's boundary."

"Which you needed to delineate the stimulation in the first place," Jaleh stated. And then she added, "What? You're conducting the wildest acts of alchemy and you think I'm not going to investigate thoroughly? Your methods are questionable, but your outcomes are undeniable. You drove the sea monster away, after all."

They had all turned away from their other searches now to look at him. All paying attention. So Siyon told them what he could—not explicitly about what he'd done with the Midnight-shells, because that wasn't his secret to share. But he explained the way the sea monster had absorbed the power he'd cast through the city barrier, and the way other experiments had suggested handling was needed to push power past a similar barrier.

Was skin similar? Siyon had no idea.

"Does it have to be you?" Nihath asked, peering over his spectacles at Siyon.

"Excellent question," Miss Plumm declared, pointing at him. "I don't think I could do the"—she grasped at thin air, mouth pursed as though she disapproved of such groping—"but we all have our own methods for *handling* matter and energy."

Melis had pulled a little notebook and the stub of a pencil out of her pocket and was scribbling—calculations, by the look of it. "If your estimations on energy frequency are correct, Jaleh, then we're going to need an awful lot of practitioners on this to even come close to Siyon's pulling power."

"We have lots of practitioners," Jaleh countered. "I'll admit a lot of the older Club members are unlikely to embrace working directly with energy, nor assisting Siyon. There'll be plenty of others, though. Not to mention those outside the upper city who—" She turned to Siyon, one hand lifted to make a point, and stopped. "What?" she demanded.

Siyon knew he was gaping at them. He couldn't help it. "I thought," he said faintly, "you'd just...tell me what I should do."

Jaleh snorted. "Yes, because you've been *so* amenable to instruction before now."

It had felt like the whole world was leaning on him. Like this was all *his* to fix. The idea that there could be help was dangerously attractive.

"Good point." Melis jabbed the chewed end of her pencil at Jaleh. "*You* can't solicit the lower city practitioners, and neither of us is going to get in to see the mudwitches, let alone ask a favour."

"Do they really exist?" Nihath asked curiously.

Siyon snorted. "Do the *mudwitches* exist? Who do you think makes the medallions for the fisherclans?"

"Excellent," Plumm said crisply. "Your people then; you can handle it. Lower city too, since you're down there."

Shit. "Wait," Siyon tried.

Melis pulled a face at her calculations. "Definitely," she declared. "I don't know that the geographical spread will be necessary, but we're going to need the numbers. We'll handle up here, you take that lot, all right, Siyon?" She tilted a professional look his way.

And what was Siyon supposed to say? No, you people who have stepped forward instantly and easily to help fix my fuckups, I'm not going to pull my part, because I'm too damn scared of a couple of women. He drummed his fingers on his notebook. On Izmirlian's journal. That he was still writing in.

Your impossibilities. Surely he could work his way around these problems. Right?

"Right," he said. "Sure. Thanks."

Jaleh tossed her head. "If handling more power helps push it out into the world and keep us all safe, that seems the only sensible thing to do. It's our city too, after all."

Their city; his plane; his responsibility.

He *had* found his answers here, after all. Now the least he could do was go asking for more help.

CHAPTER 9

Lusal, it turned out, was an absolute fountain of political gossip, lifted from all the edges of the Hisarani family affairs. It certainly made accompanying her to dress fittings and formal tea sittings more interesting. (Though when Zagiri asked nonchalantly after what Avarair was up to, Lusal wrinkled up her nose and said he was very busy with some extra and complicated project, and cranky about it. Zagiri thought it highly likely he'd been born cranky and never got over it.) She reported that the Interim Rectification Board wanted the Palace ready for the Council commencement ceremony. It was going to be a near-run thing. The central bulk of the Palace had suffered the worst damage, as the dragon clawed out through the oldest part of the original Lyraec construction. The entry hall had been completely destroyed, and the great hall where the Council had met was thoroughly unstable, the floor still liable to collapse.

Commencement was scheduled the week after the Ball, which was frankly far closer than Zagiri was really comfortable with. A scant few weeks for her to find a sponsor for her proposed reform to Council membership. She prowled through every promenade, hunting like an alleycat for the faintest mousey sign of interest. Things were so dire that Zagiri had even wondered about approaching the new Markani councillor and hoping Lomena was too unwell to pass on any gossip about her activities before Salt Night. And it might all be for nothing if Azata Filosani asking about Anahid meant she was getting skittish about it all.

In short, she had enough trouble without the bravi on her work-gang acting up. But tonight, the Awl Quarter had arrived half a bell late, claiming the inquisitors were blockading the top of the Scarp again, checking for Siyon. The Bleeding Dawn picked a fight about it, egged on by the Haruspex pair (who were constantly needling the other tribes). And when Zagiri shouted everyone to their work, the Bower's Scythe bravi started singing a little ditty about the hubris of Grand Bracken.

Sure, when Zagiri had petitioned the sergeants to lend her blades for this workgang, she'd had a fleeting, romantic thrill of reviving the supposed common ancestor of all the bravi tribes. Grand Bracken, it was said, fought nobly against injustice and tyranny in the Old Kingdoms, but split up in Bezim, where such unity was unnecessary. Yes, Little Bracken was named for it, claiming one day it would rise again, but after these nights of wrangling just a dozen joined bravi, Zagiri had *no interest* in trying it.

Latest demonstration: The Bleeding Dawn trio were nowhere to be found.

Zagiri did the rounds of the usual places they went to skive off with a deck of cards and a flagon of rakia. She was already piqued by the time she found them, apparently hard at work swinging sledge-hammers at one of the last sections of wall that still needed to be brought down. Or at least, she found *two* of them.

"Hey!" She had to shout over the noise. "Where's your third?"

The Bleeders stopped and glanced at each other. "Went for water, didn't he?"

"Don't mess me about," Zagiri snapped. "You give Hovhaness gullshit like this?"

It didn't have the impact she wanted. "You ain't no sergeant," one sneered. "You're barely even bravi no more."

It stung, all the more for being true. A handful of weeks until the Ball—fewer until Zagiri would hand back her sabre. The putting away of childish pursuits to better concentrate on the business of the azatani.

But it wasn't true *yet*. "I'll carry this blade long enough to stand up in Tower Square and call out the Bleeding Dawn for failing to keep their word." They glared at her but seemed to have nothing to say. Zagiri added: "Now where's your fucking third?"

One shrugged. "Paq has this girl, yeah? In the Avenues. She's in a tizzy about things, how the city's so dangerous these days and she never sees him. So he just popped over to make things right."

Zagiri couldn't believe she was hearing this. "He's left you here and gone to get laid?"

They winced in unison, like now that they heard it out loud they realised how bad it sounded. "Look," one of them said, raising a hand like they were going to try talking her down.

Before Zagiri could do more than draw in a breath, a shout came from the main part of the ruins. "Hey! Giri!"

Daruj. Probably not hunting for her because he'd gotten a splinter in his elbow.

Zagiri ground her teeth for a moment, then jabbed a finger toward the Bleeders. "You go get him and bring him back here. Now."

They tossed down the sledgehammers and set off across the parkland. Zagiri trudged back up the long slope of rubble toward Daruj— and then started to run when she heard the scrape of blades.

They were all facing off in the gutted remains of the Palace's entry hall, boots scuffing at the mangled mosaic tiles as the three blades circled warily. The nascent cheering and chatter of their fellows died down to nothing as Zagiri came rushing in.

One of the Awl Quarter, brandishing a short, heavy, piratical named blade; one of the Haruspex, finally called out about his behaviour, it seemed; and Daruj, the Diviner Prince bared and glittering in his hand as he shifted the point between the two other combatants. "I'll spank you both, if I have to," he said, "and not even raise a sweat doing it."

He probably could have, as well, but Zagiri had had *enough* of all this. "Hold blades!" she bellowed, charging into the middle of the circle. Her anger was boiling over now, frothing white and hot.

They all stepped back, but none of the blades dipped, and Daruj remained watchful.

The Awl Quarter twitched the point of her sabre toward the Haruspex. "*He* said—"

"I don't give a day-old fish what he said!" Zagiri rounded on her, fierce enough to make her step back. "Why did you even *come*, if this is how seriously you take our business here? If *this*"—and she swung around, encapsulating all three of them and the eager audience—"is all the respect you have for your duty, for all your bravi fellows, for your *city*. If you are happy being the bickering children here for everyone's entertainment, no more important or trusted than that, then *leave now!*"

Her voice rang off the shell of the Palace. In the silence that followed, the spectators scuffed their toes in the dust.

But the Haruspex bravi had a bitter expression. "You think it matters what we do?" he demanded. "You think *anyone* is taking us seriously? *You*, maybe. But we can't force the rest at the end of a blade."

"Not if you never try, you can't," Zagiri snapped, but it was just the anger talking. Just her frustration. Just a dire, bleeding hope. She was running out of time. She was running out of councillors to ask. She was running out of other support.

All she had was desperation, and a wild hope that she could shake the azatani out of their complacence. What if she couldn't?

But around her, sabres lowered, and then went back into sheaths. It wasn't falling apart tonight.

"Give those here," Zagiri ordered. "I'll take them back to the staging point. Daruj, get this lot back to work."

She stomped back to the staging point, three sabres awkward and rattling in her grip. Her mood wasn't improved by the clerk gasping, "Oh! *There* you are!"

Zagiri sighed and tossed the sabres onto the pile of everyone's things. "What is it now?" The fucking *paperwork* involved in this business was going to be the end of her. The bloody Council and its need for everything be filed in triplicate on the appropriate forms.

The clerk waved his board of papers off toward the nearby

trees—no, toward the ox-drawn cart waiting among them. "The delivery man *insists* on speaking with you."

Just what she needed.

The delivery man was slumped against the tailgate of his near-empty cart, wide-brimmed hat—the sort Siyon had once used as an easy disguise—pulled low over his face. "What's the matter?" Zagiri demanded as she drew closer. "I don't have any say over money or material, so you can't have anything that needs my attention."

"I disagree," said Zin as he whisked off his hat and smirked at her.

Zagiri's temper wilted under a blast of panic. "You can't be here. What if someone recognises you? Half the workforce they use for this is Laders' Guild."

Zin snorted. "Not at this time of night. Takes a bunch who can laze around in bed half the day to think this is a good time to be working."

"This is already too much attention." Zagiri looked back to the anxious staging clerk. "He's going to remember you, for starters. Why are you even here?"

"Deliveries." Zin hefted a small barrel over the wagon's tailgate.

It wasn't the sort of slapped-together make-do cask Zagiri was used to seeing delivered here. This was neatly crafted, if entirely unmarked by a brand. Was it some sort of fancy liquor? Was Zin trying to *make friends*?

Realising the answer felt like ice water down the back of her neck. "The explosives?" she hissed. "Why did you bring them *here*?"

Zin gave her a flat look. "Think I should drop 'em off round back of the Eldren Hall and say, *Never mind the lack of paperwork, just stick this in a corner and Zagiri Savani will take care of it*?"

Ink and ashes, of course he shouldn't. But that didn't make *this* a good idea. "What am *I* supposed to do?" she demanded right back, gesturing at the little cask. "Tuck that under my skirts and waddle in the front door?"

He shrugged. "Our mutual friend said you'd figure something out."

Yeva. Zagiri pulled a face. "Our mutual friend is more optimistic than sensible." Amusement tugged at his face in an almost familiar expression, but Zagiri was thinking too hard to be distracted by that. She *did* have to figure something out; it was clear no one else would. She needed to make this work.

"Open it up," she ordered. "Let me see them. Maybe I can—I don't know—sew them under my sash."

He glanced over his shoulder—much more of that and the clerk really would start getting suspicious—and then carefully pried the lid off. Inside, the little cask was packed tight with what looked almost like the cigars Zagiri had seen cousin Gildon smoke. She carefully pulled out a tightly bound cylinder of waxed paper, thick as a well-cured sausage and sealed with a little blob of red wax. There were a dozen of them in there, all precisely the same. The quality materials and impeccable construction reminded her of the devices Jaleh had made for the industrial district.

"These are impressive," she said.

Zin shrugged, like it was no big deal. "I told you. I've talked to some people."

Work like this could be relied upon. "You haven't been fucking around with them, have you?" Zagiri lifted an eyebrow at Zin's wounded innocence. "Try that on someone who didn't have to peel your last mess off the Swanneck."

He rolled his eyes, entirely unrepentant. "I swear, they're just as they were delivered to me, and I'm not going to interfere with them."

For what that was worth. But if she kept a close eye on Zin, he couldn't wriggle into anything too stupid. If any of this served any point at all.

She *couldn't* smuggle these things in, though. They were too bulky, too heavy. Shame he couldn't just deliver them.

Wait.

"If you came *during* a rehearsal," she considered aloud, "then one of us could be back at the door to let you in."

Zin seemed reluctant to admit she might have had a good idea, but eventually nodded. "I could plant them at the same time, save us having to figure out something else."

134

"*We* could plant them," Zagiri corrected him. She wasn't letting this out of her sight.

He shrugged again, like it was no concern of his if she wanted to go scampering all over the maintenance corridors of the Eldren Hall in her rehearsal gown.

She handed back the explosive tube, and he had the cask resealed and the wagon rumbling away through the parklands even as she was walking back to the staging point. Daruj was there now, waiting with the clerk.

"Misunderstanding," Zagiri told them shortly. "It's all fine."

But Daruj was frowning after the departing cart. "Who was that guy? He seemed weirdly familiar. I don't know where from, but I'm sure he's trouble. He give you a name?"

"Didn't come up," Zagiri said, which wasn't even a lie. Her heart was tripping a little fast. The last thing any of them needed was Daruj getting pulled into this by realising he'd seen Zin with the failed revolutionaries during the chaos of Salt Night. "Are the others all back at work?"

Daruj pulled his attention back to her, though his frown didn't lighten. "They are, but, Giri ... they're bad now. What are you going to do after you hand in your sabre?"

That question again. "Maybe you could take charge," Zagiri suggested flippantly.

He shook his head anyway. "This is yours. That's the only reason it works at all. *I* didn't pull the tribes together to smuggle alchemists out of the city. I didn't get them up on the roofs at Salt Night working together to keep people safe. It's all you."

For all the good that had done her in trying to pull it all together. Her family not talking to her. No other councillors interested. Even Azata Filosani gossiping about Anahid. Everything Zagiri had tried to build was coming apart.

All her, and not enough.

There were two daughters of Garabed Zinedani. Vartan Xhanari had told Anahid that, noting their respectable marriages—one to a lower-tier azata, and one to a merchant in the New Republic.

Marel Sakrani had taken her wife's name and lived in a rather fashionable apartment in the commercial district. She, everyone agreed, was where the drive to tone down the Zinedani activities came from. While her sister returned from the New Republic, Marel had taken affairs in hand and turned sharply away from the business of the barony. Even if Anahid *could* have called upon her without exciting considerable gossip, it seemed unlikely to be fruitful for her purposes.

Ruzanna Zinedani seemed more likely. She'd taken up the jewel of her father's former crown—the House known as the Banked Ember—after returning to Bezim on what must have been the first ship to sail after the news of her father's death had been carried across the Carmine Sea to her ears.

Anahid tried sending a message—as she had to Aghut and Mama Badrosani, outlining with careful discretion the shape of azatani interest in discussions of the future.

But her runner to the Banked Ember had returned with the letter still sealed in hand. Refused at the door, he said. No cards or correspondence accepted. All business via the Zinedani clerks.

Anahid tried in person, climbing the front stairs of the Banked Ember. The weak winter sunshine glinted off the office window from which Garabed Zinedani had once mocked her. She'd made him regret *that*, at least.

But she was barred at the door. All business through the clerks, the security man repeated stolidly.

Anahid *wasn't* trusting a matter this delicate to a letter via a clerk. If the only time the door of the Banked Ember opened was to admit guests during trading hours, then a guest she would be.

Laxmi loomed in her office doorway as Anahid finished pinning on her headscarf, checking her hairline carefully in the mirror. "What are you doing *now*?" the fallen demon demanded.

"Going out to play." Anahid tapped the lantern to dim its light. The sun had set while she readied herself; she could go immediately. "I'd have thought you'd approve. You can come along if you like—oh!" She smiled blithely. "But you have the fighting pit tonight."

"They can do it without me," Laxmi snarled.

Anahid insisted on no armour—this was not business, after all—
and almost regretted it when Laxmi met her downstairs in some
confection of white drapery that offered tantalising glimpses of her
muscled limbs. "They're going to think I'm touting competition," Anahid objected, her words tight with something. Indignation, perhaps.

Laxmi tossed her hair back over one shoulder; it flowed like ink,
almost as it had before she fell. "None of them can afford me," she
said, and smirked fit to make anyone want to try.

"Just…" Anahid didn't know what to say. Laxmi's collarbones
gleamed; had she been in the Flowers' cosmetics as well? Anahid
pulled her gaze away. "Don't cause any trouble."

The door to the Banked Ember was wide open, spilling strains of
music and the low hubbub of genial chatter. The same security man
was standing on the top step, questioning a guest.

A guest who squealed upon catching sight of Anahid, and came
leaping down the stairs to embrace her.

"Ana, *darling*!" declared the little blonde doll of a woman, kissing
extravagantly in the vicinity of Anahid's cheeks. "It's been too long!"

"You knew where to find me," Anahid pointed out wryly.

The Vidama Yilma-Torquera Selsan de Kith, who'd been at the
table when Anahid won Sable House from Stepan Zinedani in the
first place, waved a pale, dismissive hand. "It's no fun if you can't *play*.
And oh *my*, who is *this*?" She pressed her hand to the filmy material
covering her bosom as she gave Laxmi a thorough looking over.

Anahid resisted the urge to do the same. "Laxmi's a friend."

"I'm very friendly," Laxmi agreed, taking up Selsan's hand and
kissing the back of her knuckles.

"Shall we go inside?" Anahid interjected while Sel tittered and
blushed. As they climbed the stairs, she shot Laxmi a look. "Behave
yourself."

"Who else could I behave like?" Laxmi smirked at her. "Jealous?"

"Don't cause trouble," Anahid reminded her.

The Banked Ember mimicked an azatani townhouse, and if the
elegantly decorated parlours were far more crowded than the real
thing, the similarity was still strong enough to tighten Anahid's

shoulders. Many azatani who wouldn't lower themselves to the rest of the District came here to feel just a little daring. If didn't matter if they saw her; her secret had long flown the nest. But it still wouldn't be pleasant.

"Ana, come *on*," Selsan declared, hooking her elbow through Anahid's to drag her through two parlours in quick succession. The clatter of the lottery wheel fell away behind them, and the sight of the carrick tables knocked the breath out of her. Anahid shouldn't have been surprised; the game might not have been played under Garabed's supervision, but if Sel were here, that had obviously changed.

Anahid hadn't felt anything missing from her life, not with the myriad tangles and risks of running Sable House to occupy her attention. But still, it sent a thrill through her veins: the hiss of cards on baize, the knock of tokens into the copper ante pot, the murmur of bets and bluffs.

Selsan tugged Anahid over to a half-empty table, calling to the dealer, "Can we buy in direct, darling?"

Anahid added, as she took her seat, "And I was so hoping to convey my regards to the owner. Does she ever walk the floor?"

The dealer glanced at her, even as he produced a ledger for them to sign to receive tokens. A swift look over Anahid, and a glance at Laxmi too. "Mistress Zinedani sticks to her office, azata. But I'll pass on your message."

Anahid should press. Or she should go and find another angle of attack. She was here for a *reason*, after all. Whatever she'd said to Laxmi, it *was* business.

But one little game first wouldn't hurt.

The cards were dealt, and play began. Selsan chattered away happily, making friends with the other two already at the table, distracting them and teasing out information. Anahid watched, and learned, and savoured the familiar feel of the cards between her fingers.

The first hand she won—laying down a trio against a pair across the table—sizzled victory along her veins near as sharp and bright as—

As she'd felt when she'd killed Stepan while Garabed watched helplessly.

Anahid flinched, knocking over the stack of her winnings. Laxmi's hand landed on her shoulder, pressing warm and somehow reassuring, as Anahid hurried to gather up the tokens with trembling fingers. "I think I might just—" she started to say, rising from the table on knees she had to lock straight.

"Not leaving so soon, I hope, Azata Savani."

A new voice, yet familiar. Ruzanna Zinedani sounded just like her father, rough but well modulated, and brimming with confidence. She had Garabed's posture too, stately and relaxed, and his propensity for wearing overlarge pieces of jewelry, and the same sharp, dark eyes. She was dressed like a New Republic nobleman—brocade knee britches, snowy linen shirt, black vest and layers of colourful cravats. Her chestnut hair was even pulled back in a clubbed queue.

And at her side was Tahera Danelani. The woman who'd betrayed Anahid in public. The woman she'd threatened. The woman who'd been her friend.

Anahid opened her mouth but had no breath in her for words.

"Surely you didn't get all dressed up and come to my House," Ruzanna continued, "merely to scrape up some pocket change. It hardly compares to your last winnings, does it?"

Anahid's last winnings at a carrick table had been Sable House, won from Ruzanna's cousin Stepan. The cousin she'd murdered, before Garabed had tried to kill her and been killed in turn. "I've stopped playing for such high stakes," Anahid managed. "It's more trouble than it's worth."

Ruzanna smirked and waved one hand in a swing of frothy lace. "Oh, I don't know. At the end of the day, it got rid of my cousin, who was an ongoing waste of good rakia, so that's worth something, isn't it?" She lifted an eyebrow. "Now, are we talking, or are you leaving?"

This was what Anahid wanted, she reminded herself. This was why she came.

But she felt off-balance now, torn away from the carrick table and following Ruzanna out of the parlour, with all eyes upon them. She hadn't expected Tahera, falling into step beside her. She couldn't remember any of her prepared points.

Anahid glanced sidelong; Tahera was dressed for evening entertainments, shoulders bare in the New Republic style, her headscarf glittering with beads. She'd avoided the District before—shamed Anahid for suggesting they visit—possibly because past debts had ruined her credit down here. But here she was, with Ruzanna Zinedani herself.

Opening a discreet door into a plain staircase leading upward, Ruzanna waved toward the merriment of the front parlour. "Your associate can wait down here."

"You get your little friend," Laxmi growled, "and my mistress gets hers."

Ruzanna laughed a little. "Fine. It'll be a regular tea party. Come on."

Anahid glanced at Laxmi, relieved by the focus in her yellow eyes. No sign of teasing or flirtation now; despite the dress, the fallen demon was all business, following Ruzanna up the narrow staircase.

When Tahera hesitated, Anahid brushed past her, stepping aside when Tahera reached for her arm. They watched each other for a moment.

Then Tahera sighed sharply. "I'm not here for you. I was just catching up with a friend." She gestured up the stairs.

Anahid wondered if they'd met in the New Republic, or known each other beforehand. It hardly mattered. "Thank the Powers for small mercies, I suppose. I've had enough of you coming for me."

Tahera's mouth thinned. "Don't play the innocent victim. I merely told the truth."

"And I didn't," Anahid retorted. Her hands had folded at her waist, tight and defensive. What Tahera had done still hurt. The *anger* in Zagiri's eyes, as Anahid had had to flee.

"No," Tahera snapped, "you merely threatened to. And do not insult both of us by suggesting you wouldn't do it all again, exactly as you did."

Telling the truth again. Anahid wished it hadn't come down to blackmail. She wished there'd been another way. But yes, she would do it again. For Siyon, and for herself as well.

That had been the first moment she'd realised she could wield power. That her will could have weight. That the bars of her cage would bend, if she leaned on them.

"You could have just helped me," Anahid pointed out.

Tahera's mouth twisted. "You do fine helping yourself. Azata of the Avenues, lady of the Flower district, knocking aside everyone who opposes you..."

There was something on her face—Anahid couldn't recognise it. Not something she'd seen in Tahera before, not at the table, not in the drawing rooms of the Avenues. A truth behind the mask they'd both worn for so long.

"Look at you." Tahera sighed. "You're really suffering, aren't you?"

Was Tahera *jealous*?

Anahid swallowed. "I am sorry," she said, "about Syrah."

Tahera shrugged. "She can't hold it all over me anymore, at least. And grief has turned Enkin surprisingly well-behaved. So it's not all bad." She waved toward the stairs, almost mocking in her courtesy. "Best get on with it, hadn't you? I might go try a hand or two. There's a vacancy at the table, after all."

So it was Ruzanna alone in the office that had once been Garabed's, with Anahid taking the visitor's chair, and Laxmi prowling the room, that dress whispering around her. It didn't feel like they had an advantage. Not in the depths of Ruzanna's House. Not in the heart of the District that had been her father's, and was now hers. Would *eagerly* be hers if she just stretched out her hand to let it yield to her.

That was why Anahid was here.

Ruzanna took the luxurious seat behind the big desk. "All right, you have my attention. What do you want?"

Laxmi drifted past the back of Anahid's chair, pressing fingertips briefly against Anahid's shoulder. All right. She could be blunt as well. "I have a message, from certain azatani parties, for the baron of the Flower district. Is that you?"

Anahid hadn't really thought that Ruzanna would sit up straight and claim the title at once, eager to come to heel. But she hadn't expected the disdainful snort.

"*Barons,*" Ruzanna spat. "Barons and wars and wrestling for a slightly bigger slice of the same old pie. We *should* have left it all on the other side of the Carmine Sea. Now the world is changing even more...I'd have thought you'd agree with me. New woman, aren't you? Striking out on your own. Even palling around with the Sorcerer, I hear." She tilted back in her chair, propping her boots up on the corner of her father's desk. "You didn't pick up the baronial coronet when you took my father's metaphorical head. Why not?"

Anahid blinked away the dizzy memory of Garabed's dead weight atop her, and the look on Qorja's face as she lowered the heavy mirror. "I didn't want it," she said, half a gasp. "I don't want it."

Ruzanna shrugged. "I don't want it either. Just like you." She waved a lace-laden hand between them. "Businesswomen, both of us."

"It's not that simple," Anahid said, trying to haul her composure back into place. "I have *a* House, Mistress Zinedani. You have much more. People—a whole District—who rely on you. You have *responsibilities*. And with Midnight's disappearance, it's more important than ever that we have stability here in the District. That's better for Bezim. And more profitable for *all* of us."

Ruzanna smirked at her, almost condescending. "Better for Bezim. Like it cares for the likes of me. Azatani only come down here when there's something in it for them. Profit's in *opportunity*, za. Plenty of that to be had in Bezim right now. You should be looking around as well. I can give you some tips on where to invest in the new building. We're going to remake the face of Bezim." She smiled, like a cat looking at a saucer of cream, and then shrugged. "Can't do it if we're stuck holding everyone's hand, though. They'll get over it."

It was utterly, breathtakingly dismissive. As though Ruzanna really thought she and her sister could just take what they wanted and ignore the rest. Anahid had thought perhaps Marel was just skittish about the business, and Ruzanna could be appealed to. But this...

"You have contractual responsibilities," Anahid pointed out. "You're in danger of breaking—"

"I'm in danger of being bored to death," Ruzanna interrupted, swinging her head on her neck and fixing Anahid with a heavy look that was far too familiar. Garabed's condescension in his daughter's face. "This is a business, azata. *My* business. I'm not interfering in yours, am I? So fuck off out of mine."

Anahid opened her mouth again, but Laxmi's hand closed over her shoulder, a weight and a warning.

Perhaps the fallen demon *did* know when to beat a strategic retreat after all.

But agitation tied tighter in Anahid's chest with every step down the stairs, out into the evening. It *wasn't* just Ruzanna's business; it was that of every House manager in the District.

It was *Anahid's* business, for the weight that would come down on her if Ruzanna and Marel kept dodging their responsibilities.

It wasn't fair, for them to step aside like this, leaving everyone else in the lurch. They *did* have responsibilities—contractual responsibilities, like Anahid had said.

She paused in the street, as the idea arranged itself.

Laxmi paused with her, a smirk growing on the demon's face. "I like that look on you. We get to fight after all?"

"We fight," Anahid agreed, and smirked herself, at how little Laxmi was going to like this. "We fight *my way*."

CHAPTER 10

Redick folded his arms atop the pillar of the dock and gave Siyon a flat look. "Do you want to do this or not?"

Not was definitely the answer. Siyon absolutely did not want to go back across the estuarine river, retracing the route he'd impossibly swum as a fleeing fourteen-year-old. The mud-and-stone smear of Dockside lurked on the other side, like it had been waiting for him all this time.

This was ridiculous, of course. He'd *been* back, gathering material for his ill-fated first attempt at becoming the Power of the Mundane. He'd confronted his brothers. It had been wildly unpleasant, but nothing dire had happened.

Didn't mean this time would go so well. They knew about him now. They *might* be waiting.

Siyon pulled the tooled-leather journal out of his satchel, flipping to those last few pages. The pages that *had* been blank but were now rapidly filling up with writing—his, and the exhilarating black-ink whiplash of Izmirlian's hand. They'd written a lot, in the past few days, but there always seemed to be more pages.

You never did tell me anything about your family, Izmirlian had written.

Siyon hadn't. So many things they'd never had a chance to

explore together. Siyon had met Izmirlian's brothers after he was gone. So many things in these journals that Siyon had guessed about Izmirlian—his curiosity, his keen attention, his ability to wonder and dream—but not really *known*.

He missed Izmirlian more than ever—missed the chance to have done this *properly*—with his words floating across an empty page. With this tenuous and impossible link.

My family doesn't matter, Siyon had written back. *Not for this*.

They didn't. All that mattered was the help of the mudwitches. If this wild idea of pushing energy out through the city barrier was going to work, they needed practitioners all over the city to assist.

Siyon wasn't sure they'd even speak to *him*—not a fisherson, not someone who'd never earned his medallion, not someone who'd left— but he had a better chance than someone from the upper city.

Still didn't mean he liked the idea.

Redick heaved a melodramatic sigh. "Just get in the damn boat."

Siyon got in the damn boat.

With two of Awl Quarter's heftiest blades rowing, and the tide slack, the trip across the river took almost no time at all. Siyon tried not to hold his breath, or think of swimming the distance. Tried not to scan all the abandoned fisher-docks up this stretch of the river for the one where his brothers had thrown him in, trussed up in a sack. Shoved aside the memory of Mezin's taunting: *One day soon, we'll put you all in sacks.*

He wanted to sneak in, conduct his business quietly, and sneak back out again. Probably a flimsy idea. It was difficult to get anywhere in Dockside, let alone across the entire neighbourhood, without *some-one's* idle children seeing you and passing on the news.

Siyon hadn't expected to be met at the jetty by a Shore Clan lieu-tenant. The woman wasn't tall, but her tattooed shoulders were broad and she sprawled confidently on the stone steps leading up into the warren of riverside slums. She introduced herself as *the Knife* and gave the impression she wouldn't need help to put Siyon and the Awl Quarter rowers besides into the drink if she wanted.

If she was here to escort him, that might solve all his problems.

But as she hauled him onto the jetty, she said: "Aghut won't go against the fisherclans, so don't ask. That's all I'm here to say."

"Fine." Siyon hoped he didn't sound sulky.

From the quirk of her mouth, he failed. "You know Lady Sable, right?"

Which seemed strange from a Dockside heavy, but not so much from one of Aghut's people. "What, your boss got his manly leather knickers in a twist over an azata muscling in on business?"

The Knife snorted. "Who *isn't* muscling in? She might just be the only steady hand left. The Zinedani are shedding men like dandruff and Midnight's organisation exploded like a poorly made lantern. Every second petty gang leader fancies himself a new baron, and some of them have been down here sniffing around the mudwitches. Midnight knew better, but those he left behind are…" She considered her words and carefully went with: "Feral."

The parts of the organisation Peylek hadn't gathered up. Those who hadn't been important enough under Midnight to know their true purpose, but had been big enough to fancy themselves even bigger, now the tide was high and there was room to move. But Peylek *did* have the core of Midnight's stable of alchemists locked down.

Foolish to hunt a replacement in Dockside.

Siyon had grown up beneath the looming threat of the mudwitches. He'd never *seen* one; even messages and offerings were only ever run by girl-children, medallions passed on by clan matriarchs. In the upper city, the term was derided as superstitious quackery. By that stage, Siyon had seen enough to figure that a mudwitch probably helped Dockside women dealing with the sort of trouble Flowers (and plenty of others) used alchemists to avoid as well.

But since the Mundane power had started to rise, and magic had seeped into every nook and cranny of Bezim, Siyon had rethought a lot of his assumptions about what was and wasn't significant. Anahid's unfortunate Flower, Imelda, had known a lot of bits and pieces of useful trickery. She'd come from Dockside.

"I'm not here to steal anyone away," Siyon said quickly. "Nor try to shut them down."

She snorted. "Just as fucking well. Plenty of things disappear real easy in the marshes, and we don't go against the mudwitches either."

Siyon was feeling better and better about this little visit.

The woman waved him away up the stairs. "Just tell Lady Sable we're always open to reasonable talk. And I'd stick to the Esplanade, if I were you. Nice and public. Cut in just before the navy yard and you'll get where you need to be."

Which could be the mudwitches, or could be an ambush. But Siyon thought it unlikely. The Shore Clan had always preferred to avoid the fisherclans entirely. Don't go against them, don't get involved. In many ways, Dockside was a far more delicate balance than the upper city.

At midmorning, traffic on the Esplanade—shadowing the waterfront just above the mire of warehouses and docks—was thin. The workers were long off to their jobs, the fishing boats weren't back yet, and the few short-range free-city trading vessels on the wharves were crawling with laders and fitters and provedore agents.

There were still plenty of eyes watching Siyon, from wide-open windows and loitering crews of children in the alleyways. He hadn't worn the purple coat or anything, but he'd be naive to assume no one could figure out who he was. Or worse, recognise him.

As he walked, Siyon tried to put his finger on what felt so different. He was seeing with adult eyes the places he remembered as a child, but he'd already been back here once before, hunting for the material of the city to feed into his ritual. Dockside *felt* different from the lower city, not just to his eyes or ears or nose (a subtly different stench of mud over here) but to those other senses.

The energy here was calmer. Not tamed, but perhaps...channelled. Flowing in ordered ways. Was it distance from the Scarp? The interference of the river?

On the balcony of the big sailors' inn beside the customs house, men were sprawled at the tables, watching him pass. In the jumble of their voices, Siyon heard the hiss of that well-known word: *Sorcerer.*

"Shut it," someone else snapped up there. "One of us, ain't he? Don't get precious like a za about it."

Siyon nearly stopped. Nearly turned back to see who was—well, not quite defending him. They wouldn't thank him for the attention.

A block before the massive walled bulk of the navy yard, Siyon cut down between the warehouses. He assumed he was heading for the supply road and the marshes beyond the edge of the city; the alley taunts of his childhood had always been full of dares to venture out of sight of the road. Were there really cottages on duck legs like they'd terrified each other with? Nothing seemed too impossible, these days.

He was still very surprised when a door opened right next to him, in a brick warehouse wall he could have sworn was unbroken just a moment earlier.

In the wooden-framed doorway, an older woman snapped: "Oi." Her steel-grey hair was pinned back severely, and a stained and singed leather apron was tied over her shapeless mud-coloured dress. The stones of the breakwater were less hard than her face, and the leather thong around her neck clattered with mud medallions—dozens of them, at least, each sparking with an energy that made Siyon dizzy.

She looked him up and down, and grunted. "You've got that Velo look, all right. Get in before someone comes a-hunting you."

When Siyon stepped inside—ducking beneath the low lintel—it was into as cozy a kitchen as he'd ever been chased out of by an irate female relation. No sign of the warehouse, just a cauldron of soup bubbling on an open hearth and a long worktable overhung by drying herbs and flowers. The window in the far wall was fringed with climbing vines from a sunlit garden that must have been...in a hidden courtyard?

"Best not to think about it," the woman said briskly as she closed the door behind them again. She snapped her fingers, and lanterns sprang to full light in the corners of the room, illuminating the hanging sacks of who-knew-what, the shelves crowded with bowls and implements, the baskets of marsh grass on the workbench.

It could have been an alchemist's workroom.

"So you're the one been causing all the ruckus." The woman squinted at Siyon, grabbing his chin in a sharp grip to turn his face this way and that. "No longer just Darra Velo's little problem, are you?"

Siyon blinked. "You knew my mother?"

"Still know her. Send her liniment for her knuckles twice a month and get some nice fish and a haul of firewood in return. Know your aunts too, and your cousins. I delivered three of their babes. This is Dockside, boy, what were you expecting?" The woman sniffed and let him go, giving the soup a brisk stir before stepping behind the workbench. "You can call me Mother Marsh. Sit there. Don't touch anything. You're sparking like a firework and I don't want it in my business."

Siyon perched on the indicated stool, fighting the urge to wedge his hands between his knees like he'd been caught pilfering crab cakes from the windowsill. He wanted to ask after his family—after the Velo cousins who'd had children—but it seemed almost cowardly. If he really wanted to know, he could take a little detour on his way back to the boat, walk straight into the Velo clan hall and see for himself.

Mother Marsh brandished a hefty carving knife and set to a pile of swamp onions. "You're here to ask for something, then."

"Help," Siyon admitted. He looked around this workspace—so carefully marshalled—and realised whose hand he'd felt in the ordered flow of power in Dockside. "I wanted to ask for your assistance in handling the Mundane energy. In pushing it out through the city barrier to better feed the rest of the plane. But you're way ahead of me, aren't you?"

Maybe a little smile curved across her wrinkled face; hard to tell when she was paying more attention to the onions than to him. "Nothing runs wild down here that can be put to good work instead," she confirmed.

Siyon wanted to ask how she'd done it. Whether she could teach the upper-city alchemists how to make it work. If they'd even be able to get their heads around the way the mudwitches worked with energy and the world.

But while he was considering that, Mother Marsh kept talking. "That barrier. It's quite a neat arrangement. Had me proper surprised, until I heard your name. I knew no Summer Club tinkerer was going to come up with something that efficient or natural. All they care about is control. But you know better, don't you, boy?" Her gaze was as sharp as the flashing knife. "There's a good many things in this world we can't control."

A wild laugh bubbled up in Siyon's throat; he managed to keep it to just a little huff. "Almost everything," he admitted.

She nodded, and smiled unmistakably this time. "Almost, but not quite everything. True and truer still. You know that, so you have to know that this plan of yours won't work."

It was so pleasantly said that it took Siyon a moment to catch up. "It— What? Why not?"

Mother Marsh returned to her onions, knife brisk. "How well does it ever work? Waiting safe while others scramble? Sitting on a mountain of plenty and handing out a little at a time? You learning too much of the wrong thing up there among the azatani." She sniffed. "The mud remembers, boy. We were here before they got off their boats, and we'll be here when they fall back into the sea. And the whole time, we've told tales of the monsters and the marvellous. So who does the magic truly belong to?"

Siyon opened his mouth to protest—that this wasn't like the azatani hoarding power and wealth, wasn't about ownership or belonging—but the words stuck. Didn't he want to keep the people safe from the monsters? There was a hierarchy already, in his goals. "So what do I do?"

She shrugged her bony shoulders. "I'm not the Sorcerer. I've never set foot beyond Dockside. The rest of the world isn't my concern."

Siyon curled his fingers around his satchel, feeling the hard spine of Izmirlian's journal within. All the world that *he'd* seen. But more still that he'd gone seeking.

Mother Marsh swept the chopped onions into a bowl and fixed Siyon with a sharp look. "You won't figure it out skulking around here, boy. We'll keep doing what we can. The rest of it is up to you." She waved the knife toward the door. "You'd best get going before anyone has time to concoct a nasty surprise."

As she'd said: true and truer still.

Siyon hurried back along the Esplanade, turning all of that over in his mind. Monsters and humans. Magic and the Mundane. Handing out power and expecting others to just accept it. But it wasn't as though—

"Hsst."

Siyon jerked out of his musings; a young woman sweeping a doorstep jerked her broom up the Esplanade, where a few hefty figures were loitering out front of the customs house. Siyon's blood chilled. Impossible to tell, at this distance, just who they were. Might not be Velo cronies. The inquisitors didn't come down here a lot, but it wasn't unknown. Or maybe one of those *feral* remnants of Midnight's organisation fancied laying hands on the Sorcerer himself.

The young woman knocked her broom against the corner of her building, where a warding negation sigil was scratched into the wood, next to a lane so narrow Siyon could barely fit down it. "Nip over to Short Street," she whispered. "Get a move on and you'll fox 'em."

"Thanks," Siyon gasped, already ducking down the laneway.

Her brief smile followed him. *One of us*, Siyon heard again. Not really, in so many ways. He'd left Dockside. He'd seen more, done more, become more.

But he'd walked here before anywhere else. The mud remained, and the mud remembered.

"A blade of Bracken that was, and will be," Voski Tolan declared, for the fifth and final time that night, as she lifted Zagiri's sabre over her head. "The Star Whisper."

Not Zagiri's any longer. It had never really been *hers*—it was a named blade of the Little Bracken, loaned to her, or perhaps her to it, for the glory of its name.

Now returned. The time had slipped away from her—in rehearsals and planning and conversations at salons and on promenade as she desperately tried to find a councillor interested in reform—and now here they all were, with only three weeks left until the Harbour Master's Ball.

Zagiri's wasn't the only blade being handed in tonight. Two other azatani were retiring into society, plus one young blade taking up an apprenticeship as a shipwright and another joining the inquisitors, which Zagiri supposed, rationally, was as good a living as any other.

But hers was the only named blade, and anticipation hushed the tight-packed crowd in the Chapel. Voski smiled tightly, curling her fingers around the grip, within the spangled basket hilt. She drew the sabre from its deep blue scabbard and held it aloft. "A blade that knows," she intoned. "A blade that sees. A blade that remembers."

Part of the ritual, introducing the sergeant's recitation of the blade's history, with new additions for the most recent carrier. But as the blade gleamed over their heads, Zagiri remembered when she'd been given Star Whisper in the first place. When Voski had said she'd recited *more* history than she remembered, as though the blade had spoken.

Magic had woken fully in Bezim now. What would the sabre have to say about Zagiri? She was suddenly uneasy, clenching her fingers against the urge to grab the blade back before it could denounce her.

But it was too late. Voski said: "A blade of the Old Kingdoms, of the first tribe, of Grand Bracken itself. Carried by twenty-seven hands of the Little Bracken, to our glory, to our honour, and to our ongoing renown. Let us add to that history now the twenty-eighth Star Whisper—Zagiri Savani—and remember her name and her deeds."

Bringing the blade down to lay across her palms, Voski opened her mouth—

And gasped, as the glittering of the blade's chasing turned into a vivid glow. Light lifted off the steel, in motes and swirls, rising golden into the air above them.

All around Zagiri the crowd of her Bracken blademates drew back a little, stirring uneasily. "Like Salt Night," someone muttered.

Zagiri—who'd been busy dangling off the Swanneck when Siyon conducted his display on the steps of the Eldren Hall—had heard the stories. This was a smaller manifestation, a lesser light show, but still impressive. Sparks multiplied and swarmed, linking together and spinning into shapes and impressions, not quite images, but the sliding possibility of them.

There, quite clearly, was Zagiri on a rooftop. Lifting her hand and shouting, as a terribly familiar shape—the spreading eagle wings and snapping beak of a griffin—rose beyond her. The golden light swirled and reformed, and now Zagiri raced through the streets under a shadow—the dragon, and its fear, and its destruction. Another scintillating rearrangement, flickering like blades in action, darting and clashing, and then the light coalesced into Zagiri holding out her hand, and receiving into her grip another four hands, all stacking together, joining into one accord.

The lights twisted together, soaring upward to spread into a tall, magnificent, thorn-laden tree. The symbol of Bracken, almost exactly as it appeared on their bravi badges, hung in the air for just a moment, before the light dissolved into nothingness.

Bracken that was, and will be.

The magic faded, and hollowed out Zagiri's chest in its wake. Even the cheers lifting around her, the roars of *brave the knife* and chanting of *Bracken, Bracken, Bracken* didn't help.

"We remember her name!" Voski shouted over the cheers, grabbing Zagiri's hand and lifting it up. "We remember her deeds."

Zagiri was heavy with relief. That had been glorious, and yet all she felt was gratefulness that she hadn't been wearing the sabre when she'd flare-bombed the industrial district, or plotted the Ball's interruption. She wasn't some hero, a chivalric blade of the tribe's mythic past.

In the middle of the chaotic good cheer of her tribe, Zagiri felt weary with the knowledge that while she was trying her best, it wasn't always *good*. It certainly didn't always work. She wasn't even a bravi now—would her workgang come apart and leave her with no plans at all?

Faceless hands clapped Zagiri on the back, and someone passed her a flagon of rakia that she passed on without drinking.

Voski emerged from the press and caught her by both shoulders, holding Zagiri still amid the whirl. "Well, that was something. For you as well, I see."

"I'm fine," Zagiri insisted. "That was just unexpected."

Voski smiled wryly. "Say one thing for Velo, he makes life more interesting."

Which of course was not the only thing anyone was saying about Siyon. But it was better than what Zagiri had been putting up with all week at Ball rehearsals, where she'd heard over and over about the ongoing threat to the city's security represented by Siyon. Apparently Avarair Hisarani was saying it to anyone who'd stand still to listen.

Balian's mouth had gone a bit tight, when they'd overheard that gossip in the dance line. But he hadn't challenged anyone. Hadn't contradicted any of what they were saying. Hadn't even made an airy comment about how his brother was known to be a stuck-up twerp who constantly had sand in his trousers about Siyon.

Fingers snapped in front of Zagiri's face; Tein Geras, the quartermaster, had joined them. "I said, you coming on to the party?"

The gathering of all the tribes after their own sabre-returning sessions. It was a rare occasion of coming together in more peace than not, though any number of bravi in the same place would inevitably give rise to duels. Zagiri had enjoyed the party in previous years, though it occurred to her that of course they held this *now* because of the azatani timing, of the Ball and all the other business. As with so much else in Bezim, they just passively enforced *their* convenience on everyone else.

She *should* go. Perhaps if she spoke with the sergeants, she could keep the workgang. Keep her plans afloat, just barely. Scramble and beg, to prop up everything else that was coming unravelled. She didn't have a sponsor for her reform. She was losing what support she had. She was working with *Zin*, for the sake of all the Powers. Was any of this sensible?

Voski clapped her on the shoulder and said, "Of course she is. Come on!"

Her sergeant commanded, and—this one last time—Zagiri obeyed.

It felt strange with no blade at her hip; the thunder of Bracken boots on cobblestones seemed hollow. Her final run with the tribe. Oh, sure—once Bracken, always Bracken. She could always wear the badge, just not on her leathers, and not while drawing blade. She could hear the thunder of boots on tiles, and make the call, but she'd never be one of them again.

They ran not on the roofs, tonight, but along the streets—rattling shutters, swinging off lantern-posts, leaping over fountains. Almost like a promenade—to be seen—but far faster, far flashier, and with anything bright or interesting along the way liable to be snatched up and carried along. Soon the tribe was adorned with glittering scarves, waving purloined teaglasses, toasting with filched flagons of rakia.

More years than not, they gathered in the old hippodrome, but with the inquisitors and other ongoing workings of the Council having taken that over, there was only one place in the city large enough to bring them all together in peace.

The path up the crag was winding but well-worn; on the way, they passed the caverns and crannies in which the exiled dead of the New Republic were interred. The bravi surging past didn't precisely fall into respectful silence, but a hush settled over them, and no one started singing until well after the last of the cave openings had fallen behind them.

The top of the crag opened up—less a flat space than a shallow bowl lined in knots and bulges of shattered stone. A fire roared already in the centre and the Bleeding Dawn were clambering over the boulders and buttresses, calling raucous welcome—or possibly challenge—to the arriving Bracken. Haruspex were right on their heels, some of them clambering up the nearly sheer sides of the crag to loom out of the shadows and then mock those startled.

Zagiri stepped aside, as the tribes mingled and bellowed and cheered, to look out over the city, strewn like stardust beneath them. The view was amazing from up here, down along the headland, with the dark ribbon of the river chasm cutting through, and the blackness of the bay scooped out. Like this, it was easy to think of the city as one thing. *Bezim*. Ours.

Azatani name, for an azatani city. But the city wasn't the buildings, it was the *people*. It was everyone. Zagiri wished she could make everyone understand—but what if she couldn't?

There was the Eldren Hall. It really *did* look beautiful from up here, lantern-light making the windows glow, and the dome glittering beneath the moon.

Imagine it cracked. Imagine it leaking smoke. Imagine that certainty shattered, and the new possibilities that might be considered then.

But if she had nothing to offer—no sponsor, no reform, no way to steer—then there would be nothing but fear. She'd *fail*, worse than if she'd never tried.

As she dithered, on the edge of the crag, someone shouted from near the fire: "Hey! Hey, Savani! Get your azatani arse over here, we want to talk to you!"

It was Voski, beckoning Zagiri peremptorily over to a group of— oh, *all* the sergeants.

Hovhaness of the Bleeding Dawn smacked his knuckles against the fringe-dripping shoulder of Jerrenta of the Bower's Scythe. "Here she comes, the peddler of your little dream of Grand Bracken reborn."

Voski swigged nonchalantly from a flagon and passed it on to Redick of the Awl Quarter, beaded and glittering like a storybook pirate. "I've told you before, Hov, I'd not run together with your pack of reprobates for all the silver in the New Republic."

"What about doing so for a better cause?" asked Slender of Haruspex, her voice a serrated rasp. "What if we ran to a fight big enough for all of us?"

"That would be a pretty prize," Jerrenta purred, shrugging off Hovhaness. She leaned forward, bracing her own bottle against her knee; she always carried one, and rooftop legend said she'd once bested a challenger, bottle to blade, without spilling a drop. "What say you, little Bracken-who-was. We have loaned you our blades for half a season on grand promises of what might be. What's happening about our fight?"

Zagiri winced, and covered it with a little bow, hands open and empty by her sides; the bow of the unbladed, who could not be challenged with honour. "It—it's harder than I thought it would be," she admitted.

156

"Than she *thought*," mocked Hovhaness. Let it never be said the Bleeders weren't dramatic assholes from the top down. "This is your tribe's problem, Vos—too many *thinkers*."

"Better than none," Voski returned easily. She didn't seem at all bothered—either by the needling or Zagiri's poor showing here.

It was Redick who said, "I thought you had plans."

"I did." Zagiri drew a breath, bracing herself. "We made a good impression, with the workgang. People saw it. They marked what it meant. But everything's a mess, and I can't get a good enough grip. There's only one last, wild chance, and I—"

That was as far as she got.

"How wild?" Slender asked, keen as a blade.

At the same time as Jerrenta crowed: "My favourite kind!" She reached across the little knot of sergeants to clink her bottle against the one Redick held, before both of them drank in toast.

Hovhaness batted the oversized plume of Jerrenta's tricorn out of his face, but he didn't look as disgruntled as he might. "We haven't done all this work—*honest* work"—he sounded disgusted—"for nothing. You'd better make it mean something."

Zagiri didn't know how she felt. Her heart was a mess, hope and possibility struggling back out of the quashing mass of her earlier despair. The idea that they still believed in her, when she wasn't sure she did, was almost too hot to touch.

Before she could find any words, Voski spoke up again: "Oh, she will. She's one of us."

Bracken that was, and will be.

Zagiri smiled, and said: "Brave the knife."

She would *make* this work.

CHAPTER 11

The Siren's Cove was cunningly carved in grey stone to resemble the sea cliffs of Bezim itself, rough and daunting, with the courtyard of the House a warm and welcoming harbour beneath the gleaming archway of Lyraec marble.

Anahid wasn't really visiting, as Attabel hadn't really visited her. So she—and her attendants—waited in that courtyard. Laxmi sprawled across the rim of the central fountain, as daunting in her leather armour as the fountain's statue siren was flirtatious in her naked frolic. Anahid's other companion—the one who'd actually been invited—looked equally nervous about the fallen demon and the stone siren, as though either might be his ruin.

Legal clerks were not generally known for being intrepid. Anahid was grateful Master Gertcha had agreed to come at all. The first two clerks she'd approached had refused to be involved.

It was still quite early in the afternoon, the Fade bell only recently rung, but when Master Attabel came out to meet them, he was magnificently attired in an iridescent blue robe, his hair dripping pearls, and his long fingernails just as white and glistening. "My dear Lady Sable," he greeted her warmly, though he looked carefully at all of them. "Shall I trouble you with impertinent offers of refreshment?"

Her own words turned back at her; Anahid appreciated the

elegance. They were all dancing carefully on a shifting floor. "I won't be staying," she confirmed. "Indeed, I am here only to perform an introduction I hope will be of great benefit to all parties. I couldn't help overhearing among your associates in the gardens some confusion regarding the finer details of your tenancy agreements."

Attabel's frown was a delicate thing. Possibly he hadn't considered the problems he and the other Houses were having with the Zinedani in such a way. It had only occurred to Anahid when she started thinking about it all like an azatani, looking for the weakest seams in a well-stitched problem.

"That," Attabel said eventually, "is not untrue."

Anahid gestured toward the waiting clerk. "Master Gertcha here is a legal clerk specialising in precisely the area of property and all associated contracts. The clerk who negotiated my divorce mentioned his name, should I have any difficulties in that area." At least, he'd mentioned it when Anahid went back specifically to ask for a list of recommendations.

Laxmi snorted from the fountain. "Does he know what he's getting into here?"

Gertcha had been looking rather uncertain, clutching at his satchel, but at that he straightened his spine. "Under Bezim ordnance, all parties to a contract are legally entitled to petition for a rebalancing of the contract if the deliverance on one side has altered substantially from the initial agreement. This applies regardless of the parties or the substance of the contract."

"Indeed," Anahid added, "this is a fundamental tenet of the laws of the city, and one dearly held in the hearts of the azatani justices who would oversee any such rebalancing. And if any difficulty is encountered in the process," she added quietly to Attabel, "I know someone among the inquisitors who would be most eager for an opportunity to prosecute any oversteps."

Attabel's pearlescent-tipped fingers fluttered in front of his mouth as he considered this. It was, in its own way, a very bold step. To lodge a complaint against the Zinedani over the fulfillment of their tenancy agreements was something that would certainly draw direct attention. Attabel—or the House managers who had gathered in the gazebo—might feel that matters had not yet come to that level of desperation.

Perhaps Gertcha sensed similarly. "I can leave you a card, and call upon you later at your convenience to discuss your options."

But Attabel smiled, and waved toward the door leading into the House proper. "Oh, if we're only discussing options, let's do so inside in more comfort. Lady Sable, thank you ever so much for arranging this introduction. I suspect Master Gertcha is going to find a great number of new friends in the District."

Anahid inclined her head and turned to leave.

Laxmi fell in beside her with a creak of leather as they passed beneath the marble arch again. "*This* is your plan?" she demanded.

"This is *part* of my plan," Anahid corrected. "And may I once again remind you that no one asked you to come along."

"I'd say something about needing to keep you out of trouble, but I don't think that's possible," Laxmi shot back. "I thought you didn't want to get involved."

"This is all *about* me not being involved," Anahid snapped. The *last* thing she wanted was Buni Filosani—or Azata Malkasani, both women accustomed to victory one way or another—leaning on *her* to become baron. If she had to trap and entice the Zinedani into taking their proper place, she would eagerly take up both net and bait. "I am providing a gentle reminder that they cannot simply avoid their responsibilities while enjoying the benefits."

"You are poking them." Laxmi grabbed Anahid's arm, spinning them both to a halt. Even now, so long gone from the Abyss, her grip was always hot. "You think Xhanari is going to protect you now any better than he did last time?"

Anahid blinked. "You...know about that?"

Not that the protection had failed; Siyon had been fetched to try to get Anahid back, when she'd been snatched off the streets by the Zinedani. But that Vartan Xhanari was involved—that *she* had been involved with *him*—was a secret Anahid thought was more tightly held.

Laxmi lifted her eyebrows. "If I could walk your dreams now, maybe I'd understand what in the Abyss you were thinking."

Warmth sizzled over Anahid's skin. She'd known what Laxmi could do—plenty of stories enjoyed the notion of dreams being a playground for demons, and Siyon had complained of Laxmi getting into his nightmares like a kitten in the knitting box. But Anahid hadn't thought *her* dreams would be interesting enough. Not for a demon with the whole city at her taloned fingertips.

She cleared her throat. "There are enticements, as well. Involvement with new negotiations with certain azatani parties, even a measure of respectability. They will see, both of them, how much easier and more profitable everything is when proper roles are fulfilled. None of this need ever come to conflict, and Lieutenant Xhanari will never be involved."

The tilt of Laxmi's head was almost pitying. "You really think it's going to happen that way? You think there's any way we get out of this without blood?"

Anahid wasn't naive any longer. She knew how the District worked. She knew more than a little about the barons. "I have to try," she snapped. "I don't expect *you* to understand."

Laxmi let her go, and the winter air was cold on Anahid's skin. "Because I'm only for violence."

Her voice was flat, her eyes shadowed. Anahid didn't know how she could be surprised, standing there looking as she did, leaping gleefully into every conflict that happened their way.

"You invited me out for a drink as an excuse to start a fight with five men," Anahid reminded her.

Laxmi's mouth twisted. "I—" was all she said before stopping abruptly and shaking her head. "Forget it. Speaking of my great proclivity for violence, we'd better get back to the House. The first round of tonight's fighting starts soon after sunset."

They stalked back to Sable House in silence.

Anahid refused to feel flustered about any of it. What word had she spoken that wasn't true? And her plan *would* work. The daughters Zinedani clearly hadn't inherited their father's heavy-handed approach to things, or they would have come after Anahid already, as the killer of their family. They would have stamped their authority on the District. No one would be skittering uneasily about.

The best chance—the most sensible chance—of an outcome useful to everyone lay in an appeal to their business interests. They'd discover these risks and problems for themselves, given enough time, but Anahid needed them back on the proper paths *now*. This would be better for everyone. The Zinedani could have their business, the azatani could have their barons, and Anahid could have some peace and quiet.

Sable House was in its usual late-afternoon hubbub, everyone hustling to get their own details perfect. Laxmi stayed in the yard to get her fighting ring ready, the children flocking down shrieking and eager to help, or at least to be tossed around by "Auntie Laxmi" in some combination of game and warm-up exercise.

Anahid could hear it all from her office window as she checked through Nura's accounts. (They were always immaculate, but it would be rude not to check them.) It grew quieter as the sun set, and Anahid lit the lanterns in her office. Then noise resumed swiftly, the fighting-pit crowd flowing in almost as eagerly as the children had. Half of them must have come straight from their day of work; Anahid paused in her accounts to write a note about offering some sort of food in the yard.

When raucous applause lifted to her window, Anahid crossed to peer out and assess the turnout. The yard was nearly full, spectators perched on barrels and crates, or standing and craning their necks. A few zealous latecomers had even hoisted themselves up on the sills of the lowest windows for the vantage.

In the middle of the pit, Laxmi strutted in a slow circle, her arms spread as though to demand their acclaim. She looked still half a demon, with her braided hair an inken shadow, her eyes gleaming golden, her skin bright as scales in the lantern-light.

There were three men in the ring with her, and Anahid didn't know if the fight was to be two on two or Laxmi against all of them. It didn't seem unlikely. It hardly seemed fair. She was magnificent.

Here was a truth that Anahid *hadn't* uttered this afternoon: With Laxmi at her side, she could carve precisely what calm and order she wished out of the District, however bad things became. Even if the shards and gangs loitering in the streets tried to take more control. Even if the other barons became involved. No matter how things got out of hand.

The District *did* need a baron. Frivolity grew shrill and desperate without security, and the idea of a struggle among shards and gangs and the other barons was frankly awful. *A strong hand upon the tiller*, Master Attabel had said, looking at Anahid. *Who better than you?* Laxmi had asked.

Anahid *could* do it. With Laxmi, it might even be fun.

Look at her. It would be *glorious*.

But both of them were worth more than that.

Anahid turned away from her window and went back to her desk. Her fingers were trembling, but she smoothed them over the neat and precise pages of Nura's ledgers.

Better that the Zinedani remember their role and resume it. Far better for everyone. If she had to, Anahid would *make* it happen.

Even back in the lower city, Siyon's nerves still echoed with the jangling unease of fleeing Dockside. It hadn't really been by the skin of his teeth. No one had chased him down the slick stone stairs to the jetty where Redick and his rowers waited.

Maybe it wasn't that setting Siyon's bones to jittering. Maybe it was the difference in how the power felt, wild and surging out of the Scarp to tumble and eddy against the barrier, compared to the ordered flow that the mudwitches had braided in Dockside.

Or maybe—Siyon considered as he perched in the wreckage of an overgrown rooftop garden, looking down on the alchemists' alley of the lower city markets—it was something far more physical and tangible. *There*, below him, were all the practitioners he could possibly need to feed Mundane energy out through the city's barrier. Dozens of them, openly eager to achieve greater alchemy than they'd contemplated before this season.

And there with them were the Badrosani thugs loitering on every corner, fading into the background like tattooed scenery, watching every sale, every passerby, every happening.

They weren't *specifically* waiting for Siyon, but they'd jump on the opportunity to lay hands on him all the same.

The lower city was not much safer than Dockside, all things considered. It was just easier for Siyon to hide, down here.

Easier to not draw attention to himself. What if he just handled this quadrant of the city himself? Perched in the rooftop garden, he sketched out in the notebook a recurring system using the power of the waves against the sunken parts of the city to feed back out...

Ingenious, appeared in the margin of his scribbled diagram. *But is this really the best use of your time?*

That question mark matched the curve of Izmirlian's skeptical eyebrow. Siyon had a dizzy urge to trace his finger over it, press his *tongue* to it, which wasn't even slightly a sensible thing to consider. He swayed on the edge of the roof, digging his fingers into crumbled stone (his talons into the scree of the mountainside) and snapped the journal shut.

He'd find an alternative. Even if the options seemed flimsy. In the wake of Midnight's disappearance and the disintegration of his barony, the Badrosani had laid hold of every newly emboldened practitioner they could. But hadn't Peylek grumbled about one recalcitrant knot, out along the spine of the old Boulevard?

Siyon had asked about it, on the trip back across the river. Redick, wrestling with the tiller against the eddies of tide and river, said absently, "What, that old mansion on the southern slope?"

It wasn't much to go on, but Siyon would take it over tangling with the tentacles of the Badrosani.

Mayar had, predictably, suggested that Siyon should be able to *sense* the presence of other practitioners. Easy for them to say. They didn't wake from dreams of scenery Siyon had never beheld. They didn't tip themselves off-balance with the urge to stretch wings they didn't have. They didn't fear that, with energy sloshing around like cheap rakia, letting go enough to sense *anything* might wash him away entirely.

Siyon went and looked with his eyes, thank you very much.

The southern curve of the lower city had once been the majestic spine of the headland, a stretch of elegant and expensive homes. But the Sundering didn't care about money spent, and now few were still habitable, let alone places in which you could defend an alchemical workshop from rain or rats. This part of the lower city hadn't even attracted squatters, too far from the Scarp and the few fountains that still flowed with water.

After barely half a bell peering at overgrown walls and considering collapsed gates, Siyon thought he'd found the place. Utterly dilapidated, but the roof didn't have any holes, and the breeze carried a strong whiff of tufted sedgeflower, a common ingredient in many euphorics.

Siyon slipped through a gap in the half-collapsed gate and prowled across an empty yard. Weeds grew thick among the cracked pavers, and paint was peeling off the house's double doors, that only creaked faintly when he hauled one open. Inside seemed less abandoned, with pistachio shells crunching underfoot, and an alchemical lantern glowing to Siyon's eyes; it had been illuminated not long ago.

He crept forward to check it; the metal frame was still warm.

"Huh, there you go," someone said.

Siyon spun around, took one look at the guy on the stairs—all of Mama's boys took after her—and sprinted for the door. Too late, though: Hands seized him, shoved him against the frame. He flailed at the door and earned himself a gentle nudge that bounced his head off the wood fit to ring his skull like a bell.

Golden lights burst across his vision as an arm wrapped around his chest, marked with the curved-dagger B tattoo.

"Mum wants to talk to you." The words were limned with gloating.

What Mama wanted, in the lower city, Mama always got. He should have known better.

They dragged him back in a dizzy stagger. Bronze lightning crackled across Siyon's aching head in steady, throbbing waves. He stumbled, feet as heavy as though the ground were loath to let them go. The energy undertow pulled at him with every step. Storm clouds glowered over the ocean; real lightning stabbed across the sky as he spread wings across the waves, lolling with the shift of the seas. No land in sight, no pestiferous people with their bad tempers and pointy sticks. He could just—

Slam down on his knees, old burgundy carpet thin and sticky beneath his hands. Siyon looked up, blinking hard, and tried to get a grip on himself.

A large woman loomed above him, draped in velvet and furs, dazzling with jewels and the sharp glints of her shark-grin. "Velo, darling," Mama Badrosani said, her voice sounding a long way off. "It's been too long."

She loomed and swayed in Siyon's vision, sparks dancing around her, streaming away into darkness all around. He lifted one hand to his clamouring head. At least there didn't seem to be any blood. His fingers looked strange, so short and pale. Where were his talons?

He blinked hard, trying to focus on Mama Badrosani. *She* was the dragon here. She'd eat him up just as easily. So many stories whispered in the alleycanals down here. *The two surest ways to die: fall from a roof, or get in hock to Mama B.*

Inevitable, either way. Don't catch her eye. Don't let her get you. Don't agree to *anything*.

Fingers gripped his chin with the cold press of rings, and Siyon flinched.

Everything flinched with him, a burnished pulse in the power pooling thick around him. The very mud beneath them tensed up, pulsing the faintest tremour through the stones of the buildings.

Shit. Siyon fumbled to get a grip on himself. To get a grip on the power and the Mundane. To hold it steady.

He was helpless to stop Shakeh Badrosani tilting his face up to her frowning inspection. "You look awful. Chez, what did you do to him?"

"Just brung him in like you wanted," said another voice, beyond Siyon's ability to see. It sounded sulky. "He tried to run, yeah?"

Siyon strained to keep himself grounded. Focus on Mama Badrosani, who wasn't looking too well either. Oh, she looked well-*off*, in her furs and jewels and feathered hair ornaments. But eight years ago, to a young Dockside runaway, she'd seemed a perfect bandit queen, beautiful and potent. The lines had deepened on her face, her teeth were yellowing, and her eyebrows had been plucked thin, possibly to weed out grey hairs.

The queen had long outlived her king, but she wasn't eternal.

Siyon's mind staggered wildly, lingering on that first meeting with Shakeh Badrosani. *Call me Mama*, she'd said. *We're all family here.* Which might have reassured Siyon more if he hadn't so recently been dumped into the river by his own family.

Which might have reassured him more if he hadn't then learned about her sons.

He could hear them now, bickering behind him, words eddying around him like energy.

"Trust you to fuck up something simple."

"Shut it, Bray, I didn't see any of your street crew bringing him in."

"*You* shut it, Rippon, I've just about had it with your—"

Chez, Bray, Rippon. The three of them, but there had once been *four* Badrosani sons. "No Notan," Siyon sighed, the words slipping free without him intending it.

Silence slammed down around him. His head yanked back, fire blooming over his scalp, someone snarling into his face, "Watch your fucking mouth."

"Enough." Shakeh Badrosani didn't raise her voice, but it sliced through noise like a hot knife anyway. "You three, get lost. Leave him. He's no threat like this."

Siyon slumped on the carpet, holding on with his paltry fingernails. The Mundane weight of the floor and the mud beneath sucked at him, yearning to salve his fear. His head was a rattling jar of sparks and pain.

"You," Shakeh sighed, "must be out of your right mind indeed, to mention that traitor's name in here."

He hauled himself up onto his knees, arms outstretched for

balance—no, wait, he was gripping at his knees, but *something* was outstretched, keeping him steady.

That traitor's name. We're all family here. And then you learned that when Notan Badrosani—eldest and brightest and wickedest—had the temerity to build his own little gang, barely a dozen sycophantic followers, his mother had him staked out at low tide and stood there, with the waves inching up her hemline, as he drowned.

That's what *family* meant, in the lower city.

"What've you got in here anyway?" Mama was asking, her voice distant across Siyon's memories. He blinked, looked up again, to see her poking around in his satchel, pulling out a leather-bound note-book. "Fancy piece of work for the likes of you, isn't this?" She smirked as she flipped the book open.

The book that contained Izmirlian's impossible words.

Siyon was on his feet before he considered it, pushed up by the stone and the power as he snatched the book from her grasp. It was *his*, it was *theirs*, she *couldn't see it*.

Mama snarled, fear flashing in her eyes; she slapped him with all the weight of her rings behind it.

Back on the floor, head ringing again, and the power surging up beneath him, sharp with Siyon's panic and his pain.

Yes, came a thought from far away. *Drag it all down. Bury it and start again.*

No. Siyon clutched the journal to his chest and held on just as tightly to the energy all around him. Pressed firmly down, quelling the angry tremble of the ground; could barely feel the thud of a foot into his side over the quieting shiver of the city beneath them.

He curled into a ball, wrapped in power and desperation, and somewhere far away, a voice said, "And *this* is the Sorcerer. Pathetic."

The world calmed beneath him, destruction slowly ebbing like the urge to vomit.

Siyon couldn't have this fight, not with Mama and the entire plane as well.

He forced his eyes open, forced them to see more than just bur-nished sheen. Mama stood over him, proud and vengeful.

"What do you want?" Siyon croaked.

The toe of her slipper—fancily beaded as any azata's—tipped his chin up, making his vision swim and his head ache. "Proper respect," she stated. "That's all I've *ever* wanted."

Service. To have him on a string. To own *everything* in the lower city.

He wasn't going to get out of here without *something*. And if he didn't get out of here, perhaps none of them would. The earth beneath him was quiet, but not asleep. Too much power still curdled around him, bright in his head, frothed and angry as the sea in storm.

Siyon clambered painfully back to kneeling, clutching Izmirlian's journal to his chest. It was enough of a grounding point; he curled around it like the power curled around him, and all of them managed enough balance for Siyon to say: "What service can I do for you?"

She smiled, hungry as a shark. "That's better. Found your manners, have you? I'm not unreasonable, Velo. I just need a show. So everyone can see you've paid your dues. Say…" She tapped a stained fingernail against her lips. "Say you charm my lads against sorcery like alley gossip says you charmed the inqs."

It seemed half a lifetime ago, not barely a season, that he'd been weaving Mundane wardings on inquisitorial candle badges. And what good would those do in the current circumstances? Siyon wondered, idly, if the pixie skinks were mobbing the inqs to lick the power off their badges.

But if it got him out of here without all of them smothering in mud or magic, he'd face that question later.

"Too many," he scraped out. "I'll do your sons."

Shakeh snorted. "Fuck off. Do all my captains, or see if magic helps you breathe seawater."

Siyon shivered; the ground shivered with him, setting something nearby to rattling. But Mama didn't seem to notice, all her attention fixed on him. "Your captains," Siyon agreed, tight with desperation, if not quite the sort she believed. "But in return, I need access to the assistance of every alchemist you have on your books."

"Too many," Shakeh parroted right back at him, then shrugged one furred shoulder. "But you can have one for every charm you make me. And you'll call me—"

"Mama," Siyon chimed in with her. "I know."

We're all family here, after all. But no one was drowning today.

CHAPTER 12

Every time Anahid woke in her cramped little room in the attics of Sable House, it took her long moments to remember where she was, and why.

This morning—or rather, early afternoon, by the slant of light outside her narrow window—she lay even longer, wrapped up in missing...she didn't quite know what. She might have said *home*, but she didn't know where that was. The Joddani townhouse, for all she had been its mistress, had never really been *hers*. The apartment that had been Siyon's, and before him Geryss Hanlun's, had obviously never felt like her own.

She yearned for a belonging that she had never known. Not even in her parents' home, from which Anahid had always been destined to fly. An azata built her own nest. Anahid hadn't yet.

But perhaps she could, somewhere on the other side of all this.

She rose, and reached for the card that had come after Malkasani's unexpected—and unsettling—visit. A pale blue card, stamped with *Nurturi Parsola*, but signed with *M* beneath a handwritten message: *A reunion with news would be welcome.*

Azata Parsola, on whose terrace Anahid had taken lunch with Azata Malkasani and so many other highly respectable women. She'd been there when word came of Zagiri's mishaps, and she'd rushed home to first meet Siyon. A place of her *old* life...yet Nurturi Parsola was also on the fringes of society. Not an azata in truth, but allowed to be one by dint of her wealth and welcome.

That yearning fluttered inside her again like a caged bird. Ridiculous; this wasn't an *invitation*, it was business. The azatani needed Anahid. And she would use them in turn to achieve what she needed.

Which made it all the more annoying when Laxmi insisted on accompanying her.

"Your clerk's out there prodding the Zinedani with pins," the fallen demon growled, pacing easily beside Anahid even as she finished buckling her armour. "You think they aren't going to take a swing at you?"

"I think they'll be busy with that," Anahid snapped. "And more sensible than to bother with me. *I'm* not the pain that needs treatment here."

Laxmi muttered something that sounded remarkably like *You're a pain in my arse*, but Anahid lifted her chin and pretended not to hear.

Parsola's mansion lay in its elegant gardens just where the Avenues tipped into the not-quite-fallen neighbourhoods at the top of the Scarp—though not so far out that the genteel elite of society couldn't make the journey to be lavishly entertained on Parsola's vine-shaded terrace. Anahid steered a careful path to get there, avoiding the old hippodrome and its new bustle of the Council's ongoing functions. She realised with some surprise that the commencement of the new Council was only a couple weeks away. The Ball was just around the corner. It all seemed remarkably distant from her current life.

Nostalgia gripped Anahid at the first sight of the vine-festooned wall of Parsola's estate. She didn't *miss* the gatherings she'd attended here—they'd been a slow torture of respectability and expectations—but little things had lingered. The cut of Parsola's comments. The slow curve of Malkasani's smile. The quick debates at Azata Filosani's end of the table, into which Anahid had never felt qualified to join.

All lost to Anahid now.

They passed through the gate, beneath a trellis of black-blooming winter roses. The fountain in the centre of the entrance court was full of floating lilies, and the house nearly shrouded in trees. Azata Parsola had once told Anahid that she'd travelled for most of her life in the desert, and so now she surrounded herself with as much greenery as she could.

The trees around the back terrace—where Anahid and Laxmi were shown to meet the lady of the house—had lost their leaves for winter, letting the sun warm the terracotta tiling, and setting the window boxes to blooming with colour. Reclining on chaises tucked into a sun-drenched corner, Azata Parsola and Azata Malkasani both lifted their teaglasses in welcome. They were informally attired; Parsola had a scarf draped loosely over her head and around her shoulders, showing iron-grey hair along her forehead. It was mildly outrageous, as was the appraising look she cast over Laxmi. "My goodness. Is this one of your employees, Anahid?"

Laxmi smirked. "Not like that."

Parsola cackled, her weathered face creasing up along well-worn lines. "Sit, sit—both of you. We'll have tea before we talk business."

The tray, when it came, wafted not the sharp green of mint, but a surprising warm tang. "I hope kumquat tea is all right," Azata Parsola said as she poured into fresh glasses. "I have mint as well—for all those fashionable azatas—but I have always preferred this sort."

She passed a glass to Anahid, who had to swallow an unexpected lump in her throat. "I have as well," she admitted.

"Forgive my bluntness," Malkasani said, which was shocking enough—she'd never have asked such a thing in the Avenues; she simply wouldn't be blunt at all. "But what *is* going on with you Savanis this season? That young cousin of yours is strutting like a bull shark, flashing his councillor seal, and I've never seen an angrier sponsor than Zagiri." She sipped at her tea and added, "And I supervised *you*."

Anahid blinked. "I wasn't angry."

Laxmi snorted, and Malkasani shared an amused look with her, and this was all *outrageous*.

"I wasn't!" Anahid objected. "I'm not! I— Stop laughing."

Laxmi didn't, just grinned wider, slouching farther in her chair. "You brim over with it, Ana. Before I—" She glanced at their hosts and corrected herself: "*Before*, I could just about taste it."

"How mysterious," Parsola murmured, with the avid eagerness of an opera audience.

Anahid found herself strangely helpless, at Laxmi's grin, at Malkasani's amusement, at the idea that her anger had had a *taste*.

She cleared her throat and reached for her teaglass. "This season has not been a tranquil one for the family Savani," she said evenly.

Malkasani smiled. "Sorry, I didn't mean to drag you through the streets like a mock promenade. Curiosity just gets the better of me. Always has."

"It's why she organises things," Parsola told Anahid. "So she can stick her nose into every detail."

Malkasani nodded along. "That and to make sure it's done properly. I simply can't abide letting standards slip. Speaking of which—" And she set her teaglass down firmly on the table. "To business. Lovely as it is to sit and drink tea with both of you, I must assume you have come for a purpose."

That drew a cold finger down Anahid's spine, but it didn't entirely dispel her warmth. This *was* business, but there had surely been no need to show her such a welcome. That had been genuine. "You may find the Zinedani more amenable to overtures than they were previously," Anahid said. "Especially if you can offer building or other business permits to sweeten the deal. I'd suggest approaching Marel Sakrani discreetly."

That drew a considering hum from Malkasani. "It won't be my decision, of course, but I'm sure something like that would be feasible. I must say, my dear, I really would feel better with someone as steady and capable as—" She stopped herself, her mouth turning rueful, at whatever was showing on Anahid's face. "Well, never mind."

Laxmi shifted on her chair, but for once kept her mouth shut.

Which Anahid wasn't at all disappointed about. It was *better* this way, for everyone.

"More tea?" Parsola offered, lifting the pitcher.

But Anahid wasn't sure she could stand much more play at society. The business had been conducted now. She set a finger across the rim of her glass and smiled apologetically.

Malkasani sighed. "I suppose you're very busy, actually *doing* something with your time. Will we at least see you at the Harbour Master's Ball?"

How could she even *ask*? But Malkasani merely blinked at Anahid's astonished look. "I don't believe that would be helpful for anyone," Anahid replied, trying not to sound stern and, she suspected, failing utterly.

Malkasani didn't shrug—she'd always insisted it was an inelegant motion—but the shift in her expression conveyed the same idea. "It would liven things up. And distract a little from whatever your sister has planned."

Anahid would *much* rather speak about Zagiri's plans. "That's merely politics," she said. "She's really very keen to pursue reform through the Council commencement."

"Oh, is *she* the one who wants to widen the membership of the Council?" Parsola leaned forward eagerly. "Buni told me about that one; has she managed to find a sponsor yet?"

"I don't know," Anahid had to admit, with a quick glance at Laxmi, who was staring pointedly back. She *hadn't* spoken with Zagiri in so long. "There were some difficulties."

"And everyone's flapping around like gulls who have seen a cat," Malkasani added sympathetically. "You should bring her along the next time we do this, and perhaps we can make some introductions. Though I must admit I'm disappointed she's caught up in politics so young. I had been hoping she was planning an elopement with the youngest Hisarani."

"Ooh yes," Parsola chimed in eagerly. "All those Hisarani boys are dying to run wild, and only one of them has managed it so far."

Anahid was still wrestling with all of this. The next time they did this? Bringing her sister? But what seemed safest to say was: "Zagiri is involved with Balian again?"

Laxmi leaned forward, as though sharing a confidence, though she didn't lower her voice as she said: "Ana is avoiding Zagiri. They haven't spoken since the news broke."

That was quite enough of that. "Should I leave and let you all speak of me in peace?" Anahid demanded.

"Not angry," Parsola murmured, with a smile spreading behind her teaglass.

"Don't you start," Anahid told her.

But there was a smile tugging at her own mouth. A lightness sparking along with her annoyance. A bright engagement that she hadn't felt since...

Since playing carrick with Tahera Danelani. Camaraderie, that's what this was. The joy of being with people who were quick and interesting and welcoming of *her*. She'd *wanted* this from azatani society, and never quite been able to find it, however much she obeyed their rules.

"Do bring your sister next time," Parsola declared. "She's always sounded delightful. And give me more warning so I can have my kitchen make us dumplings. Just the thing for winter, dumplings."

That yearning unfurled within Anahid again. But perhaps—just possibly—she *could* have this little bit of belonging. "It would be my pleasure," she said.

All Zagiri had left was their plan for the Ball; she wasn't leaving any of it to chance. She and Yeva and Lusal took turns at rehearsals to monitor the schedules and movements of the staff, especially as related to the delivery doors down in the underhall. They spent so much time at it that Malkasani had pulled Zagiri and Lusal aside to ask if they were *really* ready for this Ball, and Lusal had delivered a magnificent performance of wide-eyed assurances that she hadn't been sure about this at *all*, but Zagiri had convinced her that there was a place in the city for an azata like her.

Malkasani melted. Zagiri had felt a little gratified too.

All that time, all that effort, all that careful planning, and then she got down there on the day and the back door was *locked*.

"Wait a moment," she hissed at the door, turning to survey the underhall.

From the other side of the door, Zin snarled, "What do you mean, fucking wait?"

Zagiri was busy, running her eyes over shelves, her hands beneath counters. None of the staff had ever taken a key with them when they came down to take delivery or remove rubbish, so it must be somewhere *down here*. "I mean fucking *wait*," she shot back. "And be quiet about it."

After all, the final rehearsal was underway upstairs; Zagiri could hear the faint strains of the small ensemble Malkasani had brought in to prepare the girls for the full orchestra in two nights' time.

Where was the bloody key? The underhall was spacious, but largely filled in with boxes and barrels and crates in preparation for the Ball itself. The key was often used, so it wasn't likely to be hidden anywhere too convoluted. Zagiri ran her hand down the underside of the stairs and got nothing but a splinter for her trouble. The cupboards along one wall contained only cleaning materials. She was going through the drawers on a sideboard when a bright and sunny voice behind her said, "Is this what you're looking for?"

Zagiri spun around, surprise and alarm clogging her throat.

Lusal grinned at her from just beside the back door, where she was lifting something down from a little hook, high up beside the lintel.

Relief met panic, churning at Zagiri's stomach. "Lu, you can't *be* here." Zagiri hurried over to snatch the key from her. "They're doing the promenade dances; you *will* be missed."

But Zagiri, not so much. Especially when she and Yeva had staged an argument, to give her a good reason to run away for a time.

"We'd almost finished that, actually, when one of the girls went *entirely* the wrong way, and now Malkasani is drilling everyone again." Lusal smiled innocently, folding her hands primly at her waist. "It seems that *someone* gave her confusing instructions."

Zagiri could kiss her, but this canniness felt a lot like Balian's. Malkasani might be fooled, but he saw far too much. Lusal needed to get back at once, before she got far too caught up in what was going on.

But even as Zagiri hustled her back toward the stairs, knuckles drummed at the outside of the door—gently, but unmistakably. "Come on," Zin growled. "Before someone sees me out here."

Lusal's eyes, impossibly, grew even wider and brighter.

Dammit. "Watch from the top of the stairs," Zagiri ordered. "Say something loud if anyone's coming."

The key Lusal had found was a ridiculous dainty little thing, glittering gold and barely the size of two joints of her finger, but the lock on the door matched it; they were obviously charmed, rather than mechanical. Zagiri barely had to twist it before the lock leapt open.

Lusal's pale hem was just disappearing back up the stairs as Zin shouldered his way in, hefting that familiar keg. "The fuck's that?" he demanded, jerking his chin.

"She's fine," Zagiri returned, closing the door behind him and returning the glittery little key to its hook. A faint scuff came from the top of the stairs; Lusal's feet moving in time to the strains of music, practicing her dance steps. The Ball *was* only two days away.

"Here," Zin said, and Zagiri turned around to find him holding a fistful of tight-wrapped, red-sealed explosives out to her. "I'm not lugging the whole box all over the hall, so grab as many as you can carry and let's get moving."

Zagiri took a pair of them and dithered; they were awfully bulky to tuck through the sash of her dress. But she needed to figure it out, or Zin would leave her behind and she was *not* trusting him to do this by himself. Not after everything else.

From the top of the stairs, Lusal cried, "Oh, Yeva, are you finished already?"

"Shit," Zagiri seethed, shoving the explosives back into the crate. To Zin's irate glare, she hissed, "That means Balian's coming too, and Yeva hasn't been able to stop him. Keep quiet. I'll take care of this."

She hitched up her hem and hurried up the stairs, calling: "I can't see anything down there; are you absolutely sure, Lu?"

Lusal turned to her with eyes still positively *sparkling* at the thrill. Zagiri gave her an encouraging smile—she *had* done well in giving the warning—before she turned to look down the corridor at the approaching Yeva—yes, and Balian too, looking blank-faced as ever.

Zagiri wasn't fooled. Not anymore. He was taking everything in.

"Oh," she said, "hello, you two. Lusal thought she saw a rat go down into the underhall." It seemed awfully precarious the moment it was out of her mouth. A rat?

But Lusal turned her wide eyes onto her cousin and said, "It would be an *awful* scandal, if it was, and I remembered what you were saying, Balian, about the difficulties for serving staff, so I want to be *sure*, but I just…I couldn't face going down there to check myself. What if it really *was* a rat?"

Her girlish disgust was almost comic. "It's really time we were getting back," Zagiri said, putting out her arm to usher them all down the corridor. The most important thing right now was getting sharp-eyed Balian *away* from here. Then she could perhaps say she forgot something…

Yeva met her eye. "You definitely need to get back. They're moving on to the refreshment business. I'm useless at it and Balian doesn't know the girly bits. But I could have a look for rats."

Lusal grabbed Balian's hand, breathlessly asking about the fine details of pouring punch, like she was working herself up into a state about it. Cleverly distracting him enough that he just said absently, "Yeva, you're supposed to be generating goodwill."

Zagiri forced a carefree little laugh. "How much goodwill can she generate if she tips punch on someone's dress again *by accident*?"

The reference made Yeva laugh wickedly. It definitely hadn't been an accident.

Lusal turned Balian back toward the ballroom, and Zagiri lingered; perhaps she could just stay, and they wouldn't even notice, and then she could—

Yeva shoved at her shoulder. "Get back in there," she hissed. "I can do this as well as you can, and they're already asking about you. Balian *will* come back for you. He's getting suspicious."

Zagiri hesitated, and ahead of them Balian glanced back over his shoulder, just for a moment before Lusal asked something else. But it made Yeva's point.

"You stick to the plan," Zagiri whispered fiercely.

Yeva rolled her eyes, like she'd never been dragged into any questionable schemes. "I know, I know." She shoved at Zagiri. "I've learned my lesson. I am chastened. I am a changed woman. Go."

There was no choice; Zagiri went.

Just in time as well. Balian stopped, just shy of the entrance back to the ballroom, and turned around entirely. Zagiri got there just in time to hook her elbow through his and pull him onward. "There's something I've been meaning to tell you," she insisted.

Which seemed to do the trick. His attention switched to her, one corner of his mouth twitching up. "Really? I thought you weren't speaking to me."

Then they were back in the ballroom itself. Safe. Zagiri slackened her grip, but he had hold of her now, and she'd have to make a fuss to get her arm back, with other sponsors and debutantes looking over from the crowd around the refreshment table displays. Lusal hurried over to join them.

That's all. It was just about fuss. She'd caused enough already. It wasn't that it was pleasant, to be this near him. That he still smelled of ink and warmth. Though he did, dammit.

Zagiri lifted her chin. "I don't care enough to not speak to you, Balian." As though to prove it, she looked right at him. At that tiny little smile just hooking at the corner of his mouth. "I just wanted to thank you, for all this. For saving me from having no debutante at all, and having to wait a whole other year."

"I told you," he replied quietly, though they were far enough away from the other sponsors and escorts that he could have spoken more loudly. "It was her idea."

"I'm sure she thought that," Zagiri said, more sharply than she really should have.

Balian sighed and started pulling his arm free. Shit, she'd been too prickly, and now he was going to go back and help Yeva look for an imaginary rat, except he'd find a *real* Zin.

Zagiri turned on him in a hurry, mouth open to say something— anything—to keep him here.

But he wasn't leaving, he was just looking at her, mouth slanted in something like irony. "What's it going to be? Insisting I watch Lusal pour a goblet of punch like her mother hasn't been teaching her this since she was six? Or do you want to distract me with the mural again?"

180

Zagiri tossed her head. "It's a splendid mural," she snapped. "It's our glorious history. I'm inspired by it, as a bravi. I don't care if it didn't really happen."

Balian snorted. "It did, you know."

She blinked. "What?"

"The duel." Balian nodded past her, to the back wall, and Zagiri looked as well, her eyes skating across the mural to that final panel, with the Last Duke crossing sabres with a dashing azatan.

Not just any azatan. Telmut Hisarani. Balian's ancestor.

"It really happened," Balian repeated. "Telmut challenged the Last Duke, on the steps of the Palace, and they fought right there in the entry hall. I know everyone says it's unrealistic, but it's part of our family history, and we keep all the awful secrets."

Zagiri turned her frown on Balian. "What's awful about that?"

Balian smiled bleakly. "Because he didn't win. The Duke was Lyraec nobility. He trained every day, with four different sorts of weapons. Disarmed Telmut in three strikes. A classic Fontaine opening, Avarair tells me, whatever that means."

Zagiri couldn't seem to close her mouth. "But—" she managed.

"But," Balian repeated. "Yes. But the Duke's guard, who'd been paid off by the azatani in advance, moved in, disarmed him, put him on his knees. Telmut Hisarani picked up his sabre again and ran him through. But that's not how it's done, is it?" He smiled faintly, looking a bit like Izmirlian. Something bitter, something fey. "In this city, money might be power, but *true* legitimacy comes from public spectacle. Siyon knew that, even if he couldn't have put it into words. The show is what matters. So that's the story they told."

He nodded again at the mural. The bright colours, the dramatic pose, the glory and romance of it. The duel for the city.

The spectacle. Zagiri knew it too. You had to get their attention.

Behind her, Balian sighed. "I know you're planning something," he said, barely a murmur. Zagiri spun around, and he was watching her with those clear eyes. "I know you, Zagiri. I've watched you do this before. Are you going to tell me this time?"

He'd watched her. He knew her.

She believed him. *She* was the one who'd not seen what was right in front of her face.

But she saw him now. There was a chance he could help her—he had connections to councillors who might actually take on the risk of her proposed reform, for Balian if not for her. *If* he did it. If he didn't take word of her plans straight to Avarair. If it didn't all form part of *his* plans.

He had them, she was sure. Even if she couldn't see as clearly as he could.

This was her only chance. She couldn't let it slip away.

He frowned; he'd seen it on her face. "Zagiri," he murmured, drawing closer still. "There's more going on than you know. Everyone's moving their pieces into position for commencement. The city is balanced on the edge of a blade, and whichever way it tips, it will slide *hard*."

"Do you think I'm *playing*?" she snapped. That's *why* she was doing all this.

He sighed, short and sharp. "Just…be careful."

She smiled at him, bright and false. "I'm always careful."

The look he gave her said he knew that for the lie it was, and yet—just perhaps—it didn't change his opinion of her.

CHAPTER 13

I can't believe you've got me working for Mama Badrosani," Daruj muttered as he snipped off another length of twine. "All this time, and I get pulled in sideways."

Siyon didn't have a lot to say to that. It was all true, *and* he'd dragged Daruj away from his rest to help with making all the charms that Siyon had promised for the Badrosani captains.

Mind you, he hadn't been *sleeping* but rather reading a lurid gutter romance with *The Brazen Mage* screaming from its cover in smeared purple letters. Siyon didn't want to know, and entirely disliked Daruj's smirk. Getting put to work served him right.

"I don't know why you are both so bothered about the Badrosani," Mayar said absently as they plucked the twine from Daruj's fingers to thread a charm onto it. "Everyone has been very pleasant to me."

Daruj shrugged. "Alleytales say Mama's sister married into a Khanate caravan, and they helped out during the wars after Papa was murdered. Maybe it's true."

Siyon sifted through the pile of rock chips he'd gathered from the base of the Scarp. He'd thought they'd make easy charm tokens, but now every edge was sparking bronze in his vision and a headache was churning behind his eyes. He winced and rubbed at the bridge of his nose.

He blinked his vision clear in time to see Daruj frown. "You sure you're all right?"

Daruj had been here the other night, when Siyon had been delivered home by Chez Badrosani, barely able to keep his feet under him, or the mud under *them*.

The earth nearly ate the theatre, Siyon vaguely remembered babbling at him. *It just wanted to help me. I could barely stop it.*

He'd been too distracted to see if Daruj looked terrified about that, but today's mild grumbling was the worst of the telling-off Siyon had received, which painted a vivid picture of silent concern.

"I'm fine." Siyon was reasonably sure it wasn't a lie. There was just so much energy sloshing around down here. Limning every surface and gilding every corner. Soaking in and bubbling up at the same time. Thick as well-whipped cream.

They were working on it—the whole city was working on it—but part of Siyon wondered if it was too little, too late. If the monsters weren't going to be the worst of it. If he was going to drown, pulled under and swallowed whole.

"You need a better understanding of the essences," Mayar insisted. They tossed one more completed charm aside—stone wreathed in energy, threaded onto twine, additionally tweaked for durability. "I am certain that your bond with Mother Sa is incomplete. If you could practice more meditation—"

"I've *told* you," Siyon snapped, rubbing at his eyes again. "That works for *you*. Or maybe it works for lesser essences. But if I let go of myself..."

The pull of the Mundane energy, just beneath his feet. Like the river in the chasm, leaping and gushing and merrily eager to sweep him away. Like the dragon, looming above him on a scale Siyon could scarcely comprehend.

It would be so *easy*. And what would be left of him?

Had it felt like that for Izmirlian, he found himself wondering sometimes. Not the same thing. Probably. But when he disappeared from the void, had he felt this same strange meld of simple and beautiful and terrifying?

Siyon could *ask*. If he was sure he wanted the answer. But he did, desperately, want to speak with Izmirlian. Hear his thoughts. Just see that familiar handwriting, hear those words in his head that sounded so familiar, and not nearly well-known enough.

"Let's take a break," he heard himself say.

Daruj was already reaching for that awful flimsy book again. Mayar shrugged. "I think we have enough already, actually."

It was all the excuse Siyon needed.

In his rope bunk, strung up off the floor to keep away from the rising damp, he traced fingertips over the leather tooling on the cover and spine of Izmirlian's journal. He still felt that spark of protective panic that had burst in him at Mama Badrosani's trespassing hands. As though this *were* Izmirlian, and Siyon could keep him out of her clutches. But it wasn't. Wasn't the same, wasn't *enough*. He missed Izmirlian more now than he had when all of him was gone.

He wanted all of Izmirlian back. Or wanted to be back there, before all this, with Izmirlian in his arms again.

Maybe he could just not let him go. Maybe he could do it differently, this time. Make another world, where all of this was someone else's problem.

This was weakness. This was wallowing. And yet still Siyon opened the journal, reaching for his pencil. Scribbled: *Are you where you wanted to be?*

Izmirlian's replies didn't always come immediately. Sometimes there would be nothing until the next time Siyon opened the notebook. Sometimes he found Izmirlian had filled a page with idle observations and memories, as though waiting for Siyon to return. Once, Izmirlian had asked if he'd told Siyon something already. It was possible time didn't work the same way at all, wherever Izmirlian was.

This time, words crawled across the page almost at once. *I didn't know enough to want this. But I'm glad to be here.*

Somewhere beyond. Something beyond. Siyon was still here, left behind, not knowing enough to want it.

More words appeared on the page.

You feel so close sometimes. I hear you. I taste your shadow. Like if I reached out, I could pull you through.

Siyon ran his thumb over the page, smearing bronze glow across the paper. He wanted to be pulled through. Had to fight the urge to press the journal to his face. Was so sure that if he breathed in, it somehow would still smell of orange blossom and sandalwood.

His eyes slipped closed, and the Mundane was waiting to drag him under. Siyon churned into the burnished depths, battered by energy as he clung fiercely to that thread back to himself: This want, to get back to Izmirlian, was a part of him. It spooled out behind him, a long and gilded line, as he tumbled in the maelstrom. An ocean spun away beneath him, islands like a scattered handful of green gems, and then land in a green blur, deep and leafy—*forest*, he thought, with a recognition that should be impossible for someone who'd never seen one before. Mountains reared up and fell away. The sky stained with fire and blood and memory...

And the dragon, silhouetted against it, like a glorious threat.

The bluster of the wind and the gentle curve of the horizon. The steep dive and the flare of wings, passing through clouds like a faint mist to the face, a suggestion and gone again. Golden above and bronze below.

All this was *ours*; do you remember?

(Siyon didn't. Siyon couldn't. That wasn't who he was, hadn't been *him*.)

The dragon banked tightly, wings curling and cupping the wind. She hung in the sky like an affronted bird of prey, and those star-pupiled parchment-pale eyes locked on Siyon. (How? Where? Did it matter?)

Why?

Not words like Izmirlian, but just a demand stabbed deep into him. Indignation and frustration and clawing desperate loneliness raking across his own emotions.

Why do you cling to this? To them?

"It's who I am," Siyon said—aloud, suddenly aware of his own body again, as though at a great distance. He clung to his thread of want, his only way back, and the sharp tang of lower city mud and mold elbowed aside the crisp bite of clouds.

He felt dizzy. He felt torn apart.

Then stay as you are.

The dragon snarled—a tearing crackle like thunder—and lashed out with her heavy barbed tail. The blow slammed into him, and Siyon went tumbling, streaking back across the sky, a burnished comet of energy and essence.

Reeling back in on that gilded guideline—his want and his insistence. He skidded and skipped across the ocean's salty surface, and then the Khanate desert went screaming away beneath him in a tumble of dunes and scrubland and a churning mass of massive bodies, scaled and slithering lizard-like over the stony hills, before the golden wall of Bezim rose and—

Wait.

Siyon jerked out of his protective curl and reached. Grabbed hold of the plane beneath him, yanking at handfuls of energy, hauling to arrest his flight. It didn't work like that, there were no *directions*, but he did it by instinct, hooked into the Mundane, halted his wild progress.

Insisted.

He wrenched the Mundane energy all around him to his will, and pulled himself away from the city, hand over hand, until he could see again—

There. The glimpse that had struck panic into his heart—*his* heart, in his body, that he could feel now, that lay like an anchor behind him.

But here...here were the monsters. A dozen or more of them, like massive lizards, racing sinuous over the hills. Stony hills, rippling with olive groves because nothing else would grow there, not in the hard land that lay behind the city of Bezim.

More monsters, coming for the city. For the energy. For the power. Siyon could see it, like this—a burning bronze shimmer on the horizon, like the promise of water in the desert.

They were nearly here.

So many of them. So close. Siyon looked back to the city and the soaring, pulsing, burnished dome of its defenses. Power was leaking out of it, rising in wisps like spray from the waves.

It might just be enough. It might sate them. And if it didn't, the city barrier would hold until they had enough and went away. It would do, for now.

Then sparks of lantern-light started to appear, glittering in the hills west of the city, lighting up as the sun lowered toward the horizon.

The depot. The hippodrome. The caravanserai.

Outside the city. Outside the barrier.

And right in the path of the monsters.

Siyon wrenched back to himself and lurched upright. Mayar and Daruj jumped back as his rope bunk swung wildly, Izmirlian's journal tipping to the floor.

The room was so thick with bronze power that for a moment Siyon could barely draw a breath.

"You were shouting." Daruj had his hands out, low and wary, like Siyon might bite.

"You were…" Mayar started, in a tone of correction, then had to wave a hand before they could find the right word. "*Glowing.*"

None of that mattered. "They're coming," Siyon gasped, when he could pull in air to shape the words. He struggled to get out of his bunk, wrestling with gravity and the unfamiliarity of his own limbs. "I have to—" He tipped out, nearly landing on his face before Daruj caught him. Siyon didn't have *time* for this. "Monsters," he tried again, grabbing at Daruj's shoulder. "From the west. Coming *now.*"

Mayar's eyes widened. "The caravanserai," they blurted.

Where Siyon had met their family. Where there were so many other Khanate traders. Where there was a whole little settlement, exposed and unknowing.

Daruj didn't hesitate. "Let's move. Now. Siyon, pull yourself together."

Siyon pulled, and felt, just for a moment, the whole city holding him up. Pushing him forward. A steadiness so sudden he tottered and gasped.

But it worked. "Let's go."

The evening had barely begun, but already Anahid was annoyed at Laxmi.

She was predisposed to be annoyed, because it wasn't just any evening. Anahid *should* be in the Eldren Hall, watching Zagiri make her presentation and be hailed an azata of Bezim. Her choices and their consequences prevented it. It wasn't really Laxmi she was annoyed with at all.

Except it also *was*. Because the bloody woman wouldn't leave Anahid alone.

"We're in my own *House*," she growled, after the third time she turned around quickly on the gaming floor and nearly ran into a broad pillar of buckled leather.

"A House that nearly anyone can walk into," Laxmi murmured, her yellow gaze too busy scanning the room to even look at Anahid. "Things are getting messy. I told you they would."

That she was right did nothing to improve Anahid's mood. Staff and Flower gossip was rife with altercations at other Houses. There'd been a standoff between a group of Midnighters and a pack of disgruntled former Zinedani muscle in the small hours of the morning, and a mysterious armed gang had ambushed an alchemical delivery right outside the District gate.

Things *were* messy, slipping uneasily toward outright violence. The Zinedani couldn't wake soon enough from their carelessness, but Anahid had already done all she could to that end.

"The House security is Lejman's job," Anahid snapped. "If you're implying he can't—"

"Lady Sable!"

Both of them turned immediately, Laxmi putting her shoulder in front of Anahid's, but it was just one of the trainee Flowers—a willowy youth nearly swamped by his black-banded robe. "There's an incident upstairs," he whispered, wringing his hands.

Anahid's heart clenched around a spike of panic. The last incident upstairs—in the Flowers' private entertaining rooms—had been Imelda, dead at the hand of Stepan Zinedani, who had, as Laxmi had just inferred, gotten into the House when he should have been barred.

But this, when they rushed upstairs on the heels of this trainee, turned out to be merely a woman who would not stop giggling.

The Waterfall gave his client a dirty look as she rolled about on the brocade coverlet of the bed, kicking her heels and chortling, heedlessly intoxicated on more than simply djinnwine. He referred to her as *Azata J*, but if she was here, instead of at the Ball, she must have been of a lower-tier family. "I'm still earning my fee for this session, aren't I?" he demanded.

"You'll be covered," Anahid assured him with a sigh.

"I told you," Laxmi muttered behind Anahid.

"This isn't trouble," Anahid snapped. Though it was growing more common, as the struggling Midnight shards sent out their salespeople with samples for direct purchase. The quality could be extremely variable, but the products were so conveniently available, and often cheaper than whatever the House had for sale. Messy, but not trouble.

Still, Anahid had Lejman go to send a runner to the university clinic, just in case Azata J took a turn for the worse. The woman curled up into a ball, giggling into her own kneecaps. At the very least, she was going to ache all over in the morning.

Anahid sighed. "Can you stay with her, Water?"

He wrinkled up his sharp and pretty nose. "Do I have to? Any moment now she's going to start— Oh shit, there she goes."

The woman's shoulders were still shaking, but the sounds changed—now she was crying.

"It'll only last a few more minutes," the Waterfall predicted with a sigh. "Then she'll pass out."

"She can't stay here." Anahid winced as the woman let out a great sob. "The little room, at the end of the hall. Farther from the entertaining rooms."

They all stood a moment while the woman on the bed howled like a child with a skinned knee. Anahid and the Waterfall—a tall young man, but pale and thin as sailcloth—might be able to coax her to her feet between them, though walking her down the corridor would be a nightmare.

Laxmi rolled her eyes. "Fine, I'll carry her. Out of the way."

Azata J clung to Laxmi's shoulders, burying her snotty face in the side of Laxmi's neck. "You owe me," she grunted as she carried the woman past Anahid.

The Waterfall smiled tightly as he followed Laxmi out. "Thank you, mistress."

Anahid found Nura already in the corridor, with a black-liveried House maid ready to put the room to rights. Everything was already swinging back into action, merriment rising from the entertaining end of the corridor to drown out the faint echo of Azata J's comedown.

The whole business had been unexpectedly draining. The panicked memories to start, such a strange situation, wondering how many *more* of this sort of thing they were going to have to expect, with everything falling apart...

Anahid gave up and retreated to her office. She'd just sit down for a little bit. Take a moment. Before the next crisis, and the next, and the one after that.

Things *were* getting messy. But that didn't mean Laxmi was right about any of the rest of it. The sisters Zinedani would sooner or later accept the way things had to be. They'd take the District in hand, and the remnants of Midnight's organisation would find somewhere to fit in. The storm would blow over, and the seas would return to good travelling weather.

If they could just keep everyone aboard until then.

The office was dark when she pushed open the curtain. Anahid had trouble picking her way around her furniture, fumbling toward the sideboard to find a lantern. Nura must have doused them earlier, when the evening was underway. Had she closed the curtains as well? Or was there just no moon tonight? Anahid tried to keep track of such things, as the more experienced District folk insisted that, on full-moon nights, the behaviour of the patrons was—

Her desk creaked, the way it did when someone leaned upon it. But Anahid was on the other side of the room, frozen now next to the sideboard.

There was someone else in the office with her. Someone who'd been waiting in the dark. Someone who hadn't said a word.

Laxmi *was* right. *Fuck.*

Anahid eased back toward the exit. The desk creaked again, and a chair bumped; Anahid gave up on stealth and ran for the doorway, reaching desperately. Velvet brushed her fingertips—she snatched a handful of the curtain—

Someone grabbed her around the waist, hauling her back into the room, crushing the air out of her.

Anahid held on grimly to the curtain, hearing the fabric strain and start to rip. Curtain rings rattled, and a dim stripe of illumination fell into the room. Anahid dragged in a breath.

Another hand clamped over her mouth, smothering her scream. Her attacker backed them into the room, knocking into some heavy piece of furniture that groaned against the floor. Anahid twisted, letting go of the curtain to grab at the hands holding her—around her face, around her waist. Thick wrists, canvas-protected arms. She frantically found a finger and pulled it back, back, back—

Her attacker grunted and heaved; the darkness spun around Anahid. She landed on the chaise so heavily that it teetered, on the verge of tipping over, as Anahid clung to the upholstery.

"Help!" she shouted, or tried to. Her ribs creaked and her voice was a croak.

The attacker was barely a shadow in the faint light from the corridor, cursing as he tripped over the end of the low table.

Anahid scrambled off the chaise toward her desk. If only she still had the penknife in her sash—even as she flinched away from the idea of it in her hand, of blood on the blade and her fingers and her dress and—

She swept frantically over the desk, knocking her pen aside and then racing after it, snatching it up just as a hand grabbed at her again.

Anahid jammed the pen so hard into her attacker's arm that it splintered. He bellowed: "Bitch!" Something slammed into the side of Anahid's head and knocked her clean off her feet.

The floor was cool beneath her cheek, and the world rang like a bell, the darkness now full of popping lights. A drum was beating beneath her ear, fast and frenetic, overlapping rhythms that she wished would *stop.*

"Get up," someone snarled, and a tug at her hair pulled Anahid's head up.

She was looking right at the office door when light burst through it, the curtain ripped back, and Laxmi charged in.

She was shadow and rage and the gleam of light off the buckles of her armour. She came roaring in and then dived low, something swinging over her head.

There had been another person, waiting just beside the door. Anahid could see them now, in the light from the hallway. She had walked straight past them and never known they were there. They lifted some heavy weapon and stalked after Laxmi, but she rolled and came back to her feet and *launched* back at them—it made Anahid dizzy, where she was still sprawled on the floor. A blur of violent motion, and the shadowed figure went flying across the room, slamming into the wall and slumping down to the floor.

Anahid whimpered in sympathy, but *her* attacker was no longer above her. No longer gripping her hair or forcing her up.

He stepped away, circling around the chaise, half in a crouch, hands wide, like he was stalking.

And not alone. There was another shadow on the other side of the room—how many of them had been waiting here? Both of them focused on Laxmi, who was grinning now as she rolled her shoulders and fell into a low stance.

The hand she raised to beckon them on was empty. Her attackers' hands—with a flex of their wrists, and a flash of sharp metal— were *not*.

They launched at her, both together, brutally coordinated. One knife flashed, and Laxmi kicked it away, even as she blocked another, but the third—

"No!" Anahid gasped, shoving herself weakly up.

The third slammed up to the hilt in her side, punching through her armour as though it wasn't there.

Laxmi whirled around and rammed an elbow into her stabber's chin; he went staggering back, even as she launched at the other one with a feral snarl. She tackled him to the floor, where she grabbed a fistful of his hair—as he'd tried to do to Anahid—and slammed his skull back once, twice, thrice.

An awful stillness descended, silent save for Anahid's ragged breathing. She wavered on her hands and knees, hollowed out by fear and panic and relief. "Laxmi," she croaked.

Laxmi sat back on her heels, her side heaving with the dagger still buried in it. Yellow eyes turned on Anahid, and Laxmi grinned—her teeth edged with blood. "That's my girl," she mumbled.

She keeled over sideways as Anahid screamed, and finally—*finally*—the others came rushing in from the corridor.

CHAPTER 14

Zagiri couldn't help a smirk as she climbed the stairs of the Eldren Hall under the watchful gaze of grey-cloaked inquisitors. She'd heard the whispers on the grand promenade down to the Hall: There was a fear that Siyon might try something again.

They were too late. They were looking in the wrong place. Their *something* was already inside, hissing down quietly on very precise alchemical timers.

The presentation itself was just a bright blur, for all she'd been waiting for this impatiently. The trio of senior councillors standing in for the late prefect smiled at her, and the Harbour Master said, "Thank you, Azata Zagiri Savani," and she was properly azatani now.

She barely felt a twinge of satisfaction, her eyes going to the Hall's clock even as Lusal thanked her warmly.

The Ball ran perfectly to schedule, after all that practice. It always did, which had made their own scheduling easy. The debutantes took to the floor with their escorts for the first dance, while the sponsors, who'd just announced themselves open to offers of marriage and business, were welcomed into the thick of society.

Amid the lanterns and the laughter, the face paint and the false smiles, the glittering jewels and the jostling gossip, Zagiri looked again at the clock, and at the ceiling of the ballroom. She'd done so often, during rehearsals, during their planning. She'd long ago stopped really seeing the quarter panels, the allegorical depictions of the planes, corresponding with the vices and virtues of the city. Or at least, of the azatani.

An azatani building, this. An azatani symbol of their place as the pinnacle of the development of Bezim. Their city. Their story, along the wall, in the mural of their famous rise to rule, all of it underpinned by bribery and lies.

Tonight it came crashing down.

"Hey." Yeva caught her elbow. "Maybe we should just—"

But Zagiri had stopped listening. Over Yeva's shoulder, slipping through the crowd, were Zagiri's parents.

She'd known Anahid couldn't be here, but at least she'd sent a card and a gift. It hadn't even occurred to Zagiri that her parents might come.

Kemella Savani had her chin up and determination clenching her jaw. Behind her, as he always was in social situations, came Usal, with tired shadows beneath his eyes and more creases in his sagging face than Zagiri remembered. How had he aged so much in this handful of weeks?

She'd done this to him.

"Mother, Father." She somehow got the words out through numb lips; Yeva's grip fell away from her arm. She bowed her head, giving full courtesy to her parents.

When she dared look up again, the purse to her mother's lips was still disapproving, but perhaps also the tiniest bit satisfied. "Well," Kemella said, looking pointedly over her dress. It was the pale yellow they'd always discussed Zagiri wearing for the Ball, with a blue-beaded sash. The headscarf—her first—matched. Her mother should have given it to her; Zagiri had this one from Anahid.

Their mother smiled, faint and fleeting. "You have done well, azata."

Zagiri's heart clenched. That word, on her mother's lips. She'd done it. She was an adult. She could do *anything* now. She looked at her father—couldn't help herself, couldn't stop wanting his approval.

Usal's smile was the one he wore in Council sessions and other business, faint and false. "Come, Kemella," he said gently.

They turned away, back into the crowd, and Zagiri's vision blurred. She clenched her fists in their stupid net gloves. She was *not* going to cry, not here, not now.

"Zagiri." Yeva again, back at her side, hissing in her ear. "We should go."

"What?" Zagiri's surprised blink jolted a tear free, but she brushed it quickly from her cheek. Yeva looked even paler than usual, the only colour in her face painted on. "I wouldn't have thought *you'd* get cold feet."

Yeva's mouth bunched up, pinched and whitening. "I know this was important to you, but you've *done* your little presentation now. Let's go before the chaos begins."

Zagiri's pulse tripped a little faster again. "The chaos is why we need to stay," she disagreed. "To make sure everyone evacuates. To stop anyone going the wrong way." And to see what they had wrought. Yeva shook her head; Zagiri steered her toward the refreshment table. "Yes. Come on. We planned for this. Let's just get some punch and—"

"*You* planned," Yeva whispered fiercely as she dug in her heels. "You went soft on them. These people don't deserve the grace you waste on them."

She pulled out of Zagiri's grip, skirts bunched in one fist as she shoved through the crowd, moving fast enough to draw attention. Where was she going? What was she—?

You planned.

Ice whispered along Zagiri's nerves. "What did you do?" she shouted after Yeva—*shouted*, here, at the Harbour Master's Ball. Everyone around her looked scandalised, and Zagiri didn't care, because she'd been such a fool. She'd just let them go off alone, Yeva and Zin, she'd let herself be distracted by Balian, and—

It was all going to go wrong.

Zagiri looked at the clock, but it was meaningless—this was no longer *her* plan, and she had no idea when anything might happen. "We have to get out of here," she said, and no one was paying any attention, ostentatiously stepping away from her, whispering to one another that they *knew* she was an unruly element, did you hear about the sister...

It didn't matter; she didn't care. Snide gossip and narrow minds weren't any reason to kill someone.

Zagiri turned back to the refreshment table. She planted a hand next to the enormous, glittering crystal bowl of punch, and hauled herself up, drawing gasps from all around her. Excellent. If she had their attention already, she could call out, get them *moving*, perhaps she could still—

A thunderclap tipped the world sideways, sending Zagiri to her knees, overtipping the bowl. Punch flooded over her, drenching her skirt, pouring onto the floor, and the thick scent of winter fruit and sickly sweet alcohol rose around her.

Along with shrieks and cries of alarm. People grabbed at one another, crying and blustering and looking every way but the right one.

Zagiri looked up, where the ceiling had cracked clear across, splintered like lightning, spider-creeping out from each corner. The corners where they'd planned to plant explosive devices, on a timer to go off at least a quarter bell later.

Not the plan. Not *her* plan. Zagiri had no idea what would happen next.

But she had more idea than everyone else.

Zagiri heaved back to standing, a slippered foot tangled in her soggy skirts. Her dress was a *disaster*, and that was the very least of her problems. Everything sounded far away, out past the ringing in her ears. From up here on the table, she could see people already streaming away up the stairs, out of the Hall; good instincts. Now she just had to get everyone else moving that way.

Net-gloved hands cupping her mouth, Zagiri shouted, "Hey! Get out of here!"

A few of those nearby looked up at her—and half of those turned pointedly away again. Were they *serious*? Cutting her for impropriety *now*?

A great creaking groan came from the ceiling, and a chunk of masonry slammed down in the middle of the orchestra. Wood smashed, strings twanged, and—and there were *people* under there, oh, ink and ashes.

Even as everyone froze, horrified, another section smashed down in the centre of the hall.

People scattered now, shoving toward the stairs, pushing one another out of the way, crying and coughing and covered in plaster dust.

Zagiri peeled her hands away from her horrified mouth. She'd planned—not for this, but to get everyone out. "The balconies!" she shouted, and the words vanished in the noise. She tried again, pointing at the side stairs. "The balconies lead to the terrace! *Hey!*"

Finally someone moved in that direction, soon followed by a steady stream of people. As the flood of the crowd split, it moved faster, more easily.

"Zagiri!" She actually heard that, turning to where Balian shoved out of the crowd, jostling into the side of the table. He had Lusal clutched against his side, pale and scared. Her white dress was grey with dust.

Zagiri skidded and slipped off the table, her punch-sodden skirts squelching. "Get out of here," she told him, and took Lusal's other hand.

The girl tried to smile at her, weak and watery. "Was this the plan?" she asked, barely a whisper in Zagiri's ears.

This had *never* been the plan. They were supposed to be scared, and shaken, and shown their own weaknesses. Not injured. Not killed. Not lying under rubble.

"It's all right," Zagiri reassured her. "We'll get out. It's going to be fine."

They rushed for the nearest stairs—up to the balcony, from which they could circle around to the Kellian Way.

But Zagiri had barely set a foot on the stairs when the world went white.

White and whistling, like an overheated samovar, and hot like one too. Zagiri ached all over, and the air was thick with dust and acrid smoke. Her eyes stung, and the Hall veered crazily around her; she only made it to sitting on the third attempt.

People shifted and seethed and groaned, all their finery torn and grimy. The lanterns had blown out, leaving the hall in murky gloom that didn't conceal the buckling walls, or the half-fallen ceiling. The far end of the hall, where the staircase should be, was a mess of masonry like the Palace after the dragon.

The staircase that had been crowded with people. Zagiri hadn't even planned for charges to be laid there.

She'd been such a *fool*.

Zagiri struggled to her feet, and almost fell over Lusal. "Oh! I'm so s—" The apology died on her lips; the girl's eyes were wide open under a layer of dust, staring at nothing. A chunk of masonry painted with a Lyraec legion had crushed her body.

Something jostled at Zagiri's shoulder. She pulled away—or tried to—but the something had an unyielding grip, and it was shouting her name. Even when she slapped at his face, Balian didn't let her go.

She watched his mouth shaping words, but they only came to her faintly. *We have to get out of here.*

"Lusal," she croaked.

His mouth twisted, jaw clenching. He didn't look down.

"Break a window!" someone shouted, and Zagiri heard that faintly. Up on the balcony a chair swung at the stained glass; the only thing that shattered was the chair.

Balian's eyes squeezed closed. "They're all charmed against damage," he murmured.

Of course they were. They were works of art, beautiful depictions of planar beings, you couldn't have them falling victim to randomly thrown stones. Or acts of revolution.

Her fault. This was all her fault.

Zagiri grabbed Balian's wrist. "There's a delivery door. Out the back, down the stairs."

He stared at her, and she could see him tally up the information. Possibly he couldn't help it. She knew it was there. She'd *been* down there, the other day, when he'd found her. His jaw clenched, but all he said was: "Lead the way. Get them out."

She grabbed for him as he pulled away. "You too. Come on!" What if there were more charges? What if the whole damn building came down? Zagiri had no idea what they might do, Zin and Yeva and all their wild disdain for consequences.

Balian shook his head. "Get these people moving. I'll help the injured. You"—with a prod to her shoulder—"show them the way out."

Zagiri took a reluctant step back and glanced down one last time at Lusal. She lay like a broken doll, staring accusingly. She'd wanted to be an azata just like Zagiri. There was something wrong with Zagiri's throat, plaster dust choking her. Her vision blurred.

But she turned away.

"There's a back door," Zagiri shouted as she staggered across the hall, around and over the rubble and lost shoes and discarded scarves. "Follow me!"

They did. Only a few at first, but when Zagiri looked back at the top of the stairs, there was a crowd behind her. Limping and tattered and covered in dust and blood, but following her nonetheless.

The basement was dark, with only a trickle of light down the stairs showing the faint edges of things. Zagiri fumbled at the doorframe, sweeping up, up, up...

The hook snagged at her finger, but there was no key.

"No," Zagiri gasped, and patted desperately, over and over, as though it might be hiding. It *had* been very small, so delicate and golden—had she knocked it off by accident?

But she couldn't find anything scrabbling around on the floor either, and she couldn't *see* for the press of people coming down the stairs behind her.

The people she'd promised a way out.

"Are we trapped?" someone called, on the edge of a wail.

A man beside Zagiri hammered at the back doors, rattling the lock. "Break it!" someone behind them screamed.

But the man shook his head. "Charmed."

"Get a knife!" someone else shouted. "Hack out the hinges!"

Zagiri stared at the little lock in the man's hand, gleaming gold with its charms. She wished Siyon were here, to wield some desperate piece of alchemy. Or *Mayar*, because they'd managed well enough on the Swanneck, hadn't they?

Wait.

On the Swanneck, where Mayar had used the nullification sigil to unravel an alchemical effect. All they'd needed was—

"Is there any rakia?" Zagiri demanded, lifting her voice over the hubbub around her. It stilled a little, in shock and a wave of people demanding what she was doing.

But as she shifted, her waterlogged dress rubbed against her legs. Zagiri nearly laughed out loud. Not waterlogged. Heavy with the sweet and tart punch. *Sunshine and alcohol*, Mayar had said, on the bridge.

Worth a try.

Even as the crowd around her fell to arguing, Zagiri snatched the lock and hitched up her skirt. Gathering a great wad of sodden fabric, she drew upon it with her finger the symbol she remembered: a circle and a slashing line.

No way to know if it had done anything. Zagiri just had to hope, as she wrapped her skirt around the charmed padlock, squeezing until punch ran over her fingers, dripping to the floor.

For a moment, she thought nothing was happening. That this wild gamble had failed. That people would press in, crush her against the door in their panic and desperation. It would be all she deserved.

Then the lock sprang open with a faint click inside the clump of her dress.

Zagiri let them fall, her skirts and the lock. She set her hands to the door and heaved.

When the door burst open, a press of people shoved her aside to thunder out into the night. Zagiri clung to the doorframe, pressing desperately out of their way. The fresh air from outside was almost intoxicating, free of dust and smoke and the sharp scent of panic.

She turned her back on it and climbed back up the stairs. There were still people in there. There might be more explosives.

And it was all her fault.

Daruj pointed them at the teahouse tunnel Bracken had used when smuggling fleeing practitioners, but left them to it, racing away to raise the alarm with the bravi, the inquisitors, the gate guards...anyone who might be persuaded to care.

Siyon staggered through the bronze-streaked darkness, barely aware of Mayar at his elbow over the thunder of the earth all around them. They came up into the hills as the sun was sinking in the west, a distant mire of dust casting the light in fire and blood. In another age of the city, watchmen on the golden walls would raise the alarm of enemies approaching. But no Khanate hordes had swooped down on the city in centuries. No one was watching.

No one but Siyon, who knew no human feet kicked up that dust.

The road was thin with traffic heading back to the city—traders with empty carts, merry young azatani returning from a day at the races, the less merry youths who'd laboured to make those races happen. But the Western Hill depot was never empty. The bordellos and wine bars were open all night, and the hostels were far cheaper than any within Bezim. And, of course, there was the Khanate caravanserai, where Mayar's family and more besides made their transitory, or semipermanent, homes.

No walls out here. No barriers. No protection. Save what Siyon himself could bring.

"We need to get people out!" Siyon huffed at Mayar as they ran down the last hill, into the knot of buildings.

"How?" Mayar shouted back. "No emergency bell out here. And my lot won't go anywhere without the animals."

Which wouldn't be allowed inside the city, even if a large group of Khanate traders—at sunset, with the gates closing, with monsters on their heels—might be.

Siyon gritted his teeth, settling his satchel against his side. "Get them moving. *Away* from here. I'll deal with the rest."

Somehow.

Mayar peeled off toward the stone bulk of the caravanserai, already shouting at those loitering near the entry arch. If all the Khanate caravans left, that might alert the rest of the depot all by itself.

But Siyon couldn't rely on it, not with the raucous merriment rising from the ramshackle buildings. He considered ringing the race bell, but the hippodrome was locked up tight. Hammering on every door seemed infeasible.

Siyon skidded into the hippodrome square, where an ornate fountain bubbled and a dozen dirty kids eyed him curiously. Probably thought he was just a likely mark; the Sorcerer, after all, was fifteen feet tall and—

Oh, he wasn't *thinking*.

Snagging a fistful of Aethyreal energy, Siyon twisted it around his throat, casting the loose end up into the burning sunset sky. "Hey!" he shouted, and his voice rattled windows and echoed off the hills. Whoops, maybe he'd overdone it.

From off toward the dying sun came a rending screech—a wild sound of teeth and scales and claws.

Maybe, in the circumstances, he wasn't overdoing it at all.

"Hey!" Siyon called again, as the kids cowered beside the fountain. Windows opened and heads appeared at doorways. "Get your arses outside *now*. You need to get back to the city!"

"You get back to the city!" someone shouted.

"Is it a fire?" another voice called.

"Let it burn!" someone else cackled.

People came crowding out into the rooftop gardens, still carrying their drinks, as though looking for the entertainment.

Fine. If they needed more, Siyon would give them more.

He dragged in more Aethyr, with a twist of the Abyss—for showing off, for prideful display—and a little Empyre—for brightness on high—and he wrapped it all up in a thin veneer of Mundane, for *him*, for his plane, and as some sort of apology for what he was doing with it all.

Making it up as he went. Arguably what he did best.

Siyon pressed his braided bundle of energy down, shoving against the immovable weight of the earth, until it started pushing him *up*.

Sparks of power fountained around him, satchel banging against his hip, but Siyon wasn't sure anything was actually *happening*.

Until his vision cleared, and Siyon was standing on nothing, six feet above the fountain, rising higher every moment.

"What the *fuck*?" someone yelped, down below him, and Siyon grinned.

It was working. He was...well, not flying, you couldn't call it that, not when you'd seen a dragon turn lazy circles in the night sky, felt the air curl around her wings, tasted the shimmer of clouds upon her tongue. But he was certainly doing *something*.

From up here, he could see a dense mass of livestock streaming out of the caravanserai. The Khanate traders were on the move.

"Hey!" Siyon shouted down; he could *feel* their attention through the energy around him. Voices crying out, pointing and shouting (*It's the Sorcerer!*) and one or two throwing things. Siyon pointed west. "They're coming. Get the fuck out of here."

Now people—the people on rooftops, on precarious balconies, at windows and staggering out into the street drunk and belligerent—turned to look. The dust cloud was bigger, swelling the last embers of the slipped-away sun. As the crowd hushed and the music stopped in a dozen bordellos, a rumbling thunder of many feet could be heard, faint but not distant enough.

When Siyon looked, with the plane skewing around him, he could see claws in the earth and a swaying copse of curled scorpion tails, the slithering of massive bodies and—

The depot below him erupted in screams and clatters, running feet and the banging open of doors. The evacuation resembled a rout, people streaming out of rickety buildings, leaping from low balconies, shoving and staggering in their panic. Siyon struggled to stay aloft and out of the way, the very air beneath him churning with urgency.

Probably there was a better way he could have done this.

As the mess of disreputable establishments drained like bilgewater, people streaming up the hill toward the city, Siyon clambered off his tangled mess of energy onto the top of the hippodrome wall. Keeping one hand looped in the power he'd pulled together, he squinted west against the gathering gloom. Were those shadows now, at the base of the rising dust? They were running faster than petty little humans ever could.

Siyon straddled the outermost edge of the wall, bracing one foot against the anchor point for the uppermost awnings, and churned his bundle of energy around his arms.

Those monsters wanted power. They were hungry for it. And here was Siyon, with plenty.

He didn't so much throw the energy as push it out, like a boat's hull against the water. The wave surged westward, widening and sparkling, gouging up *more* energy from every hill it raced over—sparkling Aethyr and glimmering Abyss and burning Empyre, but barely the faintest dredged-up burnishing of the Mundane.

Would that be enough? Would it even serve as a distraction?

"Hey!" Not Siyon this time, but a smaller and far more human voice.

Down in the square, Mayar waved both arms over their head. "Come on!" they shouted. "Everyone's moving!"

The road back up to the city was a solid mass of people, dotted with lanterns and torches. Khanate caravans choked the trade road winding north through the hills, but the camels and donkeys were moving fast, like they could sense what was coming.

Siyon could feel the rumble of the monsters' approach now, vibrating through the brick wall beneath him. "Go!" he shouted down to Mayar. "Make sure they get inside!"

He turned back to the west. The dust loomed high over the writhing, skittering mass.

They wanted energy. They wanted power. Siyon reached out again—not for anything and everything, but *his*. The Mundane, thick and bronze and pooling in the roots of the city—

But he wasn't *in* the city. Siyon's senses found the barest trickle of energy, like dipping his fingers in a puddle when he'd expected the ocean.

There wasn't enough, out here. Despite all the practitioners working at it, there still wasn't enough coming through the city barrier.

Siyon reached farther, stretching his awareness out behind him, laying a metaphorical hand against the boundary—*his* boundary, that he had built, that knew and recognised him.

He pulled at it. Demanded. *Insisted*. And the energy came—sluggishly, reluctantly, in thick and syrupy clots. He had to drag at it like a fishing net. Too little, too slow.

This wasn't going to work. Siyon couldn't stand between the city and this incursion, couldn't stave them off with *this* paltry trickle of energy. It was not going to be enough.

With a snarl, Siyon sank what he'd gathered into the biggest, most Mundane anchor he could find—the hippodrome itself, built by hand, of manufactured brick, and gilded with the energy and industry of generations. It sucked in everything he could feed it, churning power around its track, sparking off the spina, sizzling between the seats. Once Siyon opened a conduit, it pulled more energy from the city, burning along the paths beaten into the hills, connections of habit and intent.

It was better than Siyon had hoped, but still not enough.

Siyon leapt down to the square, snagging at Aethyr to slow his fall. He hit the ground already running, the approaching threat beating at his heels.

The road back up the hills was cluttered with debris. Siyon could hear the crowd, shouting and shoving as they fought their way into the city—

No, wait…

They were hammering at the gates. The closed gates.

Siyon snarled in frustration. Everything he'd done, and they were all going to die anyway, ground up against the wall by monsters that weren't even here for *them*.

Another screech came from the west. The last light was dying in the sky; everything below was seething shadows. Siyon plunged into the back of the desperate crowd, ducking between agitated men craning to see over the crowd ahead, skirting women clutching crying children, insinuating his way between little knots of nervous people clinging to one another.

The hammering at the gates was almost as loud as the skittering approach of the monsters; people shouted up at the white-tunicked guards holding lanterns over the wall's crenelations.

There was someone else up there, *not* wearing white. The lantern-light glimmered on the metallic embroidery of a longvest. There was an azatan up there.

He was shouting something, voice faint at this distance. "—by order of the Interim Rectification Board."

Even distorted by the charmed megaphone, Siyon recognised that voice. That crisp Avenue accent. That well-armoured arrogance.

"I repeat," called down Avarair Hisarani, "the gates are closed until and unless the criminal Siyon Velo turns himself in."

Siyon stopped, pressed in on all sides by trembling, nervous, wild-eyed people. People who'd seen him, floating above the depot, telling them to get out. People who hesitated, stiff with silence.

A massive crash sounded from behind them, loud enough to judder the hill beneath their feet and make everyone duck, hunching their shoulders.

Behind them, the hippodrome collapsed beneath scrambling weight, the high wall of it disappearing under a shadowed mass. The monsters cracked it open like an egg, sucking at the power Siyon had left inside. They screeched at one another; the rattling clatter of snapping claws set Siyon's teeth on edge.

"He was here!" someone shouted from the crowd. "We all saw him!"

Then *everyone* was shouting. A voice bellowed over the hubbub: "He *saved* us. He got us out!"

"He's the reason for the monsters!"

"There he is!"

"Here! Here! Drag him forward!"

The crowd shifted and jostled and staggered this way and that, but no one was pointing at Siyon, no one grabbing at *him*.

"Stop!" a woman screamed. "Stop! No!"

Siyon looked back down to the depot. Darkness covered everything, but amid the buildings, a glow sprouted. Not power, but fire, licking at curtains and wooden walls as the monsters went crashing through the buildings. They'd soon be pushing up toward the city.

Avarair Hisarani waited, gripping the parapet. Grim and implacable as he'd been, facing off with Siyon before Salt Night. He might just hate Siyon enough to let everyone here die for it.

The crowd churned into a frenzy, shoving and shouting in chaos. Any man slightly taller than the rest was being set upon. They weren't going to *need* the monsters, at this rate, but they were coming anyway.

Siyon couldn't let this happen.

He pinched a twist of Aethyr and shouted: "I'm here!" Pulled energy, and kept pulling, from the crowd and the hills and the city wall, right there, eager to feed him. He sucked it all up until his vision turned a shimmering bronze, the power glowing beneath his skin.

He stood in a halo of burnished Mundane power that sent the crowd scrambling away from him. Siyon stepped forward, until his energy sparked reflections in the metallic thread of Avarair's longvest. It shone in the satisfaction in his eyes.

"Open the fucking gate," Siyon snarled, voice crackling with energy, harsh as a rockslide. "When every last one of these people is inside, you can do whatever you want with me."

There was a moment's silence—except for the grinding noise of monsters wading through the depot below.

The gates started to creak open.

The tide of humanity flowed urgently inside, like water bursting through the gap in a dam, scurrying with panicked looks over their shoulders.

At *Siyon*. Not at the monsters.

Someone slipped out of the crowd—Mayar, catching at Siyon's elbow, hissing, "Douse the light, get among us."

They weren't alone; a dozen other people loitered, tight with fear but staying. Some of them wouldn't look at Siyon, but they'd stand with him. They'd try to smuggle him inside.

They'd fail. Avarair would never let Siyon get whisked away.

"Go," Siyon grated. With all this energy burning in his veins, he could feel the monsters at his back. Feel their claws digging into rock, feel their hunger, feel their attention turning this way, hooked by his brightness.

The gates needed to be closed before they got here.

Mayar hesitated a moment longer, but the group was disintegrating around them. They fled toward the gate, and Mayar went too, the last ones rushing inside.

Safe. Siyon had managed *that*, at least.

But now what? Now he walked into the trap? Now he gave himself up to Avarair Hisarani?

How did he think that would end?

Better, perhaps, to stay out here. Turn and face the monsters. Give them everything he had, all the energy hammering beneath his skin. Maybe he *could* fend them off, like this.

Maybe he couldn't, and it would still be better to die on their claws than in the hands of the Council.

Siyon didn't want to die. He had Izmirlian back, just a little. He had so many questions and so much to find out. He wanted to *fix this*.

The gate was starting to creak closed again, Avarair watching from the top of the wall. He, it seemed, didn't care which way Siyon died.

Well, *fuck him*.

Siyon slammed down his foot, on the hard-packed dirt of the road, and sent everything he was holding—all his power, all his fear, all his rage—into it. Turned the road into a river of energy, slipping and sliding back down toward the depot, a bronze torrent.

Then he sprinted for the gate, sliding in with it skimming his shoulder, hooking one last wisp of power into the wood and sealing the barrier behind him.

Even as hands seized him.

CHAPTER 15

Sable House closed entirely, every last guest politely but implacably evicted, some still clutching a forlorn bundle of clothes. Qorja called in favours she wouldn't specify to fetch the healer from Gossamer House, a fussy little stick of a man who ordered them all out while he attended to Laxmi.

He also brought news of what else was happening in the city tonight.

Explosions at the Ball. The Eldren Hall collapsed. The dead and injured laid out in lines on the Kellian Way.

It seemed impossible. Anahid should have known, somehow. She should have been there.

"Go," Qorja urged her, hands around Anahid's trembling ones. "The healer knows his business, but it's likely Laxmi will sleep for half the night at least. Find your sister."

Anahid didn't want to step outside. Not without Laxmi. There could be anything—anyone—waiting for her out there. She hadn't even been safe in her own House. In her own *office*. Three of them, waiting in there.

There was something in that she should pay attention to, but her head was still ringing, and her sister's Ball had been blown up...

"Go," Nura repeated. "We have everything in hand here. The healer will look at the surviving intruder next."

211

Bitterness rose in Anahid's throat, metallic as the blood—*Laxmi's* blood—on the floor of her office. "I don't care if he dies," she snarled. But sense caught up a moment later. "Wait—"

Nura nodded, already a step ahead. They'd only know who was behind this if they could wring it out of the survivor.

Anahid didn't know what she'd do with that information. She couldn't think about it now. She left behind her House, and her mistakes, and ran for the Eldren Hall.

Or what was left of it.

The crowd started just past the opera house, people clustered and milling, collapsed beneath the trees, ashen and ash-smeared, crying and calling and staring blank-eyed into the night. There were those in torn and grubby finery, those who'd come running in their night attire, those in the uniforms of inquisitors or the university's healing schools.

Anahid waded farther up the Kellian Way and deeper into the grisly, grimy aftermath of the Harbour Master's Ball.

The road had been closed off into a makeshift hospital, tents raised for those less able to sit up or speak. Around them, people were laid all over the wide, tree-lined street, glittering and groaning, a carpet of torn lace and uncomprehending tears.

Smoke hung thick on the air. Anahid hurried onward, scanning the patients for familiar faces—and they *were*, many of them. She'd known these people all her life.

At first, Anahid didn't even recognise the Eldren Hall—her eyes kept sweeping past the shattered mass, looking for the four towers that must be here somewhere...

It was only when she stumbled over the first spill of rubble—crumbled masonry and glass crunching underfoot—that she understood. The towers *weren't* anymore. They had toppled, some out across the Kellian Way, one sidelong into the neighbouring building. The dome had fallen in on itself. The grand stairs leading up to the portico—that Anahid had climbed so many times; upon which Siyon had stood to call the city together—were strewn with rubble.

It was a disaster.

"Let them through!" someone called, up near the shattered portico. "Get them out!"

Another voice—a voice Anahid would know anywhere, even smoke-cracked and shattered by effort—shouted, "Get him first, get him *out*; Balian, *move*."

Anahid raced up the stairs, ducking around a man who stepped out to restrain her. "Zagiri!" she called, barely audible in the rest of the chaos. "*Giri!*"

There she was, streaked with grime and ash, hair draggling wild and wet out of its pins, no sign of the headscarf Anahid had given her—no, wait, there it was, wrapped as a makeshift bandage around the head of Balian Hisarani, who lolled, barely conscious as he was hauled out of the wreckage.

"I'm fine." Zagiri jerked her elbow out of someone's grasp and tottered. "See to the others who—oh, ink and ashes."

She was staring at a nearby body, half buried under fallen masonry, when Anahid hauled her into a wild hug.

"Ana," Zagiri gasped and clung to her, one arm tight and desperate around her. By all the Powers, was she *crying*? "Ana, it's all my fault."

"What?" Anahid tried to wipe the mess of Zagiri's hair out of her face. "What's your fault?"

"Her fault she's a hero!" one of the men nearby declared, as Balian was helped away down the stairs. "She got half a hundred people out the back, and then she went back in, started boosting more out this way over the rubble!"

That sounded like her bold and heedless sister, but Anahid staggered under Zagiri's weight, rocked by a sudden anguished groan into her shoulder. She wrapped her arms anew around her sister, and there was something warm and sticky under her palm. "Not everyone," Zagiri wailed, her words mushed together. "Not Lusal. My *fault*."

"Zagiri," Anahid started, trying to get a proper look at her sister, in her dirty dark red dress.

But the dress had been pale. That was *blood*, all over her sister's shoulder, her dress shredded along with the skin beneath.

Her sister swayed, face pale beneath the dust. Anahid held Zagiri tighter and shouted, "Help!"

The man who'd called her a hero dashed back up, catching Zagiri as she fainted. "Easy does it," he said, hefting her in his arms. "We'll get her down to the tents. No need to fret."

Easy for him to say, though the healer who hurried over to take a first look wasn't bothered either. "Not as bad as some I've seen," he said grimly, peeling Zagiri's eyelids up. "Arm's likely broken, but the blood's largely stopped already. Let me look her over properly, get that arm set, then you can take her somewhere to rest."

"Of course." Anahid stepped back to give him room to work, and then was in someone else's way. She scuttled out of the tent entirely, finding a quiet spot to the side.

Where the sounds of shouting reached her. Fresh shouts, angry and fearful, coming down from the Boulevard.

"Monsters!" someone screamed.

And another voice, faintly over the ruckus, "The Sorcerer! The Sorcerer himself!"

All Anahid could make out was a lot of people up on the Boulevard, flickering between the street lanterns. She glanced back into the tent, at her sister who needed her.

Her sister, who would be unbelievably irate when she woke up if something had happened to Siyon and Anahid didn't know what.

Anahid hurried away up the hill. The crowd thickened as she went, the Ball survivors mixing with a new surge of wild-eyed people covered in the pale dust of the stony western hills; they must have come in through the city gate. Half of them were silent and overwhelmed. The rest were shouting, grabbing anyone who'd stand still to tell their story.

"What do you mean, *overrun*?" someone demanded, farther off in the crowd. "What monsters?"

Anahid shoved through onto the Boulevard. The crowd only grew thicker, stunned and tearful and rowdy, as far as she could see toward the gate. What had *happened*? What more was being done to her city? Where was Siyon?

Spurred by curiosity, Anahid slipped into the back streets, circling the Boulevard crowds to reach the wall. One of the access staircases was nearby, and the usual guard nowhere to be seen, so Anahid went up.

The wind whisked brisk off the ocean behind her, carrying the faint tang of smoke from the Eldren Hall and blowing the loose strands of her hair across her face. But beyond the wall was even more chaos. The depot in the western hills was on fire, every building ablaze and the flames even dancing along the top of the hippodrome walls. The noise of it was a roar, even at this distance.

Or maybe that was the monsters silhouetted clearly against the glow. The largest of them stood half as tall as the hippodrome, even on four feet, and they moved like massive versions of the skinks that skittered in the cracks of the city. But their tails curled up into scorpion stingers, and they swiped and hissed at one another as they rolled and writhed amid the burning depot.

Anahid cowered behind the crenelations of the wall and gaped.

"Clear the road!" someone bellowed, behind and below her. From the city side—the *safe* side—of the gate.

Anahid crossed to the inner edge of the wall and peered down to the street, where a double squad of white-tunicked guards formed up around a prisoner. Light loomed and veered crazily from this angle, as lanterns were raised swinging.

An azatan in full evening dress stepped out in front of the prisoner and his escort. He shouted again: "Clear the road, or I'll have you all arrested."

What was Avarair Hisarani doing up here? Shouldn't he have been at the Ball, objecting to Zagiri sponsoring his cousin?

The crowd did *not* clear the road. They shifted and seethed, and someone shouted back: "Let him go! He saved us! Let the Sorcerer go!"

Only then did Anahid recognise the prisoner, stripped down to his shirtsleeves, bowed head covered in dust.

Siyon looked a thin copy of himself. He looked...beaten.

"There is a warrant for his arrest," Avarair announced to the crowd, even as he beckoned to someone back in the gatehouse. "And he has delivered himself into Council custody. Disperse *now*, or there will be consequences."

Another squad of white-tunicked guards marched forward—that explained why there was no one on the wall, at least. They paraded out in front of Siyon and his guard, in front of Avarair, and turned to face the gathered people.

As one, they lifted their crossbows to point at the crowd, setting the stocks against their shoulders.

Anahid had seen one of those, in her parlour. She'd seen what it could do. They were illegal, save on trading vessels. Or in times of emergency. Anahid was too far away to see if any of the guards were at all bothered about pointing them at unarmed people.

The crowd flinched back. On the fringes, in the shadows, people started to melt away. For a few moments more, a tight huddle of people held firm, staring down the guards and their bows. Then they too broke and hurried away, some into the side streets, some streaming away down the Boulevard.

The last to leave glared right at Avarair, lantern-light gleaming off a shaved head. Anahid recognised them—the young Khanate person who Siyon had been working with before Salt Night.

Then they were gone, shifting away in shadows.

"Move out!" Avarair shouted, full of satisfaction.

Anahid half wished she had a crossbow of her own, up here. She wouldn't even shoot him anywhere fatal.

The guards marched forward, the front rank with their crossbows still hefted, though no longer raised, and the others following behind, in a protective circle around Siyon.

Who shuffled and stumbled, barely looking up. Exhausted and dejected.

They all moved out in a circle of light, showing the people waiting on the Boulevard. The front ranks were silent and sullen, but as the parade moved farther along, just before they turned the corner out of sight of Anahid's position on the wall, she heard other shouts.

"The Sorcerer! They've caught him!"

A cheer.

The wind was brisk in her face, whipping hair against her neck, and the tears away from her eyes.

Zagiri woke more gently than she had in weeks, drifting slowly up from clinging sleep as she snuggled deeper into a pillow that smelled—

Just like home.

Suddenly alert, Zagiri opened her eyes to a bedroom—*her* bedroom, in the Savani townhouse. She lay beneath the familiar Revarri patchwork quilt, in the bed with her old sabre hanging from the post, with light edging around the curtains in the way she *knew* meant it was after dawn, but not so late that she couldn't make breakfast.

Beside the bed, slumped half out of an armchair and onto the quilt, was Anahid. She was wearing a headscarf again, an old one of their mother's. Even asleep, she looked tired. There were the faint beginnings of wrinkles between her eyebrows, and starting to tug at the corners of her mouth.

Zagiri's sister was getting old.

What were either of them doing *here*?

Memory crawled back to Zagiri, scratched and patchy and awful. The Ball, the destruction, Lusal Hisarani's staring eyes. Balian's refusal to leave while anyone else remained, even as the ceiling creaked above them and the smoke thickened, as he started to stagger and cough.

Until a balcony collapsed on both of them, stone bouncing all around like cast marbles, and Zagiri had thought maybe that was it, they were both dead.

Not so. She'd dragged them both out. Blood streaming from his head, blood all down her dress, one of her arms just not working at all, pain screaming along every nerve she had.

Anahid on the stairs, frantic. And then darkness.

Zagiri half wished she could crawl back into it, into that blissful nothing where she didn't have to learn just how many people had died because of her mistakes.

At least she'd saved Balian. He'd never forgive her. He shouldn't. *Lusal.*

She rolled away from Anahid and nearly startled right out of the bed.

"I see you're awake," her father said, from a rather less-comfortable chair.

He was properly dressed for morning, in the plain shirt and trousers he had always worn to family breakfast, freshly shaven and with his hair oiled and dressed. But his eyes were almost hollow with sleeplessness; had he even gone to bed since she'd seen him so briefly at the Ball?

When he'd been still angry with her, and rightly so.

Zagiri's vision blurred, and she wiped at her eyes, sniffling as she gulped, "I'm so sorry. I never wanted any of this."

True about so many things. She'd made so many mistakes this season.

The words were spilling out of her. "I'm sorry about cousin Gildon, and I'm sorry I was so impatient. I should have—"

"No," Usal said with a sigh, as he leaned forward to cover her outstretched hand with his own. "No, my little gull, *I* should have. I am the head of this family, and I should never have let you feel so unheard that you had to resort to such stunts. I should have ensured you knew more about our position, my concerns, all of it. I..." His smile was a small and painful thing. "I did not see how you had already grown up. What you are capable of."

All those dead bodies, crushed beneath the rubble. The stairs exploding beneath them. What she was capable of.

Her father was still smiling at her. "You are a hero, Zagiri. There are dozens of people who live today only because you made a way out for them."

An awful, terrible part of her wondered if she could use that. Be their hero, and steer them all toward the necessary change.

But he had it all backward. There were dozens of people dead today because she thought she could control everything. How could she ever make it right?

Her father was still talking; Zagiri made an effort to listen. "But it is no longer my concern, and not without its pleasant side. Council is already convening, in emergency session, and I can be here instead, with my daughters."

Council was convening? Already? "Why is—?"

"You're awake," Anahid said from behind her.

When Zagiri tilted back, her sister was sitting up, rubbing at her linen-creased face, and staring in sharp disbelief. Just how terrible had Zagiri looked last night, when she'd staggered out of the ruins of the Eldren Hall? She didn't *feel* too bad, right now. Still stiff and sore, especially in the shoulder that had taken the brunt of the falling balcony, which from the feel of it had been bandaged very tightly.

If there were any justice in this plane, Lusal would have walked out, and Zagiri stayed under the rubble.

With a creaking sigh, Usal levered up to his feet. "I will go and see about some breakfast for the pair of you."

"No," Anahid said faintly, sitting up straighter. "I should go. The gossip will be—"

"Who cares about gossip anymore?" Usal declared, with that bitter smile again. "We all have far better things to worry about today."

He closed the door quietly behind him, and Zagiri turned back to Anahid. "Has Council convened early?" She'd thought she'd have time to get herself together. She hadn't planned on . . . any of what happened.

Anahid wiped over her face. "A lot has happened, Giri. But are you all right?" Zagiri nodded impatiently, but Anahid continued, "No headache? Are you feeling sick? Is the light too bright?"

"I'm *fine*," Zagiri snarled.

"You're not," Anahid snapped. "That shoulder was broken, and they've dosed you with all sorts of things and basted you like a Salt Night ham, and it will still be weeks until it's fully healed."

Zagiri couldn't help reflexively shifting her elbow, feeling the stiffness and soreness. "Ana, what has *happened*?"

Her sister frowned at her a moment longer but finally said: "The Western Hill depot was overrun by monsters last night."

Zagiri gaped. *"Overrun?"* She couldn't even begin to understand it. There'd been *one* monster previously, in the harbour, and it had been terrifying.

Anahid shook her head. "I don't know any of the details. I don't think anyone does, except perhaps Siyon, and…" She trailed off, pressing her lips together, brows creasing.

Oh shit. "He died?" Zagiri barely recognised the small scrap of her voice.

Anahid shook her head. "No. No, he's alive. But they arrested him. I saw him marched off in custody. They say he turned himself over, so that the gates would be opened to allow those fleeing the depot to enter the city." She huffed a little bitter breath. "They also say he called the monsters in the first place. They are saying a *lot* of things, right now. Including that he was somehow responsible for the Ball."

Zagiri absolutely would not let him get tarred with that. Even if she had to turn herself in and drag Zin and Yeva along with her bare hands.

She needed to speak with Yeva. She needed to find out just what the girl had been thinking. Or if there was even more to this that Zagiri wasn't seeing.

"What do you think you're doing?" Anahid predictably demanded, grabbing at Zagiri's uninjured arm as she started getting out of bed.

"I need to see someone," Zagiri insisted. "Yeva was at the Ball with me, but I don't know if she got out."

Surely she would have; she'd fled early, knowing what was coming. Too cowardly to face the consequences of her choices.

"Send a message," Anahid insisted, but she was losing the wrestle, unwilling to truly put weight on Zagiri. She stood up, as Zagiri wriggled out on the other side and looked around for a dress. "Zagiri, *no one* is accepting visitors at the moment. Between the Ball and Siyon's arrest and the emergency session to discuss all of it, everyone's hiding at home and waiting to see what comes next."

Zagiri grabbed something out of her cupboard—old, and plain, but perfectly serviceable. "This can't wait," she said, stepping into the dress and then—damn. "Can you help?"

Anahid rolled her eyes, but she came around the bed to help Zagiri get the dress on over her injured arm. "I should come with you," she muttered, as she fastened buttons up Zagiri's back. "But I can't. I have to get back to the District."

There was a catch in her voice, like a crack in her impeccable composure. It had Zagiri craning over her shoulder to see her sister's face. "What's happened?"

Anahid shook her head tightly. "I thought I could control it all," she said, and Zagiri almost flinched, to hear her own recriminations on her sister's lips. "A foolish thrill. Violence spills and overflows. That's what it *does*. But I had my eyes closed so tightly, I couldn't even see it." She took a steadying breath, tied off Zagiri's sash, and said more evenly: "I was attacked. In my office. Laxmi accounted for them, but they stabbed her." Her face grew cold as stone, and her voice colder still. "I am going to ensure they regret it."

For just a moment, Zagiri was afraid of her sister.

Anahid pulled up a smile. It was almost more frightening, given what had come before. "But that's my business, and not your concern. I will help you leave the house if you *promise* me that you will speak with Yeva and come straight home again. Is that clear?"

Now that Zagiri was on her feet, the walk over to Yeva and back again seemed ambitious. She certainly couldn't manage any farther. "I promise."

It was easy enough, in the end, to slip out the front door while her sister was taking her leave from—and making her own apologies to—their parents in the breakfast room. Zagiri wished she could stay and help support Anahid—who had done nothing wrong but find herself a wonderful life society could die mad about.

But she had her own business to attend to.

Anahid was, of course, entirely correct: No one was accepting visitors, including the Bardhas. Zagiri had her own calling cards now, as an azata, but they were back at the apartment. She'd taken a moment on the way out, though, to write a message on the back of a family card. She presented it to the Bardhas' housekeeper, for immediate delivery to Yeva; go ahead, she'd said, I'll wait here for the reply.

The message read: *Talk to me or I'm telling them everything*.

The housekeeper was back remarkably quickly, to show Zagiri into the upstairs parlour.

Yeva stood by the cold fireplace, chin up, arms folded. Her

eyes flickered over Zagiri's face—which the front hall's mirror had informed her was a mess of bruises and scrapes.

"Yeah," Zagiri said in greeting, with a tight smile. "Those of us who *stayed* at the Ball, instead of running away, didn't have such a great time. Speaking of, were you planning to come to Lusal's funeral? You remember, the debutante you sponsored and then left to die?"

The housekeeper quickly closed the door behind her.

In the silence left behind, Yeva folded her arms tighter, hunched in silent defiance.

Zagiri sighed. "Look, I don't... blame you. I knew what you were, both of you, and I trusted you again. Because it was easy, and because I was angry. It's my fault. All I want to know is who else was involved. How much bigger was this than I knew?"

Yeva shook her head. "No one. It was just us."

"No, it wasn't." Zagiri had been thinking about it, to distract from how painful and unsteady the walk over here had been. She'd figured out a few things. "Zin talked about a backer. Who was it? *Someone* got him those explosives. They were good work. *You* couldn't afford them, so he certainly couldn't."

With every word, Yeva's eyes grew wider. "What?" she bleated. "I didn't... It's just alchemy. Isn't it easy here?"

Zagiri growled with frustration. Yeva had no idea. She didn't know a thing about Bezim, and she'd just walked in here determined to change it.

There was no point in staying further. Possibly hadn't been any reason to come in the first place, but Zagiri had wanted to see her. Wanted to know this for sure.

Zagiri paused, with her hand on the door, and looked back. "I'm going to unravel this," she warned Yeva. "I'm going to make sure everyone involved is exposed. Us too, if it comes to that. So I suggest you tell your mother you want to go home."

For the first time, Yeva looked genuinely stricken. "I can't—there's no one back there for me. She'll have to come too. I can't do that to her!"

She should have thought of that earlier. Then again, there was plenty Zagiri should have considered more fully before she acted.

"Wait." Yeva stepped forward, hands up now, almost beseeching. "What are you going to do?"

Zagiri didn't know yet. But she was going to figure it out.

CHAPTER 16

Siyon didn't remember much of being paraded through the city. Bronze power had swamped him anew, on this side of the barrier, and everything came thickly through that—shouting faces and angry words, stumbling steps and the reek of smoke.

By the time he fought his way through the wash of energy, he was lying on a narrow cot in a small room. Stone walls, dirt floor, stone ceiling, all of it shining with Mundane effort. Siyon knew where he was—under the old hippodrome—just by the weight above and the way the city draped around him.

Which unsettled him enough to jerk him the rest of the way out of his daze.

Siyon had heard that the government—the actual *useful* part, unlike the Council itself—had taken over the old hippodrome. He hadn't really cared, blithely assuming that none of it mattered to him in the lower city.

It mattered now. Siyon was no longer safe in the lower city. And whatever the Council had in mind, what it meant for *him* seemed quite obvious.

Nothing good at all.

The azatani were scared—again and still, of what had been happening, of losing their stranglehold on alchemy, of *him*. So unused to problems they couldn't buy or bully their way out of, they'd *started* scared, clinging to tendrils of panic from the summer and autumn. He'd confirmed all their fears when he released the dragon. Nothing since had helped. Not the endless bubbling magic of the city, nor the monsters hammering at the city bounds.

Siyon could hardly blame them. Those shadowed glimpses of the giant scorpion-tailed lizards smashing through the depot had been the stuff of nightmares.

Something else had happened as well. Something at Zagiri's Ball.

That much had been easy to glean from fragments of overheard conversation, as inquisitors and clerks went back and forth along the corridor in front of Siyon's cell. Something awful had happened at the Ball, something that had the azatani terrified.

They weren't good at feeling afraid and powerless. They preferred to be angry and vengeful.

And now he was in their custody. At the mercy of their justice.

They were going to kill him. It made it a little hard to concentrate on anything else.

He had to keep a tight cork in the flagon of his panic, though. Siyon remembered all too well his audience with Mama Badrosani, and the eagerness of the Mundane energy to shape itself to his fear. Easier to keep a grip on things when his head wasn't aching with a recent knock, but Siyon could still feel the power licking along his urges, whispering at the edge of his mind. Even more eager now, as though hopeful that the amount he had drawn to hurl at the depot monsters was just the beginning.

If he let it, the earth could shake his captivity to dust around him. All his own fears would be flattened. It would just take destroying the city.

Maybe the azatani were right. Maybe he *was* a risk and a danger.

Footsteps outside jerked Siyon from these dire thoughts. Grateful for it, he sidled over to the door. There was a narrow grille above it, allowing in air but no vermin. If Siyon braced a boot on either side of the door's shallow niche, he could push his way up.

"—Velo," one voice said, and Siyon paused in his shuffling climb to listen more closely. The voices were too quiet.

The footsteps came to a stop right outside. Shit, were they coming in *here*?

But there came the sound of a door opening, and it wasn't his. Across the corridor? Siyon wriggled up in a hurry, wedging his cheek against the ceiling to peer out through the narrow gap.

A grey-tunicked inq stood in the doorway opposite. "Right, bring him in."

Another pair nudged forward a big guy, burly as a lader, with a reddish glint to his hair and beard. He didn't really struggle, but he didn't make it easy for them either, dragging his heels and staggering a little to bang one of the inqs into the doorframe.

"Hey," the other snapped, and the guy turned to sneer at him.

Siyon slipped from his perch in shock, his heel skidding against the frame.

What was his *brother* doing in inq custody? How had they even laid hands on him? He didn't think Mezin deigned to ever come into the upper city.

"This'll go easier if you cooperate," the inq snapped as Siyon pushed back up into position.

"Fuck your cooperation," Mezin growled, "right in the ear."

Charming as ever.

They shoved him into the cell opposite and clanged the door shut behind him. As they went off down the corridor, one of the inqs said, "Looking forward to seeing that one on the poisoner's slab, frankly."

The other two made wordless noises of agreement, and Siyon pressed his face harder against the door, trying to keep them in view. They were going to kill Mezin? What *for*? What was going on?

A new voice spoke up, right outside Siyon's cell. "Aren't brothers troublesome?"

Just that voice made him flinch—the sharp corners of the Avenues accent, the painfully familiar edge that tipped it from teasing into sneer. He skidded down the door, getting a splinter in one scrabbling hand.

Ow. Fuck.

"Oh, don't be shy," said Avarair Hisarani from the other side of the door. "I'm certainly not coming *in*. You've already threatened me once, and who knows what your demon is capable of."

Siyon hissed as he pulled the splinter out of the heel of his hand. He wasn't going to admit anything about Laxmi's changed state. He didn't want to see Avarair's smug face in here.

He desperately did, so he could put it back through the door. He couldn't hear the guy's voice without seeing him again atop the city wall, threatening to let everyone out there die unless Siyon turned himself in. The energy trembled all around him, eager and agitated and tugging at Siyon's control. It could bring down the whole hippodrome on both of them.

Probably wiser to keep him outside. "Made a formal complaint about me chasing you up some stairs, did you? Figures you're a tattletale."

"And you're a menace. Along with your whole family, it seems."

Siyon expected that to sound more smug. Surely this was the highlight of Avarair Hisarani's winter. He'd apprehended Siyon himself, after all.

But Avarair didn't sound silky with satisfaction. There was a sharp edge to his voice. Still something to prove.

"Are you expecting to get anything out of Mezin?" Siyon asked casually. "Or are you going to try to lean on some sort of brotherly bond? Either way, you're wasting your time."

The closest the brothers Velo had come to *bonds* had been the rope they'd knotted around his wrists before they threw him into the river.

But Avarair laughed—even that was wound more tight than Siyon had expected. "Nothing's going to save either of you. Want to tell your brother what you did, Mezin?"

From behind the door opposite, Siyon's brother growled, "Fuck the lot of you."

But he *did* sound smug, like whatever he'd done, he was satisfied about it.

It didn't surprise Siyon as much as it could have when Avarair said: "Your eldest brother blew up the Harbour Master's Ball. He killed three dozen azatani, and injured many more."

No wonder they were executing him. No wonder they'd laid hands on him. For that casualty count, they'd have stormed into Dockside, into the Velo compound itself, and dragged him out. What had he been *thinking*?

But Siyon remembered the last time he'd seen his brother, facing off down a Dockside alleyway. Remembered Mezin snarling, *Soon we'll put you all in sacks.*

Not Siyon's problem. He had plenty of his own.

"You should hear the things he says about you," Avarair mused, like Siyon hadn't heard them directly from Mezin's mouth. "But most interesting of all has been your satchel. We finally got it open—and what a collection you have there. Makes me nostalgic for the days when we could have poisoned you for sorcery. Don't worry, the Council are meeting in emergency session right now, figuring out what to do with you instead."

Yeah, that really put Siyon's concerns to rest. He'd had just about enough of this. "If you're here to gloat," he said to the door, "you're doing a shit job. You're supposed to sound smug. Didn't you learn anything, running as a freeblade?"

The words surprised Siyon even as they came out of his mouth. When had he learned that about Avarair? He remembered Izmirlian mentioning his brother's skill with a blade, but surely they hadn't spoken *that* much about it.

"But what I'm really curious about," Avarair said, as though Siyon hadn't spoken. "What I *really* want to ask you about, is how in the Abyss you came to have one of my brother's journals in your possession."

From the corridor came a scrape of paper and leather, as of someone flipping a notebook open.

Siyon scrambled back up the doorframe, dragging his face to the gap so he could look down at Avarair Hisarani.

Who had Izmirlian's journal in his hands. *That* one. The one Siyon had been writing in. The one in which Izmirlian had been writing back.

Panic bit at him, and anger too. It wasn't his to look at. It was private. It was *theirs*.

The old hippodrome rattled faintly, every stone of it tremouring against the next.

Just for half a blink, before Siyon clamped down on the plane, on the energy, on his own emotions. His vision burned bronze for a moment, and then it was clear again, just Avarair and the notebook in his hands. Dislodged dust drifted down from the ceiling, but he didn't seem to notice.

Too busy sneering. "Are you *that* sentimental about him? To keep his maudlin self-indulgent scribbles?"

Avarair flipped through the pages dismissively, swiping past Izmirlian's careful drawings and keen observations, not caring about any of it, and brushing through the final pages.

Which were—all of them, every one in front of Siyon's disbelieving eyes—absolutely blank.

He let out a dull little sound, and Avarair looked up. "Does this make you feel *closer* to him, even after he abandoned you, like he abandoned every duty he'd ever had?"

Siyon couldn't have answered, even if he'd wanted to. He couldn't stop staring at the journal in Avarair's hands.

Those blank pages. Those blank pages that had *not* been at all blank, when he'd last closed the journal on Izmirlian's impossible words.

Had Siyon *imagined* it? Had it only happened in his head? But Jaleh had seen the writing as well, hadn't she?

"Hey!" Avarair's flash of anger pulled his face farther from Izmirlian's than ever. "I'm talking to you!"

Lost as Siyon was, he knew the answer to that. Knew the answer to any question in that tone, from someone like Avarair Hisarani. He'd never be too far gone in floundering not to have it readily to hand.

"Get fucked," he said.

And dropped back down into his cell, even as something hard bounced off the door, rattling the hinges. Siyon took two hurried steps back, setting his feet, rolling out his shoulders. Ready in case Avarair was pissed off enough to ignore his previous good sense. Laxmi might not be at his beck and call anymore, but Siyon had plenty of dirty, angry violence of his own.

Part of him hoped Avarair would come in. Fuck that strange edge to his voice, like he was still nervous and irritated about something. Fuck his brittle attempts at beating the brother who was long gone. Fuck *him*.

But the noises from the corridor were faint. Perhaps the sound of a book being picked up again. The sound of footsteps retreating.

Louder was the laughter rolling out of the opposite cell. "Maybe you're one of us after all," Mezin called.

"Fuck you too," Siyon called back.

He curled up again on his narrow cot, more alone than he'd felt in weeks.

Anahid didn't get back to Sable House until after the midday bell, hurrying through empty streets where the air hung still and hushed. It felt like the nervous days after Enkin Danelani went missing.

"Did I miss a curfew announcement?" Anahid asked the man who ushered her through the District delivery gate.

He kept one hand on his heavy staff. "Nothing official. But the city is nervous. Aghut's got people on the Swanneck, and there are crowds up around the old hippodrome, I heard. After everything else..." He shook his head and nudged Anahid along.

She hurried past quiet corner discussions and watchful knots of Flowers. None of them knew what sunset would bring. Would anyone welcome frivolity in the face of destruction and monsters? Or would the shards of Midnight's gang see this as an opportunity to push harder while the inqs were distracted?

The District needed a firm hand, now more than ever. They needed a baron. For other reasons too—with the Council meeting already, even in emergency session, Buni Filosani's interest in a new arrangement became more pressing.

None of it was Anahid's business. Except someone had *made* it her business, with three knives lying in wait in her office.

Nura met Anahid on the stairs, saying only: "She's awake."

Laxmi was sitting up in her bed, shovelling baked eggs and

vegetables into her mouth. Occasionally she'd pause to scratch irritably at the bandaging around her ribs, exposed by the almost lewd disarray of a robe clearly borrowed from one of the Flowers. She still looked hale and hefty; the little attic bedroom seemed smaller than ever with Laxmi in it, taking up far more space than simply the physical. But there were hollows beneath her yellow eyes and her cheeks were nearly as pale as the sheets.

Something twisted in Anahid's chest, to see her this close to weakness. But the frantic bird fluttering at her ribs stilled. She'd *seen* the knife go into Laxmi. Heard it too, which had been somehow even worse.

She wasn't going to lose Laxmi. Not yet.

As Anahid sagged in the doorway, Laxmi smirked and cupped a hand around her ear expectantly.

So Anahid said it: "You were right."

"Too fucking right, I was." Laxmi went back to scraping the sauce from her dish. "So now you're going to do as I tell you, and we'll make sure they can't get at you again."

"At you, actually." Anahid settled onto the rickety seat at Laxmi's bedside. She smiled tightly at Laxmi's quizzical look, but first said, "Are you quite well? Feeling any pain? Qorja tells me the healer was quite complimentary about your physique, but you *are* human now, and our bodies have their frailties."

"I'm fine," Laxmi snapped. "He smeared some shit on me that itches like kelp lice, but it sure is healing. What do you *mean*, at me?"

Anahid took her dish and held on to it. Something for her hands to do that wasn't far too improper, like smoothing back the sweat-damp hair at Laxmi's temple, or twitching at the fall of that robe. "I think it's quite obvious that they weren't here for me. I didn't even know two of them were there until *you* came in. Perhaps I was just bait, or perhaps they were assuming you would be the first into the office, as you'd have preferred, I'm sure. But *you're* the weight that's been causing trouble in the District, Laxmi. You're the threat."

Laxmi's frown deepened with every word. "They should have sent more people, then. I'll show them a threat."

"No," Anahid said, short and sharp. "You will not." Laxmi's eyebrows went up, but Anahid did not pause for interruption. "This isn't your fight. I know you don't care, that you just enjoy the struggle. And that's part of why. You have more worth than merely as a weapon. There are other strengths than that of the knife. I refuse to play by their rules."

She took a breath, left a space now, but Laxmi just watched her, leaning forward a little. Golden eyes on Anahid's mouth, as though waiting for the words that came next.

What came next was: "I am going to make new rules. I am going to make a threat so large it can't be cut to shreds or beaten down."

Laxmi's mouth twitched. "What does *that* mean?"

"I don't quite know yet," Anahid admitted, and felt a smile tug at her lips. She *should* be terrified about this. She was stepping out of the corner where she'd barricaded herself. But it hadn't been safe there. Not for her. Not for the people she cared about. "There needs to be someone. Or some*thing*. But I won't be the baron. I won't live with that knife in my hands. Not even if it's you. I'm sorry, Laxmi, but I won't."

Laxmi tilted her head, considering Anahid. "You won't let yourself." Her tone was almost gentle.

"But there must be something," Anahid stated. "We all have an interest in it. So perhaps..." She was starting to see how it would work, like sitting at the carrick table and knowing who was bluffing, and who played true. But in this hand, they needn't all play *against* each other. "Perhaps there can be another way. A way that leads to *less* violence, rather than more."

Laxmi rolled her eyes. "Boring," she sang.

Her teasing smile was a new relief. "I'm aware," Anahid said, feeling for gentle words, unsure if she was wary of bruising Laxmi, or herself. "That what I'm proposing may not be your idea of fun."

She would feel the loss of Laxmi, Anahid realised, if the fallen demon didn't want to play along. She'd felt the loss, when the knife went in. She'd felt *bereft*. She wanted Laxmi at her side. Not for the protection. For *Laxmi*.

But she wasn't the one who got to decide that. Laxmi was her own woman now—not a demon bound to anyone's service or obedience.

"Are you kicking me out?" Laxmi asked, entirely nonchalant. But her hand clenched on the sheet, nails curled tight as talons.

"Of course not." Anahid looked up, and was caught by the golden glow of Laxmi's gaze, clinging like honey. "You'll always have a place with me," she said, without entirely intending to.

Laxmi's hand relaxed its grip on the sheet and lifted toward her. "Anahid."

A knock rapped at the little room's door—brisk, no-nonsense, and familiar.

Anahid turned aside, and wondered what on earth this flush was in her cheeks. "Yes, Nura?"

The door opened, and Nura glanced between them—Anahid's flush inexplicably deepened. "The third man is awake, mistress."

The one of Laxmi's attackers left alive. Anahid leapt to her feet and then turned back to press at Laxmi's shoulder as the woman shoved back the covers.

"I'm coming too," Laxmi snarled up at her.

"I may get further," Anahid growled right back, "if he thinks he was successful."

Laxmi stopped her struggle, thinking about that, and Anahid became abruptly aware that the business of restraint had brought her very close indeed. Near enough that Laxmi's ink-dark hair brushed her knuckles, and when Laxmi tilted up to look at her—amused as though she'd noticed too—they were breathing the same air.

"Come straight back," Laxmi ordered, not quite a purr. "And tell me all about it."

Anahid straightened, cleared her throat, and followed Nura out.

They'd put the surviving thug in a small locked storeroom in the basement of Sable House, not far from the cold room where Imelda's body had lain. There wasn't room for a bed, so the man—bruised and injured as he was—slumped on the cold stone floor.

Coming straight from Laxmi's recovery, Anahid found it hard to muster too much sympathy for the man.

His hands were bound with hempen twine. The doctor had cleaned up his face and the new gaps where he'd lost teeth from Laxmi's blow to the chin. *This* was the one who'd stabbed her, Anahid recalled.

She was doubly glad she'd not allowed Laxmi to come down as well.

He was awake and alert enough, his gaze running over Anahid, before moving on to Qorja and Lejman. The room was crowded, with four of them in here, but Anahid wanted that. Wanted *him* to feel outnumbered and alone.

"What?" He ran a nervous tongue over the split in his lip. "Time to turn me over to the inqs?"

"Hoping for it? Does your employer have a deal to winkle you out?" Anahid shrugged. "They've come and gone. There were two bodies to be dealt with, after all."

A flicker on his face, at the confirmed fate of his associates. Or perhaps at the news that the inqs wouldn't be taking him. Didn't, perhaps, even know about him.

Anahid smiled and folded her hands over her sash. "Just us now."

Behind her, Lejman shifted with a creak of his leather armour over his bulky shoulders. Laxmi wasn't the only threat in this House. She was just the flashiest.

The man huffed a little laugh that sounded more like surrender than mirth. "Yeah, look: I don't know who's picking up the tab. Word's out all over, that there's plenty of rivna in messing up this House. In fucking up the Harpy."

"The who?" Qorja sounded startled.

But Anahid knew. "That's what they call her in the fighting ring."

The man looked up at her, like eye contact could convince of his sincerity. "But I didn't make the deal for this job. I was just along because Sten thought another knife might be wise."

Part of Anahid wanted to object. To wring the price of her own fear out of him. To bring Laxmi down here after all and let her have whatever revenge she wanted. Perhaps his memory might improve.

When she merely made an impatient noise and turned on her heel, she saw emotion flash across his face—worry, fear, panic.

He considered all of that likely.

But he didn't call her back. In the basement corridor, with the door locked again behind all of them, Anahid forced her breathing even. "You believe him?"

Lejman inclined his head, his beaded braids clicking gently. "I've had people out asking, and had similar whispers back. There's no name attached. That checks out."

"I believe it more than any name he gave up easily," Qorja agreed, though she didn't look happy about it. "There are certainly plenty of free agents on the streets, at present."

And—thanks partly to Laxmi's machinations—plenty of former Midnight agents who viewed Anahid, and Laxmi, as potential impediments to their plans. Anahid winced in frustration, rubbing at her forehead. "It may not even have been a proper job, just a misunderstanding about complaints against our interference."

"Oh no," interjected a new voice from the top of the stairs. "It was a real job."

Anahid whirled about, as Peylek came swaggering down, with Nura just behind her. Midnight's lieutenant smiled tightly, tipping a nod each to Qorja and Lejman before turning an almost assessing gaze on Anahid.

But the next thing she said was: "Is it true they've taken Siyon Velo?"

Anahid probably should have expected that. Peylek had only come to her in the first place to get to Siyon, however well things had turned out for them both. "I saw him arrested and marched away," Anahid admitted.

Nura's eyes widened. Behind Anahid, Qorja gasped: "What? That really happened? I thought it was another wild tale."

Bezim was made of wild tales, this season.

Peylek nodded, like the worst had been confirmed for her. "What are you going to do about it?" she demanded.

As though there were anything Anahid *could* do. She wasn't even an azata anymore, not really.

Though she had the ear of those who were. Of those seeking stability in the city, even with the barons. "I am going to work to strengthen the elements of the Council who have no interest in punishing Siyon,"

Anahid answered. Would there be enough time? For them to strike a deal with Buni Filosani, for her to use that to build support among the azatani, for any of it to lean on Siyon's side of the scales?

Peylek pulled a face, thoroughly frustrated, and Anahid snapped: "We can hardly break him out of custody. An attack on the inquisitors? On the Council? What will *that* do to the city?"

For a moment, Peylek weighed the question, as though it might yet be worth it. Anahid was glad Laxmi wasn't here, also eager to break and snatch.

"Fine," Peylek grumbled, dragging a hand over the russet stubble on her scalp. "But push hard. I don't know what happens to any of us if he falls now." Her eyes looked almost haunted; Anahid wasn't sure why. But then Peylek waved an absent hand and added: "The contract for offing your lady warrior came from a broker. Former Zinedani thug, usually works out of a teahouse near the top of the Scarp, but no one's seen him today."

Lejman grunted behind Anahid. "I know the man, mistress. I'll set people to find him."

If he hadn't been gotten rid of, like so many others who had disappeared recently.

Anahid shook her head. "No. It doesn't matter who wanted us quiet and out of the way. They won't get their wish. And I haven't time to bother with them. There's too much to do."

She had a District to take in hand, and a new kind of baron to make. Something that worked for all of them. Something all of them could work for. Something different.

Anahid looked up at Peylek, consideringly. "I have a proposal."

CHAPTER 17

Prolonged bed rest was out of the question; Zagiri was alive, when so many weren't, and she needed to make that count. At least her half day in bed, drifting in and out of a not-quite-feverish doze, gave her plenty of time to think.

Justice wasn't often a simple business, but at present Zagiri suspected that the Council would prefer it to be so—which meant blaming as much as they could upon Siyon, who was already in their custody.

The truth couldn't be relied upon to float, not in such stormy seas. Zagiri knew what had happened at the Ball, who was responsible, that there was more lurking behind it. How could she build that into a raft, and sail it into harbour?

She'd meant what she said to Yeva: She'd stand up and tell all about what they'd done. But only if that would *achieve* something other than airing her own guilt. At the moment, it might only play into the hands of Avarair Hisarani and the rest of the Pragmatics. Zagiri's association with Siyon was well-known, and she could easily be painted as his accomplice.

Unless—Zagiri realised, waking in clarity to the delicate light of dawn staining her bedroom ceiling—*unless* she turned herself in to the right person. Someone who asked hard questions, and demanded justice, even if it discomfited the azatani or would be more sensible to stop.

A sign of how strange things had become that instead of laughing at the idea, she struggled into a dress, grabbed a pastry from the breakfast room, and walked up to the old hippodrome.

The nearby streets were strangely quiet, even for this hour of the morning. But the approach to the hippodrome entrance itself was clogged with people, two groups facing off across the square.

Behind those on the seaward side, someone had pinned a banner to the building. It read: *Sorcerer save us.* The landward group carried a tall pole bearing a scarecrow in a bright purple coat, surrounded by bright felt tongues of red and orange.

Outrage sparked in Zagiri's chest. They didn't even burn people in Bezim! Poison was far more humane, even if you no longer believed in the old Lyraec superstition about curses attaching to spilled blood.

She was pleased to see that the *pro*-Siyon group was at least twice as large as the *anti* group. But quiet as the water seemed now, the air was heavy with the anticipation of a great and roiling boil to come.

Zagiri slipped between the groups, to the nervous-looking white-tunicked guard at the hippodrome gate. "I need to speak with Cap— Lieutenant Xhanari."

It was as easy as that; they ushered her inside, summoned an escort, apologised for the *rabble*. Zagiri touched the beading on her headscarf, her magical symbol of being azatani.

The escort apologised further for the dilapidated state of the corner of the old stables that now housed the Special Crisis Task Force. Zagiri hadn't realised Xhanari had been demoted so thoroughly. What a coincidence; he could so easily have accidentally run into Anahid, in the Flower district.

The rest of the make-do office was empty, and Xhanari himself was clearly preparing to leave. But he paused in the buttoning of his plain coat, took in her face and her headscarf, and gave a little nod. "How may I assist you, Azata Savani?"

Just as stiff as ever. Just as proper. Just what she needed. Zagiri waited a moment, for her escort to hurry off again, before she said simply: "I know who attacked the Ball—"

That was where Xhanari interrupted her. "We already have Mezin Velo in custody, though I am curious as to where you acquired your information."

Zagiri gaped at him. "Mezin *Velo*," she repeated.

Zin. Mezin. Another member of the Velo fisherclan, the Dockside relations that Siyon was so loath to speak about. Every time Zagiri had thought he looked familiar now flashed back through her memory. She could *kick* herself. Had he been laughing at her this whole time?

"You didn't know," Xhanari diagnosed, watching her closely. "Who were *you* going to accuse?"

She shook her head. "No, I—I knew him as just *Zin*." And they had him already in custody? "How did *you* find him?" There was absolutely no reason why he should tell her, of course. Zagiri's plan now tangled around her, choking her with panic. Had Zin already dumped *her* in it? Or did no one care what he had to say when his name delivered all the guilt they needed? Mezin *Velo*. "They're blaming Siyon."

Xhanari's mouth pressed tight, just a twitch. "More alchemical explosives were found in a Cliffside apartment rented to Mezin Velo."

Cliffside, where Zagiri had met with Yeva and Zin. Where Zin had said he had a *backer*. It was all so neatly tucked together.

Like it had been arranged that way.

Xhanari was still watching her; he hadn't brushed this aside and left already. "You don't believe any of that," Zagiri realised.

He cleared his throat and straightened some files on his desk. "That investigation isn't within my remit," he said casually. "And I have been warned more than once about staying within the bounds of my assigned duties."

But he *didn't* believe it. He knew there was more to be discovered. It burned within him like the last coal in the dying fireplace.

Zagiri took a breath and did what she'd come here to do. "The explosives were about this size—" She lifted her hands to demonstrate, and her fingers didn't even tremble. "And wrapped tightly in high-quality waxed paper, very even. Sealed with red wax. All of them the same, perfectly made. *Expensively* made. I'm pretty sure they were manufactured by someone in the Summer Club. Zin—*Mezin*—said he had a backer. That's how we could afford such good-quality material." She lifted her chin and met Xhanari's black gaze. "I let him into the Eldren Hall, during the final rehearsal for the Ball. I wanted— it doesn't matter. This is all my fault, and I won't rest until *everyone* responsible is facing justice."

He hadn't expected that, though the only sign was the slightest widening of his eyes. The next moment, Xhanari tapped the lantern on his desk, plunging them into darkness. "My shift is over. I should be leaving." But even as she opened her mouth, frustrated words hot on her tongue, he added, "Why don't you walk with me?"

They left through a small side gate, unattended by those protesting either for or against Siyon, though the wind carried the rhythmic chant of voices. Zagiri glanced down toward the main gate, where there were milling bodies, and raised placards.

"The crowds are smaller than yesterday," Xhanari noted, leading her away into the narrow streets. "But they aren't leaving. The Council needs to act."

Act on Siyon, he meant. Zagiri didn't think either group outside the hippodrome would accept simply being told the matter was resolved. They'd want to see it happen.

That's what mattered in Bezim, after all. As Balian had told her. It was all about the show and the story.

Xhanari had a stride almost as long as Anahid's; Zagiri fell into a familiar quick pace to keep up, hugging her injured arm close to her body. "Here's what I know," he said, clipped and curt as they went. "If Mezin Velo were living in Cliffside, he could not have been working his family's fishing boats, and therefore would not have been paid. He couldn't have afforded the rent in Cliffside."

Zagiri remembered seeing Xhanari there, when she was meeting with Yeva and Zin; he *lived* there. He knew what it cost. "So who owns the apartment rented to him?"

But Xhanari shook his head. "It's mostly azatani-owned, out

240

there, administered through agents and managers. Who offered the information that led to the discovery would be more interesting, but marked in the files merely as *anonymous community complaint*."

He'd already read the files. Zagiri couldn't help a smug smile as she hurried along beside him. The smile faded as she realised what that *anonymous* complaint likely signified. "He was set up to take the blame for this all along." His *backer* had wanted chaos—possibly not the Ball itself, but *something* to cause fear and concern—and wanted someone immediately to hand to blame for it. Had they known who Mezin was? Who he was related to? Had that been a part of their plan?

"I also know," Xhanari continued, "that the explosives as recorded in the evidence files are not at all consistent with what I know of the work of Siyon Velo who"—and he glanced sidelong at Zagiri—"I am sure you'll agree is rather more slipshod than precise in his approach to most things."

A loyal part of Zagiri wanted to protest that Siyon always tried his best. She swallowed against it, as they turned down the Boulevard, heading toward the commercial district. "So you agree with me? They're probably Summer Club made?"

Xhanari steered them into the commercial district, where the shops were starting to open, though the streets were still very quiet. "The third thing I know," he said, as though she hadn't asked any questions at all, "is that *I* will get no answers if I march into the Summer Club and demand them."

He came to a stop, and Zagiri looked up at a familiar black door in a respectable brick building, with that little plaque engraved: *Summer*.

Vartan Xhanari, who'd led the raid on the Summer Club, before he'd been kicked out of the alchemy division of the inquisitors entirely.

Zagiri touched at her headscarf, the beading cool beneath her fingers. "What if you stand next to me while *I* ask the questions?"

He very nearly smiled as he held the door open for her.

When Zagiri had first come here with Siyon, they'd gone around to the back, but she was an azata now. The steward at the front desk greeted her with great politeness.

But not much assistance. "I'm afraid the charter is quite precise that for the safety of members, the general public, and indeed the entire city, there are to be *no* visitors on the premises save those signed in properly by a member in good standing."

Zagiri gave him an Anahid sort of smile. "Of course. Could you send someone for Nihath Joddani?"

She was sure he would be here, though when he came down he was, almost inevitably, still reading a book, only glancing up when he stumbled at the bottom of the stairs. He blinked behind his glasses—once at Zagiri, twice at Xhanari. "Miss Savani. And, uh, Captain."

"It's Lieutenant now," Xhanari replied, with almost brutal equanimity. "And I think you mean *Azata* Savani."

Nihath blinked at her again.

It hardly mattered right now. "We have an alchemical puzzle that needs unravelling," Zagiri told him. "So I immediately thought of you."

The flattery worked, or maybe Zagiri was being uncharitable and Nihath would have helped regardless. He even closed his book entirely, without a finger marking his place.

Xhanari produced a folded piece of paper from inside his coat that turned out to be the evidence report on the explosives—when had he grabbed *that*?

Nihath peered at the detailed specifications of the devices that had been recovered—in pieces from the Eldren Hall, and whole from the apartment. "Oh, what exemplary utilisation of Negedi's third principle of energy thresholds," he effused. "The wrapping is seagrass paper, I assume, which permits a cyclical build-up of propulsive force to reach the shatter point calibrated by the waxing." He nudged his glasses back up his nose. "Some sort of mining device, was it? Clearing out the mess under the Palace?"

No real way to be gentle about it, so Zagiri just told him. "These were used to blow up the Ball."

His mouth dropped open, and the page slipped out of his fingers; Xhanari caught it before it hit the carpet. "The Ball was blown up?"

"Where have you *been*?" Zagiri demanded, though the answer was clear—he'd been here, in the hush, and the isolation, and the endless books like sand in which to bury his head.

Nihath collapsed a little, wearing an echo of the chagrin a school-boy might for being told off about daydreaming.

Zagiri snatched the page from Xhanari before he could object, and thrust it back in front of Nihath. "Can you tell us who made it?"

"I, ah..." He seemed uncertain, but Nihath was reliably incapable of not being a know-it-all. He was soon talking his way through possibilities aloud—there were a dozen practitioners capable of this, but some of them weren't in Bezim at the moment, and another would *never* use red, for ridiculous superstitious reasons, and as the wrappings were conducted *this* way around, it suggested a dominant left hand, which meant—

Azatan Diryani wasn't anyone Zagiri thought she'd met before, but he was so entirely generic—in his simply patterned longvest, neatly trimmed hair, and plain azatani features—that she couldn't quite be sure. He had a lens squashed in one squinting eye socket, and he greeted them with: "Look, is this absolutely urgent, only I've really got to finish these diorite samples?"

"Afraid so," Xhanari said blandly, nudging his coat aside so that the candle badge of the inquisitors caught the light. "We need to speak with you regarding a shipment you provided to—"

"Commission," Diryani corrected absently. "I'm not some manufactory, to produce *shipments*. I practice the Art."

"We need to see your records," Xhanari pushed on, "regarding this."

Diryani looked at the evidence sheet as it was held up, even as he said, "I don't keep records; I just told you, I'm not..." He trailed off, eyes skittering over the details of the report. His jaw went slack, his eyes wide. "Oh, ink and ashes. *These* were used at the Eldren Hall? But I only deal with *reputable* people! I don't take commissions from Dockside riffraff!"

"Which reputable person," Xhanari asked, the words taking on a sharp edge of disdain in his mouth, "commissioned *this*?"

"I don't know," Diryani wailed. "I don't keep...But it couldn't have...Not any of *my*...Perhaps it was stolen?"

There was nothing useful to be found here. Nothing to say, standing on the steps of the Summer Club, the door closed behind them again.

"Why?" Zagiri demanded. "Why would any azatani want that to happen?"

Xhanari sighed, buttoning up his coat. "Why did you?" As she gaped at him, he continued: "Because you thought you could achieve your objectives through these means, be they ever so unsavory. Because you thought they were *tools*." He gave her that nod again, precisely correct. "Good day, azata."

For she was, after all, one of them. She'd worked hard to be so.

The rushing energy of the Mundane, churning within the bounds of Bezim, never slept. It was waiting for Siyon when he did, just beneath the surface, eager and clinging. If he slipped too deep, he could feel the edges of it catching at him, pulling him in, ready to wash him away.

Every time he jerked awake to the stone ceiling of his hippodrome cell, Siyon wondered if it might not be almost a relief to drown.

He rolled off the cot and paced the narrow confines of the cell. It didn't really help. By the third circuit of the little room, Siyon's senses were starting to crawl between the stones, wriggle into the earth, seep out to the streets and the energy that simmered there.

There were people out there. A lot of them. Siyon could hear them even in his cell—or he thought he could, but perhaps he was using a different sense. A constant low murmur, as though of a distant sea with chanting waves. *Magic rise, people rise.* Or perhaps simply *Monstrous.*

Somewhere, people were debating what to do with him. About him. To him. It seemed the least important thing to consider. What were the monsters doing, out beyond the city's barrier? Had they fled the depot or settled in to stay? Were there more on the way? Did anything Siyon had set in motion with the practitioners of the city matter at all?

He couldn't tell, from in here.

Or perhaps he *could*, if he just stretched out. Just a little more. Lean out over the river. Don't fear falling in. Was this what it was coming to? Him, or the city.

Siyon stopped pacing when he started to feel that perhaps his steps could sink into the hard-packed dirt floor. He lay down again on the cot and closed his eyes. His fingers twitched for something to do. If only he had his satchel. If only he had Izmirlian's journal.

If only the words were still there to give him comfort.

Siyon heard again Avarair sneering: *Are you that sentimental about him?*

Yes, Siyon was. A weakness. A wallowing. A wish.

Instead, he sank—into sleep, and into the dark. Even as he clung to himself, *insisted* on himself, he was still pulled along, bumping and buffeting against the world.

The Sorcerer, said a storyteller in the central square of a Lyraec village, beneath the long spreading branches of a parasol pine.

The Sorcerer, called a turbaned news-crier on the bustling corner of a Khanate town.

The Sorcerer, whispered a white-haired woman, pen scratching across paper, overlooking a waterfall chasm surrounded by a city Siyon did not know at all.

He was there, in every mention. He was trapped more surely than he was within this stone cell. He belonged to every single one of them.

They pulled him down deeper still.

The Sorcerer, the dragon thought, wrapped around the peak of a mountain like a fur stole around an azata's shoulders. She laughed and sent drifts of snow shivering down the mountainside. More blew all around her, whiting out the sky, descending like fog between her and the other mountains around them.

Now you know, Siyon heard—or felt, or perhaps thought himself. He wasn't really here, and yet he *was*, more here than he was anywhere else in the world. *Now you know what it's like. Wait a few hundred years. It's not so long.*

Siyon looked around her—snow and stone and clouds and ice. *You're alone*, he realised.

She had been, almost every time he'd seen her. She was always alone. Alone in the cavern, before he released her. Alone in the sky, flying away. Alone now, in the wildernesses of the world.

Because you choose them. The dragon snarled, lashing out with her tail, and slipped on the mountain's peak. Her talons ripped into stone, and the noise echoed off the peaks around them, sent snow and stone shaking free.

Sent Siyon bouncing away like a pebble skipped on a calm sea.

Of course she was alone. Who could match her? Who could understand? Who wouldn't look upon her and quail with fear?

The Sorcerer, the world murmured, whirling beneath him.

"Siyon!"

He blinked, and winced, shading his eyes from the piercing light clutched in someone's hand. Fingers curled like talons around the glaring whiteness, and Siyon remembered a scream on the wind, wings against a burning sky, the shriek of a vengeful angel.

"Olenka," he croaked.

She shifted, and now she was just a woman with her hair pulled back severely, holding up a lantern that burned after so long in the dark. She put it down beside his narrow cot. "Well, you've fucked up comprehensively this time."

Siyon managed to pull his feet up before Olenka sat on them. The cot certainly wasn't big enough for the two of them, but she sighed like the load her feet had been carrying was more than merely her weight. She scratched at her head, and some tight dirty-blonde curls sprang out of their restraint, fizzing around her face.

It certainly didn't seem like she was here to drag him off to anything.

"I barely remember the Empyreal plane," she said thoughtfully, staring at the open door of Siyon's cell. "Funny, that. I was decades old, as you count things here, and yet it all feels a blur. Sand slipping through my fingers. Not as vivid as humanity." She finally looked at Siyon. Her piercing pale eyes seemed almost soft. "They're putting you on trial. Day after tomorrow. In public, for all to see."

Of course they were. The only surprise Siyon could really summon was that they were bothering. But the process mattered, in Bezim. The story they told themselves was that this city was fair.

Everyone must see the Sorcerer conquered by law and order.

He had to swallow hard before he could say: "What's going to happen, when they kill me?"

"They may not," Olenka objected quickly, but when he just looked at her, her mouth twisted. "I don't know. The things you've made will likely come unravelled. The way the plane has rebuilt itself around you will dissolve again. Last time—so my elders told me—it took a long time. But the last Alchemist before you had held the role for..."

Siyon smiled bleakly. "A lot longer than half a year, I'm guessing." And probably hadn't felt like they were wrestling an eel the entire time. Coming unravelled. Dissolving. What had he even *made*? The city boundary, of course. "Maybe it's for the best. The monsters will go back to sleep, the magic will stop flowing, alchemy will be manageable again... The barrier around the city can come down, and whoever tries next can do a better job of everything."

"Siyon," Olenka said, like a sigh. Sounding disappointed, like always, but perhaps not *only* with him. "It's not as bad as all that. You dealt with the sea monster. Even the depot monsters were gone when the sun came up. You've solved other problems. You can solve these."

That almost made him laugh. As though frantically stamping out fires meant he could stop a spinning wheel of fireworks. He hadn't yet. He didn't know where to start. "Can't if they kill me."

If they couldn't look at him without fear and panic. If they shoved him out.

Alone on a mountain peak.

He blinked, and Olenka was gone again, lantern and all. Had Siyon slipped back into sleep? He was still sitting up, his back cradled against the stone wall.

You can solve these, Olenka had said, with all the certainty of the Empyreal plane from which she'd fallen. He was less certain, but she made him wonder. Made his thoughts turn that way, to the burnished dome he'd laid over the city, curved around it all.

Siyon reached up toward it...

And slipped into the flow of energy, whisking him away, pulling him under, even as he traced his senses along the inside of the barrier dome. He was anywhere, everywhere, nowhere. He wished he could tell Izmirlian—*show* Izmirlian—but the journals were out of reach, out of reality, perhaps never real at all. Was Siyon's mind coming apart at the seams? Thinking he could fly with the dragon. Imagining places he'd never seen. Feeling like Izmirlian was close enough to touch, and if he just reached a little more, stretched out just so...

His fingers grazed at the edge of something—the barrier, or some other boundary, hooking around and tugging...

Skittering sidelong, into darkness. True darkness, the deepest darkness.

The void.

Not what he wanted. Not where he needed to be.

But even as Siyon turned, reaching toward the familiar burnished rush of the Mundane, something hooked into his collar—or perhaps directly into his soul—and hauled him back.

A voice like an angry can of bees snarled, "Well, *finally*."

Siyon blinked, and blinked again, forcing his mind to scrape together sense from the absence around him. He'd done this before, with Izmirlian dying in his arms. He could do it again now.

The Demon Queen unfurled like several nightmares braided together, in loops of black-scaled snake body, the slash of taloned hands, the gleam of golden eyes.

"Did you summon me here?" Siyon asked, actually curious. Could they do that? He'd met all the Powers here in the void, when he'd become the Power of the Mundane himself, but that had seemed like special circumstances.

"Not quite, but you strayed close enough to snag my hook." The Queen grinned—another horror of too many, and too sharp, teeth. "The hook you gave me, or have you forgotten your promise? You owe me twice over, Velo. Where is my warrior, hmm? Where is my favourite blade whom I lent to your aid?"

"Ah." Siyon tried frantically to remember precisely what deal had been done there. He'd been rather more focused on the not-dying part—from the rage of the Demon Queen, or that of Prefect Danelani—than the details. "She's still here. Not here here, but—"

"You think I didn't feel her fall?" The Demon Queen was abruptly closer, her breath clawing sulphurous at Siyon's face, for all that neither of them really *had* faces here. "You owe me for her aid, and you owe me for her loss, and you owe me your power."

Siyon felt something teeter—beneath him, around him, within him. As though her claim had claws sharper than her own. As though it mattered. But he didn't stand alone, and the Mundane came bubbling up through the cracks of him, bronzed and thick as tar. "I owe you thanks," Siyon countered.

"You owe me something dear to you," the Queen returned, her voice a low rasp, like sand insinuating into a crack. "You owe me something magnificent, and unequaled, and powerful."

Siyon wouldn't have let Laxmi hear him do it, but he could admit she was all of that.

"Even your life is not unfettered," she muttered, rustling around him, tongue flickering in the darkness, grazing his forehead where the touch burned. "So many claims on it. So many grasping hands. But ... Ah. Yes. Give me *him*. Your memories. Your yearning. *Izmirlian*."

Siyon flinched, and she laughed, looping her tail around him, coiling and caressing. "Yes," she hissed. "Why struggle on with them? They are weight to carry. They hold you back, keep you from your true purpose. Give them to me, so deliciously bittersweet, and I will call us even."

For a moment—a moment that might have been an eternity here, between the planes—Siyon considered it. He could move on, as Izmirlian quite literally had. No more clinging. No more wallowing. No more wishing things had been different.

No more keen observation. No more wry humour. No more Izmirlian. No more memories of the brief time they'd shared.

"No," Siyon said, and shoved the Demon Queen away.

Shoved hard enough that he felt the void start to fray around him.

In the disintegrating darkness, she made a harsh rattling—of scales and scorn and displeasure. "Then you will *fight*. Stop selling yourself so cheaply. Make them pay. *Fight*, Power of the Mundane. That is my price."

Siyon fell out of his narrow cot, in his stone cell. Hands and knees on the stone, and the breath coming harsh in his throat. *Fight*.

He wanted to. He didn't want to die. He didn't want to let go of any part of who he was.

But he couldn't help thinking that what the Demon Queen wanted—what she demanded—was rarely good for anyone else.

CHAPTER 18

It was more difficult than ever, with the Flower district on tenter-hooks, to arrange a casual meeting. But that was just why Anahid couldn't call upon anyone formally. She had much to ask of the managers of the District; she wasn't going to start off by asking them to officially welcome the women who'd been attacked in her own House.

What Anahid needed was just that casual meeting. Qorja and Lejman had been asking delicate questions of their contacts in other Houses; Anahid set a handful of Peylek's people to watching the streets of the District and reporting back.

And she found herself lying in wait in the pleasure gardens for Master Attabel, who was taking his daily walk, which served as both exercise and advertisement for the refinement of the Siren's Cove. She hid from the wind in a little bower wreathed in star jasmine, where she could make Laxmi sit on the bench with her. It had been obvious that no force in the Mundane was going to keep Laxmi in bed for another day, but Anahid was certainly not letting her put strain on the healing stab wound.

"Worried about me, were you?" Laxmi asked, sprawling over the stone bench with an expression best described as a leer.

Anahid ignored her, leaning out to peer down the path. "Here he comes."

The star jasmine was thick with winter growth, also sheltering them from inquisitive eyes. Anahid was quite sure Attabel would appreciate the discretion, even if he had been the one to approach her previously, with his concerns and his gathering of other House managers. The troubled seas he'd mentioned to her had only grown more tumultuous.

So Anahid didn't take it personally that Attabel flinched back when she rose from amid the star jasmine. She merely waited, while he hesitated, and considered, and glanced around.

She *did* feel gratified that he stayed, coming to meet her. "I am so pleased to see you out and about, Lady Sable," he began. "I had heard such awful rumours. And is your more, ah, physical associate—?"

"I'm doing fine," Laxmi said from the shadow of the bench, and grinned at his startled twitch. She stretched ostentatiously in her leather armour—now patched with extra studs over the stab hole—and crossed her ankles. Being seen had been part of her argument for coming along. *Let everyone know that it takes far more than three men with knives to bring me down.*

The idea of someone trying again made Anahid furious and fearful. It stiffened her spine and pushed her forward with her plan. "I'm glad to have stumbled upon you," she said.

That earned a little smile from Attabel. As always, he was highly decorated, in billowing satin trousers and a gauzy tunic heavily embroidered with fish in a golden thread that matched his painted nails, and the gilding on his long eyelashes. "My dear Lady Sable, the pleasure is all mine. I have been wanting to thank you, for introducing me to that charming clerk. The acquaintance has been quite fruitful for me, though I must admit, not for all of our concerned associates."

Anahid could guess why. "The Zinedani are cutting the rent of major Houses like yours, but inviting the smaller ones to terminate if dissatisfied?"

Attabel gave a gilded but bitter smile. "You should go into fortune-telling."

"All they care about is the business. But there is more to being the baron of the District, isn't there?" Anahid smiled thinly at the careful lift of Attabel's eyebrows. "Which, yes, is why I'm here, but not in the way you might think."

"What other way is there?" he asked, with a showy spread of his gold-tipped fingers, and then blinked violently. "You can't be suggesting that *I*—" He couldn't even finish that, one hand on his chest as he grimaced.

She nearly laughed. "Yet you'd merrily suggest me for the role."

His eyes still wide, Attabel objected, "That's different. You..." She didn't help him out of his speechlessness, this time. Just waited until he finished: "You have already indicated a proclivity."

Laxmi snorted from her sprawl on the bench. "She's already offed the last fucker, is what you mean. Though actually, that was—"

"Not important," Anahid interrupted, with a sharp look at Laxmi, who just grinned in return. No one needed to know that it was actually Qorja who'd killed Garabed Zinedani. Let the weight land on Anahid; she was already carrying one murder. "I have no wish to continue or cultivate that *proclivity*, as you so charmingly term it. It is my deeply held wish to avoid violence altogether, though I am hardly stumbling along defenseless."

Taking her cue, Laxmi braced her hands on her knees in a way that made her arms flex and gleam. Rather distractingly ostentatious, really. Anahid forced her attention back to Attabel.

Who was looking thoughtful. "Then what is your proposal?" he asked, with curiosity rather than challenge. Good.

"I don't want to be baron," Anahid reiterated. "Nor do you. Nor, it must be observed, do the Zinedani. But we need someone in the role. Or something. Or, perhaps, all of us."

He blinked at her in a flutter of gold. "You..." His lips pursed, his brow furrowed—he was giving that sufficient consideration to risk appearing unflatteringly serious. "A *committee*," Attabel finally said. "What a remarkably azatani suggestion."

But he wasn't scoffing. He wasn't waving her away with one gilded hand.

"You're halfway there already, aren't you?" Anahid pointed out. "This *concerned citizens* group of yours is where we'll start. The barony of the District will be held in common, driven by the decisions of all interested parties. Everyone will contribute and benefit. Even the Zinedani can join in, if they wish."

That made him snort most indelicately. "There will be objections, and not just from them." Attabel glanced sidelong at Laxmi, who was making a good show of lazy unconcern with her head tipped back. "You'll need more muscle backing this proposal than just the Harpy here."

Laxmi's lips curved smugly at that name.

"I won't do this by violence," Anahid emphasised. "But yes, I can bring more backing to this proposal. The Zinedani are not the only baron to have abandoned their organisation."

His eyebrows went up again. "You think you can harness *Midnight's* people to this wild plan? They seem thoroughly invested in stirring the chaos to their own benefit."

"Some," Anahid corrected. "Not all. There are always those who would prefer stability and order. And who are prepared to hold firm in seeking it."

Attabel made a considering noise and tucked his hands inside his sleeves, though Anahid could hardly see such a flimsy garment providing any shelter against the winter breeze. "You'll come to our next meeting. Bring proof of this Midnight partnership. And we will see what comes of it."

Anahid stepped out of his path. "Thank you. I believe this will benefit all of us."

He sniffed and continued along his path, passing out of the bower and along the avenue of pencil pines.

From the bench, Laxmi grumbled, "I didn't even get to be threatening. Not really."

"You'll have your chances," Anahid predicted. However much she might prefer it otherwise. "And don't pretend you didn't enjoy preening."

Laxmi shifted on the bench, drawing Anahid's attention as she lolled even further, leather-clad knees spreading like her grin. "Don't pretend you didn't enjoy it just as much."

Anahid cleared her throat and checked down the avenue—where Attabel was now turning out of sight onto another path. She lifted her voice and called, "It's clear."

Peylek appeared from around the back of the bower with barely a rustle. She brushed her hood off the russet fuzz of her hair and gave Anahid a slanted look. "Bit presumptuous with our involvement there, weren't you? There's no agreement yet."

Anahid adopted an airy expression of mild concern, one she hadn't used since she'd stopped attending drawing room parties full of careful gossip, but it still came with the ease of practice when she needed it. "Oh, I must have misunderstood when you told me that you'd be on board if the House managers were going ahead with this."

The plant of Peylek's hands on her hips said she saw through Anahid's gullshit, but the twitch of her lips said she wasn't entirely angry about it. "What I said was that we *wouldn't* be on board if the managers weren't."

"Ah, my mistake." Anahid shrugged easily.

From the bench, Laxmi started to laugh.

Peylek's mouth twisted farther toward mirth. "There'll be arguments, at this gathering. They'll all be in a tizzy about it."

"They'll need reassurance," Anahid agreed. "They'll want to have as much say as they can, without taking on any responsibility. They'll be skittish about crossing the Zinedani, even now. They'll challenge my right to organise it at all, to be the figurehead, but in the end, none of them will want to speak with the other barons, or negotiate as one of them. And in the end, none of them will want to be left out, because there is no alternative to this other than further chaos." She smiled tightly. "Yes, this is a committee. It's also a negotiation. Both of those things are the water in which azatani swim. This *will* come to pass, if I have to drag them all along individually."

"Sure," Laxmi drawled. "*You'll* do the dragging."

"You'll sulk if there's nothing for you to do." Anahid flicked her a sidelong glance. Safer that way, with her grinning like that.

Peylek tilted her head. "Oh, I see. It's like that, is it? Maybe you *should* just take the job yourself."

Anahid's smile tilted toward satisfaction. "No, this will be better. You'll see."

She was sure of it. Sure in a way she hadn't felt since Salt Night. Sure in a way she'd missed. It felt good, to take action. The fear still laced her bones, but there was an edge to it like exhilaration.

She was *doing* something now. She had bought into the game. But she would change the rules. And she would *win*.

She needed to. There was no time to waste.

The business of the dead in Bezim was usually quiet and private. Not everyone followed the city traditions, even if they'd been here for generations; that was entirely their own business. There were the caves up on the crag for those who preferred interments, and platforms out in the hills for the various rites of the Khanate, and Zagiri had heard there were specialists in the city who could embalm in either the modern or ancient Lyraec traditions. But even the azatani, who otherwise made a minor performance of much of their lives, usually gave their dead to the sea in small and silent ceremonies.

Usually, three dozen of their number hadn't died in the same catastrophe, many of them newly flowering toward their adult lives. Even the tallying after Salt Night—when the dragon bursting out through the Palace of Justice had killed the prefect and her husband, along with many of their influential friends—hadn't seemed such a communal outrage.

Scant few azatani families were untouched by the Ball attack, but even they turned out to join the parade of mourning down to Dockside.

Zagiri walked with her parents, and the trio of girl cousins, who were in oblivious and endless tears over a school friend who'd been killed. One more stone weighing at Zagiri in this tangled and dragging net.

The heavy and sombre procession began in the Palace parkland, trailing down the Kellian Way past Tower Square, across the Swanneck, and down to the docks. It made a terrible, elongated echo of the promenade to the Harbour Master's Ball. It felt somehow final. As though there was nothing left, and they might all take ship into the Carmine Sea.

Their ancestors had allegedly done it before, fleeing the Old Kingdoms to come here in the first place. But Bezim was theirs now—named for it—and they would strangle it with the strength of their grip if they had to.

Zagiri had no idea how to stop it.

As they passed Tower Square, Zagiri caught a glimpse of someone under inquisitor supervision scrubbing at the tower face, where words had been painted: *No Sorcerer, no Bezim*. It buoyed her heart, to see support for Siyon, at the same time as it clenched her stomach with unease.

The city was simmering with tension, with a public trial announced for tomorrow. If someone tapped too hard on the straining edges of it, the whole thing might explode.

The azatani procession accumulated an audience; unlike the Ball-night promenade, there were no cheers, no joy, no merriment. The gathered shopkeepers and clerks and university students watched in silence. As they turned down into Dockside from the Swanneck crossing, the alleys were crammed with the harder faces of laborers and factory workers, watching with a sullenness that bordered on disdain, save where they turned to one another with mutterings and sidelong looks.

Down on the central quay, opposite the harbour master's office, the water was already bobbing with the bundled-up bodies of those earlier in the procession. The linen wrappings darkened with seawater, pulling the bodies down into the depths, activating the alchemical charms that would help turn the dead back into salt.

The Savanis, without a body of their own to commit to the waves, stepped aside to allow others easier access to the wide stone steps leading down into the ebb tide. Zagiri turned away for a moment, scanning the families already gathered in grieving clumps, their hands empty as their hearts. They all nursed bruises, scrapes, bandages like Zagiri's own.

Every body now sinking into the sea was her fault, but one hurt more than the others.

She finally spotted Balian farther down the quay, sitting alone on a bollard and staring out to sea. He seemed oddly rumpled, with his hair a mess and the shoulders of his longvest sitting crooked. Zagiri supposed that was only to be expected, in the circumstances.

Intruding seemed appalling, but Zagiri wouldn't get another chance. She stopped a little distance away and said: "I'm so sorry."

The wind clawed at her voice; for a long moment she thought he hadn't heard her, or perhaps was just ignoring her. Zagiri knew she deserved it, but she stayed nonetheless.

Eventually he turned and looked at her, bleakness overlaying all of his usual genial cheer. When he stood, and turned to face her, the reason for his crooked longvest became apparent; his left shoulder was bandaged, bulking beneath his shirt.

Zagiri knew well that alchemical tricks could only do so much to hasten the healing of anything more complicated than a slice from a sharp and clean sabre. She lifted her own arm a little, still wrapped in a sling. "We match," she said quietly.

"We survived." His voice was tight and blank. It gave her nothing.

Survival was guilt, with so many bodies sinking into the sea. "We were lucky."

"You pushed that luck," Balian pointed out, still flat. "I'm told I wouldn't be here at all, if not for the *heroic* azata who hauled me out." He didn't sound grateful.

He knew. He knew it was her fault. He knew *her*. Once, it had warmed Zagiri through. Then it had enraged her. Now it left her cold and hollow.

"It wasn't supposed to go like that," she choked out.

"You're a fool," Balian stated, crisp and stinging as a handful of flung gravel. "I *told* you to be careful. I expect this blithe shit from Yeva, but I thought that *you* had greater sense. Powers know why, after that mess with the sorcery reform."

He had told her. He was right. He was justified. Zagiri wanted to hide from these excoriating truths, but she deserved the flaying. She needed to endure it. She needed to try to make it just a little bit right.

Zagiri swiped hard at her face; she couldn't afford blurred vision, not when she needed to see clearly. "It wasn't supposed to go like that," she repeated, more fervently. "Except *someone* wanted it to. It's not just my fault."

"What?" That faint line creased down beneath his brows, and Balian looked at her—actually *looked*, for the first time today. "Are you trying to pin this all on Siyon's brother? He's already on the poisoner's slab for it, what more do you—"

"No." Zagiri took a step closer; she didn't want any of this overheard. Didn't want any of it whisked away from Balian before she could make him understand. "Even Mezin is...He's just someone's tool. *Someone* gave him the explosives—they were Summer Club made, Balian. By some snob who only deals with the *respectable*. And they were expensive. Like the apartment he was allegedly living in."

She hadn't realised Balian's eyes were glazed with grief until they sharpened against the whetstone of his swift-moving thoughts. She'd always loved to watch him haul in realisation, like an implacable fisherman.

"The link to Siyon," he muttered, the words barely audible over the gusting breeze off the harbour. Someone farther down the quay was crying, low and continuous. "And the prompt of fear."

"I don't know that the Ball was the intended target," Zagiri added in. "It's possible whoever it was just gave Mezin supplies, and *he* decided. And the Ball was possible..." No way around it, much as the admission burned in her throat. "Because of me."

She hated that it made sense. Some azatani—wanting more fear, wanting that reason to crack down, wanting a black mark against the Velo name—provided Mezin with the ability to cause trouble. But it was *Zagiri* who gave him the ability to strike against the Ball. Against all of these innocent bodies sinking into the harbour.

"You think my brother's involved," Balian said, barely louder than a breath.

Zagiri looked at him looking back at her. It wasn't quite an accusation. It wasn't *not*. "I think the Pragmatics benefit most from the excuse to tighten their grip," Zagiri confirmed.

Balian's chin lifted in the barest nod. "If this were Rowyani's scheme, he'd have chosen an intermediary to work through. Someone to handle the details." Someone like Avarair, Zagiri realised, as Balian hesitated before continuing. "The apartment that was allegedly used—it was in one of our buildings. A Hisarani building. I handled the paperwork from the inquisitors' raid. And Avair would have been at the Ball, for Lusal if no one else, except for what happened at the Western Hill depot that night. Since then he's been…prickly. Distracted. I thought perhaps it was just having Siyon in custody, but he's not here today. Our parents asked him directly to come, and he snapped at them and stormed out."

As though perhaps he felt guilty. Zagiri eased closer again. "Can you look into it?" she asked. Begged; she wasn't too proud to do it.

But Balian hesitated again. "Zagiri," he said, low and serious, "what is it you hope to get from all this?"

Justice. The truth. To drag them all kicking and screaming into the light of day, so *everyone* knew.

Even as she thought it, as she *felt* it, Zagiri knew it wasn't going to be enough. Balian's impressions of his brother, and circumstantial evidence? She could take it to Xhanari, but nothing official could come of it.

Certainly not while the fear had them all in its grip. The fear caused by the attack. The fear of Siyon Velo. The fear of their own loss of control.

She'd been a fool to think she could ever make use of it.

"You have to realise," Balian whispered, close enough now to do so. "If it comes to a straight challenge, Rowyani will just throw Avarair overboard and sail away."

And Rowyani would only step higher off the back of it, climbing the fear.

"They're going to kill Siyon, aren't they?" Zagiri's voice sounded underwater; she was crying again.

Balian sighed, a warmer gust against her cheek. "I don't see how they can't. They need to show that they can control something, to themselves, to the city. They need law, and process. Or Bezim is more broken than they can countenance."

"It *is*," Zagiri gasped. She dragged a hand over her face, wet and salty. "It is broken."

She only felt distantly the one-armed tug as Balian pulled her close; she turned to sob helplessly into his shoulder.

This is what it must have felt like, for the alchemists she'd helped, back in the summer. The friends and family of those who were executed, and those who were fleeing the possibility. Because there was nothing else they could do. There was no way to save themselves, in a broken city.

This was what she'd wanted to prevent ever happening again. And now here she was, right in the middle of it.

She couldn't change it. Couldn't fix it. Not in time to save Siyon.

CHAPTER 19

When the door of his cell creaked open, the last person Siyon expected to see was Vartan Xhanari. Yet Siyon blinked, and he was still there, standing next to Olenka.

"Huh," Siyon said, not getting up from his narrow cot. "I'm so dastardly you're forgiven your transgressions and welcomed back to alchemy, is that it?"

Xhanari sighed, long-suffering. "It's not all about you, Velo."

"Except in the ways that it is," Olenka commented wryly, but her smile was short-lived. "Turns out there are precious few inquisitors who aren't scared of you right now. Someone's been spreading stories of what you can do that don't seem quite so wild given what's been happening since Salt Night."

Siyon snorted, flopping back on his cot. "You think I'd still be here if I could just walk out?"

But even as he said it, he wondered. The stones around him vibrated with his words, crawling with bronze glow. Maybe he *could* just walk out of here. But what would it get him? He could stop being trapped in this hole and go hide in another one? Still have no way out. Still not know how to fix anything.

Xhanari stepped into his line of sight, looking down at him like he was a suspect piece of evidence. "I think you turned yourself in when you didn't have to."

"And let everyone out there die?" Siyon challenged.

Xhanari's mouth thinned, but all he said was, "Come on. It's time."

Part of Siyon wanted to cringe, cling to his cot, kick and scream. But there was no point in making things harder for himself, and he knew just how easily Olenka could manhandle him. So he stood, held out his wrists for the bonds, and went quietly.

Energy billowed around them as they marched down the corridor, Siyon wading through power that he suspected even Olenka couldn't see. It dragged at his legs, pulled at his senses; it was a shock when he was marched out into the winter sun, beating down on the open hippodrome track like a hammer on an anvil.

Siyon squinted, blinking away painful tears, stumbling on hard-packed dirt long washed free of its original sand. There hadn't been races run here since the Sundering had sent every horse in the city into a frenzy. The former spine down the centre had long ago crumbled into a low ridge. The course still carried the memory of thundering chariots, and the circling banks of seating carried an echo of the cheers and stamping feet.

No, wait. That wasn't an echo. The stands were full of people, and Siyon gaped as he stumbled after Olenka. The crowd roared, and jeered, and over there was a knot of people cheering, waving wildly, holding up a massive banner that read—oh shit—*Velo for Prefect*.

Nice to have someone on his side, but *nope*.

Over on the other bank of the hippodrome stands, amid jeers and hisses, the signs read *Monstrous magic* and *No shelter for sorcery*.

But the majority of the crowd was quieter. Shifting, and murmuring, and watching. Faces and people all blurred in Siyon's vision—Dockside leathers and university robes and merchants in all manner of garb.

Here to see. Here to hear. Here to make up their minds, perhaps.

At the northern end of the hippodrome rose the grand curving stand for the old Lyraec nobility. Still shaded by awnings hung from ancient poles, today it was packed full of azatani, here to see their justice in action.

A balcony curved out in front of the noble stand, where once the Duke had watched the races in elegant state. Now it had been cleared, occupied only by five people whose white sashes were trimmed in gold. The senior magistrates of Bezim, all five of them, here for Siyon.

Siyon didn't see any way this ended well for him.

Olenka and Xhanari led him toward a single stool set out below the balcony. At least they were letting him sit, though it was an ominous indication of how long this was likely to take. Xhanari and Olenka stepped back, close enough to lay hands on him if Siyon tried anything, but far enough to leave him terribly alone.

The central magistrate lifted her hand and the shimmering, brassy strike of a gong stamped down on the arena. In the slightly shocked silence that followed, the central magistrate rose and started to speak, her voice coming loud and clear through the charms still at work in the hippodrome.

"This special investigation of the full Justice Committee of the azatani Council is now convened. Any disorder will result in ejection and fines for interrupting justice." She beckoned off to the side, adding, "All right, Kurlani, get on with it."

A man stepped out onto the platform, neatly presented in a grey longvest. The superintendent of inquisitors himself, here to lead the session. Despite everything, Siyon felt a tiny spark of hope. Back before Salt Night, Kurlani hadn't been as negative about Siyon as might have been expected. He'd possibly even ensured that Siyon's brief inquisitorial detail was as useful as possible.

But that had been *before* Salt Night. Before Siyon woke a dragon from beneath Bezim. Before he helped destroy the Palace of Justice, and apparently bring a whole lot of other monsters to their doors.

"As determined in special session by the emergency Council of Bezim," Kurlani began in a voice that could cow a squad room of unruly inquisitors, "a special investigation is enacted into the actions of one Siyon Velo, sometimes acclaimed as the Sorcerer. It must determine whether Velo has been working to undermine, damage, or destroy the city of Bezim or its interests, activities, and security, including through collusion with extraplanar entities, foreign actors, and domestic insurrectionists. The Council suggests, but does not limit the scope of investigation to, the charge of treason."

Noise crested in the crowd behind Siyon, but he could make out no specifics through his own moment of dizziness. When sorcery had been struck from the register of crimes, it had been argued that any effects of alchemy could be covered by other charges.

Treason was certainly another charge. They could poison him for that, as well.

And Siyon was quite sure, looking up at the avid azatani, with the noise of the people of Bezim pressing like a hand against his back, that they were going to. All of the rest of what happened today was merely the spectacle required for any momentous happening in Bezim.

He didn't want to die. He didn't want any of this to be happening. He wished, for a moment bright and blazing as the sun off the white awnings, that he'd left the city along with the dragon on Salt Night. Just flown away, into the wild.

For a moment he could even feel the wind on his face.

When Siyon opened eyes he didn't remember closing, the trial—sorry, investigation—had moved on. There was some azatan in a virulently patterned longvest up there facing questioning from the magistrates. Some practitioner that Siyon had provided with extra-planar material, back in the day.

Technically illegal, of course. Apparently worse for Siyon, in the doing, than the practitioners in commissioning him to do it.

After him came Master Unja, giving stern and critical details about everything from Siyon's first attempt at Summer Club membership—that had ended abruptly when Enkin Danelani went calamitously missing from another room—right up to their recent gathering in the university library. The words *temerity* and *unsubstantiated* featured heavily.

Well, fuck him too.

The crowd was starting to shift and seethe by now; this wasn't exactly exciting. A fight broke out in the general stands and grey-tunicked inqs broke it up, marching a half-dozen people away.

The magistrates didn't even pause in bringing out the next witness.

Which was Miss Plumm. However impatient she'd sometimes been with Siyon, she was more so with the Justice Committee, brushing questions aside as irrelevant, giving terse and unhelpful answers, and telling off the magistrates for sticking their noses into alchemical matters without any advisers who could—

"Thank you," the central magistrate interrupted crisply. "That will be all."

There was another witness, and another, and another. Inquisitors who'd been present during various exciting events of the past year. One who'd participated in the Summer Club raid and conveyed the salacious news that Siyon had been there, but evaded capture when no one else had; obviously it didn't occur to them now, any more than it had then, that he might have hidden on the roof. Another from the Eldren Hall stairs when Siyon, with Balian's assistance, had fast-talked his way past to conduct his performance that had led to the waking of the dragon.

They faded one into the next, as Siyon blinked in the sun. The murmuring of the crowd swirled around him like an eddy of burnished energy. There was so much of it, pouring out of the stands, mingling with that seeping up from the stone beneath him. It beat in his blood, louder than the alchemically amplified words.

Siyon slipped gently out of himself, didn't even need to reach, he could just *feel*…

The city all around, as though this hippodrome, crowded with people, was a heart pumping blood.

The sluggish thud of Mundane power, boiling up within it, pressing like a hangover headache against the skin of Bezim.

That skin, that barrier, that line that Siyon had drawn, between us and them, between the city and the world.

They'd needed this, once. Now they needed it gone.

You're so attached to them, the dragon had said, and Siyon was. He was attached to this city and to its people. He needed, if nothing else, to fix his mistakes.

One way or another.

Carefully, he reached out, stretching up to press against the inside of the boundary, to see if he could—

"Stop that," Olenka hissed, knocking Siyon's arm down. "Don't give them more reasons to worry."

And the crowd *was* bothered, shifting and muttering, the azatani fluttering about as Siyon blinked and swayed in the sun, in the here and now, in his physical body. Sparks danced around him. Tilting back, he could see—past Xhanari's frowning face—the curve of the bronze dome of the city barrier skewing the colour of the clear winter sky.

As Siyon reeled, Kurlani called out: "Bring out Mezin Velo."

The big man was brought out jostling between two white-tunicked guards, shrugging off their grip as they shoved him to a halt. Some of the magistrates shifted uneasily, but the central figure showed no sign this witness was any different from the azatani and inquisitors who'd come before.

"We note," she said, consulting some papers, "that you are convicted of terrorist assault on the Harbour Master's Ball. But you have been offered commutation of your execution to ten years labour in the Archipelagan depot in exchange for testimony as to the nature of your conspiracy with your brother."

Siyon's head jerked up. What conspiracy?

The hippodrome skewed around him in bronze-smeared sharp edges that Siyon couldn't quite blink away. The energy was hooked into him, urging, demanding. Even with it hammering away at him, Siyon knew one thing for certain:

His brother wasn't going to die for him.

But Mezin just laughed, and it rang in Siyon's ears like a bell. "You want me to dance for you?" he demanded. "I might have chucked my brother in the river once before, but fuck if I'll do it again just to please *you lot*." Those words were a massive bellow, that shook the arena into silence for a moment.

"Such language is not—" The central magistrate began.

"Fuck your language," Mezin roared, and squared his shoulders; the crowd roared with him, more entertained than they'd been all day. "Yes, I tore your hall down on your heads, and I'd do it again. I'm not the only one, so sit comfortably while you can!"

Kurlani waved a hand glowing bronze to Siyon's sight; more guards came out to assist in hauling Mezin away again.

As he disappeared back into the tunnel, Mezin shouted, "He's got you running scared, and you should be!"

The crowd was in an uproar, the main stands a tumult of outrage and raucous approval and boisterous shouting. The azatani were a quieter flutter, with shades of the same expression on all their faces.

Oh, they papered over it with affront and distaste, but Mezin was right: They *were* afraid. Between the strike at their Ball and the monsters on their doorstep, they had no answers. They had no policies. They had no precedent.

They were scared.

"If there are no further additions to the investigation," the central magistrate called, over all the noise.

"I would like to question the defendant."

It was an azata, descending through the crowded northern stand. No one Siyon knew, though she frowned down at him like many an older woman had, as though everything from his personal grooming to his life choices could use a little sharp advice.

"Azata Filosani," the central magistrate said sternly. "This is not usual procedure."

"I only have one question," Azata Filosani said, with the mild determination of a woman who will not be evicted from tea until she's had as many biscuits as she wants. "And there is no one so qualified to answer as Velo himself."

Filosani stepped to the front of the balcony, looking down at Siyon on the sand. Just another azata. Not a practitioner. Not anyone Siyon had ever met. What on earth did she have to ask?

"Will all this stop?" she asked, and waved one illustrative hand in air that billowed around the gesture to Siyon's eyes. "The magic and the monsters and everything else. Will it stop, if we kill you?"

The question startled Siyon no less than, from the sudden sharp spike of noise, it did the crowd. Not even the question, so much as the words chosen. *If we kill you.* No refuge in impersonal words like *execution.* Filosani was reminding everyone of exactly what was being chosen here.

But the question itself went through Siyon. He looked up, at the curve of the bronze dome over all their heads. Pressing down on them. The way he'd trapped them all.

The things you've made will likely come unravelled, Olenka had said.

If *he* couldn't break the city's barrier, his death would, sooner or later, one way or another. But would it be soon enough?

"I don't know," Siyon admitted. His voice cracked, and seemed to fall dead to the sand where all the azatani voices had soared around the stands. But silence had fallen, and everyone still heard.

Azata Filosani's face folded into disapproval, like she'd expected better from him.

"But what other problems will it cause?" someone shouted from the azatani stand.

"The balance of the planes!" someone else insisted.

And then everyone was shouting, the stands bursting with demands, bristling with banners, hammering at Siyon with the noise, the noise, the noise.

Over it all, he could still hear the central magistrate, her voice made piercing by the grace of alchemy. He didn't need to hear it. He knew what she'd say.

Siyon Velo, held guilty of treason, through action or ignorance or accident. It hardly mattered. The result was the same.

He'd be executed by poison in three days' time.

CHAPTER 20

After everything, the Winter Picnic was still going ahead. Apparently the azatani simply could not do without the opportunity for all the new members of society to mingle, even if it had to be delayed by the funerals and relegated to a rather unfashionable corner of the parklands by the ongoing works in the Palace.

Before the Ball, Zagiri had planned to use the Picnic to have strategic discussions about how the city could be strengthened by bringing everyone together, angling toward the Council commencement that was just around the corner. After, she hadn't planned to attend at all, until Anahid had insisted that this *was* the chance for the right conversations.

If Anahid was coming—braving society to make connections for Zagiri's goals—then the least Zagiri herself could do was grit her teeth and endure the colourful tents, the stalls of boutique alchemical liquors, the buffet tables of late winter treats, the dancing and fortune-tellers and avid gossip. All anyone wanted to talk about was their relief that Siyon Velo had finally been *properly dealt with*, as though he were someone's troublesome lapdog.

One of the white-clad serving staff went past, carrying saucers of rakia-tinged djinnwine; Zagiri's hand twitched with the desire to grab one, but she'd probably just end up throwing it on someone. She couldn't make a scene and storm out. She couldn't even make a political point and insist everyone *think* for once.

She was here to make better choices.

Zagiri glanced toward the copses of winter-bare trees and glossy pines in this part of the parkland, where a figure moved quietly along the edge of the Picnic's frivolity; Anahid, skirting society.

She was angry as well, but in that way Anahid always was: tight and frosted over with icy politeness. She'd come in drab shades of grey, all the better to blend into the winter distance, especially when the rest of society was dressed in their hopeful spring colours.

Today, Anahid's attire put Zagiri in mind of nothing so much as a blade, held ready, glinting sharp. Those who *did* glance her way looked away again in a hurry. Anahid had always been a little daunting—had struggled to find a husband because of it—but now she was downright intimidating.

Zagiri thought it suited her. She wished she could feel her anger the same way, cold and clean, instead of tangled up in a frustrated, guilty knot, wrapped around the black pebble of her despair. It had lodged in her chest at the funerals, and only tangled tighter while she sat through the farce that had been Siyon's condemnation.

She'd almost cheered during Zin's outburst. But that pebble wouldn't let her. They were going to kill Siyon. Unless someone found a way to stop it.

"Azata Savani!" someone cried in the crowd, and Zagiri's head whipped around, looking for who had spotted her sister.

But Polinna Andani came out of the crowd, trailing her little coterie of fellow gossips behind her, coming toward *Zagiri* with hands spread and a simper in her voice and so many others turning to look. "My dear, I simply must thank you, for myself and for *everyone* who survived the horrors of the Ball."

The words burned, like salt rubbed in the wounds where guilt had already flayed her raw. But Zagiri couldn't scream. Certainly couldn't slap Polinna's wide-eyed face.

Everyone was here today. The injured, the grieving, the avidly curious—all of them. Somewhere were those who had wanted this to happen—maybe not the Ball, but some manner of destruction and chaos. Those who had funded and enabled it. Who were just as responsible as Zagiri herself.

Somewhere else were those who could help her foil all the rest of their plans. Who could possibly save Siyon. The people Anahid had brought her here to meet with.

"I'm sure," Zagiri said—to Polinna, and to everyone listening, "that I only did what anyone would have. But it made me realise what truly matters. Please excuse me."

Too brusque. Too pointed. Possibly unwise. She might need influence with the Andani family before this was over. But anger was choking Zagiri, as she stumbled toward the quiet fringes of the Picnic gathering. Damn Polinna and all her kind. Whatever happened, it wouldn't change what they thought or did, prodding and picking at each other until someone told them what it was fashionable to believe right now.

They could afford to be heedless, when azatani privilege swaddled them in safety.

Twigs crunched beneath Zagiri's slippers; a hand caught her elbow, guiding her away from the crowd, and Anahid said, "Easy. Take your time."

Zagiri dragged in a breath. "I hate all this. I hate that I can't afford to hate it. I need to be more polite."

But Anahid—her sensible sister, her canny sister, her careful sister—just shrugged. "You've always found your own way of doing things. You'll be fine."

Zagiri's throat clogged, her vision blurring. She shook her head. "You wouldn't say that," she managed, words broken, "if you knew what I'd done."

A tug at her hands, and Zagiri stumbled after her sister, blinking away her stupid, useless tears as Anahid steered them into the little copse, hidden away between the trees. "What?" Anahid asked. "What have you done?"

It was a question, not a demand, and the worry on Anahid's face was for Zagiri, not for the consequences; the gentleness shattered the dam of Zagiri's guilt.

The tears came in a flood—for Lusal and all the lost, for her own helplessness, for the respect Anahid would no longer have for her when this was done—but Zagiri told her everything. All her foolish decisions, all her mistakes, all the mess she'd made.

Somehow, when she was done, Anahid was still looking at her with love and concern, holding Zagiri close. "It's all right," Anahid murmured.

"It's *not*," Zagiri burst out.

But Anahid was undeterred. "No, it's not. But you will work to make it so, as best you can. We aren't defined by the mistakes we've made, or the worst things we've done, but by what we choose to do about them. What we do next."

Zagiri snuffled—very becoming of an azata, no doubt. "You really believe that?"

"I have to." Anahid drew a great breath, as though bracing herself, and said: "I have made my own mistakes. Done terrible things."

Zagiri couldn't help a snort. "Yeah, *you're* the impetuous idiot in this family."

"Zagiri." Her sister's grip tightened, her voice trembling; Zagiri looked at her, really looked, and Anahid said: "I'm the one who killed Stepan Zinedani."

For a moment, all Zagiri could do was stare. "I thought it was Laxmi who..."

"I let you think it," Anahid said. "Because I didn't want to be someone who could do that. But I am. Hiding from it doesn't help. I killed Stepan, and I would have killed Garabed too, given the chance. But that doesn't mean I have to kill anyone else. It doesn't mean that's all I am, always. I get to choose, every time, who I am, what I do. I can make better choices, that build rather than destroy." She touched Zagiri's cheek. "So can you."

It helped—the shock and the reassurance both. Zagiri pulled herself upright, scrubbing tears from her face with a net-gloved hand. "Oh. I've cried all over your dress."

"Never mind." Anahid smiled. "Grey is very practical like that."

"*There* you are," came a new voice, and to Zagiri's surprise, Azata

Malkasani came bustling around one of the tree trunks in a delicately patterned pink gown. Surprise gave way quickly to horror; what must she look like? But all Malkasani said was, "Oh, my dear, how fortunate that you're young enough not to feel the need to wear all that kohl; *that* would have been a mess. I do hate to hurry you along, in the circumstances, but—"

"But there's no time," Anahid agreed. "Let's go."

As they moved quickly around the fringes of the Winter Picnic, Malkasani angled herself toward them in just such a way as to serve as a shield. The posture pulled her gown askew at her shoulder, revealing the shiny pink skin of alchemically healed injuries—surely her scars from the Ball. To Anahid, she said, "You didn't bring your brooding and bounteous associate today?"

Anahid's mouth twitched. "I'll tell her you called her that."

It took Zagiri a moment to catch up. "Laxmi's met Malkasani?" It seemed the sort of thing that might cause spontaneous combustion.

Malkasani laughed merrily as she held open the rear flap on a lemon-yellow tent and ushered them all through.

Inside, a great round table had been set up, draped in a pristine white cloth, and covered in food and drink. But it was the people who really caught Zagiri's attention. A dozen azatani were arrayed around the table, all of whom she could name, from having researched their subcommittee involvement, general interests, and likelihood to take on a new clerk. A dozen former azatani councillors—who likely would be again when the new Council commenced next week. Councillors whose politics had seemed friendly to Zagiri's desired reform.

And nearest, standing to greet them, was Buni Filosani, who Zagiri had met when she'd been touring the Palace works. Whose support Zagiri had despaired of, after Anahid's scandal.

"You found them, excellent." Azata Filosani beamed as she took Anahid's hands. "How wonderful to see you again, Azata Savani—or do you prefer another mode of address?"

The question was genuine, not snide, and Anahid smiled in response. "For daylight hours, that suffices."

"Then thank you for bringing us the newest Azata Savani, who

I've already met in rather different circumstances." Filosani held out a hand to Zagiri, who took it and offered a nod by carefully drilled instinct. When Anahid had said there were people she should meet, she hadn't expected *this*. All these councillors. Buni Filosani smiling at her in welcome. *Malkasani* involved. "I warn you, the honest work of your night gang may soon seem far more appealing than what we're about here. At least when you shift a stone, it stays shifted."

"Not always," Zagiri responded, and felt near as nervous doing so as she had first taking up a sabre. "And lives are of rather more significance than stone."

"Well said," chipped in an elderly azatan from the table— Gentani, Zagiri's memory provided, who had been the driving force behind funding the university's medical clinics for most of his career. He beckoned to Zagiri. "Sit down. Have a drink. And let's hear this proposal of yours."

Better than her wildest dreams, *this* group of azatani keen to hear what Zagiri had to say. But still, Zagiri hesitated. "My proposed reform would be for the Council commencement," she noted.

The somewhat scandalously blonde Azata Hilogani looked over her spectacles and snapped, "There's much to do before then, if we want it to succeed. We'll need careful conversations, *and* a neutral sponsor on board, or the Pragmatics will simply—"

Zagiri hated to interrupt, but she couldn't let them run away with her. "They're killing Siyon Velo tomorrow!"

A hush fell across the table. That pebble of despair grew larger in Zagiri's throat. None of them seemed *uncaring*—all serious, some regretful, others clearly displeased.

Azata Filosani sighed. "Unfortunately, we are, unless something very dramatic happens between now and then. I don't know that even Master Velo has command of the sorts of powers that would be required to bring an emergency halt to a decision of the full justice committee. But I must admit, he has surprised me before, more than once."

Zagiri wanted to shout at her, but what had she said that wasn't true? And what could Siyon do, to escape his fate? If he blew a hole in the hippodrome and fled, he would be hunted even more. If he did something dramatic, it could only make everyone more afraid of him.

But Zagiri couldn't just give up on him. He had caught her, when she fell. How could she not do the same for him?

"I'm sorry," Filosani said, very quietly, as though it were just the two of them there. "I will understand if you do not wish to be involved further, given such disappointment. But I want most deeply to build a better Bezim. One in which this will not happen again."

For a moment, all Zagiri wanted was to walk out. To refuse to compromise. To go *find* a way to help Siyon evade his fate.

She looked to Anahid, still waiting beside her. Anahid turned slightly, toward the tent flap. She would go with Zagiri. She believed in Zagiri. *You've always found your own way of doing things*, she'd said. *You'll be fine.*

But Zagiri needed to make better choices. She needed to stop flinging herself heedless into mistakes. She couldn't think of a single sensible thing she could do to save Siyon. Not on her own. Not even with Anahid.

She hated this. But she hated the alternatives more.

All she could do was hope that he could do the impossible, as he had so often. That, and ensure a better Bezim for him to do it in.

Zagiri turned back to Azata Filosani, and all the councillors behind her, and said, "I'd like to stay. I'd like to help."

Anahid watched Zagiri step forward to take a seat at the table. The councillors rose from their own to give greeting and offer their names, not quite as equals, but certainly as colleagues. The pride that warmed her was not uncomplicated. She wished Zagiri could remain that flaming arrow of a girl. But no fire could burn forever. Seeing her sister's determination tempered was better than seeing it broken.

Azata Filosani sidled up beside her. "Will you join us also, Azata Savani?"

Anahid glanced around the table full of councillors, none of whom had done so much as glance sidelong at her in disapproval. Perhaps she could have joined their discussions. They promised to be far more invigorating and refreshing than any she'd had in azatani society. But they paled in comparison to the tangles that engaged her now.

With a smile, she said, "I don't think this is really the place for me, do you?"

Filosani tilted her head, not accepting that entirely. "If your sister's proposal goes ahead, as I hope it will, there will be all sorts of new Council places. Representation for the lower city and Dockside. For the Flower district, too."

Which was an interesting—though not tempting—possibility. Anahid certainly didn't want to stand up in front of the Council and represent the District, but would the option entice other managers to join her strange new baronial committee, or cause greater fights than ever?

"We'll see," was all Anahid said, for now. "There is much still to discuss and decide."

Filosani glanced at her. "Do I detect a softening of your previous position? Our mutual District friends have remained unhelpful, and I would prefer to have the beginning of a consensus before commencement."

Barely a week away. Anahid felt time squeezing around her like a too-tight sash. They were killing Siyon tomorrow. Unless something impossible happened. The entire world could be changed by this time next week.

"I cannot speak for the District," she said, and took a careful breath before she added: "Not yet."

That last word tugged a satisfied smile onto Filosani's mouth, but she merely nodded and said, "Good luck, then," before stepping back to her own seat at the table of councillors.

Anahid waited quietly near the tent flap as the discussion commenced, and Zagiri laid out her proposal for widening the Council membership in clear and sensible terms. It was satisfying to see her taken so seriously—answering questions, engaging in discussion—but mostly Anahid stayed for the respite from the Picnic outside. Even lurking on the fringes was tense; Polinna Andani would love to make some public display of disdain, and Tahera Danelani was also here, bright and beaming in the heart of society.

It brought to mind her last meeting with Tahera, at the Banked Ember. *You do fine helping yourself,* Tahera had said, and there'd been something in her face... Something Anahid thought she might have seen glimpses of among those glancing sidelong at her this afternoon.

Jealousy. Or perhaps frustration that *Anahid* had done these things, and those people—and *Tahera*—didn't quite dare.

Tahera Kurlani, as she'd once been, had married the brother of the woman everyone knew would soon be prefect. The cage of *her* respectability had been even more rigid than Anahid's self-built construction. Far less easy to dismantle. A far greater fall, if she had.

Around the table, conversation shifted to practical matters of votes and procedure. How to make Zagiri's idea palatable, to introduce it to those who might vote in favour, without offering too much warning to those who would obviously be against.

"I hate to say it," the elderly Azatan Gentani noted, "but the agitation of the city surrounding the execution of Master Velo may be a significant problem."

"Or it could be an asset," Zagiri jumped in, with an unhappy cast to her mouth. But she pushed forward, being practical, even as her heart must be as pained as Anahid's. "If—*when*—the city boils over, order cannot be maintained by only the inquisitors and guards. There are too few. They'll need the bravi. They'll need the trade guilds. They'll need the barons." She glanced back to Anahid.

Who nodded. Chaos would receive short shrift in the baronies; neither Aghut nor Mama Badrosani would care for disorder in their affairs, and all of Anahid's arguments in the Flower district were based on the desirability of stability.

"We still need that neutral sponsor," Azata Hilogani put in, jabbing a finger on the table as though she could physically pin one down. "If this comes too obviously from your camp, Buni, then Rowyani will chew off his own arm rather than let it get up."

"He'll do that anyway," Filosani shot back, then waved a hand. "We'll lose more of the centre, though. We need to imply that Syrah would have supported this. I'd hoped you could bring us that"—she nodded to Zagiri, who winced a little—"but the new Savani councillor seems unlikely to oblige. I've no great leverage with the new Danelani councillor either."

Anahid knew no Avenue gossip, but from what she knew of the family, it seemed likely to be the brother. Demian. Tahera's husband.

An idea lodged in Anahid's mind, clear as knowing who had the fourth power at the carrick table, made obvious by so many little details. She stepped up to Zagiri's side, and leaned down to whisper to her startled sister: "Perhaps I can help with the Danelanis."

"What?" Zagiri whispered back, and then scowled. "No, Ana, you shouldn't have to deal with Tahera any further, after what she did!"

Maybe she shouldn't. Maybe she wanted to. Maybe Anahid needed to know if she *could* turn these cards her way. The thrill was in her veins now. She wanted to see it through. Wanted to see the hands on the table.

"I'll be fine." She squeezed Zagiri's shoulder, "but don't rely on anything until I get back to you."

Anahid slipped out of the tent and into the edges of society, sliding past notice and curiosity, ignoring the occasional sharp glance and skirt twitching out of her way. Easier when she had a purpose.

She found Tahera in a pretty little bower, where strings of alchemical lights illuminated a fountain of djinnwine, centrepiece to a refreshment table of winter delicacies. Anahid drifted closer, as though considering the cured meats and pickled vegetables, while Tahera spoke with two older azatas—one of whom, Anahid suspected, was the wife of Azatan Gentani. The conversation didn't seem to be going the way Tahera wanted. The azatas were soon slipping politely away, leaving her frustrated.

When Tahera turned toward the refreshments, Anahid met her gaze and lifted an eyebrow.

A challenge accepted; Tahera hissed across the table: "Are you shameless, to come here?"

Anahid let herself smile at that; her shame had shifted in ways few here could understand. "I want to speak with you," she said. "But I could call upon you of an evening instead, if you prefer it."

That tightened Tahera's face further, both of them remembering Anahid's visit to the Danelani townhouse, seeking Tahera's intervention with the prefect over Siyon's arrest. Remembering how she'd twisted it out of Tahera, with the pressure of the gambling debts she couldn't let anyone know about.

The first violence Anahid had done. Her first taste of power over another person.

The very thing Tahera had pointed out she'd do again.

"Whatever you've come to threaten," Tahera began, low and vehement.

"Offer," Anahid interrupted, still smiling. As Tahera paused, her head tilting just the way it did when she picked up a new card, Anahid added, "Shall we step aside and discuss things properly?"

Tahera glowered at her. Perhaps Anahid had played and lost. She'd raised the bet, and her opponent was going to fold and walk away from the table.

Then Tahera said, "Around the back of the copse of spruce."

She walked away without a backward glance.

It did occur to Anahid, as she made her way around the Picnic toward that copse of glossy green spruce, that this might be a ploy. Tahera might get her out of the way and...what? Something worse than what she had already achieved? If Anahid spent half a bell waiting in the chill while Tahera laughed at her, that paled in comparison to everything that might yet happen in the next few days.

As it was, she'd barely had a chance to find a spot where the trees shielded her from the worst of the wind before Tahera came striding around the other side of the copse.

"Speak quickly," she snapped, crossing her arms over her chest. "I have things I actually want to achieve today."

"With the spouses of other councillors?" Anahid asked. "Are these things in support of your husband?" When Tahera's expression grew more sour still, Anahid nudged a little more: "He *will* be confirmed as the new Danelani councillor at commencement, won't he?"

"So I hear." Tahera's jaw clenched; her voice tight. Her laugh was a short and sharp bark. "Ink and ashes, you really *are* out of things now, aren't you? You haven't even heard that I've moved back into the Kurlani townhouse. I'm assisting my mother; she's *also* going to be confirmed as a councillor, after my uncle took this chance to retire."

The words were as quick and sharp as a hammer on a nail, and there was far more at play here than Anahid had realised. She couldn't help a sharp tug of something—sympathy, perhaps, or simply recognition—as she put the pieces together. "You're leaving him?"

Tahera's mouth twisted. "Aren't you kind to frame it that way. In truth, Demian hasn't spoken three civil words to me since my past indiscretions were brought back to haunt him."

Which, of course, had been Anahid's fault. "Ah. I—" She stopped, at Tahera's glare. *Do not insult both of us by suggesting you wouldn't do it all again*, Tahera had said to her. But still, Anahid offered: "I'm sorry that happened. It's most unfortunate."

"What's *unfortunate* is that everyone seems to believe that *he* was the useful one in this marriage." Tahera considered Anahid and snorted. "You wanted to speak about *him* as well, didn't you? You can go away disappointed, like everyone else, and take with you whatever you were going to *offer*."

These weren't the cards Anahid had expected to draw, but she could still make a hand with them. "The offer was for you," she said, arresting Tahera in the process of turning away. "A chance to be involved in something new. Something daring. More like your Zinedani friends. Or, I suppose, like me."

"I don't want to be anything like you." Tahera put on a very good show. She lifted her eyebrows disdainfully and added a sneer to her voice, but it didn't make the words any less a lie. She was still here. She was still listening.

She was burning to be more.

Anahid shrugged. "Then you could carry this to the Zinedani themselves, perhaps. I've not heard from them regarding my invitation to join the management of a more organised District, but I imagine the possibility of a Council seat of their own would catch their attention."

It certainly seemed to have caught Tahera's. "How? They aren't anything like eligible."

"At present," Anahid agreed. "But that could change if a proposal was raised at commencement to broaden membership beyond the azatani. To other parties of significant interest to the running of Bezim."

Tahera's mouth hung open for a moment. "You can't possibly believe that will work. With the Pragmatics in everyone's ear about the threat of the Sorcerer and the need for control?"

"Does the city currently feel under control?" Anahid asked. "Will it feel so once they've executed that Sorcerer? Or will it feel *worse*?"

Zagiri had a point, much as it made Anahid want to weep: Siyon's death might help, if they could harness it. If they had to. If he couldn't surprise them all yet again. (Please let him surprise them all.)

Tahera was thinking about it. She *was* a canny player, perhaps even more so now that she'd been burned by her debts. "You want Demian to make the proposal. Or *someone* does. Too bad for you."

Anahid allowed that with a tilt of her head. "They'll find someone. There are a number of councillors working on this."

"I can imagine just who," Tahera noted.

It was possible Anahid had miscalculated. If Tahera took this to the Pragmatics, traded it for some advantage of her own, all the care about not letting word spread would be wasted. But Anahid didn't think that would get Tahera anything she truly wanted.

"If this happens, you're offering the Flower district seat? To *me*?" Tahera's brows lifted. "Not keeping it for yourself?"

Anahid found it easy to smile, and easier still to show her rueful chagrin. "I don't want it. Not the attention, not the significance and certainly not the drain on my time. But I do think it best to have someone who understands how the Council and the azatani work, as well as the District."

Though Tahera had her game face on now, calm and showing nothing, Anahid knew she was interested. How could she not be? She *did* want the significance. She wanted something to do, someone to be. Something just a little closer to respectable than Anahid had managed.

Tahera pursed her lips. "They'll be furious about this, you know.

Ruzanna and Marel. Marel, in particular. Everything she's done to shut you up, and you're *still* pulling gullshit like this…"

She trailed off pointedly, like a line in the water. But even if Anahid knew the hook was there, the bait was undeniable. "What she's done to shut me up?"

A smirk tugged at Tahera's mouth. "Surely you know. The Zinedani have always thought you a problem. They're the reason I called you out at that party." She shrugged. "At least the last of my debt is now cleared. But haven't you guessed who's put a bounty on your ostentatious lady guard's head?"

Anahid could feel her surprise showing, could see Tahera's satisfaction with it, and yet she couldn't reel it in. It didn't matter who was behind it, she'd said when she thought it could be anyone, just some former Midnight gang leader with a grudge against her. When she didn't know it was *them*, rubbing at her all season, like salt under her collar.

Just like their father after all, ready to squash everything and everyone to get their own way. Willing to kill. This anger bubbling up inside her felt so familiar. Terrifyingly so.

Anahid swallowed hard against it. "It doesn't matter," she said. Tried to convince herself.

Even as Tahera's smirk deepened. "But it *does*," she said, stepping forward now. "Because here's *my* offer. I'll be your councillor for the Flower district, *and* I'll talk my mother—the new Kurlani councillor—into being the sponsor. Not as good as Danelani, I know, but you'll have trouble finding a better candidate between now and commencement. But my price, *Lady Sable*, is the elimination of the Zinedani."

"What? I thought they were your friends." Anahid blinked, even as she realised. Of course. "Not really. They've dangled the debt over you, and even now that it's cleared, you don't trust them."

"Would *you*?" Tahera demanded. "They're sharks. It's just how they were raised. And the only sensible thing to do with a shark who knows the taste of your blood is…"

Kill it.

Tahera wanted Anahid to kill the Zinedani sisters. That was her price. Just blood on Anahid's hands again. Just revenge against those who'd ruined her life, and nearly killed Laxmi.

That was all.

Tahera smiled sweetly. "Let me know. I'll be waiting."

They were killing him tomorrow. It made it difficult to think clearly.

After two days, Siyon was mired in desperation—soaked deeply into the stones around him, leeched down into the entire headland of the city beneath his feet, where the Mundane energy quivered with the need to spill over, flood the world, do his bidding.

Just holding the plane steady was exhausting.

Don't bother, the bronze glow whispered to him, curling around his ears, flowing gently through every part of him. *Give in. Sink down. Let yourself be carried away.*

It would be so easy. Siyon could almost taste it. If he just relinquished his hold—on here, on now, on himself—he could slip between the cracks in the stones of his cell. He could vanish. He could flee.

He could cease to be Siyon Velo.

As the time ticked past, it was increasingly tempting. After all, tomorrow he'd cease to be anyway.

But if he did that, would the barrier remain? He could stay here forever—not really him, and not really *here*—sloshing around in the energy he'd bound inside the city. As the monsters clawed at the dome of the barrier, as the people inside ran out of everything but fear, as the world changed totally.

It wouldn't matter to the plane. It wouldn't matter to the magic itself. It would matter *deeply* to everyone Siyon had ever known and cared about.

He couldn't. He wasn't worth a whole city. And he wouldn't even be *himself*, if he let the Mundane swallow him whole. He had fought hard—to be Siyon Velo, to manage all this. He hadn't given Izmirlian up to the Demon Queen; he wouldn't give himself up to the Mundane.

To death, perhaps, if he had to. If there was no other way.

He still hoped it wouldn't come to that. He *could* still flee, if he found a way to break the barrier. Too much to hope the azatani wouldn't fear him. But they'd all still be alive to chase him, and that would be enough to be going on with.

Time, however, was running out. They were killing him tomorrow. And Siyon had tried everything he could.

He finished another stumbling lap around his cell, trailing fingers against the stone walls in a vain attempt to reground himself in his own body. The stone whispered to him now, throbbing with a burnished glow, and Siyon had the strangest feeling that his fingertips were sinking in, feeling the subtle nuance in texture between the stones and the mortar between.

"Stop it," he muttered, and the glow diminished.

Like he'd kicked a puppy. The energy just wanted to play. Wanted to help. Wanted to flow and tumble and show him *everything*.

Siyon couldn't. He *couldn't*. He was just a person. Just this person. He couldn't be everything, everywhere. He wasn't the dragon.

He could feel her as well, constantly now, even when he was here, in his body, in his cell. (At least, he thought he was here. He could no longer be quite sure.) He could have pointed straight to her, though at the moment that would have involved pointing at the floor near the corner of his cell, which seemed decidedly strange, but Siyon *knew* that she was there, far away, nestled in the corner of his mind.

None of this helped. None of this was going to save him. He didn't know what could.

With teeth-gritting effort, Siyon pushed the energy away from him, clearing himself just a little space, so he wasn't utterly awash. He closed his eyes again and concentrated.

Mayar would be impressed with how much meditation practice Siyon was doing, in here. Then again, they might be horrified with how he was doing it. No relaxation here, no surrendering, no letting himself drift. Instead he kept the energy at arm's length, shoving against it with his purpose, an endless wrestle like swimming through seaweed.

He lunged out into the plane, rather than reaching, and pushed for the city bounds.

The dome loomed brighter than ever, as though every trace of power that was being fed through the practitioners of the city—through the existing order of the mudwitches and the manipulations of the alchemists—was only strengthening the damn thing. The surging bronze power of the Mundane pressed and battered against it, a storm against cliffs. It seemed impossible anything could stand it; surely Siyon need only add the faintest of pressure for the whole thing to give way in the face of the flood.

Except it had withstood everything he had to throw at it yesterday, and the day before.

Siyon fought his way through the turbulence of energy to lay palms against the barrier (or at least, that's how it felt). He braced his heels against … something; *himself,* perhaps, the only fixed point in a wildly fluid space. Braced, and *pushed*.

It worked as well as every other time he'd tried. He might as well have set his shoulder against the Scarp.

Siyon tried gouging with curled fingers, tried to gently ease a hand through, tried to sink down to the edge of the barrier and peel it away—but there *was* no edge. The barrier curved down beneath the earth, and Siyon slid down the lower round of it, trapped in an enormous bubble. He kicked against it, screamed at the uncaring smooth surface that rippled endlessly, and never gave way.

They were killing him tomorrow. *They were killing him tomorrow.*

His desperation was a knife, carving down the length of his spine, and Siyon took it—laid a hand on the back of his neck and *gripped*, drawing that frantic need out of himself like some barbarian blade in an opera. It came long and sharp and shining.

Siyon wrapped both hands around it, put his weight behind it, and plunged it into the barrier.

The faintest crack appeared in the smooth shining dome, just a sliver beside the shining blade of his urgent mortality.

Energy rushed past Siyon, out through the crack, but every pulse of it clung a little to the edges, gumming up what Siyon had so desperately opened. No, no, *no*. He couldn't let this get away. If he could make this little flaw, with all of himself, then he needed... what? *More*. More weight. More urgency. More *people*.

Siyon reached, behind himself, beyond himself, in a way he couldn't describe at all. For the city, and all the people within it. For Bezim and everything it meant. He reached for more weight, more anger, more desperation, and he found it flowing in the streets, clustered around the hippodrome, leaping easily to his bidding. Siyon leaned against the blade in the barrier, teasing open a little more, just a little...

He felt the world turn around him, the whole plane watching him. Parchment-pale eyes blinked as the dragon lifted her head to consider him, and damn all the distance between. She was curious. She didn't think he could do this. Didn't think it was possible.

Didn't *think* it was, but was interested to see if he did it anyway.

"Fuck you," Siyon growled, leaning harder against his own need, pulling with the weight of a city. "I'm Siyon Velo, and we know about me and the impossible."

We knew. Izmirlian knew. As though the thought was a summoning, the faintest whisper of a voice came into Siyon's mind. *Are you buying the city with your life?*

He was trying *not* to, but he would, if he had to. If it came to that. If there was no other way.

The faint doubt was too much. The blade snapped in Siyon's hand, the barrier sealing up in the barest blink, and Siyon *fell*.

The city caught him. It was right there. He'd called it to him.

He woke flailing, in his cell, on his cot, leaning back against the wall—

No, he was *in* the wall. The stone cradled his head, curved around his shoulders. When Siyon lurched forward, it scraped against his skin, clinging and eager. Siyon staggered into the middle of his cell and stared back, breath coming harsh in his throat.

The wall behind his cot held a perfect impression of his head and torso, smooth and natural as though it had always been there.

Worse when he looked around. The dirt floor—too hard-packed

to have shown more than the faint scuff of Siyon's pacing for all of his stay there so far—was covered with markings.

Not markings. *Writing.* The hand was eerily familiar—whiplash and elegant, curving around and around in endless lines, save where Siyon had stumbled through it.

Another way, Izmirlian had written, over and over, spiralling into the centre of the room, where another word had been carved deep with vehement lines.

Avarair.

Siyon stared at it, too confused to even panic. The floor, he realised, was the only surface in the cell not dripping burnished Mundane energy. As though it had been swept clear by some other force, before or during the writing.

Another way. Avarair. He finally got a miracle and couldn't even make sense of it.

Siyon's heart was still hammering when someone beat a similar rhythm on the door of his cell.

"Stand back, Velo!" someone snarled from the other side. "I'm coming in."

"No!" Siyon yelped, lurching forward. No one could come in, no one could *see* this, they'd think even worse of him, they'd—

What, kill him twice?

But the moment Siyon's foot touched the floor, the dirt shivered, and shimmered bronze, and the writing vanished.

Siyon was still gaping at it when the door creaked open in a wash of lantern-light that made Siyon squint; he hadn't realised it was pitch dark. He raised a shading hand and vaguely made out the face of—

Avarair Hisarani.

Possibly he should be astonished, but with everything else that was churning inside him, Siyon couldn't summon much unease. Nor could he summon any words. Avarair. Another way.

What was going on?

Avarair glared at him. "Why are you even still here?" he demanded, which frankly seemed a baffling question from the person who'd arrested Siyon in the first place. He waved the lantern toward the wall. "There's a crowd out there claims you're the Power of the Mundane, you're our saviour, you're far more than human, but you're still stuck in this cell, aren't you? You're just a man."

In the light of the lantern, Avarair looked both more and less like Izmirlian. Less in that Avarair looked—for him—almost rough. As though he hadn't shaved in a day or two. (Siyon was closer to a beard than he'd ever managed before.) As though his hair had been dis-arranged by careless clutching at it. Siyon had rarely seen Izmirlian looking anything less than immaculately groomed, unless it was in the bed they'd shared.

And yet, there was a driving fire behind Avarair's eyes, and an energy to the way he paced across the cell, that made Siyon think of Izmirlian's coiled and frustrated purpose. The things he'd wanted, and not known how to grasp. Not thought he *could* grasp. Been ceaselessly annoyed about the need to make a life without.

Something was bothering Avarair.

"With everything that has happened," Avarair muttered, whirling around to glare at Siyon. "We are *right* to demand more order in this city. We are right to *shape* more order in this city. It is the right thing to do!"

His voice rang off the stone walls. But Siyon wasn't sure Avarair was shouting at *him*.

He answered anyway. "Order for who?" Siyon's voice was the rasp of stone on stone. "Shaped by who?"

"Shut up," Avarair snarled, and marched forward; Siyon gave way, but soon his back hit the wall. Avarair lifted the lantern, like the light might show truth; it certainly showed the shadows beneath Avarair's eyes. "Why are you still here?" he demanded again, but hard on its heels: "How did you do any of it? How did you stop the monsters at the depot? How did you wake up the dragon? How did you *do what he wanted*?"

It rang with desperation—Siyon knew what that sounded like, intimately. He'd forged a sword from it, but Avarair's shook too much to be held steady.

"How?" Avarair repeated. "It wasn't possible. It *wasn't*. When he

289

first suggested it—we asked. We asked *everyone*. All the most reputable alchemists of the Summer Club. It wasn't *possible*." His head shook, almost helplessly. "But he wouldn't put it away. He wouldn't *compromise*. We have to, there's no other way to live, there's no other way to achieve anything in this world but to bend your goals to what can be achieved, to what is needed, but *Izmirlian*—"

The name was a snarl in his mouth, the sound of a bitter, long-standing, twisting grievance.

That Izmirlian hadn't bent to reality. He'd forced reality to bend to him.

Or, perhaps, Siyon had forced it.

"He believed," Siyon answered. That was all he had. Izmirlian had always believed. In his goal. In *Siyon*. Nothing would have been possible, without that.

"I believe!" Avarair snapped. "I believe in the proper truths of this city! In what's real and proven! In the need to keep this city safe, from itself if need be..." He trailed off, looking like he'd ventured too far out on the cliff's edge and now feared the ground.

"What's real and proven," Siyon repeated. "Like that I *can* do these things? Like that there is so much more in the world than the old order can wrap its head around?" He eased forward, as though he were stalking Avarair across the roof tiles.

This man's name, written uncannily on the floor. Another way. Was this it? Was *Avarair* somehow the loose thread that might unravel the knot of Siyon's fate?

Almost choked by the possibility, Siyon could barely find the breath to finish: "Your *correct order* is going to kill me. Because you're all too stuck in your compromises. Because none of you believe that you can reach for more." He took another step, close enough and tall enough that Avarair had to tilt up to look at him. "Or can you?"

For a moment, there was something in those clear brown eyes. A hesitation, a possibility, the faintest wondering. Like the cousin of Izmirlian's curious consideration of anything and everything. A moment, when Siyon thought perhaps he'd done it. Perhaps Avarair was going to help him.

Then panic clouded over Avarair Hisarani's eyes, and he gulped, "No."

Turned on his heel. Wrenched open the cell door. Slammed it behind him.

He took the last faint gasp of Siyon's hope with him.

CHAPTER 21

They were killing Siyon today, and the old hippodrome was under siege. The crowds had swelled, shouting and smothering, chanting and crashing, noise washing through the streets like a storm surge smashing against the shore of the Council's justice.

Yesterday, the forceful merriment of the Winter Picnic had managed to drown it out. Today, Anahid caught the faint murmur from the moment she stepped out of Sable House with Laxmi at her side.

In the square out front of Sable House, Lejman was debriefing the final security patrol of the night, made up of two of their own, alongside three from other Houses, and one of Peylek's people. The patrol were laughing and jostling, though Lejman looked sour; Anahid paused to ask: "Any problems?"

"No, mistress," the patrol chorused, like she was their schoolmistress.

Lejman sighed. "Only if you count this lot encountering so little sign of trouble that they decided to stage a mock fight to advertise their Houses."

The patrol grinned and shoved one another.

"Leave the foolishness to the bravi," Anahid suggested, which didn't seem to quell them at all. Truth be told, she felt quite pleased herself. The more effective—and visible—their combined efforts were, the more Houses would ask to join.

But those were secondary considerations for today; as the patrol was dismissed, Anahid pulled aside the former Midnighter on the crew. "Where's your mistress? I sent her a message yesterday."

He gave her a look like it should be obvious. "Up at the hippodrome, ain't she?"

Of course she was. After all, Peylek had grilled Anahid about what she intended to do about Siyon. If only there were anything she *could* do.

The noise only grew as they neared the old hippodrome, joining a flood of other people streaming up to witness whatever might happen—students in their robes, merchants of all tiers, shopkeepers and clerks, bravi in leathers, Dockside workers in canvas vests. And here to prey on *them* were all manner of vendors of food and drink, small troupes of entertainers, the fleet forms of petty thieves, and hawkers of souvenirs and alchemical tricks.

Knots of protesters clotted the intersections, beating drums and waving signs, one group singing an opera aria about the dangers of the planes, another chanting in short, sharp repetition: *Break free, fly free.* Down one side street, a parade of people held a massive banner depicting a strange crawling shadow it took Anahid a moment to recognise as a dragon.

A scrawny Lyraec woman ducked through the crowd, shaking a fistful of cheap, clattering amulets. "Protect yourself from the Sorcerer's curse!" she cried, brandishing her wares in Anahid's face.

Laxmi growled at her. "Protect yourself from me!"

But the woman was already gone, buffeted in the crowd.

Anahid pushed onward, chasing a glimpse of familiar russet fuzz above dusty black. She shoved her way across the flow of people, and into the quiet opening to a building courtyard, where Peylek was leaning against the wall. She barely spared Anahid a glance from what she was doing, hands busy rolling up some sort of blue powder in a tight cylinder of waxy vineleaf. "Little busy," she grunted.

"Did you get my message?" Anahid swallowed the urge to apologise. This wouldn't be such short notice if Peylek hadn't been so difficult to find. "Are your people ready?"

Peylek jerked her chin toward the crowd without looking up from her rolling. "They're all out there. Look for the loudest shouting in favour of Velo. We have better things to do than help you become baron of the District today."

"I *told* you, that's not what I want." The response was almost reflex; Anahid frowned down at the little cylinder in Peylek's hands, now wrapped up entirely and sealed with a greyish blob of something. It looked roughly like how Zagiri had described the explosives for the Ball, though with far less Summer Club precision. "What are you doing?"

"Something." Peylek shot Anahid a fierce look from under her eyebrows. "None of your business, if you're more concerned with what might happen *later* than what's just about to happen."

Of course Anahid was concerned; Siyon was her friend, the first person who'd told her she could do whatever she wanted. She wouldn't *be* here if not for him. But she reached out to grab the little vineleaf cylinder, glaring when Peylek whisked it behind her back. "You can't blow this up. Who will that help?"

"It might help Siyon," Laxmi chipped in unhelpfully.

"You think if you get him free, the city will rally behind him?" Anahid demanded. "You think half the people shouting out there will still be on Siyon's side if more people die today? You think the Council won't come down harder than ever, until they've smashed you all to pieces? You'll just make a mess. Think about the *future!*"

"You think!" Peylek snapped back. "What kind of future do you see for people like me if they can just kill Siyon Velo? He's the *Alchemist*. What am I? What are all of my people? Just some weird leftovers of more mysteries they don't understand. Why shouldn't I make a mess?"

She could so easily be right. Part of Anahid wanted to let her do it. They were going to kill Siyon. There *should* be consequences—immediate and messy. What if Peylek *could* stop them?

Except it would never, ever work. It would be the Ball all over again. It would be the dragon. It would be one more thing that made the Pragmatics look *right*, to people who were afraid and desperate.

"We can do better," Anahid promised. "We *can*. We can make something better. Slowly but surely. If we work together."

Peylek stared at her for a long moment, before her mouth twisted up, bitter with resignation. "Yes, I got your message. We're ready for your little job." Her mouth twisted further, and she spat, thick with derision: *"Better."*

Anahid refused to be ashamed about what she was going to do. What she *had* to do, to get Tahera on board, to get Zagiri's reform happening, to—yes—build something better. It wasn't pretty, and she wasn't glorying in it, but she wasn't going to suggest there wasn't more than a little satisfaction in all of it.

But that was for later.

They rejoined the crowd and were swept into the hippodrome through the same entrances that had once admitted crowds eager for a different sort of spectacle. The more things changed in Bezim, the more they stayed the same; the crowds today weren't flying the coloured bunting of the hippodrome teams, but they were just as avid and antagonistic, shouting and singing and shoving at one another.

The stands were packed already; Anahid had spent too much time arguing with Peylek. They wedged into a corner, Laxmi standing firm against the buffeting crowd while Anahid scanned the stands around them. She hoped there was still one last chance to do something for Siyon.

"Up there." She pointed to a quieter space in the otherwise churning crowds.

They were pressed close by the jostle of passing people. Laxmi murmured in Anahid's ear, "Are you sure about this?"

"Now you ask?" Anahid shot back, and the curve of Laxmi's smile—in the moment before the other woman turned away—buoyed her up.

They rejoined the flow of people, pushing up farther into the stands. In that still spot that Anahid had found, Mama Badrosani and Aghut sat amid half a dozen each of their biggest, burliest lieutenants. Catching Anahid looking, Mama lifted a heavy-ringed hand and beckoned like an opera queen calling her knights to her side.

Anahid took a breath and inclined her head.

But she'd taken no more than two steps when noise surged all around them. Anahid startled and whirled around; Laxmi steadied her shoulder, but all around them the crowd had paused, fixing their attention on the hippodrome floor.

Or what there was of it, free of more surging crowd. There was only a scant half-circle, up at the end near the nobles' stand, where a line of grey-tunicked inquisitors held people back from the executioner's slab on its raised dais.

Of course, everyone had to see. That was the point of all this. Let everyone see justice. Let everyone see that the Sorcerer died like any other man.

The doors had opened in the wall beneath the azatani stand. The inquisitors were bringing someone out.

It was beginning.

The crowd around Zagiri surged forward, carrying her like a storm-swell.

"For the rigours of justice," some white-sashed person announced up on the Council balcony, "bring forward Mezin Velo!"

Zagiri wriggled her way through the press, treading on toes in her bravi boots. She'd braided her hair—wincing against the weight of her half-healed arm—and left off the sling, along with both her tricorn and her headscarf. She wasn't bravi; she wasn't azatani; she didn't know what she was. Not today.

She was one last, desperate hope. She was a slippery, scrabbling need to get to Vartan Xhanari. She'd seen him just up here, part of the line pushing the crowd back, making way for the prisoner being paraded for everyone to see.

There he was in front of her, silently marshalling the crowd. Zagiri ducked under someone's uplifted arm, around a woman hefting a rot-softened apple, and lurched forward, staggering into Xhanari's restraining arm.

He glanced at her, then again and sharper, a quick glance taking her in. Zagiri had never known anyone who saw so much, so quickly, save her sister. "If you're thinking about trying something," he muttered, barely loud enough to hear over the hooting and hollering all around them, "*don't*."

Zagiri couldn't say she hadn't considered it. The despair that had lodged so heavily inside her was fizzing into desperation. This was the last chance. And yet her choices seemed worse than ever before. When she licked her lips, they were bitter with the potential for violence that hung heavy in the air.

This was already going to go bad. But if she'd learned anything in the last half year, it was that there were many sorts of bad, some worse than others.

"Can *you* try anything?" she asked. Her last, faintest, barest hope. "You kept looking, didn't you? In the files, in your investigations, in your questioning, did you find anything?"

Xhanari looked fully at her, and his black eyes were as bitter as burnt olives. He *had* looked further, as she had. He'd looked, and whatever he'd found had been enough for *him*, but would never be enough for actual justice.

The crowd shoved and screamed; someone leaned on Zagiri's back with the weight of a hundred people behind them, and she staggered into Xhanari's arm, linked to the inquisitor next to him. They were all wrapped around with some sort of alchemical rope that glowed gently as it took the pressure of the crowd with only a little flex.

Grey-tunicked inquisitors marched their prisoner to the dais, six of them surrounding him. Mezin Velo had his head up and a challenge in his eyes.

Zagiri shrank back, but his gaze passed over her like an uncaring summer storm. He didn't point or sneer or bother to damn her.

She was already damned enough.

"Look at all this," Xhanari muttered, barely audible over the crowd's clamouring. "It's not justice. It's a circus. A spectacle."

On the raised dais, Mezin was pushed down flat on one of the marble slabs, bound with lengths of white silk. The poisoner was waiting, all in white—tunic and hooded mask and the supple leather gloves that shielded his hands and forearms. He raised one hand—holding a vial of something dramatically black—and then the other—palm upward, in something like supplication.

Here, preserved in one of the oldest of Bezim's rituals, was the last shred of the divine superstitions of the ancient Lyraec empire. A moment for the intervention of *something else*, if there was anything else that cared to get involved.

The crowd seethed and shifted impatiently. They weren't here for *this*. No one, it seemed, cared too deeply for the fate of Mezin Velo.

"Get on with it!" someone shouted, over to Zagiri's right. There was even laughter.

It made her feel faintly sick.

Not just her, it seemed. "This isn't justice," Xhanari growled again. "This isn't order. This isn't *right*."

"He deserves it," Zagiri objected. He'd done it all intentionally—deceived her just to kill so many young girls and their families. He'd taken and stolen all the help he could to make those dead bodies.

She still wasn't convinced. How could death for death help?

The poisoner uncorked the black vial, approaching the slab. Despite the white silk bindings, Mezin heaved and thrashed. But the poisoner knew his business. He laid a firm and bracing hand over Mezin's face. Pinched at his nose, probably. Waited for his mouth to open, as it inevitably would.

"Maybe," Xhanari said. He was moving. Untwining his arms from the alchemical chain, which glowed and hauled his neighbours a little closer. What was he doing? "But if he deserves this, so do others. And none of them will ever come close to this." He jerked his chin toward the dais.

Where the poisoner tipped the contents of the vial into Mezin's gasping mouth, and clapped his other hand down over it.

Mezin arched up, straining at the white silk bonds, his exposed skin burning suddenly red with desperation. Or maybe that was the poison. It was supposed to be quick-acting. It was supposed to be painless and humane.

It looked anything but.

"So much of this city is just for *show*," Xhanari muttered, close beside Zagiri. His face twisted. "Fuck this."

And he walked away.

Along the line of inquisitors, striding with determination. One of the other guards said something, and Xhanari shook his head. Yanked something off his uniform, and cast it down glittering in the trampled dirt.

His candle badge.

Zagiri gaped after him, but a moment later, he was gone, swallowed up in the chaos and newly eager crowd.

They all knew what came next. *Who* came next.

In his cell beneath the hippodrome, the noise of the crowd wrapped around Siyon, thick and pricklesome and smothering as a rough woolen blanket.

He tried to breathe. He tried to remain calm. He dug his fingers into the floor, clutching fistfuls of burnished stone.

What if he let himself sink into it? What if he let the energy carry him away? What if he gave up on being Siyon Velo, before that man could be killed?

He didn't want to die.

But letting the Mundane swallow him would be just the same. Who he was, gone. Everything he held on to—his friends, his city, his memories—swallowed and washed away.

And all the problems still there. The energy churning up inside the city, while the monsters bore down, thirsting for a taste. The barrier still there, despite Siyon's best efforts. All of his mistakes, that had brought him here.

Siyon wanted to run. He wanted it so badly his heels were jiggling with it. There had never been a time in his life when he hadn't run—from the life his family had chosen for him, from the risks of the lower city and the threats of the barons, from everyone who'd disapprove and try to shut him down. From angels and demons and inquisitors and responsibility.

But running away now wouldn't solve anything. There was nowhere he could hide from everything he had done, and what it had caused.

The whole world had been leaning on him. And shouldn't they? He was the Power of the Mundane. If someone had to make it right, it should be him.

I'm sorry, he said, to no one who could possibly hear him now. *This is how it has to be.*

The door opened, and two guards came in, flanking the door. Two more, out in the corridor. And one lone inquisitor, with her frizz of hair pulled back tightly, and the memory of righteous wings in her posture.

"It's time," Olenka said, not ungently.

Despite everything, fear twisted in Siyon's chest. "Don't do this," he begged. "Please."

The pair of guards had stepped forward with a looped rope, ready for his hands; they glanced at each other, and one shrugged uncomfortably. "Sorry," he said. "Way it is, innit?"

They bound Siyon's hands. They hauled him to his feet. They pulled him out of the cell.

"For the rigours of justice," the chief magistrate announced, "bring forward Siyon Velo!"

The crowd roared, loud and vehement enough to shake the stones beneath Anahid's feet. It rattled her ribs, and made her stagger back against Laxmi.

"Oi!" someone shouted, right next to them.

It was one of Mama Badrosani's sons, looking sulky as he shouted: "Ma wants to talk with you."

"Now?" Anahid demanded, glancing down to the arena.

They were bringing him out, a lone figure in a ring of grey and white tunics, taller than all of them save one. Still very much visible to the seething masses who shoved and stretched at the bounds of the cleared space.

The noise was immense, a thick blanket of overlapping voices—some shouting Siyon's name, some screaming the evils of sorcery, some crying for mercy, some simply jeering.

"The Sorcerer saved us!" a woman shrieked, from somewhere down in the arena.

"Then why can't he save himself?" a man shouted back.

"Yeah," the Badrosani son bellowed over the ruckus. "Now. Come on."

It was what Anahid wanted—to speak with the barons. But not now, not when her friend was being led to his execution. She didn't want that to be happening at all. None of them had any choices.

They climbed up with the Badrosani boy pressing a path through the crowd by sheer force of his bulk. Down on the sand, someone screamed, and the crowd surged and staggered. The chaos was already starting. Anahid found Laxmi's hand and held on tight.

The little island of muscle-shielded calm around the barons seemed surreal in the midst of all this chaos. Aghut took one look at them and snorted in derision; Mama Badrosani shooed another of her sons off the bench to make room for Anahid to sit. Laxmi crowded in behind her, squaring her shoulders and glowering at the world.

"Look what the seagulls dragged in," Mama Badrosani drawled, her voice even rougher when lifted to be heard. "What a face, though. What's wrong, don't enjoy a nice public execution or two? What's not to like, eh, Aggie?"

Aghut pulled a face like he might spit, were there enough clear space. "This whole mess is as welcome as a shark in the rain barrel."

Anahid's hope, that she'd so carefully crushed down, gave a desultory twitch, like a fish on the quay. "I'd have thought if anyone could influence today's events, it would be respected figures such as yourselves."

"Such flattery!" Mama cackled. "You think we haven't tried? Fucking debacle, all of this." She tilted close enough for Anahid to see how her make-up was running in the heat of the crowd. "You come up here to ask us to spring your mate?"

"I hoped," Anahid admitted. But no, that wasn't why she'd sought them out. She had other reasons, and hollow and pointless as they felt with the crowd baying—for Siyon's blood, for his life, for the sheer joy of it—she still had plans to enact. "I came to let you know that I intend to take the District in hand, though in a rather different manner than you might expect. I hope we can achieve a balance regardless."

Aghut snorted. "Yeah, good luck with that, za."

But Mama seemed very pleased. "Ain't she polite, though? Coming to see us. More than the fucking Zees have bothered with. Good luck with your little plans, Lady Sable." She glanced down at the sand, and her expression soured again. "You got a plan for this?"

The crowd was one massive scream now—banners had been torn, and fights started. All the order to which Anahid had belonged for her whole life had come to this. There was no way to stop it. Save another feat of impossibility. A different sort of violence, breaking the bounds of order, breaking out entirely.

"He shouldn't need our help, right?" Mama said, from a long way away and right beside Anahid. "Sorcerer and the Power of the Mundane. I heard he could walk through solid stone, if he wanted. Yet we're all still here."

"Ain't no one doesn't benefit from a little aid," Aghut declared, and tipped a nod down toward the arena. "We got people in place, ready and waiting, if a chance comes up. But I don't see one. Unless something happens."

Something. Something like only Siyon could create.

The sand blurred in Anahid's vision. Laxmi gripped her shoulder, and Anahid wrapped her hand around those scarred knuckles, gripping tight.

Zagiri clung to the guards' alchemical rope, in the gap where Xhanari had been, trying to hold her place at the front. She didn't want to see, but she didn't want to miss the moment she could *do* something.

Please, let there be a moment when she could do something.

"Why isn't he *doing* anything?" someone wailed behind Zagiri. "They said he flew, out at the depot. Why isn't he flying away?"

"He's a fraud!" someone else bellowed. "He's been lying all this time!"

"He's in league with the monsters!" another voice screamed.

And Siyon *didn't* do anything. Didn't fly away. Didn't even struggle. He did balk for a moment, up on the dais, saying something to the guards. Something that made them look embarrassed, wincing apologetically even as they shoved him over to the second marble slab.

Mezin had been unbound, where he lay still as the stone beneath him. Declared dead, by the poisoner's careful assessment of heartbeat and breath and eyes.

Siyon lay down on the other slab, with his eyes closed and his lips pressed tight together. He grabbed hold of the edge of the marble with a grip so tight his fingers seemed to sink into it.

No, wait; there was no *seem* to it at all. Zagiri could see the marble somehow *squished* between his fingers, like it had no more resistance than bread dough.

If he could do that to marble, what else could he do? If only he *would*. And yet, if he did…

The crowd screamed and shoved around Zagiri, wild as water on the boil, just *waiting* for an excuse to spill over. They churned with uncertainty. There were so many ways they related to Siyon—son of the city, bravi and alchemist, someone who'd shown them wonder— but also so many ways they feared what he'd become.

If Siyon fought, they would *explode*.

Maybe he should. Maybe they should.

Zagiri closed her eyes against the threatening tears, then blinked hard. She wouldn't turn away from this.

The least she could do was watch. She should *remember*, for the rest of her life, the reason *she* was fighting. The things she was fighting to prevent from ever happening again.

She'd change the city, she swore it. Even if it took her whole life.

The poisoner lifted his hands—the vial, and the supplication. The invitation to the world to intervene.

The crowd howled all around Zagiri. She wished she knew how to pray.

That white-gloved hand came down on Siyon's face, but he opened his mouth without coercion. He lay there, and let the poisoner pour the black vitriol down his throat.

Zagiri's knees gave way, and she sagged against the rope. She wanted to scream, to rage, to tear her hair out. She forced herself to watch, as Siyon's body went taut—like Mezin's had, arching up against the white silk bonds—and then collapsed in sudden stillness.

It *did* look peaceful, like that. Quick. Unbelievably sudden. He was there, one moment. *Alive.*

And then gone.

The crowd was still screaming, but the noise was already ebbing. As though the water of their rage was draining out of a holed bucket. As though there was nothing to keep it in, now that Siyon was gone.

The poisoner pulled off his gloves again, to lay a bare palm against Siyon's chest. Then in front of his nose and mouth. And finally, peeling back one eyelid. The formal motions of checking for signs of life.

He folded hands over his chest, and bowed to Siyon's dead body, before starting to unfasten the silken bonds.

It was done. It was *over*. Siyon was gone.

Zagiri still couldn't look away. Couldn't believe it. Ran her gaze over the inert body, even as the crowd around her shifted and seethed and shook itself out of this strange dream. *Was that it? Was that all? What now?* The guards and inquisitors along the boundary rope were relaxing their grip. Starting to call that it was all over, and people should move along. Starting to lean in, listen to questions, offer answers.

But up on the dais, the poisoner frowned and pulled up one of the silken bonds. It looked strange, peeling off Siyon's skin like it was sodden. Was that a faint wisp of something, rising off it?

Rising off *Siyon's body*?

Because Zagiri was still watching, she saw the moment Siyon's chest jerked, and his throat convulsed, and he *coughed*.

Zagiri ducked under the boundary rope before she could even think about it, sprinting for the dais.

The poison poured black and viscous straight into Siyon's mind. It hooked sharp into every corner of him, engulfed him in an instant of excruciation and thick, clogging darkness, and dragged him straight—

Down.

Out of his body, slamming into the earth. He shattered out of his skin and scattered to every corner of the world. He fled—like reflex, like a flinch, like instinct—in more directions than he could comprehend.

But the bounds of the Mundane caught him and would not let him past.

He belonged here, after all. He was the Power of the Mundane. He was *more* than Siyon Velo. More than merely human. He was...

Everything.

He spun in the darkness, a gyre of awareness and pain. Was he still falling? Was he still anything at all? Maybe he could stay here. It barely hurt at all, really. Everything seemed distant—the noise, the light, the concerns of reality.

He'd been so afraid of this. Of losing himself. He remembered that, dimly and distantly, before it crumbled to nothingness.

Something brushed against his hand. He *had* a hand. There came the faintest whiff of orange blossom and sandalwood.

Izmirlian. Siyon remembered him, and then remembered himself. It hitched at him, as though his descent had been momentarily arrested.

Enough to tip Siyon out of the gyre, plunging in a new direction now. The way he could always have pointed, like a compass to north.

A massive scaled claw hooked him out of the darkness and back into reality.

Parchment-pale eyes, with their star pupils, blinked down at Siyon, lying insignificant within the cage of her claws, sprawled on her fine-scaled palm. For a moment, in a strange echo, Siyon remembered Salt Night, looking into that same eye as he tried—and failed—to bind the dragon again.

Her strength, her glory, her denial.

He'd been so foolish.

But this wasn't memory, and they weren't in Bezim. Weren't anywhere Siyon had ever seen. The air scraped frosty against his gasping throat, and cold pierced him, here on a mountaintop with snow dusting the black-scaled bulk of the dragon.

Siyon had never been this cold, the sensation seizing him like a fist. His gaze skittered away from the dragon to the white clogging the air. The snow was so *soft*. In the operas, they'd always just scattered sequins on the stage or—in the cheaper productions—fish scales. This was...

Magical.

The dragon huffed a hot breath, blasting over Siyon like he'd opened a furnace. Her *teeth*—ink and ashes, they were even more enormous than he remembered, as though he'd tried his best to erase the memory entirely.

Finally, she said. Or rather, she conveyed the *sensation* of it, the impression of having waited such a very long time for a thing that you started to believe would never come, and yet you were patient as the earth, and could wait forever if you had to. The word itself was a pale shadow.

The dragon lifted him up—and Siyon grabbed desperately at the slight webbing between her talons, so he didn't go skidding off her palm. And yet—

He didn't move. Gravity didn't pull at him.

He wasn't really here.

She realised it a moment after he did; Siyon *felt* the twitch of her surprise. Surprise and then, rising swiftly up beneath it, anger.

He could feel her awareness stretching—it was enormous, it was the whole world, it was an echo of everything he'd feared about giving himself to the energy. Clearly he'd been a fool. For here she was, both *everything* and also, at the same time, wholly and completely and manifestly herself.

She stretched out and comprehended in an instant what had happened to Siyon. How he was here. Or not here.

He knew, because she knew, because the thought passed from her to him in a blink. He'd fallen into the Mundane, because all his resistance was gone. The flesh, dead. Lying unbreathing on a marble slab in the old hippodrome of the city of Bezim.

They'd killed him.

Like they'd tried to kill *her*.

How dare they?

The hot rush of anger came boiling up so fast, so scaldingly, that Siyon was shouting with rage before he realised it wasn't his.

They may not. They must not. This cannot be borne.

"No," Siyon gasped—actual words, with his actual mouth, and he felt a spasm in his chest. He had a chest, he had a mouth, he had a *body*, far away. "No, wait—"

Too late. As though the realisation had woken reality to the impossibility of what was happening, pressure tightened all around Siyon and whipped him away again. He was gone from the dragon's grasp, but she was still *right there*, with him in everything and everywhere. Even as Siyon hurtled back through darkness and energy and the Mundane, he could feel her wings stretch, her defiance screaming at the sky.

How dare they?

She leapt, wings clawing at the night. She turned herself unerringly toward him.

Toward Bezim, with all her wrath for those who would dare to try killing *her* Power.

Siyon slammed down, flat on his back, the sky a dazzle over him, the world pain beneath him, and every part of his body heaving. *His* body, real and shuddering—choking, heaving, slick with a sticky, slimy sweat. Siyon kicked and convulsed.

"Siyon!" someone screamed, and then Zagiri was at his side, grabbing at his shoulders and hauling him off the slab.

Siyon nearly fell over, staggering and tilting, slipping against the syrupy mess on the marble and he would have gone over, save for her catching his weight.

She grunted, a pained sound on the verge of a scream, but held them both steady. Held on to him despite the thin grey ooze that slicked down his skin, spattered into the dirt.

"Are you *sweating out the poison?*" Zagiri demanded, voice high and thin. "What did you *do* to the slab?"

Around them, the guards who'd escorted him here backed away, horror twisting toward fear on their faces. The poisoner crouched as though trying to hide at the foot of the slab—the slab that looked rumpled and pocked as a moth-eaten blanket.

Siyon's mind squelched like three-day-dead fish. His bones shifted like sand. His vision skewed, thick with a bronze overlay that shimmered with the echoes of the entire world.

"Hey!" someone shouted—not for the first time. A woman, over at the mouth of the tunnel in the deep shade beneath the balcony. She looked familiar, in the white tunic of the Palace guard, but when she pulled back the sleeve, there was the *S* and baling hook of the Shore Clan. Siyon knew her: Aghut's lieutenant who'd met him in Dockside. "Come *on*," she snapped. "We have a way out, but you need to *move*."

CHAPTER 22

Zagiri had so many questions—how was the Knife here? Why was she wearing a *guard* uniform? Why was she helping them?—and no time to ask any of them.

"*Move,*" the Knife snapped, and they did.

Or tried to.

Siyon was impossibly alive. His eyes were open, but his gaze skittered and skewed; his feet were hardly more stable, sliding beneath him in ways that Zagiri didn't understand. He paced steadily beside her for half a dozen steps, and then his knees gave way. All his weight sagged across her shoulders, where she'd pulled his arm, and the not-quite-healed bones ground beneath her grip, turning her vision white.

Both of them hit the floor, sand digging into Zagiri's bracing palm.

"Fuck's *sake,*" the Knife snarled.

Zagiri couldn't blame her for the panic behind her anger. From the roar following them, everything was going to the Abyss in the arena—"*The Sorcerer!*" someone was screaming, over and over, in fear or exultation—but they couldn't rely on the chaos covering their escape for long.

The Knife grabbed Siyon's other arm to haul it over her own shoulders, then pulled a horrified face at the thin greyish slime that seemed to be *coating* Siyon's skin. "What the absolute *fuck* is this?"

"You think I know?" Zagiri demanded right back, pushing herself upright, and gritting her teeth through the agony in her shoulder. "You think I know *anything* about what just happened?"

She heard her own voice as if from a distance, shrill and tremulous, and forgave herself for it. This was a mess.

"Mess," Siyon murmured, head lolling, and had he picked that out of her *thoughts*? He grimaced and got his feet beneath him again. When his eyes opened, the wide black pupils had a burning bronze spark in their depths. "She's coming," he said.

"Not yet," the Knife huffed, peering ahead in the gloomy tunnel. "But they will be, very soon. We need to keep moving."

Between the two of them, they got him stumbling forward, even as Siyon shook his head, blinking like he couldn't see straight. "What happened?" he mumbled.

"Good bloody question, fisherlad," the Knife grumbled as they staggered onward.

He peered at her, and then at Zagiri, wincing at a particularly loud scream from behind them. "I didn't want this," he murmured. "Better if I'd di—"

"*No*," Zagiri insisted, tugging at his hand despite the twinge in her shoulder. "No, Siyon, *listen*. This is our chance. We can hold this together. We can…" She didn't know. She was trying to find a landing while in free fall. She'd hoped for this, but planned for everything else. But she was bravi—or she had been. She could adapt on the fly. "*Everyone* is looking right now. Everyone knows the Council is fallible. That their order is *wrong*. We can change everything. We can push."

"How?" the Knife snarled, from his other side, as Siyon's head lolled between them. "The azatani won't—"

"*I'm* azatani," Zagiri snapped at her, pain sharpening her tongue. "We're not all the same. We can *decide* what we are. We can choose something different." She had to grit her teeth—against the pain of Siyon's stumbling, and against the tears that threatened. She had to believe this impossible chance could work.

"How," the Knife continued, "without turning that into a city-wide battle?" She jerked her head toward the racket behind them. The thunder of feet against the aged bench seats of the stands. The roar of the crowd, like a fresh-sparked inferno.

Zagiri nearly challenged her—concern for peace was rich coming from someone who'd tried to blow up the Swanneck bridge. But Zin had made that accusation, she remembered now, and he had hardly proven himself trustworthy. In the end, it didn't matter. The answer was the same, regardless.

"We all pull together," Zagiri panted. All the organising the councillors had done around that table—the councillors and *her*. But more than that too. She looked across Siyon's slumped-forward head at the Knife. "There are more than just azatani and *their* order in this city. Don't tell me Aghut hasn't planned for unrest."

The Knife didn't deny it. "We can't keep a lid on things forever, though."

"Until commencement." If their plans still held. If everything came together. If, if, *if.* But they had Siyon now. They *had* to make the most of this. They had to make it work.

"Five days?" the Knife growled, heaving at Siyon and not letting him stagger. "And how are we going to hide *him*?"

Siyon's head lolled back, his eyes full of bronze sparks. "I can," he started, and then collapsed entirely, jerking both of them down with him; Zagiri's shoulder twisted, and her knee slammed into the stone floor. She cried out.

A spark of light appeared in the tunnel, far ahead of them, and a faint voice called, "Who's there?"

"Shit," the Knife hissed. "*Shit.* Get him— *What the fuck?*"

Beside her wide-eyed horror, Siyon was down on his knees—

No, wait. Siyon was *buried to the knees in the floor.* Like the stone had given way, except there was no breakage, no gaping hole like where the Palace had once been. The stone had simply swallowed him, like water.

Zagiri remembered Siyon's fingers digging into the poisoner's slab, the state of it when he'd impossibly risen from it. She'd been too busy getting him out of there to think much about it. Too busy dealing with yet another impossibility.

"How is he doing this?" the Knife asked, faint and tremulous. "What *is* he?"

Zagiri didn't know. It didn't matter. "He's my friend," she snapped. "He's the only one who can fix this. He's Siyon Velo."

As though answering to his name, Siyon's eyes snapped open. And they were glowing—not just with sparks, but burnished bronze from edge to edge. "Let me go," he said, and his voice was the slow grind of stone.

The Knife did, springing away with alacrity, but Zagiri said, "No, wait, *Siyon*—"

"They're *coming*," the Knife whispered furiously. She was right; the tramp of approaching boots was echoing down the tunnel. "Even if we get him out, we can't get him *out*."

Zagiri tangled her fingers in Siyon's ruined shirt, tacky with the grey goo. Despite that sheen to his eyes, she hoped he could still see her. "Siyon, are you all right?"

Ridiculous question. He'd just been *poisoned*, and he shrugged it off. He was being *swallowed by rock*.

But Siyon smirked a little, like he could see the funny side of it too, and *that* was him; she knew that smile. He blinked, and the glow in his eyes faded a little—not entirely, but enough that she could see his natural grey beneath. "Commencement," he whispered. "Five days. Fix this."

"We can," Zagiri said. Promised. Hoped. "Together, we can."

"I'll be there," he said.

And slipped into the rock like a pebble disappearing into the sea, silently and instantly and *gone*. Nothing left but the poison-sweat drying on Zagiri's palms.

"Come on," the Knife growled, and grabbed Zagiri's elbow to haul her up, sending a fresh spike of pain zinging along all her nerves. "What?"

Zagiri shook her head, cradling her arm close to her body. Least of her problems, right now. She looked back, the way they'd come, where the arena had turned into a howling storm. Someone was shouting for the crowd to disperse, voice booming under alchemical amplification.

A closer voice snapped, "Hold there! Don't move, or we'll shoot. This egress is for judicial personnel only."

It was a squad of inquisitors, two of them with big black crossbows lifted and loaded. Like the one Xhanari had shot Izmirlian with. Like the ones Anahid had reported from Siyon's arrest. The ones that were illegal, save aboard ship in foreign waters, or amid emergency, war, or riot.

This probably applied.

The Knife grabbed Zagiri's other arm, hauling both of them around. She straightened her shoulders in her white guard tunic, though she was careful to keep Zagiri in front of her Shore Clan tattoo. "Thank goodness you're here. Everything's gone to shit back there and I have to get this one"—she gave Zagiri a little shake—"to my captain."

The squad leader glanced nervously down the tunnel behind them. "You can't come this way. I have my orders."

"Which have just been countermanded," a new voice announced from behind the squad. It was a voice that snapped with authority in every crisp Avenue word; the inquisitors reacted instinctively, standing aside and lowering the crossbows.

Balian Hisarani stepped between them with hauteur and arrogance to match his eldest brother. There was another squad— of white-tunicked Palace guards—just behind him. "I'm glad you haven't actually *abandoned* your posts," he said, with a snide edge that had the inquisitor captain flushing—more likely with rage than embarrassment—but Balian gave him no time to respond before continuing: "All units are ordered with immediate effect to crowd control. The hippodrome needs to be cleared *now*. You and your men proceed with all haste. I'll ensure these two get where they need to go."

He hadn't even looked at Zagiri or the Knife. She knew, because she couldn't stop staring at him.

The inquisitor squad turned sharply, and the Palace squad fell in behind them, and all of them went trooping away down the tunnel.

Balian barely waited until they were out of earshot before he muttered, "What a fucking debacle. Well, where is he?"

"Who?" the Knife asked, in a very good show of confusion.

Zagiri shrugged out of her grip. "You wouldn't believe me if I told you."

Balian looked far more tightly wound than she'd ever seen him. She wondered if it was anger, or panic, or simply his lingering grief and the pain of seeing *her*. "Of him," he said, "I might believe anything."

He stepped aside, jerking his head to the empty tunnel in front of them.

The Knife clearly had no idea what was going on, or why he was doing this, but she wasn't going to question it. As she hurried past him, Zagiri called, "Wait! Five days, right?"

Until commencement. Until they could take their chance at building a better Bezim.

Balian's eyebrows ticked up, but the Knife just called over her shoulder, "We'll do what we can."

As she ran away down the tunnel, Balian turned those considering eyes—those eyes that saw too much, always—on Zagiri. "Five days," he repeated. "You're part of whatever Filosani is planning for commencement?" But before she could even express surprise that he knew, his eyes widened a little, and he added: "Ah, no, *she's* part of *yours*. Your proposal for reform."

Zagiri winced, holding on to her shoulder and wishing she could just...stop. Just for a little. "It was supposed to be a secret," she muttered.

"Don't worry," Balian said, which was ridiculous advice right now. "Avarair's been pacing and muttering about Filosani's lot being up to something, but I heard about your wild ideas from Lusal." His mouth tightened. "*She* thought it was the most wonderful notion she'd ever heard."

Zagiri barely remembered telling her. Not that she had a *proposal*. Just...in passing, wouldn't-it-be-nice, Bezim could be a better city for everyone, not just us.

Lusal, full of dreams, choosing what sort of azata she wanted one day to be. Looking at Zagiri, and choosing *like her*.

It still hurt sharp as new.

"This is our chance," she said through the pain. "This is the best chance we'll have."

"Maybe," Balian said, but it sounded like agreement. He was considering. Measuring. "You'll need a sponsor, someone neutral who can—"

"I *know*," Zagiri growled. Did he think she was—

He was *smirking*. Asshole. "Will Siyon be there?"

That flushed her with cold uncertainty. "He promised he would," Zagiri noted. But he'd promised while literally *sinking into the floor*. After having risen from his own execution. The wild and unexpected victory of it still shook her. She wasn't sure if Siyon still lived in the same world as the rest of them. If he was still made of the same flesh and blood. Would she even recognise him in five days?

Balian nodded. "I'll do what I can. Keep the Pragmatics off-balance and looking the wrong way. It won't be difficult, they're in a state already. And Avarair…" He grimaced, too complicated an expression for Zagiri to even start unpicking it. "He's a mess. If he *was* involved in what happened, with the Ball, he really doesn't like it. He's…unpredictable. Which is not something I ever thought I'd say about *that* brother."

There seemed little she could say to that, save: "Thanks. And for showing up here as well."

Balian huffed a little breath. "I didn't even realise it was you until I was already halfway down here. And then I asked myself, who would run *toward* the wildly impossible?"

Zagiri smiled, thin and pained. She scuffed her boots on the sandy stones that had swallowed Siyon up. "Yeah, well. He did it for me first."

And she was going to do everything she could to make it count.

The streets were still crowded with people now streaming *away* from the old hippodrome. The vendors were gone, and the protesters part of the wholesale panic.

Anahid had planned to make use of the inevitable disruption, but she hadn't expected *this*. Not the executioner's recoil, not her sister—of course and always—leaping into the chaos. Nothing Anahid could do but try to adapt her plans, clutching at the back of Laxmi's leather armour as they shoved out of the battering storm of the crowd.

They found Peylek back in the same courtyard entrance, as though no time had passed. She greeted them with a wide grin. "Even better chaos than you anticipated."

Far better. Siyon had *survived*. Anahid could have wept from joy and relief. But she still had business, and her entire plan might have been scuttled before they had even begun. "Can we still manage?"

"Don't worry." Peylek waved a hand; something glinted on the back of it. "Everyone's already in place, and I have a pin in the target."

"You think you can keep eyes on someone in *this*?" Laxmi demanded. Even Anahid was skeptical; Peylek couldn't have inherited *that* much from her former baron.

"I didn't say eyes." Peylek lifted her hand. That glint on the back was a bronze-tipped sewing pin, the sort a dozen dressmakers had stuck into Anahid by accident.

Peylek had it neatly tacked through the skin of the back of her hand.

"Still in there," she said, pointing with her other hand back at the old hippodrome. "Coming out the more landward entrance, I'd wager, but if she goes an unexpected way, I'll feel it."

"How useful," Anahid said faintly, once she'd managed to close her aghast mouth. "Let's get in position, then."

They hurried through the streets, trickling downhill like water with the others fleeing the chaos. The noise followed them, a distant roar of surf against cliffs. This might all be too much. There might not be any sensible place to build from, when this fire had burned out. But Anahid had to lay foundations as though there *would* be.

If Zagiri's reform was to be raised at commencement, they needed a sponsor. To get one, the Zinedanis had to be dealt with.

Anahid couldn't flinch now.

The commercial district was shut up tight, the shops hurriedly shuttered. One broad street had been blocked entirely by an overtipped cart, and two burly delivery men shouted at each other over the placid ox.

One of the men stopped gesticulating long enough to tip a wave at Peylek as they went past.

The next street along was narrow, not quite a lane, but rarely travelled. Unless, of course, you were on your way from the old hippodrome to a fashionable apartment in the next block over, and the main road was blocked.

A mismatched bunch of trouble loitered halfway down the block. One of the security guards from Sable House stood alongside half a dozen odd-job crew members from Peylek—more used to running messages than wielding the enforcer's clubs that hung from their belts—and two former Zinedani heavies lifted from the new communal pool of Flower district security. None of them precisely had Anahid's trust, but all she needed for this, she hoped, was bodies.

That and Laxmi at her side.

"Relax," Laxmi suggested, rolling her shoulders beneath her leather armour. She grinned. "It's not like we're storming the Banked Ember. Though I still say that would've been more fun."

"You and your fun," Anahid said, just to see the widening of Laxmi's grin.

Then Peylek flexed her pin-pierced hand and said, "They're heading this way."

Anahid nodded to the gathered group. "Take your places. Close at my signal and do *nothing* else unless specifically instructed."

They scattered up and down the narrow street, slipping into niches and loitering in doorways. Lying in wait. Anahid ducked behind a flight of stairs, Laxmi's breath hot on her neck as both of them watched the entrance to the narrow street. Time seemed to creep past, until three figures appeared.

Marel Sakrani, the lower-tier azata who had once been Marel Zinedani, certainly wasn't naive. She always travelled with a manservant—not uncommon for azatas, though Marel's was rather broader across the shoulders than one just there to carry shopping or a parasol. Today she'd shown her wisdom in taking a second fellow along to the hippodrome as well.

Anahid let them get well into the narrow street before she stepped out; not a very impressive roadblock, save for Laxmi behind her.

One manservant laid a hand on his mistress's shoulder, the other immediately turning back. But three of Anahid's motley—one of them perhaps recognisable to Marel as a former employee—now blocked that exit.

Say this for Marel: She lifted her chin and walked on to face Anahid with perfect poise. The only resemblance she had to her late father was in the hardness of her eyes. She was in many ways everything that Anahid was not: short, generously curved, and pretty, complete with a dimple that pressed into one cheek even when she was looking annoyed. She was wearing a simple but elegant day dress, a beaded headscarf, even net gloves.

"I don't know what you hope to achieve here," she snapped in greeting.

Anahid's heart beat fast, but she forced a slow smile. "Well, if I were your father, I'd be whisking you off to ask the other barons for your death."

Marel blinked. "What?"

"A thing," Anahid continued, "I'm quite sure you *didn't* do before you hired a crew to kill my guard."

At the edge of her vision, Laxmi wiggled her fingers in a coy little wave.

Marel's face pinched tight. "I don't know what you're talking about."

"Yes, you do," Anahid corrected. The blood was singing in her veins now, thrumming against her fingertips.

Marel's gaze whisked over them, catching on the others of Anahid's crew who'd stepped out behind her, ready to catch anyone who made a run for it. (Well, not *anyone*. Anahid had other plans for the servants.) Marel drew herself up. "You've been *interfering*. You know you have; don't play innocent with me. You brought it all on yourself."

Anahid slapped her. *She* wasn't wearing net gloves, and her hand made a most satisfying *crack* against Marel's stubborn jaw. Almost as satisfying as Marel's outraged gasp, or the tears that glimmered in her eyes as she turned back to stare, outraged but also fearful. Her servants took a half step forward, arrested again at Laxmi's growl.

"I didn't *want* to interfere," Anahid snapped, the words tight as knots in a line. "I just want a stable and safe District in which to run my business. But *you* have made that impossible." She lifted her gaze, meeting the eyes of one manservant, then the other over their mistress's shoulder. "You," she said pointedly, "are free to go."

"Unless you'd prefer to stay," Laxmi added, with almost lascivious emphasis.

They lasted longer than Anahid had expected before they broke and ran, back the way they'd come. One of them was stopped briefly by those blocking the street's entrance, but then they were both through, and away.

Marel lifted her chin, trying her best to look imperious with the mark of Anahid's hand starting to flush on her face. "They'll be going straight to my sister," she declared.

"I do hope so," Anahid replied with a smile. "That's the whole point of this."

She stepped aside, and Laxmi grabbed Marel, hoisting the azata over her shoulder with apparently no effort whatsoever, leaving her kicking and shrieking, both ineffectually.

Cheap theatre, but that's what Bezim liked best.

They didn't have far to go—part of why Anahid had chosen this spot, rather than anywhere closer to the hippodrome. Plenty of time to get settled in before Marel's manservant came back with Ruzanna and reinforcements, bringing them to the location he'd been given.

A location still, after months, so festooned with alchemical protections that no force the Zinedani could still muster would be sufficient to batter a way inside.

"Don't mind the mess," Laxmi said breezily to Marel, setting her back on her feet in the apartment over the milliner's on Glass Street. "We haven't really been tidying up recently. Very busy, you realise, getting stabbed." Her grin was equal parts menace and amusement.

Marel froze, her eyes darting around what had once been Siyon's workroom, and Geryss Hanlun's before him. "This is the Sorcerer's apartment."

"It was mine too," Laxmi objected, nudging a pair of her knives aside so she could hoist herself up to sit on the workbench. She moved easily enough, but she pressed a hand briefly to her side. Marel curled in on herself, doing her best, it seemed, not to touch anything at all.

They waited in silence thereafter, as time ticked past and Anahid worried that something had gone awry. Had Ruzanna gone to the inquisitors instead? But surely *they* had no time to spare today. From the open balcony doors, the roar and rush of the crowd at the hippodrome sounded like the ocean had gotten loose in the city.

Time ticked past, until one of the motley—a former Midnighter, lean and fast as a fish—came racing up the stairs from below. "They're coming, mistress," he gulped. "Like—fair a dozen or more."

About what they'd expected. Anahid ducked out to the balcony, calling up the spiral staircase to the Midnighter waiting on the roof, "Anything?" But apparently Ruzanna had declined to send further trouble over the rooftops.

Too long away from Bezim, perhaps. Not thinking like someone who lived with the bravi.

Anahid hooked her hand through Marel's elbow and said to Laxmi, "I've got this, but you can tag along if you like." The golden flare of her eyes might have been affront, or something else. Anahid didn't have time to consider it right now.

She marched Marel down the stairs, to where Ruzanna was kicking at the leaf-and-vine gate that Siyon had liked so much.

The *well-charmed* gate.

Anahid shoved Marel ahead of her, calling, "You'll just hurt yourself if you continue."

"Fuck you!" Ruzanna snapped through the ironwork bars. "How fucking *dare* you?" She grabbed the gate with both hands.

Then yelped, leaping back, shaking out her hands like she'd

plunged them instead into boiling water.

"Let's all stay civil," Anahid said. Her heart was racing. Fear, at least a little. This could still come unstuck. But not only fear.

She liked this. She liked the control. She always had. The thrill of having these people, these events, in her power.

She *could* kill them, perhaps. Step back and let Laxmi leap into the fray. Signal the crew on the roof to let death fall like rain. She *could*. But she wasn't going to. No one was even bleeding yet. No one needed to be.

Fuck Tahera's smug certainty that she could make Anahid her monster. Anahid was doing this *her* way.

Ruzanna snarled from the other side of the gate, snatching a knife from the hand of one of her minions and jabbing it toward Anahid. She was pale with outrage. "You are starting a *war*."

"I'm not *starting* anything," Anahid countered, and then realised. Her mouth rounded in surprise. "Oh. Your idea alone, was it, Marel?"

Azata Sakrani's mouth pinched tighter as her sister snarled, "*What* was her idea?"

"I was attacked in my own House," Anahid told her, her voice rough with the emotion she wasn't allowing to spill over right now. "My guard was nearly killed."

From behind her on the stairs, Anahid heard: "Not *that* nearly."

"Yeah, I heard. Pissing off everyone, aren't y—" But Ruzanna stopped mid-word, her expression turning thunderous. "Marel, you *didn't*. We agreed—this is *business*."

"We can't do *business* with thirteen of our Houses presenting demands for contract arbitration due to unmet conditions," Marel snapped.

They both looked at her, matching expressions of accusation. But Anahid just shrugged. "You can't take the barony without the responsibilities. But either way, here we are. What happens next? Are we going to war—brutal, drawn-out, *expensive* war?" She smiled, as though that idea didn't bother her. A sharp and slicing smile she hadn't allowed herself since she'd stood in the Badrosani theatre, blood upon her blade.

Her hands were clean, this time. She smiled all the wider for it.

"Or," Anahid suggested brightly, when neither of them shouted enthusiastically about doing battle. "*Or* are you renegotiating your contracts as landlord only, walking away from the District with rents in hand, and being fucking grateful for it?"

After that, it all went fairly smoothly.

By the time Anahid climbed the stairs again—alone now—Laxmi was back sitting on the workbench, sagged on one bracing hand, the other lifting a flagon for a swig. She raised an eyebrow at Anahid and offered the rakia. "Celebratory toast?"

"Idiot." Anahid stepped around the offering to frown at Laxmi's side, where she'd laid a hand earlier. "Is it bleeding again?"

Laxmi wrinkled up her face. "Maybe a little. Not enough to bother."

"I'll be the judge of what bothers me," Anahid snapped, stepping between Laxmi's knees and reaching for one of the buckles on her armour.

Laxmi grabbed her wrist, tight enough to stop her, not quite enough to hurt. "You should've kept the little one. Hostage to good conduct."

Anahid met her golden gaze. She was very close. But Anahid felt steady. "I'm not running things that way," she stated firmly. "I'll hold them true; I'll face them down as many times as it takes, but I won't be cruel. I'm doing this *my* way. And if you don't like it, I can take my things and go."

The grip on her wrist tightened, just shy of pain. "I didn't say I didn't like it," Laxmi murmured.

Anahid found herself watching the words on Laxmi's lips. Watching the slow curve of her smile.

She lifted her other hand and curled it around Laxmi's head, pushing her fingers into the ink-dark spill of the fallen demon's hair. It felt wildly daring, but then again, she had just faced down the children of a baron, who'd wished her and hers harm, and been foiled in that wish. She *was* daring.

And with Laxmi this close, the curve of her mouth less an

invitation than a challenge, she felt all the more so. She liked it. *Laxmi* liked it.

Anahid let her laughter bubble up. "How," she asked, barely more than a whisper, "did you fall in love with *Enkin*?"

Laxmi's mouth twitched. "Shut up," she growled.

And hauled Anahid in to kiss her.

CHAPTER 23

The city seethed, bubbling and bumping like a cauldron of fish stew on the boil. By the time the sun was setting, sinking blood-red over the ruins of the depot in the western hills, the chaos had long overflowed the old hippodrome into the rest of the city.

Zagiri swung one-armed—her *good* arm—from a lanternpost at the corner of the Boulevard and Kellian Way, watching the churning mass of people still clogging the intersection farther up, close to the old hippodrome. She'd have a much better view from a rooftop, but what she *didn't* have was two working arms to climb up there with. In fact, her injured shoulder ached so badly she'd fashioned a new sling from her waist sash. The tassels tickled at her neck, but the damn thing hurt less when it wasn't jostling around.

She was far too busy to go and see a healer again right now, even if any would be open for business, and not hiding behind thrice-locked and barred doors.

"They're not moving," Zagiri declared, sliding back down the post to firm cobblestones again. "I think we— Are you even listening?"

Mayar blinked at her—hard and squinting, as though trying to clear something from their eyes. "Sorry, it's just..." They stretched out a hand, like they were standing on the deck of a heaving ship instead of the cobblestones of the Boulevard. "The energy is *vigorous*. I feel like I'm in a full waterskin strapped to a galloping camel."

Zagiri bit her tongue on asking—yet again—whether Mayar could tell where Siyon had gone. If he was all right. The answers were always more troubling than precise, and in any case, it didn't matter. She'd see him again at commencement, in five days. He'd promised. As long as commencement happened. As long as the city didn't shake itself apart.

That was her job tonight.

Craning back to look up at the nearest building, Zagiri whistled sharply, and a tricorn-topped head appeared over the edge of the roof. Daruj waved, and whistled back—the lifting note of a Bracken blade asking for orders. Zagiri cupped a hand around her mouth and bellowed: "Keep an eye on them. Call in the others if they start causing trouble."

As Daruj raised a thumbs up, Zagiri was already turning away, down the Kellian Way, and whistling again—the short, sharp blast of one of the few all-tribe signals: *alert, on me.* She strode down the hill, with Mayar trailing behind her like a vague shadow, and a half-dozen other bravi emerged from alleyways, jumped down from the trees, flowed in behind her.

They weren't all Bracken, but they *were* all known to Zagiri—they and many others now scattered across the upper city, watching the trouble points and unruly clumps of people, had worked together on the Palace ruins in the bravi nightshift workgang. The blades she'd pulled together to make a political point.

They'd been waiting for her when she staggered out of the hippodrome. Not all of them, but someone from every tribe, sent by the sergeant, ready and waiting to rally the rest of their crews.

As she'd stared at them in astonishment, one of the Bleeding Dawn—Zagiri thought it was actually Paq, the one who'd shirked his duties to see to the needs of his Avenue girlfriend—rolled his eyes and said: "The seventh runner just saved one of us from the final fall. You think we're going to turn our backs on that?"

Not every bravi blade turned out to their tribe's whistles, and Zagiri couldn't blame them. The hippodrome had been a churning cauldron, and the stories were already sizzling wild through the streets—that Siyon had turned into a dragon and eaten the executioner; that he'd vanished into thin air; that he'd disappeared into the earth and could now appear *anywhere*, like Midnight had once been said to.

That last one…well, Zagiri wasn't speculating.

Her scraped-together pack of bravi had tried to bring some safety to the mess as the former protesters had spilled from the hippodrome, now turned merry or menacing in the wake of the execution's outcome. It had all been a mad scramble, whisking fearful families down narrow alleys and through building courtyards, and even opening routes to the rooftop where the worst of it could be waited out. The chorus of bravi-whistled signals had seemed incongruous in the bright afternoon, but more blades—tribes and freeblades both—had rallied to their cause with every passing bell. They'd been able to spread out, creating a cordon of more-trouble-than-they're-worth to steer the rambunctious mobs into larger spaces where their energy could splash out harmlessly.

Out into Cliffside, and down into the commercial district, where the havoc had already blocked streets and broken windows. The Flower district had their gates heavily guarded, spreading calm out into the surrounding streets, and offering safe haven for anyone caught in the upper city and in need of shelter.

Meanwhile, the guards and the inquisitors had locked down the hippodrome, escorting the azatani back to the Avenues and their securely charmed townhouses. It was the *rest* of the city left at the mercy of the storm. As always.

Zagiri wasn't going to hide. She wasn't going to keep her head down and assume everyone else was just as safe. She *was* an azata now, but that didn't mean she had to cower.

It could mean something else, for her. For Anahid. For Lusal. For every azatani blade who'd come when she whistled. For any of them who willed it so.

Dusk slipped quietly across the city, but only half the lanterns lining the Kellian Way kindled. One lantern-post had been knocked askew, the lantern smashed in another and simply missing from a third. Darkness spotted all the way down to Tower Square, which was glowing merrily with the remains of the bonfire of smashed café tables that had been built around the statue of the Last Duke earlier in the afternoon, before Zagiri and her bravi had pushed down this far.

Zagiri paused in one of the remaining pools of radiance holding the gloaming at bay, and stared up at the wreckage of the Eldren Hall. Fuck, they'd really done a number on it. The towers had all toppled, and the dome had collapsed into a slumped pile of rubble.

Perhaps she felt a flicker of pride. It had taken a dragon to make this much of a mess of the Palace, after all. But the thought was fleeting, chased away by guilt and exhaustion.

From here, Zagiri could hear a faint wash of sound from the group she'd left up on the Boulevard—hopefully settling down, even if they weren't going home yet—and other sounds twitching through the city. Running feet and distant shouts, the drumming from university hill where two colleges were holding some sort of vigil, the ongoing amplified declarations from the hippodrome that everyone was to clear the area. But that was it.

Was this the first moment she'd had to draw breath since she'd stepped into the hippodrome this morning? Today had felt half a season long.

And it wasn't over yet. Even as Zagiri turned to consider the group with her—a mismatched bunch of bravi from all five tribes—a whistle sounded from over toward the Scarp. It was long and piercing, calling all blades urgently.

Zagiri lurched into a run, and the others were already moving, all of them racing to answer. They pelted along a side street and raced down the staircase into the fruit market.

It wasn't as much of a disaster as it could have been. Half the stall-holders hadn't bothered opening this morning, with the city so distracted, and many of the rest had shut up quickly once the shouting started. But still, there were knocked-over poles and torn awnings, smashed boxes thick with the tang of citrus pulp, shattered glass jars and a lingering miasma of pickling vinegar.

And shouting, over on the eastern fringe. Zagiri ran with the others through the market, skidding in the remains of a cabbage as she rounded the corner.

There were a dozen hefty figures outside one of the shops lining the market, cast into strange shadows by the lanterns—possibly pilfered from the street posts—held aloft by two of them. More of them *inside* the shop, having entered through the smashed display windows. As Zagiri steadied herself, a sack came flying out, scattering pale purple leaves in its wake. A crash sounded from inside, and then a raucous cheer.

Just *looters*, taking advantage.

"Hey!" Zagiri shouted, shouldering forward, before she really thought about it.

But though her bravi crew shifted nervously, they stayed behind her, standing firm as the thugs noticed them, one calling, "Oi, Lev!" into the shop.

A broad-shouldered man—presumably Lev—came crunching back out of the shop and swaggered over toward them. He had a chunk of wood propped against his hefty shoulder—not exactly a weapon, but not exactly *not*, either.

Zagiri didn't even have a blade at her hip, but she had a dozen behind her. Would it even matter? There were just as many of these guys, and they all looked dauntingly well built—laders or off-duty security for warehouses.

Their fight wouldn't be a bravi duel, that was for sure.

"I told them already," Lev said, gesturing with his lump of wood up toward the shop roof, where Zagiri could just make out the faint silhouette of two more people—probably the blades who'd whistled for help. "And I'll tell you right now, this ain't none of your business, get it? This lot"—he held up the wood, showing Zagiri that it was part of the shop's sign, reading: *Alchemical Tools*—"they think they can get away with anything. It ain't right. What happened up there ain't right!"

He pointed up the hill, to the old hippodrome, and his friends all cheered, a loud bark of noise that made Zagiri flinch.

But she didn't step back. "Nor is this!" she shouted back, and if her voice seemed thin after his, they still all turned to glare at her. "That's someone's livelihood you're trashing. Or are you just thieves?"

"Zagiri—" someone said nervously behind her.

Far too late. Lev roared and charged them, and his mates came as well.

Zagiri fell back with the other bravi, sabres whisking out of sheaths all around, but they needed space to bring them to bear. She wasn't armed at all, and Lev had an alarming turn of speed on him for such a big man.

She ducked away, behind a heavy table still half piled with massive winter melons. Lev came too, snarling with a glint in his fist now— a knife, one of the long and heavy Dockside working blades. Zagiri grabbed desperately for the first useful thing to hand—

And caught the thrust of his knife in the pale green swell of a winter melon. The impact jolted the fruit out of her hands, spinning away to thud heavily in the dark, but it took the knife with it.

Zagiri's relief was short-lived; Lev lifted his chunk of wooden sign over his head with both hands.

A new voice cut through the gathering gloom: "Stand down!"

It came with the tramp of boots and more shouting; Lev growled again, turning to run into the night, his friends clattering away with him.

Zagiri held up a hand against the glare from a well-maintained hand lantern, held aloft by—"Lieutenant Xhanari?"

He shifted the lantern enough that she could see his stony expression. "Just Xhanari now, it seems." He was still in grey, but his candle badge was gone; she'd seen him throw it down into the sand of the hippodrome arena as he walked away from his duty.

No, just from the execution. Because here he was, still keeping order.

Along with a dozen other grey-tunicked people, formed up in disciplined lines and armed with regulation short truncheons. There wasn't a candle badge among them.

Apparently Xhanari hadn't been the only inquisitor who felt what had happened this morning wasn't in keeping with the job he'd signed up for.

"Thanks," Zagiri managed. She wiped sweaty palms against her trousers; one shuffling foot kicked something heavy under the table.

Xhanari considered her. "So the bravi on every second rooftop, shouting down about where the trouble is...those are your doing, are they?"

Zagiri shrugged. "It's our city too, right?"

"Ours," Xhanari repeated, with a strange twist to his mouth.

What the name of the city meant, of course. But *ours* had been said by the azatani. It was supposed to be *their* Bezim.

"Yeah," Zagiri said. "Ours."

Hers, and Xhanari's, and everyone else's. Not *just* the azatani. Not anymore. Not if she had anything to say about it.

He cocked his head as more shouting came on the wind, from farther toward the Scarp. With a lifted eyebrow, he said, "Hope you weren't planning on getting home anytime soon."

"Wait a moment," Zagiri ordered as she ducked down and groped under the table until she found—*there*. She straightened with the knife Lev had left behind clutched in her melon-sticky working hand. It wasn't a sabre, but she'd make do. With a bright smile, she lifted her voice so not only Xhanari could hear. "Don't you know, the bravi go all night!"

They cheered, all around her, up on the rooftop. Answering levity tugged briefly at Xhanari's ranks of former inquisitors.

Even Xhanari almost smiled. She could have sworn it. But he was serious again as he said: "Then let's get to work."

Siyon slipped out of Zagiri's grip and sank.

Sank like an anchor, cast out in search of solidity in a storming sea.

Sank like a stone, into stone.

Sank like he had once before, thrown into the river trussed up in a sack. (Not *intended* to drown, but accidents happen.)

The same helplessness tightened his throat—there was no one who could help him, nothing he could do, nowhere he could run even if he made it out of this. The same panic twisted his limbs—he couldn't breathe, he couldn't get out, he couldn't survive this!

He *had* to survive this. He'd made Zagiri a promise. Five days. He'll be there.

He'd survived before. He could survive again. He was more than he had been, in that sack.

More, and yet also...less.

Something had been left behind—on the executioner's slab, in the darkness of the Mundane, in his thick and tacky sweat. Or perhaps in the air above, unable to sink into stone as he had. Some part of *him*.

Without it, the rest of him frayed easily at the edges. It would be so easy to sink forever. He couldn't remember why he'd resisted before. He could just dissolve into the stone and the world and the Mundane itself. He could be here—be this, be a part of his plane—forever, and that wouldn't be death.

It had happened this way before. The very earth itself had been the Power. That might even have been how the dragon came to be chained, asleep, in its cave. Siyon *knew* it, seeping into his mind like the slow accretion of stone over centuries. He could relax. This would be fine. This would serve.

But it wouldn't save the city.

The stone smoothed over his mind, pressing at his concerns. Never mind the city—that was fleeting, a thing of mere centuries, barely the spark of light from a shooting star against the velvet night of Mundane eternity. The Power needn't be troubled about such small things; the whole plane was his, and he was the plane. Let it go.

No. The city was people, and people *mattered*.

He planted his feet on that certainty and halted his descent. He shook the encasing stone away from his mind, like shrugging out of wet canvas. He reached out to grasp and pull around him—not power, not energy—but *himself*.

A person, not merely the Power of the Mundane.

His senses skittered and skidded, spilling out over hills and into valleys, delving and curling like curious roots, seeping down like water into the earth, leaping up like mountains to the sky. He felt every grain of sand, every unfurling leaf, every creeping beast, every person, every monster, every beating heart...

He was everywhere. He was everything. He was.

But he was *Siyon Velo* too.

He scraped at the Mundane, like scaling a fish, gathering himself back together one glittering fleck at a time. He winkled the scraps of himself out of the cracks between things and peeled the thin veneer of who he was off the apple curve of the world.

He had become the Power. And he would remain as such.

But ink and ashes, it was difficult. He worked one-handed, clinging with the other to the city, to *his* city, to his home. He could feel it trembling in his grip, feel it shaking as though another dragon were birthing itself from the depths. He could hear—

People running through the streets, tangled in fear and panic, splashed by anger and brutal victory, but overhung by care and succour, like vines trailing down in tendrils and delicate blooms.

Siyon scraped up shards of his own memories—of a spreading-tree badge and the weight of a sabre in his hand. Kiss of midnight air on his skin and the press of his bladebrother's shoulder to his. Daruj and Voski Tolan and Zagiri, plummeting with the sunlight behind her, landing on his chest with the weight of impossibility...

He could see—

Words crawling across walls in empty streets, scraped with chalk, splashed with paint, carved with desperation and possibility. The Sorcerer Lives. Unnatural. Rise Bezim. *Other words too, written across the city in running feet and acts of cruelty and kindness. Words that told of what the city could be, what its people could do, what it all could mean.*

Siyon wrapped himself in hope, and fear, and determination. He bound himself with selfishness and generosity and all the ways people were the same and yet different. He painted the bruises of blows upon his own flesh, thus calling it into being, and he held up new arms to shield those who had no other protection.

He could taste—

Stone. Dust and the ages and the depths.

Too hard. It was all too hard. He was still sinking, despite everything. There wasn't enough left of him to resist.

He could feel—

The barest touch against the base of his spine, hardly there at all. A voice against his skin, no sound but only breath, shaped like words: "Let me help you. As you helped me."

Siyon stopped sinking. He drew a breath into ragged lungs. He opened his eyes.

"Izmirlian," he said, the word bittersweet on his lips.

He reached out, and no one was there.

No one but himself, alone in the dark.

But he was here. He was real. He'd stopped falling.

He was Siyon Velo again.

Not Siyon alone, though. As he unfurled, the Mundane hung sticky as a cobweb from every part of him. He felt it shift and sway around him, even as he moved through it—a part of it and yet distinct. Within himself, he found an awareness, and a knot of rage, coming swiftly nearer.

A scream in a throat not his own, wings tearing the sky, claws ready to rend.

They tried to kill you. They tried to kill me.

The dragon, coming fast as the ballista bolt that had torn through her side. Coming *back here.*

Siyon reached out to her, trying to explain, trying to reassure. He was fine, he was alive, they were both too much to be brought low, they could—

She shoved him aside, and came onward, ever onward.

Siyon set his teeth and pushed himself upward. He'd be there to meet her, then. He hadn't pulled himself back together, hadn't come back to this city, just to let the dragon tear it all down.

He rose again, through the earth, through stone. Back into his streets.

He clawed out of the darkness, like the dragon herself. Tore himself out of his interment. Ripped upward, to the light, to his life, to—

A fire, burning in the heart of Bezim, built of the life and hopes of the citizens, of their daily lives, of the things they were prepared to give to build a better tomorrow. It sent Siyon spinning upward like sparks and chances, swirling around the statue of the Last Duke on his horse, daubed in charred paint: *Ours.*

He reached out and grabbed hold of familiarity, of solidity, of something that was *his*—

And went tumbling across a warped and damp wooden floor, fetching up on the rag-twisted rug that Anahid had brought down to them in the lower city, insisting he should have *some* of his things in the place that he was living.

The lower city squat skewed strangely around him, more twisted and buckled than it had really been. He wasn't *only* here, or perhaps he wasn't only *now*. The rickety room smeared and stretched. Mayar was here—on the rug right beside Siyon, knees folded and breathing steadily in meditation; they were also over at the table, rummaging through Siyon's left-behind things; and also pacing, searching, a blur of movement. They were talking to someone—*It's been nearly a day now, if he was going to come here, he would have. I'll try*—

They were gone again, and Siyon was alone.

Not at all alone. The whole *city* was with him. Warmth enveloped him, bright and burnished, as more power welled up around him, slipping into the churning surge that was the city already. Too much, bound up here. Siyon needed to fix that, needed to make it right.

But he needed his feet beneath him, his head on straight. Needed to *not* be washed away by the flood of power, flowing along the streets with nervous gossip and patrolling feet. Lower city alleycanals, upper city avenues, cobblestones and pavers and hard-packed dirt. In his wake, the pixie skinks crawled out of cracks and fluttered their wings in the sun. Ahead of him, people peered out their windows, cracked their front doors, assessed the quiet of the city—truly calm, or merely biding its time? Siyon pooled with the Mundane power in fountain yards and building courts, where neighbours dared to come out and draw water, speak to one another, say: *Do you think it's over?*

Not yet, not yet. Five days.

How many had it been already?

Siyon opened his eyes, standing...somewhere. It wasn't only him; his city had *changed*. He was on the Kellian Way, with trees shading both sides of the wide street, but there were branches broken from

them, and posts missing their lanterns, and beside Siyon a set of stairs
scattered with broken stone rose to...

Oh. That *was* once the Eldren Hall. But his brother—his dead
brother, his executed brother, his brother who'd tried once to kill
him—had destroyed it. Attacked the azatani. Planted his anger in the
heart of the city and set a match to it.

The street around him—the Kellian Way, main thoroughfare from
the top of the city all the way down to Dockside—was empty. The sun
beat down with the steamy heat of storms brewing, as though winter
was long gone. It was midday, or close to it. *(It's been nearly a day.)*
Siyon turned, blinking in the glare, as warm bronze power sloshed
around him, crawling between the paving stones, dripping from the
bare tree limbs, crackling through the very air.

Where *was* everyone?

Even as he asked it, he knew the answer—knew it in the minds
of every Mundane thing around him. They were elsewhere. They
were hiding. They were scuttling around corners and lying as low
as they could. They were waiting to see what happened. Whether
the city exploded or stayed standing. Whether a future happened.
Whether—

"Hey! You there!"

Siyon didn't turn. Instinct kicked in, and he was running before
he thought about it, and even then he *knew*. Drumming boots with
the hard steel nails of the inquisitors, thundering across his cobbled
streets. Silver badges coiled with charms.

He didn't *need* to run, not like this, not through the streets, but
when he was so newly returned to this mortal form, he didn't trust it
to be waiting again if he left it. So Siyon ran, with his footsteps burning bronze in his wake as he flowed downhill, like water.

He didn't need to flee, because what could they do to him that
they hadn't already tried? Could they play this out a dozen times or
more, tragedy turned comedy, the man who couldn't be poisoned? Or
would each time kill a little more of him, until he slipped into the
sloshing of power like one more scrap of it?

So Siyon fled, the streets flashing by beneath his charmed heels, until all of a sudden there were no more. Just the cliff edge, flashing by, as Siyon leapt.

Out, into the river chasm. Like the path the griffin had taken, when he'd hurled it from a rooftop. Somewhere in his mind, the dragon flew—fast as an arrow—with her wings outstretched against the wind.

But Siyon had no wings of his own. He plummeted. He hit the water, and sank.

Like he had before.

Deep and deeper still, with the Mundane wrapped around him.

CHAPTER 24

"T his is entirely ridiculous," stated Rodesin, the manager of Gossamer House, in the prim manner Anahid suspected was simply the way he said *everything*. He sniffed disapprovingly. "Working together. Comparing methods. Drinking *tea*."

Anahid rather agreed; agitation twisted her stomach, sitting here sipping tea the day after Siyon had not quite been executed, and had very much gone missing. The city had calmed somewhat, overnight— partly because the inquisitors and guards were now patrolling at least the upper city, and partly because those patrols were being assisted (or occasionally circumvented, as necessary) by a mismatched amalgamation of bravi, District security, other scraps of baronial forces, and a squad of former inquisitors led by, Anahid had heard, Vartan Xhanari.

She was extremely curious how *that* had happened. But there was no time for distractions. Not when she needed the District under control, the Zinedani swept aside, and confirmation that the barons would make a new deal with Buni Filosani, if she became the new prefect. There were four more days until the commencement of the new azatani council.

There was no time to waste.

Yet here Anahid sat, in the pleasure gardens of the District, drinking tea with the managers who'd already joined, or newly expressed interest, in their federated barony. It was very good tea— she'd had Nura make it specially. Refreshing, *calming* tea. A sign of what she wanted to build together: something civilised.

And because she was building something civilised, she couldn't force them into it. She couldn't run roughshod over them, stamping her control. She *wasn't* becoming the baron. Not like that.

So Anahid sipped her tea and said nothing.

Attabel, from the Siren's Cove, waved a languid hand, fingers tipped today in a shimmering emerald green. "Roddy, darling, *you* are being ridiculous. We worked together under the Zinedani, after all."

"I wouldn't say *that*," reflected the manager of the Blueflower, tilting her head. "We jostled for position and favour, under the Zinedani."

"We *were* working together," Attabel retorted pointedly, "under the neglect of the Zinedani daughters. And I, for one, have no desire to go back to *that* set of circumstances. So unless anyone has a better idea...?" He lifted his eyebrows imperiously.

"We need a baron," snapped the manager of the Dragon's Flight— who insisted upon being called *Draconia*, though Anahid supposed as Lady Sable she really didn't have sail to spare for criticism. "You think the Badrosani and the Shore Clan are going to respect a *committee*? You think the *Zinedani* will?"

"I think," Anahid said as she lowered her teaglass; every eye turned to her. The attention was terrifying, but perhaps a little thrilling as well. "Mama Badrosani and Aghut are eager to avoid a confrontation with each other at this time, when it would be very easy to tip back into a full-blown war." And *none* of them wanted that. The last half-season had been bad enough. "If we show strength in the District, they will respect it. And I have made it quite clear to the Zinedani that they are welcome to join our federation as an interested party—" There was the expected outcry; Anahid raised her voice to continue. "—but otherwise, they are landlords only and will abide by all appropriate regulations and ordnances."

"Or what?" Draconia demanded. "You think they'll just go meekly?"

There was a creak of leather behind Anahid, as Laxmi sat up from her slouch and said, "Or *else*."

Anahid swallowed the urge to smile and said chidingly, "Laxmi. No. We are not engaging in violence in the District anymore. Not unless thoroughly provoked. Together, we can find other ways." She looked around the collected managers, the light glinting off their sparkling earrings and the gilding on their teaglasses. "That is the one thing I insist upon."

"The *one* thing," someone muttered.

But it was almost drowned out by Crosef of the Twist of Fate slamming down his teaglass with unwarranted force. He was a hefty man, looking more a fisherman than a House manager. "Enough of this meaningless chatter. I'll sign on to anything that keeps my House working, and working well. So all I came here to learn is whether the District will be open tonight."

They hadn't been, the night before, though the chaos in the streets had diminished significantly by then. But the District had been crowded with those residents of Bezim who'd been unable to make it safely back to their homes, and keeping the gates closed had meant a significant portion of the communal security forces could be sent out to aid in the maintenance of order in the wider city.

But tonight… "Why not?" Anahid said, and shrugged. "Let us offer both the thrill of a distraction and the warm glow of normality. Bezim is not broken, nor is it bowed."

Draconia tilted her head, the spikes of her hair making the gesture pronounced. "We could ensure a large and avid crowd," she said, eyeing Anahid in a somewhat alarming manner. "If we could suggest that the Sorcerer himself was hiding within the District. What say you, Lady Sable? Did not you offer him shelter and succour once before?"

Anahid *particularly* didn't like the way the woman wrapped her full lips around the word *succour*; she ignored Laxmi's snicker. "I am acquainted with Master Velo, yes. But I assure you, I have no more idea of where he has gone than you do."

Draconia pouted, but Crosef snorted. "Just as well. Last thing we want is the guards crawling all over us. They haven't set a curfew or anything, have they? Do we need more permits?"

And everyone looked at Anahid. Of course. This was what she'd gotten herself into. But someone needed to be in this role. Someone needed to be the person they looked to. And Anahid didn't trust anyone else to do it *properly*.

So Anahid snapped her fingers, and Laxmi rose from behind her, heading out of the gazebo to find a runner. "I'll ascertain at once," Anahid declared. "If you hear nothing from me before sunset, assume we are operating as usual."

They all relaxed. Anahid wasn't sure they were even aware of it, this tension that they lost in the face of someone else making the decisions—even the ones who were tutting into their teaglasses and making snide remarks to one another about the high-handed ways of azatani.

She'd get them there. Anahid was sure of it. But there was a long way to go yet.

As she opened her mouth to push on with her agenda, there was a sudden rattle of boots on paving outside the gazebo, and Laxmi swung back in through the door. "Ana!" she snapped.

A message runner ducked around her to gasp: "Master Attabel! There's—at the House!" She'd clearly come fast; she was gasping for breath, but managed: "The Zinedani!"

The meeting shattered like a dropped glass, managers scurrying away to check on their own establishments. Anahid hurried with Attabel—with Laxmi and *his* security trailing them—back to the Siren's Cove. Their own message runner had already gone to check on the curfew situation, and even if he'd been here, Anahid wasn't sure where to find Peylek at the moment, enmeshed as she and her people were right now in the city's security and the search for Siyon.

She wouldn't need more people, Anahid told herself. She'd *dealt* with the Zinedani.

But part of her fluttered with doubt.

There were only half a dozen people in the central yard of the Siren's Cove, including Ruzanna Zinedani, in her knee britches and black vest. She planted her hands on her hips and surveyed them like *they* were the trespassers.

"I'm still the landlord here," she declared. "And I'm here to inspect my property."

The Flowers of the Siren's Cove were lining the upper balconies, enjoying the warm afternoon sun and watching avidly if quietly. They knew a test of power when they saw one.

Anahid stepped forward with a polite smile and an outstretched hand. "Of course. You'll have your advance notice of inspection as delivered to the tenant at least three days ago, yes?"

She smiled at Ruzanna, and Ruzanna glared back, and the silence stretched.

"At least," Anahid said sweetly, silently thanking Master Gertcha, who had gone on at *length* about such details as she escorted him down to the District, "that is the standard clause included in the usual lease of property. But perhaps you and Master Attabel negotiated some alteration of the terms?"

From behind Anahid, Attabel said: "I cannot say I have any memory of such negotiation."

Anahid took a step forward, almost close enough to hear the grind of Ruzanna's teeth. Close enough that she could lower her voice to reach no farther than the two of them. "Our agreement is barely new-minted, Mistress Zinedani. If you break it now, I'll be very cross."

Ruzanna's gaze shifted for a moment, from Anahid's face to a point behind her. Where Laxmi waited like a walking threat, no doubt. But *only* Laxmi, with Attabel's security man to back her up. Ruzanna had five men with her. The numbers were on her side.

This time.

"I thought you and your sister wanted to be respectable business-women," Anahid said quietly, and Ruzanna's gaze jumped back to her. Anahid lifted an eyebrow. "But go ahead, if you want to follow your father after all. Take up the knife. Take what you want. That's how the barons do it."

Ruzanna's mouth twisted. "How are you going to stop me if I do?" she snarled. "I've heard all about it, how you don't want a fight."

"I don't," Anahid admitted, and smiled. "I never did. Until your father forced me to it."

And look how that had turned out for him.

Silence stretched between them, Ruzanna's eyes furious and her fists clenched. Anahid hardly dared to breathe, wondering if all her plans were about to come unravelled, with Ruzanna's fist slammed into her jaw.

Then the woman spat on the paver just next to Anahid's slipper and snarled, "Fuck you, za."

Anahid nearly flinched, nearly sagged in relief, nearly let her walk away; but she couldn't afford the weakness, not with time against her. She grabbed Ruzanna's wrist—barely holding on at all, just a touch. "Not so hasty. We do have a deal, Ruzanna. Where's what I was promised?"

After only a moment's seething hesitation, Ruzanna said: "You'll have it in hand by the end of the day."

"That would be excellent," Anahid said lightly. "I'd hate to have to come and get it."

Ruzanna shook off Anahid's hand, gestured for her men, and marched out of the courtyard.

Anahid smoothed down her skirt, far more easily than her emotions. Her ribs ached, breath rattling against them, and cold sweat trickled down her spine.

And yet there was an awful thrill to having the other woman bend to her will. Of making events turn her way.

She folded her hands over her waist sash, so no one could see them tremble, before she turned back to the others.

Laxmi smirked at her, in a way that curled in Anahid's stomach. The Flowers chattered and tittered up on the balconies; word of what had happened would be everywhere by sunset. Attabel's managers were already hurrying out to flap around him like a flock of colourful birds, but he waved them away as he stepped forward to meet Anahid.

And here, in the courtyard of his own House, he gave her a careful nod. Not a bow. Not even a genuflection as deep as he would have given Garabed Zinedani. But an acknowledgment.

"Standing together," he said, his voice pitched to carry, "seems to benefit us all. I am most grateful for your support, Lady Sable."

Anahid smiled. "And I yours, Master Attabel."

She could do this. She could stabilise the District and be a part of the new shape of the city. It would *work*.

But there was still so much to do, and only four days until commencement to manage it all.

As the Tower sounded the midafternoon Fade, Zagiri sat down for the first time all day on the rim of the fountain. The bell didn't so much ring, since the ructions of Salt Night, as it gave a flat *clank*, but Zagiri supposed it hadn't seemed as urgent a thing to fix as any of the actually destroyed buildings. Or possibly a new bell had to be forged in the Republic and shipped over the Carmine.

Her mind was drifting; ink and ashes, she was tired. The only sleep she'd had since Siyon's failed execution had been half a bell snatched shortly after dawn, when she'd staggered up to the apartment off Glass Street, passing Anahid and Laxmi on their way out. A relief to hug her sister, to know she'd come through the chaos well, even if she was going back out into it. Something *had* seemed a little odd with the pair of them, but maybe Zagiri had just been so exhausted she could barely tell one plane from another.

Her work was paying off; the city was almost back to a nervous, jittery normal. Tonight she could *sleep*, and then tomorrow, start lining up all the details they needed for commencement.

The flurry of chaos had left its mark, though. With her working elbow braced on her knee, Zagiri frowned at the low, still-smoking mound of bonfire. The café furniture that had escaped burning had still been smashed. On the side of the statue of the Last Duke, the painted word had smeared thick as tar, no longer reading *ours* so much as *oops*. The statue's raised arm had been knocked clean off, along with the horse's ears and most of its tail.

Zagiri wished she could take the statue to commencement to show all the azatani. This is what comes of those who don't pay attention to the people of Bezim. Deposed. Disarmed. Chipped away at.

Honestly, it had been far less of a mess than Zagiri might have expected. Thanks to the bravi, and Xhanari's troupe of former inquisitors, and the barons' crews. But she was quite sure that while they'd been out here fighting it, Rowyani and Avarair and all the rest of the Pragmatics were scurrying around the nervous Avenues, fanning fears and planting the seeds of their own control.

Azata Filosani and all her other councillors would be there as well, setting forth *other* whispers. Having other conversations. Preparing as best they could.

That was their fight. This was Zagiri's.

The scuff of a boot behind her was all the warning she had before Daruj whisked her tricorn off her head and danced away again.

"Fuck you," Zagiri sighed, squinting at him against the afternoon sun.

Daruj delicately tossed her tricorn back onto her head, only a little askew. "What's with the sling? You ran the tiles for years without breaking anything."

"You should see the other guy." Zagiri's mouth twisted; it still stung, to walk past the cordoned-off pile of rubble that had once been the Eldren Hall. "What's with still having the energy to play hat thief?"

Daruj flung himself down on the edge of the fountain next to her. "I am renewed by the vigour of love!"

Zagiri revised her estimate of his energy; when Daruj got this expansive and poetic, he was either extremely drunk or extremely sleep-deprived. "You went to check on your mysterious lady friend? Who *is* she?"

"Ah!" Daruj raised a chiding finger, but his grin was almost glowing. "I am sworn to deepest secrecy. A delicate flower such as she cannot be besmirched by the—"

"It's Gayane Saliu," said Jaleh Kurit.

"What?" Zagiri yelped, startling in surprise—she was so tired that she hadn't even heard Jaleh approaching, and now here she was, all severe dress and primly tied-back hair. "Wait, *what*? Gayane *Saliu*?"

"No!" Daruj shouted, but his gape-mouthed surprise was as good a declaration of Jaleh's accuracy as him adding: "How do *you* know?"

Jaleh looked coolly down her nose at him. "You've been canoodling in front of her personal alchemist, with whom I share a provisioner." She assessed his exhausted sprawl and his leathers battered from the past two days of activity. "And to think, she could have *anyone*." With Daruj spluttering, she turned to Zagiri and demanded, almost in the same breath, "Well, where is he?"

Even reeling in surprise from *that* revelation, Zagiri didn't need to ask who she meant. "You think I know *that* and I'm just trotting around scraping together order with my bare hands for the fun of it?"

The face Jaleh pulled suggested that was no more than she'd expected, but she'd still hoped for another answer. "He's such a debacle," she muttered. "Though when I look around at the world, it makes a certain sense that *he* became the Power."

"*Doesn't* it, though?" Daruj said heavily, then looked a little surprised to have agreed with Jaleh.

She ignored him, planting her hands on her hips and saying to Zagiri, "Well, what are we doing?"

"We?" Zagiri repeated, feeling like she'd been entirely left behind.

"We," Daruj repeated, fluttering his fingers at Jaleh, "is not *you*."

"We is all of us," Jaleh told him sharply. "You think alchemists who can't shelter in the Avenues have enjoyed the past two days? My father's neighbours want to burn his shop because of *me*, and I haven't lived there in over a year. But fortunately my brothers still do."

"I remember *them*," Daruj muttered.

"I thought you might." She smirked at him, then her expression twisted toward a frown. "Honestly, you look *awful*. You went to see Gayane Saliu like this? When did you last sleep?"

"Fuck," Daruj stated, with careful overemphasis, "you."

Zagiri interrupted them. "If you or the other alchemists have any sort of brew good for exhaustion, that would be extremely handy."

"*Sleep* is good for exhaustion," Jaleh snapped, and gave Zagiri a long look. Whatever she saw made her mouth purse, and she flipped open a cross-slung hip purse that Zagiri hadn't even realised she was carrying. It was a dainty little thing, compared to Siyon's satchel, but at a quick glimpse seemed almost as crammed full of glass vials and linen sachets and twists of coloured paper. She pulled out an enamel powder box that contained little pellets the precise pale blue of a robin's egg.

"Take *one*," Jaleh warned sternly. "Let it sit under your tongue until dissolved. Send anyone else who needs one to me. This is *not* for long-term use, you understand."

After a long and unimpressed look, she offered the box to Daruj as well.

The pellet started to fizz immediately under her tongue. Zagiri could have laughed, and not from the sensation shivering out through her mouth, whispering into her blood. "As long as I'm coherent for commencement in a few days, then I can sleep for a week."

"Tomorrow," Jaleh corrected absently, still frowning at Daruj as she snipped the box closed and slipped it back into her little bag.

Zagiri wasn't so distracted by the bright singing in her veins that she didn't catch that. "Wait, what?"

Jaleh blinked at her. "Commencement has been brought forward to tomorrow. I was delivering something to Markani when the message runner arrived to tell her son. Something about the necessity for strong leadership in this troubled time." She snorted. "They're not wrong about *that*."

"Shit." Zagiri lurched to her feet—and her head barely spun at all. "Oh, that is *good*. Thank you. I'm going to—wait." She stopped, her thoughts running clear and cold as water from a fountain. She didn't need to go and tell Filosani; they'd have been informed as well. But plenty of others wouldn't have. "Jaleh, can you go to the District and tell Anahid about the change? Ask her to spread the word. And, Daruj, you spread it too, but also can you find Mayar and tell them I need to speak with them?"

The two of them exchanged looks. Daruj was already sitting up straighter, under the effects of the blue pellet; he shrugged. "Yeah, sure."

That was all Zagiri needed; she turned and sprinted out of the Square.

Let Filosani take care of the political preparations. Zagiri trusted

Anahid to take care of the sponsor, as she'd indicated she could, as long as she knew the timing. But this needed *more*.

Never mind strong leadership; they were bringing commencement forward to avoid the city's attention. But the Palace still wasn't ready, and no work had been done in the last two days. They'd have to hold it in the hippodrome, right where the city had just witnessed Siyon defy the will of the azatani council.

Zagiri would make sure they—and as much of the rest of the world as she could arrange—were back to watch again.

Through the bravi and the Flower district, the word would get out. She had no way to tell Siyon, of course. Could only hope. If there were any Khanate merchants still in the city, after the destruction of the caravanserai, Mayar would be able to get a message to them. And that left...

Zagiri hammered on the door of the Bardha townhouse with all the energy Jaleh's little blue pellet had sent sizzling into her bones. The streets were still hushed up here, but there were signs of life emerging. Household staff had stopped about their errands to gossip quietly on street corners; a coffee shop had one shutter cracked, dispensing little cups to customers standing and exchanging views in the street.

Bezim wouldn't be kept quiet for long.

But no one answered the door, and when Zagiri craned her neck to see into the front parlour, the room was full of packing crates.

No. Shit. *"Shit."*

With a heavy grinding, a window opened on an upper storey of the building; Zagiri stumbled back out into the street so she could see up, even as a familiarly accented voice shouted down: "Last time you just climbed up." Yeva leaned against the sill and added: "I guess that would be difficult now."

With all this new energy, Zagiri felt unwisely like it might be possible. To distract herself from bad ideas, she called up, "Are you leaving?"

"Soon as we are given leave to depart by the Council." Yeva shrugged one shoulder, but Zagiri thought there was a twist to her mouth. "So you can stop worrying."

She'd told Yeva to go. For a moment, Zagiri wondered what would happen to them, back in a North that was still not settled. Hadn't Yeva said something about Madame Bardha coming to get them out of some mess up there?

But her main concern, right now, was keeping Bezim from tipping into even deeper trouble. "Come to the commencement tomorrow," she called up. "Get your mother to attend."

Even from down here, she could see Yeva's dubious frown. "Attend and do what?"

"Nothing," Zagiri said, to Yeva's clear confusion. "Just…be there. Watch what happens. Be a witness. Sometimes that's all it takes."

Yeva hesitated, one hand on the window, before she said, "I'll see what I can do."

It was more than Zagiri had any right to expect, really.

Whistles sailed on the breeze over the city as Zagiri turned away. They rang oddly and incomprehensibly in her ears—was the blue pellet already wearing off and her exhaustion clouding her mind again? Or were these just another tribe's codes, rather than the universal signals they'd been using for the past two days?

Were the tribes out and running again? The sun had only just touched the horizon, but Zagiri couldn't blame them for being eager. She didn't know how they had the energy, though, after the past two days.

She turned onto the Boulevard and stopped dead. The entire width of it—enough to run three carts together—was packed with bravi. There were sashes and feathers in the orange and brown of Bracken, but also the blues and purples of Awl Quarter, the pinks and greys of the Bower's Scythe, the deep green of Haruspex, and the brilliant red of the Bleeding Dawn.

They were *all* here, at least a double-six from each tribe, standing shoulder to shoulder or even mingling. Someone laughed from among the press, and someone else started singing—probably a Bowerboy—and was hushed to silence again.

Five figures stepped forward, as mismatched a group as one could possibly imagine. The sergeants of the tribes, facing her here in the last of the daylight.

Why?

Zagiri turned to Voski Tolan, short and battered as a pigeon among a bevy of preening cormorants, nursing a tight little smile.

But it was actually Hovhaness who spoke, stepping forward with that sneer he must have practiced in a mirror. "You promised us certain things, little one."

It struck like a blade to the ribs. Zagiri *had* promised them. She'd promised herself. She'd hoped for so much. And she'd caused so much pain because of it.

Now she was scrambling just for the edge of a chance. "I'm sorry," she said, plain and honest. "I'm still trying. And if we make it anywhere, it will be on the back of the work that we did together, all of us. I thank you for that."

Hovhaness wrinkled up his nose and flipped a gold-flashing hand. "Not good enough."

Redick nodded along, the golden beads in his braid chiming. "We came to your call. Not just the once, but many times. On the rooftops in chaos."

"Sneaking quiet through the streets," Slender added unexpectedly, in her scratched voice. "Getting our unbladed brother and sister practitioners to safety."

Zagiri really *had* been pulling the tribes into the thick of things all the way through. "I'm sorry," she repeated. "I...I had no right to demand so much."

"Demand?" Jerrenta repeated, with an elaborate frown on her beautiful face. "Sweetest of little sweet things, you *asked*. You *offered*. And we accepted." The frown transformed into a wicked and gleeful smile. "Because it has been *fun*."

Voski nodded sharply. "And if there's more fun in the offing, we want our slice. All of us." She spread her arms, including all the blades behind her. All the tribes. "We want to see what happens tomorrow. We want to see what alchemy you and the Sorcerer can cook up. And, if it becomes necessary, we want you to stand for us. Speak for us. For all of us."

They *what*?

Hovhaness sniffed and added: "We're not calling it Grand Bracken again. I refuse."

"We're not calling it the New Dawn either, you plonker," Jerrenta shot back.

Zagiri closed her gaping mouth, but she still couldn't find any words. "I'm not Bracken anymore," she finally managed.

"Just as well," Redick muttered, with a sidelong look at Voski.

"You are the one who asked," Slender declared.

Zagiri swallowed. "We may still fail," she admitted. And if they failed, and if *Rowyani* became prefect on the back of that failure... "It may not go well, for those who stood up."

Voski snorted. "You think they'll take *us* on?" Her voice was strident, her words ringing, like a challenge called.

Behind her, the bravi—all the tribes, all together—raised a mighty cheer, ringing in the empty streets around them.

And Zagiri *believed*.

This was Bezim, standing together. From azatani to Dockside, and everyone in between, this was all of them, crying challenge.

They could do this.

They *would* do this.

CHAPTER 25

The world curved beneath Siyon, like a ripe apple perfectly made to fit in his palm. He didn't want to sink his teeth into the firm flesh so much as he wanted to admire it. Shine it against his shirt (*his what?*) and let the light play over its polished skin. Every little detail was fascinating.

Yes. Ours. It will be as it should.

The sun on a scaled back. The wind beneath leathery wings. The world spread out beneath them.

As it should be...

The whisper—of sound, of sensation, of satisfaction—coiled around him, lulling and luring him. It was a tangle difficult to escape, like dragging himself out of heavy and expensive sheets.

He remembered that, remembered himself again—easier this time. Remembered being Siyon Velo, waking in a bed on the Avenues, the mattress soft as blandishments beneath him...

Except there was salt in his mouth, gulls calling high and clear, and something hard nudging against his side.

Except he had somewhere to be. He'd made a promise.

Siyon opened his eyes and blinked at the underside of a rotting dock. He was bumping against one of the pillars, part of a bed of flotsam and seaweed and a single wretched boot.

Now the stench hit him like a rotten fish to the face. He flailed in the water, grabbing at the pier, churning up muck, and jabbing splinters beneath his fingernails. He coughed, hawking up thick, salty unpleasantness, and shook his sodden head.

"Ah, shit," a voice said from above him, and the light between the warped dock boards shifted. "I think he's alive after all."

"Help," Siyon croaked.

But the kids were off—and that's all they were, half a dozen Dockside brats, too old to cling to their mothers' skirts any longer, but too young to haul a catch or cleat a line or sling a load. Too young even to run a message, but from the speed with which they fled, not for much longer.

He'd been one of them. And then he'd been a lean and lanky problem, fighting every way life pushed him. And then…

And then he'd been tipped into the river, in a sack, by his brothers. Possibly right here. Clinging to the pier, Siyon could see the lower city across the water, all the jumbled jetties and sunken warehouses and mucky make-do buildings.

He'd swum that, to start his new life. *His* life.

Which had brought him back here. To the very place he'd fled.

Not quite the same place. Mezin was no longer here to torment him, dead of the poison that had failed to kill Siyon.

He'd survived. He had another chance to fix this. To be who and what he needed to be. To fulfill all the promises he'd made.

Siyon hauled himself out of the water in an ungainly sprawl. The world seemed new, in a way far beyond the gentle morning light. Sparkling. Sharp-edged and full of glowing promise. Power limned each droplet of sea bilge that Siyon wrung from his ragged trousers. It sparked on each gust of the breeze off the drowsy afternoon harbour. It traced every line of the alleys and rooftops of Dockside when he squinted up at them.

The power was *in* the world. In every part of it. In *him*.

Siyon tottered dripping off the dock and into the warren of his youth. He was drawn along by a trail of memories—this drain, that public house sign, the geraniums blooming stubbornly in the window

352

box on the corner house. He staggered along unthinking, letting the stones pull his feet.

In hindsight, it was obvious where they'd lead him.

The compound of the Velo fisherclan hadn't changed at all. The stone arch still had moss growing in the crevices that never saw sun. The tunnel between the outer storerooms was still cold and dank. The sunlit yard at its end was still festooned with drying and mended nets like some strange festival bunting. Siyon didn't recognise any of the children playing a game in that yard, tossing fish bones and counting chants. They hadn't been born when he'd left, but if they were here, then he must be related, somehow, to all of them.

Know your aunts too, and your cousins, Mother Marsh had told him. He remembered that, distantly, like it was a story he'd overheard in a wineshop one night. *I delivered three of their babes.*

"So you're here," a voice said, just beside Siyon; the street reeled in umber shadows when he whirled around. It was Bayan, the brother just older than Siyon. He had grey eyes, the same grey as Siyon's, the same grey that their mother had inherited from a sailor father she'd never even met. "You'd better come in."

Siyon followed, helpless as though he were a little rowboat tied to the stern of some larger craft.

In the yard, the children swarmed around them. "Who's this soggy mess?" asked a girl who stood a head taller than all the others. When her demands received no answer, she planted hands on hips and shouted, "Uncle Bayan, you mind your manners when a fisher-woman addresses you!"

Right now, that got her naught but a cuff around the ear, but the blow was barely enough to muss her hair. In another handful of years, her orders would be obeyed.

The women ran the fisherclans. The shorebound, the net makers, the deal brokers, the babe carriers. They held every future of the clan in their clever fingers, and that was just the way of it. Couldn't change the pull of the tides. Couldn't change the lines of power.

"Where's your gran?" Bayan demanded as the girl glared at him.

Darra Velo lurked in the tally room like a spider in the centre of her web. As Bayan led Siyon down the corridor, two runners went scampering out past them. Laughter from the big hall farther along, where women would be knotting nets, or spinning twine, or some other work not allowed to those like Siyon. Farther again was the scaling hall, still stinking of fish on the faint breeze from the outer delivery doors.

Siyon dawdled, reluctance dragging at his heels. He made himself follow Bayan, across the threshold, into his mother's throne room.

Figure of speech. In Siyon's youth, the room hadn't even had a chair; his mother was always standing, always *moving*, trailing an endless tail of runners and questioners as she strode the halls of the Velo compound, keeping an eye on and a finger in every aspect.

But now she perched on a high stool, one ankle hooked around a leg, the other foot flat on the floor as she leaned between the sideboard with its array of abacuses, and the high table laden with manifests and bills. She still looked spry enough, lean and hungry, but her tilt against the table, with stiffness in her shoulders and a hand bracing against the edge...

When had his mother grown old?

Send her liniment for her knuckles twice a month, Mother Marsh had said. Siyon's eyes darted to the fingers splayed over the worn wooden surface. Gnarled and red, bent and twisted. There'd be no more nets from those hands.

"Well now." Darra Velo's voice was just the same, rough but reedy, thin as a scaling knife and twice as serrated. "Ain't this a thing."

"Found him out front, Ma," Bayan reported. "Figured you'd want to see him."

Darra sniffed. "Not sure as how I do, but he's here now, so I guess I'm seeing. Run along down the kitchen and have us brought a mug of tea, yeah?"

Bayan left without so much as another glance at Siyon.

Siyon looked around the room, with every crack in worn-smooth stone edged in the glimmer of power. Even here. Perhaps especially here. This was all Mundane business. It was all his.

His mother sighed, leaning back on her stool. She was shorter than him even atop it. Siyon's father must have been tall as a tree. Her mouth pinched same as it always had when she looked at him. More grey in her hair, twisted up at the back of her neck. More lines on her face, worn as any surface exposed to the sea.

"Hear you finally bested Zin at something," she said, but her attention had already moved on; she snatched up some papers with one red-knuckled hand. If she regretted the demise of her eldest son, there was no sign of it on her face. "What is it you want, then?"

"I don't know," Siyon admitted. He felt damp and drained. Energy skittered about him, aimless and ebbing. "I don't know why I'm here."

"Same as ever then," she snapped, and slapped the papers down on a pile of others. *Then* she looked at him, flat and cold. "Always clear you didn't want *this*. But you wouldn't bloody leave, would you?"

Siyon blinked. "What?"

"Stuck about like mud refusing to be turned into useful brick." Her mouth pinched tighter still, such a familiar expression from Siyon's childhood that it made him momentarily dizzy. "You think you'd be here even now, if we hadn't made you leave?"

"If you hadn't . . ." Siyon echoed, trailing off. *Made* him leave?

He'd left in a panic. He'd left because he had no other choice. He'd left because, when he'd miraculously got out of the sack they'd tied him up in, all he'd wanted to do was *escape*.

He realised now—of course, so clear, seeing her here in the centre of everything—that it hadn't been their own idea. Fishermen did as they were instructed, and the sons of Darra Velo were all good fishermen. Except Siyon. He'd known that she knew, at the very least. Had likely told them to pull him into shape. But he'd somehow thought that perhaps she'd left the details up to them. He hadn't wanted to think that his mother had ordered him thrown out like trash.

Darra braced both hands on the table and eased off her stool with a wince and a grunt as she straightened her back. But that was her only sign of weakness as she fixed a hook-sharp glare on him. "*Years* you spent, hating it here. And what did you do about it? Sweet fuck all!" She made a sharp gesture, like she was throwing something away. "Bad as your father, wafting around waiting for someone else to point the way."

Siyon gaped at her. "You think you did me a *favour*? By getting my brothers to nearly kill me?"

He wondered if she'd even known how close it had been. His brothers might never have told her what precisely had happened. *Siyon* certainly wouldn't have, in their shoes.

But his mother didn't flinch. Didn't even blink. Barely lifted an eyebrow. No indication either way. "You're not the one who's dead, are you? Seems the nudge helped you along."

"*Nudge*?" Siyon repeated, and it was only when his voice rang off the stone walls that he realised he was shouting.

Not that his mother was cowed. Not that she cared at all.

Had she ever? *Had* she thought that he might become something else, if he could just be winkled out of Dockside like an oyster from its shell? Or had she just wanted this useless boy out of her hall?

Did it matter? Siyon was not defined by her, not her wants nor her orders. He remembered Anahid, tipsy on the tiles in the lower city, telling him that he could become whatever he needed to be. A magic that had always been his.

Siyon turned on his heel, striding out of there. He took the fastest way out—past the hall, and the big kitchen where Bayan called his name over two steaming mugs of tea, and out through the scaling hall into the late afternoon.

Anger steamed within him, roiled like thunderclouds, pushed into the power of his wings—

Those weren't his, but this anger...some of that *was*.

Siyon turned and looked back, to the low-domed shingle roof of the scaling hall. When he was fourteen, and feeling this way, he'd climb up there and sulk between the chimneys, avoiding the world.

No one had ever come looking for him. No one had demanded he get back to his tasks.

Why had he only ever gone that far? If he turned left, and climbed a staircase, cut through the cooper's yard, the Kellian Way was *just there*. Climb the hill, cross the Swanneck, and he could have gone *anywhere*.

Why hadn't he?

Because this had been his world. This had been all he knew. Like Mother Marsh, never setting a foot outside. Creatures of the mud, the rest of the world not their concern. Siyon had thought this was all there *was*, for someone like him. Until it was made clear it wasn't for him at all.

Fuck his whole family, they hadn't been *right*. But maybe they hadn't been entirely wrong either. Maybe he had needed a *nudge*.

They still could have done it without nearly killing him.

"Siyon!"

Bayan stood in the wide double doorway of the scaling hall, still holding a mug of tea in each hand. His brother looked bewildered. He often had, looking at Siyon. He'd never understood. Or maybe they'd all understood more than Siyon realised, but less than they'd thought.

Siyon knew, now, what a duty was. What a promise meant, to people who actually cared about him. What it was like, to leave and start anew.

Terrifying, but exhilarating too.

He had things to break, and things to keep. He had a problem that needed solving before he could—

Siyon blinked. "What day is it? Has the Council commenced yet?"

"*What?*" Bayan spluttered, as well he might. What did such things matter to the fisherclans? "Wait, where are you going?"

"Everywhere," Siyon said.

He reached out, toward what he needed—

And stepped sidelong out of reality, to the crack and splash of a dropped mug of tea.

Laxmi eyed the abandoned teahouse with a suspicion that bordered on distaste. "Are you sure about this?"

"No," Anahid admitted, looking over the building herself. The three upper levels had windows shuttered tight, but in this part of the city, barely a block from the renewed noise of the old hippodrome, Anahid could hardly blame the residents for having left altogether. The teahouse itself had had its windows smashed, and the once-cheerful curtains were now stained and hanging crooked. Figures moved inside, though, illuminated by lanterns.

Waiting for Anahid. She took a breath, hand pressed to her waist sash, which crinkled with the paper wedged behind it. So many matters she still needed to attend to. There was no time for dawdling, weighed down by hesitation. But there was also no room for error.

"There's no other way," Anahid said aloud, reminding herself. "So let's get on with it."

The teahouse floor had been swept in a wide swath from door to the central table, but glass still crunched beneath Anahid's slippers. Smashed tables and broken chairs had been shoved into the corners, leaving a mismatched array of furniture beneath the lone chandelier that glowed with remnants of its alchemical charms.

The raw orange light glinted from Aghut's shaved head and carved lines into Mama Badrosani's face. The shadows loomed deep and impenetrable in the corners, where anyone at all could be lurking. It didn't matter; Anahid could hardly walk out again, or renegotiate this meeting. There was no more time.

But the other barons felt the pinch as well. "What a fucking mess," Mama was saying as Anahid came in. "Can you imagine this shit happening under Syrah?"

Aghut snorted. "Many things would be different if Syrah Danelani still sat in the big chair." He eyed Anahid, as brutally considering as ever, and for once it didn't bother her.

She wasn't just *her*, after all. Not taking a seat at this table. Not looking the other two in the eye. She was the Flower district, and all the House managers who'd joined together with her to become something new.

"So you came out on top after all, did you?" Aghut smirked, beckoning across the table. "Pay up, Shakeh."

"Ah." Mama jabbed her pipe at him and sneered at Anahid. "You ain't actually the baron, are you?"

She seemed very certain of that; Anahid wondered who was feeding her information from within the District. But that was a problem for the future. If they pushed through to have one worth the word.

"I am a representative of the barony of the Flower district," she responded easily, "with all due authority to make binding agreements, should it come to that."

Mama snorted. "Don't get ahead of yourself. And you stop waving your pretty fingers around," she sniped at Aghut, "or I'll chop 'em off. I ain't paying out the bet until she's an actual *baron*."

"I'm the best you're going to get," Anahid snapped. "Are we talking, or not?"

"Calm your perky young tits," Mama snapped back, settling back in her chair with a disgruntled expression and a creak of protesting wood. "We're bloody here, aren't we? Little as I want anything more to do with that lot than I have to." She tipped a nod out through the shattered teahouse windows, where the crumbled upper edge of the hippodrome wall was just visible.

The street was already growing crowded. The people were quieter than those at Siyon's execution, and filing into the hippodrome in far better order than they'd all come flooding out last time. But they were here, and in numbers, with a bell still to go before the hurriedly arranged commencement.

Bezim was coming. They wanted to see what happened next. They wanted to see if the whispers they'd heard were true.

Aghut considered the flow of people for a moment, then glanced sidelong at Anahid. "What've you lot got on the boil?"

"You'll have to be more specific about which *lot* you mean," Anahid told him. She might have smirked, had things felt more certain, but there *were* so many groups at work, with contradictory goals. It must have been Rowyani's faction who'd pulled the date forward; what plans were *they* hurrying to enact?

While Anahid scrambled to get her last pieces in place.

"I don't care what you're about," Mama stated. "I just want my piece and I want the acknowledgment that it *is* my piece." She leaned forward again, bracing one ringed hand on the edge of the table as she glared at Anahid. "I've heard what that asshole Rowyani is saying. *Our city should be ours*? He can keep his sticky fingers to himself."

"Which doesn't mean," Aghut added with far less vigour, "that we're willing to take any crumbs thrown our way."

He made a very good show of being relaxed, even tilting his chair back on two legs to prop his boots up on the table.

Anahid wasn't fooled. He was here—they both were—despite the scurry to arrange this meeting. It should have been Filosani, negotiating the arrangement she intended to honour as prefect, but they were out of time, and they all knew it. It *didn't* mean they'd take any crumbs.

But she had rather more to offer than crumbs.

"A proposal is going to be raised at today's commencement," Anahid said, and touched her fingertips to her sash again. She certainly *hoped* it was going to be raised. "If voted up, it will expand membership of the Council to more of the citizenry, organisations, and interests of Bezim than is currently the case."

They grasped her meaning at once. "Non-azatani?" Mama's too-thin eyebrows went up, and she glanced at Aghut. "Never thought I'd live to see it."

"You still might not," he pointed out. "Because that's never going to get voted through. Not by the azatani. Not to relinquish their stranglehold on power."

"And share it with the likes of you," Anahid completed for him.

It visibly gave him pause, even this scarred veteran of Dockside. "With *us*?"

Anahid let her eyebrows lift a little, as though surprised he hadn't made the connection himself. "Well, the lower city is a quarter of Bezim, and Dockside almost another quarter in itself. Once the bounds of the Council are being renegotiated, it seems almost certain that there will be a seat for such significant areas."

Mama narrowed her eyes. "This is the ploy, is it? You've shoved the District ducklings into an orderly line and now you think you can pull *us* into respectability as well?"

Yes, that was exactly what Anahid thought. What's more, when she looked across the table at the woman who'd seen off the Bitch Queen, ruled her family and her quarter of the city with an iron grip... Anahid thought it was going to work.

They were *here*. They wanted to make a deal. They wanted the stability and security of a place in the organisation of the city. Syrah Danelani had already broken them to the leash when she crafted the deal that ended the Baron Wars. They'd taken food from her hand. Eventually, like it or not, the city would make pets of them.

Anahid shrugged. "It needn't be *you*, of course. Someone else could take on the role. Do the paperwork, attend the meetings, be spoken to as a councillor, equal among all the others."

Aghut gave her a sharp look; perhaps that bait had been a little blatant. But it was no less tempting for it. The acknowledgment they wanted, their piece, and more besides.

"Details like that can wait, though." Anahid brushed that dangling lure aside. "All that matters, all I need to carry to Buni Filosani today, is whether we will make new covenant with her, for the stability of the city and our own endeavours, should she be elected to the prefect's role."

Mama frowned. "*That's* not happening today, is it?"

"No," Aghut answered, before Anahid could. He was frowning as he stared out the shattered windows, at the thickening crowds streaming past. "But if she has us in hand, that's power she can swing today. And if the Council membership *does* change…" He looked back at Anahid, a new consideration in his eyes. Perhaps he was actually impressed.

She finished for him. "An expanded Council would change the landscape of the prefecture election quite significantly."

Aghut smirked. "Not going to suggest we attend? Show our weight in support? Perhaps speak to any councillors with whom we might have undue influence?"

"I wouldn't dream of trying to orchestrate your behaviour," Anahid said, allowing herself a smile. "After all, you have your own endeavours and interests to protect and advance."

He snorted, and whipped his feet off the table, letting his chair crash down. "Of course we do. So you can trot off and tell Filosani that I look forward to negotiating the price of the Dockside vote." He paused, knuckles resting against the edge of the table. "And if she lets that fucker Rowyani win, I'll be disappointed. You coming?" he shot across to Mama.

She pursed her lips, and screwed up her nose, but said: "Yes, of course. What have we to lose?"

Everything, if Rowyani won. If he beat down the reform today, if he rolled on the back of that into the prefecture, if he stamped down on the city so hard that the barons rose up and had him removed...

If order failed entirely, and the city sank into a more bitter war than it had ever seen before.

Anahid dragged a breath in, and shoved aside this sudden dire vision of a future she *must* ensure they avoided. She rose to her feet as well, and said, "Thank you."

Aghut waved a hand, already striding out with his hefty lady lieutenant at his shoulder. One of the Badrosani sons came out of the shadows to drape a fur around his mother's shoulders.

She gave Anahid a considering look as she shrugged more deeply into it, coming around the table. "Aren't you a dark fish in the night? I really didn't think you had it in you. Could've sworn you were off to hide, after that business in my theatre." She sighed. "Federation. Council seats. When I think of what the Bitch Queen would have made of this nonsense."

"The Bitch Queen is dead," Anahid pointed out.

Mama's mouth twisted. "Watch it, girl. *I'm* not. Not yet. And nor is your opposition. So get out there and see to it."

CHAPTER 26

Zagiri paused in the tunnel that let out onto the sand of the old hippodrome, squinting against the glare and the dazzling colours of the assembled azatani. Possibly it was just as well the Palace was still in ruins. The formal Council Hall couldn't have held even a fraction of the crowd currently crammed into the stands of the hippodrome. Nearly as many as Siyon's execution day, filling all the seats and overflowing into standing areas, with bravi and other daredevils perched on the high outer walls.

The azatani themselves had the freedom of the arena today, mingling among rows of bench seating. With their delicately patterned spring longvests and lacy parasols, the azatani seemed determined to carry on as though everything was normal, lifting their voices louder in idle gossip to cover the simmering noise from a crowd they refused to acknowledge. Their nervousness was made manifest, however, in the thick line of grey and white that ringed the arena, where the inquisitors and palace guards stood between the azatani and the regular people of Bezim.

They were here. They were watching. Awe curled Zagiri's fingers at her side—that the word she'd sent out had seen *this* great a response. That the people cared as much as she'd hoped they would. There hadn't been such public scrutiny of the Council since...

Well, possibly since the first azatani Council had marched upon the Palace, and Telmut Hisarani had challenged the Last Duke to that controversial duel over the fate of the city.

Just looking at the crowd—people sitting quietly and people shoving and chanting, enterprising refreshment sellers and even more cunning bet takers—filled her with certainty that the city *would* change. Perhaps not today, with so much against them, with everything so rushed, and Siyon still lost. But so many azatani were here. They were seeing this—that the city cared. They would witness the question being asked: What if these people had more of a say?

It was all Zagiri had wanted, with her ill-considered attack on the Harbour Master's Ball: to make her fellow azatani *think*.

Because each azatani was a person, just like her. They could think, and consider, and choose. For so long, the azatani had been choosing the same thing, the old thing, the ongoing thing, but they didn't *have* to.

Lusal had shown Zagiri that. People *could* choose otherwise. If they knew there were options. If they knew they could.

And, this being Bezim, if the spectacle was grand enough.

Ink and ashes, but Zagiri hoped Siyon showed up.

"Giri!" she barely heard, over the hubbub.

It was Anahid, which was momentarily astonishing. She was *here*, gowned and scarved, even if it was all-black, glinting with jet beading. The very sight of her was a jarring combination of familiar and unthinkable: her sister where she'd always been, dressed as she always had, and yet in a place where she would *not* be made welcome.

Which made it all the more amusing when the first thing she said was, "What *are* you wearing?"

Laughter bubbled out of Zagiri. "I'm not getting stuck in something I can't run in." But leathers hadn't seemed appropriate, not when she needed to look at least something like a proper azata to be allowed entry.

So she'd settled on trade-voyage attire, with wide-legged but comfortable trousers and a many-buttoned jacket, though the headscarf she'd chosen was rather fancier than would be worn aboard ship.

Zagiri felt much better in this getup than in a gown. Even if she still couldn't climb, with her arm yet in its sling.

"Are you expecting to have to run?" Anahid asked, but her smile was warm. Proud, even.

Zagiri shrugged. "I'm expecting *anything*." She scanned the tops of the walls again, where a long line of bravi kicked their heels and tossed toasted walnuts at one another.

"Any sign of him yet?" Anahid asked, edging closer. As though anyone were likely to overhear a thing in this ruckus.

Zagiri shook her head. "Not yet."

She had no reason to expect Siyon. He'd promised, sure, but he'd promised to be here on another day entirely. Even Mayar had no idea where to find him. They were on their own.

Yet Zagiri's eyes wouldn't stop searching. He'd survived an execution. He'd fallen into solid rock. Showing up a few days early would be the *least* of his achievements.

A gong strike shimmered over the crowd, which barely quietened at all. But enough for them to hear, from the balcony in front of the nobility's stand, a woman calling out: "The assembly will come to order for the commencement of this fifty-eighth session of the Council of Bezim."

"Damn." Anahid straightened to look over the crowd. "That's the start, and I still need to…Have you seen Tahera?"

Ridiculous for her to ask Zagiri, who'd need to *climb* Anahid to be able to see anything. "I thought you said the sponsor matter was all arranged."

"It *should* be," Anahid said, still peering around. "But she hasn't responded to my message. I'm here to make sure." She flashed Zagiri a pinched-tight smile. "Good luck with everything."

She strode away into the crowd before Zagiri could answer. A crowd that parted when people saw her coming, skirts twitching out of her path as though Anahid's disgrace might be contagious.

Anahid was here, braving society, to make sure. Not lurking about on the fringes, where she could avoid the worst of society's disapproval, but striding right into the middle of it all.

For Zagiri, and for the future they could build.

"Let the roster of seats be filled," called the registrar, from the balcony overlooking the hippodrome arena. "Abbisani, do you send a councillor?"

The noble stand behind the balcony was empty now, but would soon begin to fill, as each family's duly chosen councillor was called up to sign the register, make their oath, and take a seat. Down in the arena, the azatani milled about, gossiping and showing no inclination to file into the orderly bench seating. In the stands, the rest of Bezim simmered in anticipation; they certainly hadn't come to see the boring bureaucracy.

Zagiri pushed into the crowd, only to whirl around abruptly at a glimpse of purple. But it was only a headscarf—which was quite daring all on its own, with that colour quite out of fashion since Salt Night.

It was Azata Parsola, with the purple scarf tied in her idiosyncratic fashion—and there with her, laughing and accepting her kiss upon the cheek was Buni Filosani.

Zagiri wriggled through the press, even thicker around Filosani. Some of those loitering nearby were familiar to Zagiri from the discussion at the Winter Picnic, and others she thought might be hopeful of influence, or even just trying to overhear interesting gossip. Parsola caught sight of her, and Filosani made a gesture that had two young azatans—clerks, probably—effortlessly nudging the crowd aside and ushering Zagiri closer.

Filosani's eyebrows went up as she looked Zagiri over. "Setting forth on a new adventure, Azata Savani?"

"I hope so," Zagiri replied, with her best attempt at a confident smile. "But I'm planning for the unexpected." She glanced around the stands, unsure what she was even looking for. Where would Siyon come from, if he came? Up from the earth? Down from the sky? Out of the crowd?

"What wisdom that seems," Filosani declared merrily, "after the season we've had. We'd be fools to think everything is right where we want it." For all her geniality, a lifted eyebrow gave significance to that last sentence. *Was* everything right where we want it?

"We can try our best," Zagiri replied, and very much *hoped* that

Anahid had found Tahera. That everything was in order. "All luck with your endeavours today, azata."

Filosani inclined her head graciously. "And you with yours, azata."

Zagiri moved away, as the registrar called for the Danelani family councillor to ascend. There were still many families to go, but time was ticking away. She looked around the crowd—and found many people looking back, giving her a nod, or merely measuring who she was, and why she'd been graced with Filosani's attention.

She was one of them, after all. She was azatani.

Faintly, over the wash of other noise, came a shout. "*Zagiri!*"

From the timbre, it was someone shrieking at the top of their lungs. Zagiri turned, and spotted them—a small knot of bravi, clustered right down on the railing of the stand, two of them nearly tipping over as they waved furiously. A prime position, possibly only relinquished because one of the waving bravi was Daruj, the city's beloved Diviner Prince. Mayar was next to him, one foot atop the railing and the sun glinting off their fresh-shaved head.

Zagiri picked her way through the crowd, until she reached the white-and-grey fringe. A white-tunicked Palace guard looked from her to the cheerfully waving bravi and frowned before he stepped aside. "They can't come down," he warned.

"As if we want to!" Daruj grinned, tilting against the railing as Zagiri crossed the last distance to the base of the wall. "*Much* better view from up here. When does it get interesting?"

A good question. "They'll be most of a bell yet, swearing in the councillors."

"And then comes the chance?" Mayar squinted up at the nobles' stands. "Are you going to do it?"

Zagiri laughed. "No! It's all taken care of." She hoped. She *really* hoped Anahid hadn't misplaced her trust in Tahera Danelani.

"Still," Daruj called cheerfully, "can't hurt to be prepared, so you might want this!" He hurled down a long bundle.

Zagiri lunged to make the catch on instinct, one-handed and juggling the surprising weight, the clank, the sudden smell of oiled leather and well-cleaned steel.

It was a sheathed sabre, wrapped up in its belt. "What?" she asked, not even looking up as she flicked the belt loose enough to get a good look at the hilt—plain cup guard, a little battered.

This wasn't a named blade. This wasn't even *her* blade, the ordinary sabre that was still hanging off her bedpost.

Zagiri frowned up at the pair at the railing. "Whose is this?"

Daruj's grin widened—bright and wicked and full of promise. "Siyon's!" he shouted down, loud enough to draw attention from all around. The centre of attention was where Daruj was most comfortable. He tossed his head, glinting with ornaments and prizes, and nodded at the blade in her hands. "He keeps leaving it behind—at the Chapel, in the lower city. Someone should remember it. And you can hardly stand for the bravi without one, can you?"

Siyon's blade. He hadn't kept it like this, Zagiri would lay money on it. Someone had seen it cleaned, sharpened, oiled. A very plain blade, but made as good as it could be.

"Thanks!" she called up, and managed to lash it around her waist on the second try, using the elbow of her injured arm to brace it so she could get the buckle done up. She barely felt a twinge for it, so maybe the damn shoulder was finally healing again. The weight at her hip felt reassuring; she lifted her good hand in salute to the stands. "Here's hoping I don't have to use it."

"Wrong attitude, Savani!" Daruj hollered after her as Zagiri sauntered back between the guards into the azatani crowd.

She took a smile with her. For the reminder of who the bravi were, for the blade at her hip, for the little piece of Siyon she could carry with her, whatever else happened today.

The registrar called family after family. Zagiri paced through the crowd, watching the periphery, watching the stands, watching the skyline. Her gaze snagged on a strange bright spot, tucked into the corner of the seating near the noble stand: both of the Bardhas, Ksaia and Yeva, in full Northern finery with their golden hair braided into crowns. They'd come after all, to witness what would happen today. The world, or at least part of it, was watching.

The registrar called the Savani family councillor; Zagiri hunched her shoulders and prowled onward, refusing to even watch cousin Gildon smirk his way up to his new seat. They'd do this anyway. *Fuck* him.

The sun beat down out of a gloriously clear blue sky. Gulls floated over the hippodrome, calling to one another. The crowd simmered, waiting with varying levels of patience. There was no sign of Siyon.

And finally the gong rang out again, the sound shimmering away as the registrar's voice lifted. "The Council roster is filled and all seats are accounted for. The fifty-eighth Council of Bezim may now commence!"

The azatani paused their chatter to mark the announcement with an ovation—and some of the people in the stands followed along. Zagiri's heart tripped faster.

Now things really began.

As Anahid strode away from her sister, into the arena crowds, she felt the dizzy exhilaration of leaping overboard into the cold and uncertain depths of the sea. Instinct told her to stay—with Zagiri, on the fringes, away from this disapproval and disdain.

But timidity had proven no defense.

Anahid squared her shoulders in her glittering black gown and marched into the midst of azatani society. The registrar was calling the first councillors, and the crowd was starting to shift. A knot of Pragmatic councillors was forming around Matevon Rowyani, rather larger than Anahid liked to see, with another clump forming, as though in balance, around Buni Filosani. There were smaller, looser clusters, of those less firm in their affiliation, and great drifting swathes of those just here to mingle and gossip.

And all of these people—in their embroidered longvests and beaded headscarves, who'd invited her to their parties and welcomed her into their homes—were turning their backs upon her.

The sting didn't matter. She didn't need them. Or rather, she needed only *one* of them.

Where was Tahera Danelani?

She'd intended to call upon Tahera, and explain that the Zinedani threat had been neutralised, if not quite in the manner that Tahera had preferred. To make clear the ways in which this was better, and to confirm precisely what would happen in return. But there'd been no time. Anahid had only been able to send a message runner, and she'd heard nothing back.

This was too important. Everything rested upon the Kurlani councillor. Anahid needed to know it was all in hand, and she needed to know *now*.

A flash of bronze in the crowd snagged Anahid's attention. She turned just as people shifted, bringing Tahera Danelani into view, the sun striking sparks off the beading of her headscarf.

She was in the very centre of a group of other azatas, laughing merrily, deeply engaged in conversation. Though not so deeply that she couldn't glance up and meet Anahid's eye.

Tahera pointedly looked away again.

Anahid recognised all the women she was standing with. Respectable azatas—*belligerently* respectable. The sort of women who would turn a shoulder the moment Anahid—and the tarnished tatters of her reputation—was spotted in the crowd.

She hesitated, hands knotting in her skirts. She wished Laxmi were down here, that she could at least have that steady menace at her shoulder, that smirk in her ear, that warm press of fingertips at the base of her spine, as she confronted these sharp-biting birds.

But Laxmi had other tasks today, and Anahid didn't *need* her. She was enough, on her own.

Anahid marched across the sand as the registrar called for the Filosani councillor to ascend. There was a scattering of applause, which Buni acknowledged with a modest smile and a lift of her hand as she climbed the stairs up to the balcony. The group with Tahera turned to watch, tilting against one another to exchange sidelong remarks.

When they turned back to their conversation, they noticed Anahid's approach.

Sleeves were tugged, and whispers hissed. Even as Anahid eased her way around a pair of azatans exclaiming over the disaster of the hippodrome's destruction, the women she was approaching turned as one.

Their shoulders fit together against her like an impenetrable wall, with Tahera on the other side.

Anahid almost laughed. As though *she* were going to play by society's rules *now.*

She marched right up to the beaded wall and tugged lightly on Azata Gahotani's earlobe. When the woman spun about in outrage, Anahid elbowed through the space left and into the thick of the little group.

"Azatas!" Anahid declared, with a wide and pleasant smile—too much for the Avenues, but not quite enough to be outrageous. "What a wonderful turnout there is this afternoon. Such an interest in the governance of our city. Perhaps we should always have these things in the open air!"

But she wasn't looking at any of them. She wasn't *interested* in any of them, save one.

If Tahera would rather stand with these women—rather have their respect and their inclusion—then Anahid already had her answer for whether their deal was going to be honoured. And everything would unravel.

Behind her, Polinna Andani huffed: "Even for *you*, Anahid, this is outrageous. Come, I think we have business to be about elsewhere." People to tell, she meant. She whisked her skirts around and flounced off.

The other azatas drained away with her. Tahera stayed. Her lips pursed. "That could have been done a *little* more judiciously," she suggested.

"Fuck judicious," Anahid suggested right back, and Tahera's mouth quirked toward mirth. Anahid almost wanted to smile back. Almost, but there was *no time*. The registrar was calling for the Joddani councillor. "Did you receive my message? I've done what you asked."

"You haven't," Tahera countered stiffly. "I was quite clear as to my requirement."

Elimination of the Zinedani, she'd said. She'd wanted more blood on Anahid's hands.

She could go hopping into the Abyss. "It's better this way," Anahid told her coolly, and continued as Tahera opened her mouth. "No, shut up. Think with your head and not your spleen. Death is not the hard line on a balance sheet that you seem to believe it to be. It leaves unreconciled figures and many loose ends, and you never know who may pick them up and decide to pull. Finality is better achieved through other means."

Tahera took a sharp step closer, fists bunched in her bronze skirts. "I'll think however I like," she snapped. "And *you* can take your request and—"

She stopped abruptly as Anahid removed from her sash the roll of paper she'd carefully tucked away there. The pages were reluctant to unfold smoothly, after their captivity, but she opened them sufficient for Tahera to see what the document was.

The record of debt under the name Tahera Danelani.

The record Ruzanna Zinedani had delivered to Anahid as part of their agreement.

Tahera grabbed for it; Anahid twitched the pages out of her grasp. "*Such* an amount," Anahid noted quietly. "I'm almost impressed."

"Give it to me," Tahera snarled.

Anahid stared her down. "Honour our deal."

In that moment of silence between them, the registrar called: "Kurlani, do you send a councillor?"

A cold fist closed around Anahid's stomach. Too late.

Tahera's mouth twisted. "Don't overreact," she snapped, and reached for her own sash, only to pause. "The rest of our deal holds? The District Council seat is mine?"

"*If* there is one," Anahid reminded her.

With a smirk, Tahera pulled something from her sash—a knife, Anahid thought for one panicked flash of a moment. But when Tahera flicked her wrist, a folded hand fan snapped open, pleated in the New Republic style, of an eye-wateringly orange satin.

Tahera raised it over her head, bright as a flag, and halfway up the stairs, the Kurlani councillor-to-be—her mother—lifted a hand to the crowd.

Anahid felt a weak flush of relief, but tightened her grip again as Tahera grabbed for the paperwork. "Ah!" she chided, meeting Tahera's glare. "You get it after the proposal is made, and not a moment sooner."

The orange fan was shoved back through Tahera's sash with vehemence. "So I'm supposed to just stand here with *you* until the Council commences?"

Everyone had seen them together already. Word was spreading. Tahera would learn soon enough that she couldn't catch her fish and still watch it jump. "We're going to be working together in any case, aren't we?" Anahid pointed out. But sympathy tugged at her. It hadn't been easy, taking a step outside society. It still wasn't. "This is the price," Anahid said, more gently now, "of daring to do other than we're supposed to."

The look Tahera gave her was cold. "Do you think I'm going to fall upon your neck and name you sister in fellow feeling?"

Anahid had a sister. She could have used a friend. But whatever trust there had ever been between Tahera and herself had been long poisoned. "I am grateful to you, you know," she told Tahera as the registrar called the Markani councillor. "I would never have even imagined all I could be, had you not shown me the first glimpse."

Tahera sighed, looking up to the noble stand, where the seats of the Council were now half full. "You seemed so tightly tied in your own little knot, that first time we met on Parsola's terrace. If I'd known how things would turn out, I'd have left you there to set forever in your tangle."

But her eyes drifted to the paper in Anahid's hand. It was her freedom from the consequences of her past mistakes. This *was* working out better for both of them.

They waited together in silence, as the last councillors were called, and the general stands grew as restless and murmuring as a late spring sea.

The registrar had to strain to be heard over the rumble. "The fifty-eighth Council of Bezim may now commence!"

A brief ovation from the gathered azatani. The rest of the crowd were starting to chatter, nearly drowning out the ritual opening of the first session. Anahid could almost hear their questions. Wasn't something going to happen? Was the Sorcerer going to show up? Was it all going to be this boring?

She glanced up at the stands, to the place where she and Laxmi had sheltered at Siyon's execution, next to one of the entrances. A dark smudge could just have been a hefty woman in black leather armour, her arms folded unmovingly over her chest. And probably that dustier darkness was Peylek at Laxmi's shoulder as well.

All of them waiting to see how things would unfold. To be there if needed. To do what needed to be done.

The registrar worked through the usual opening procedures, all of them empty and meaningless, until she called for the carrying over of rules from the fifty-seventh Council, unless there were any proposals for additions, amendments, or alterations.

Anahid's grip tightened on Tahera's debt paperwork, clutched against her sash.

One of the newly sworn councillors popped immediately to his feet and proposed a limit to the duration of Council sessions. *Someone* had raised it at every commencement Anahid could remember, but *still* other councillors immediately leapt into argument, about the vicissitudes of the job against the necessity for thoroughness in governance.

Impatience coiled beneath Anahid's skin like an itch. Tahera gripped her orange fan so tightly, the varnished wooden spines of it creaked.

The registrar hurried the proposal into a vote—which failed to pass, as always—amid the rising muttering of the general stands. Then she asked for any further proposals.

Up in the fifth row of seats, an azata stood, lifting her hand. Azata Kurlani sounded quite a lot like her daughter as she called down: "I propose that the membership of the Council be widened to include representatives of city interests outside the tiers of azatani families."

The crowd hushed; Council members turned to one another; the azatani in the arena gaped.

"Yeah!" shouted one of the bravi perched atop the walls. And then the crowd was on its feet, cheering and stamping and applauding.

A dozen Council members shot up, half of them talking before they were upright, no one waiting to be acknowledged by the registrar. Azata Kurlani resumed her seat with her hands folded tightly together at her waist sash.

And Tahera snatched the debt paperwork from Anahid's hand. "I hope you know what you're doing," she said, quiet but fierce, "or my mother's just ruined herself."

She stalked away as the registrar shouted for order. White-tunicked guards were moving among the Council, and the general stands cheered to see the azatani getting told off.

With the chaos settled, debate began in earnest, arguing intent, definitions, consequences, history. The general crowd shifted and grumbled, chatter drifting toward jeers. Few of them, whether they were robed students or somber merchants, Dockside laborers or brightly dressed Flowers, had much patience for all this bureaucratic back-and-forth.

Among them all shifted the dark specks of Peylek's crew, scattered like seasoning. Altering the flavour with a question here, a nudge there, a settling joke or a shouted response or a cry of outrage.

This was too important to be left to chance.

A councillor noted the value to the city of non-azatani trade groups and commercial interests, and the crowd gave a full-throated roar. He had to lift his voice over the approbation to add that perhaps some sort of consultative committee would be more appropriate. The crowd hissed at that.

Azata Filosani rose to speak, her voice carrying over a crowd hushing itself to hear. "Has not the past year shown us what our city is capable of? Yes, I speak of the Sorcerer, risen from the mud of Dockside and the lower city to amaze us all, but he is not alone. We have faced fear together. We have fought. And we have triumphed! We are still standing!"

The crowd came to its feet, roaring their defiant victory and drumming against the wooden benches.

"I say we are *all* Bezim!" Filosani shouted to be heard. "And I say it is time we made that official."

The applause continued after she'd taken her seat, the crowd cheering and clapping and collapsing into rhythm, chanting: "Bezim, Bezim, Bezim!" as the registrar shouted for order and eventually gestured for the gong. The shimmering tone smothered the noise like a blanket.

And in the hush, Azatan Rowyani stood.

Tension cramped Anahid's stomach. Of course he would speak. Of course he must be allowed to. And yet nothing good could come of it.

Rowyani spoke of the strength and prosperity and splendour of Bezim, and how that encouraged and produced a worthy populace. He even got a few scattered cheers from the crowd.

"But this grand ship of Bezim," he continued, "was built by azatani hands, stocked and outfitted and crewed by our forebears! We have the experience—centuries of it, in our family traditions. We have the vision. And we have the control."

The crowd muttered mutinously, but all around Anahid on the course of the hippodrome, her fellow azatani were straightening their shoulders and giving one another little nods, as though to confirm that, yes, they had all those things, and wasn't it good?

"I agree with my inestimable colleague Filosani," Rowyani said, not so much as tipping a nod in her direction, "that we have seen much in the past year. We have seen the mistakes made by those who are unused to responsibility and power. The accidents. The destruction. The unexpected. The *fear*."

There were people crying out in the crowd now—jeers and boos, and a general stewing of grumbling dissent. The guards squared up at the bottom of the wall, and the azatani drew together, away from the stands, toward the noble stand and the balcony. Rowyani was telling *them* what they wanted to hear, fear of the people driving them closer to him.

And they were the ones who would vote on it.

Rowyani tilted his head, and Anahid could imagine his condescending smile from here; it clenched her fists and ground her teeth. "This is a proposal most earnest and well-meaning, but ultimately misguided. Sailors who can tie a knot most ably cannot captain the ship of state better than those trained to the task. *We* have always had the best interests of the city—the *entire* city—at heart. And so I must—"

A voice cut across him—so loud the words echoed off the walls and set the gong to shimmering faintly in its stand: "Is that what the Last Duke was told when he was cut down?"

Anahid *knew* that voice.

Between the planes was the void, and the void was perfect.

Siyon hopped across it like the gap between wharf and boat, one foot leaving solid ground outside the Velo compound, and the other landing with a squelch in the shallow marshes on the northern edge of the city, where he promptly sank up to the ankle in mud.

"Fuck," Siyon sighed, even as he blinked against the lingering dark-and-dazzle of the void. He knew what he had been aiming for, but still could have known where he was by smell alone. The combination of mud and brackish water really caught in the nose, like he'd never be free of it. They'd come out here as kids, hunting duck eggs and swamp garlic, daring each other to stay out all night and meet Mother Marsh.

Siyon had met her now, in truth. *She* had better sense than to live out here.

A cart rattled by behind and above him, along the old supply road to the bastion at North Point. Siyon shifted, tilting to get free of the mud without leaving his boot behind. He nearly tipped over entirely, flailing back and then pitching forward to lean heavily against...

Against the city barrier, he realised, when he finally had both muddy boots planted among the reeds. They whispered and whistled around him, waving in the breeze off the water, passing through the bronze curve of the boundary as though it wasn't there at all. It *wasn't*, of course, in any sort of physical sense. But Siyon flexed his hand against it, pushing off it to stand upright, and it barely rippled beneath the pressure.

That, of course, was the entire problem. Why Siyon was here. He'd taken a step toward the problem he had to solve, in the place it might be easiest, where Mother Marsh and the other mudwitches had been keeping the energy so orderly and controlled. Out on the northern fringes of the city, where it didn't so much stop as dribble off into the encroaching marsh. Officially, the city stopped at that old supply road on the rocky ridge behind him, but there were a handful of ramshackle houses clinging to the slope, dipping their toes in the mud. Siyon's city boundary had been drawn for people, rather than geography, and there *were* people living in these tilting shacks, even if they all dreamed about one day making a shift to somewhere slightly sturdier.

The marshes spread out before Siyon, boggy and overgrown and stinking, stretching north as far as he could see, though his other senses carried him farther, over the sturdier hills and the little streams that ran between them, bare mud right now but flowing strong when the summer storms crashed into the mountains to the west...

Siyon blinked hard, pulling himself back to here and now, his own body among the reeds. The barrier in front of him.

From his cell beneath the hippodrome, armed with his desperation and the flow of the power around him, Siyon had thrown himself at this dome, and achieved nothing. The barest crack in the barrier, that allowed power to flow out into the rest of the world, soon sealed up again.

But now he was more, and less. Part of him *had* died on the poisoner's slab, and because of that he could slip between the cracks of reality, inhabit both his plane *and* his body. Now he could feel the sheen of energy in the bronze curve of the wall, like the shift of colours and shine in a bubble. It had been polished by every skerrick of power that passed into it. It was *perfect*, no weakness at all.

Siyon laid both hands against the barrier, braced his heels against the last stony outcrop of the hill, and *pushed*.

The barrier didn't so much as flex beneath his weight. Siyon might as well have pushed against the crag rising over the city. Strange as he was, now, he might have moved that more easily.

A seagull flew overhead, passing straight through the barrier, and then ducking back again. Show-off.

Fine. Siyon hadn't really expected that to work anyway.

When Siyon held his hand up toward the surface—not quite touching this time—he could see the crackle and snap of the power through his own flesh, the energy of the barrier calling to that beneath his skin. This time, he *pulled*.

Pulled the energy into himself, more and more and more, like some opera tale of a fisherman swallowing the sea to find his beloved. The power rushed into Siyon, glowing in loops and coils, melting into an endless puddle. There seemed no limit to how much he could take. He *was* the Power, and he could swallow it all down, the endless burnished flood of energy.

But the barrier grew no thinner. As though it was—

"Hey," someone called, up behind Siyon.

He tried to whirl around, staggered and tripped over the rising bank, and sat down hard in a tuft of reeds. The winter-pale sky spun above him. A dark shadow poked into it, leaning over the rickety railing of one of the shacks on the slope. Siyon blinked, and the man came into focus: mud-smeared face beneath a wide-brimmed hat.

"Hey," the guy called down again. "You're him, ain't it? The Sorcerer."

He wasn't even wearing the purple coat. But for all Siyon knew, he was glowing like the city barrier did to his eyes. "Yeah," he said, voice a croak. "That's me."

A gapped grin split the muddy face looking down at him. "Nice one! Show them they can't just have it all their way!" The guy cackled and slapped at the splintered railing. "Say, you need a hand?"

Yes, Siyon did. But from where he was lying, he could see endless threads of power, streaming across the sky, pouring into the city barrier. One from this guy, and one from the baby crying in another shack, and one from someone else clanging away with pots and pans. Each sign of life a tiny tendril of bronze energy.

The whole city, pouring into its own defense.

Siyon had *made* it that way. He'd built it on the people of Bezim.

Fucking inconvenient as it was, he'd apparently done a really good job. He couldn't break through the entire city.

He needed more than a hand. He needed something bigger than Bezim.

He needed the Mundane.

Fitting, really. He'd done nothing alone, since he started on this path. He'd walked willingly with Izmirlian, and suspiciously with Midnight. He'd had help from Zagiri, and Anahid, and the bravi, and the whole damn city. He'd so rarely been alone, even when he'd felt so.

He would never *be* alone now. The entire Mundane was with him. If he let it in.

Like Izmirlian had, leaping into the unknown. *Outside* everything they knew. But also *into* something new. Something bigger. Something waiting to be discovered.

Siyon clambered to his feet. "Thanks," he called up to the guy hanging over his railing. "I'll be all right."

He would be. He knew it.

But he still waited until the mud-smeared guy went chuckling into his little shack.

Siyon didn't let himself sink. Nothing so passive. This time, he dived straight in.

Like leaping from the southern cliffs, plunging into the cold sea. Siyon shot down like he never had, not falling into the water, not slipping into the earth—he pushed forward, eyes open, without any struggle.

And so he saw the dragon's cavern open up around him. Not as a cold and stone-lined prison, but as the space inside a person, cradled safe within their ribs, where a heart beat. Where power arose to drive the world. Where everything began.

Siyon floated here, suspended as though deep underwater. He found it hard to believe he'd ever been afraid of drowning—that panic now seemed distant as a moth fluttering against a late-night window.

Harder still to think he'd been afraid of this surrender. Everything here was *him*—the energy, the earth, the entire Mundane.

He was the Power, and the power was him.

This wasn't who he'd always been. There were parts of him that had been left behind. There were new things he was becoming. But that was no more than the fact of living—the new, the old, the choice and the changing path. With every step Siyon had ever taken, he'd become someone new. No longer the son of a fisherclan. No longer a mere provisioner. No longer the man who'd had poison poured down his throat.

But always Siyon Velo. Becoming who he needed to be.

Anahid was right. *Izmirlian* was right. Change was not death, it was growth. And the unknown could be beautiful as well as terrifying.

Siyon settled—delicate and impossible as a bloodgull—in the power-scarred place where the dragon had been chained. Where Siyon had woken her, released her, and then *failed*.

He realised that now. Could see it so clearly. He'd failed to greet her—*meet* her—properly. Failed to see in her the other half of the Mundane—the monstrous to his human, the wild to his tamed.

Failed to embrace all of who he was and could be.

No wonder she was lonely, angry, lost out there in the world. No wonder he was trapped in here.

He'd opened the rakia and then dropped it. But it wasn't too late. He'd stopped the flagon from rolling away. He could pick it up again.

She was coming back.

Standing here, where she'd slumbered for so long, Siyon could feel the weight of her, bearing down upon the world in this place for so long. Perhaps this *hadn't* been the font of energy, before her long confinement. Had she worn thin the barrier of the world, to let the power seep in and pool around her?

So much Siyon didn't know. But he had a long time to find out. Centuries, perhaps.

But first, he had a promise to keep.

Siyon didn't know *when* it was; that felt less important, down here. He'd felt adrift in time since first sinking into the stone. If he tried, perhaps he could be wherever—*when*ever—he needed to be.

He could stretch out every sense he had—those of the earth and the plane and his own body, all of them equal—and find . . . *there*.

The tight-bound knot of people, the heart of Bezim, the beat of their curiosity and their purpose. The stone that encircled them, built by their hands and design. The weight of their attention, bending the past and the future to encircle this moment. Those Siyon knew among them, searching for their vital goals, and with the barest flick of his thoughts, Siyon nudged the sparks of the world into a more useful order for them.

Not enough to keep his promise. Not enough for who he needed to be. So Siyon sank down even deeper, soaking in the power, and he—

Reached.

Up, and out, and through.

He travelled in a blink. He stretched out toward the sky. And he was halfway there when he realised—by the sweep of earth around him, by the brush of stone through his bones, by the burn of the magic in his veins—that he might not arrive in the manner that anyone had expected.

But here he came, the Power of the Mundane.

As he truly was.

Stone stretched and time bent and the sky opened around him; the Alchemist arose.

CHAPTER 27

The azatani crowd parted, like they were the sea and Zagiri the ship cutting through.

She couldn't blame them. That had been *loud*. Zagiri shot a glance sidelong at Nihath, who winced a little and twisted his fingers in their tangle of nothing.

Possibly her fault for just saying *make sure they can hear me*. But they were working in a hurry here. She *wasn't* going to let Rowyani roll over this entire business.

He didn't get to decide what being azatani meant.

"This is out of order!" cried the registrar of the council, up on the balcony. She waved a furious arm. "Azata, you have no right to make a submission!"

Nihath tipped her a nod and fell back with the rest of the crowd, leaving Zagiri in the middle of a little empty space, alone with her words and all their attention.

Whatever the rules were, Bezim *loved* a spectacle and was always willing to give time and space to one.

When Zagiri spoke it was still loud, but not stone-shaking loud. "This isn't a submission." She hadn't been tasked by the bravi— by the city writ small in the tribes—to offer comments, had she? She set her shoulders (as best she could, with the left one still in a sling) as she laid her hand on Siyon's sabre at her hip. "This is a challenge."

The registrar objected, and various of the azatani councillors behind her were shouting as well, but they were all lost in the roar from the stands. The people of Bezim approved.

Indeed, the people of Bezim gave every indication that if they'd known azatani politics was this exciting, they'd have come along to watch sooner.

On the balcony, the registrar gestured for the gong, but the Aethyreal charms Zagiri had wrapped around her—crafted by the best alchemical practitioner in the city, after all—were stronger. "The rituals of the duel predate those of the council," she said, even over the shimmering tone of the gong. "You used them when you took power from the Last Duke. *You* did not wait for him to agree to share the ruling of the city. You did not doubt your capacity to steer the ship. You stepped forth, and you said to him, as I say to you now—*This is unjust.*"

The crowd was wild and jubilant; the sound swelled all around Zagiri, cheers and catcalls and the bravi drumming against the stones of the hippodrome as if they would bring the whole thing down.

She was standing for them. She was standing for *all of them*.

But not *just* for them. "I am one of you!" Zagiri had to lift her voice, despite Nihath's charm, to be heard. She raked her gaze around the arena, over the shifting and whispering splendid in all their finery. "We are azatani. And Bezim is ours, not to own, but to keep. To guide. Yes, to steer, but what *some people* forget"—she dared a glance at the balcony, where Rowyani was shouting at the registrar and waving to the palace guards—"is that a captain cannot shift a ship by himself. I remember who we are, azatani. We are the ones who stand up and say: This is not the best way of doing business. Who say: *We can do better.*"

Around her, the azatani shifted, muttering to one another. Zagiri wasn't sure that she'd convinced anyone.

But actions, in Bezim, always spoke louder than words.

"I call challenge!" Zagiri said again, hand still on the sabre at her hip. "I call challenge against the Council, on behalf of Bezim."

There was agitation in the noble stand—shouting and pointing and knots of frantic consultation. But in their midst, Rowyani beckoned to someone. He gestured firmly down, into the hippodrome course. Pointed at Zagiri herself.

Someone broke out of the ranks of clerks and assistants lining the side of the stands, and descended to the registrar on her balcony. Someone with a posture very haughty, and very familiar.

Avarair Hisarani spoke with the registrar, giving a peremptory jerk of his chin, and a dismissive cut of his hand, before he headed down the stairs to the arena.

The registrar stepped to the railing of the balcony and shouted something entirely smothered by the crowd's ongoing commotion. Zagiri held up her hands, turning to scan the stands—and ink and ashes, there were so *many* of them, waving hippodrome team flags and bravi sashes, standing on the benches and hollering. They quietened reluctantly at her soothing, quelling gestures.

But they did hush just enough for the registrar to be heard: "The Council accepts your challenge."

Shit. She hadn't thought it would come to this. If she'd thought at all, which Zagiri acknowledged hadn't quite been the case, she'd reasoned that if there wasn't a *prefect*, surely no one else could be compelled to stand for the Council. It hadn't occurred to her that someone might just step up.

The crowd was going wild with renewed jubilation. This was just what they wanted to see. A spectacle. A show. A simple fight.

The azatani in the arena drew back even farther, leaving Zagiri in the gap between the rows of benches that no one had been using anyway. At the other end of the long corridor, Avarair Hisarani now waited, with a sabre in his hand.

He knew what he was doing with a blade. Zagiri wasn't sure if she could tell that just by the way he was standing, or if she'd already known it. The knowledge couldn't have just appeared in her head, after all, and she knew it very clearly. He might not have run the tiles with a tribe, but he wasn't some azatani amateur.

Unthinkable to back down now. The crowd was louder than ever, clamouring like a storm. Even the azatani were shifting restlessly, crowding around and jostling for position. Eager to witness.

All of Bezim loved a spectacle.

Fine. Zagiri drew her sabre—*Siyon's* sabre, a little rough in her hand, a little heavy against her arm. "Draw the circle," she said, and Nihath's charm carried her words to the entire stadium. "Let's do this."

There was a moment of confusion, but then three azatans stepped out from different parts of the crowd, pulling the wooden benches aside. They worked together to curve benches around in a barrier, and then carved a sparring circle in the packed dirt of the former hippodrome course. Zagiri stepped up to the line on her side of the circle as Avarair paced forward to his. He looked different than usual, in some way Zagiri couldn't quite pin down, but also just the same: stern, and untroubled, and faintly disdainful.

Maybe he was right to be so. She had only one working shoulder, and someone else's blade.

Zagiri twisted around, finding Nihath in the azatani mob jostling behind her. She beckoned to him around the hilt of the sabre, sliced her hand. *Stop this.*

Nihath frowned fussily and mouthed: *Are you sure?*

Zagiri nodded vehemently. If Avarair landed a hit on her—*when* Avarair landed a hit on her—the last thing she wanted was the whole city hearing her scream.

He shrugged and did something with his hands that caused a brief flash of silvery sparkles. A pressure in Zagiri's ears that she hadn't even noticed until that moment suddenly eased.

"Thanks," she said, and her voice fell flat in the air around her.

One of the azatans who'd marked out the circle stepped up beside her; through the strange distance of her nervousness, Zagiri realised it was Beren Josepani, one of her former Bracken blademates.

"Are you sure about this?" he muttered. "I heard Avarair once beat the Blessed Jester herself."

That was a bladename Zagiri knew—the whole *city* knew— though she'd retired from the Bower's Scythe before Zagiri was old enough to run the tiles. So maybe Avarair was out of practice.

A thin hope to hold on to. No, she was not sure about this at all. "You have a better idea?" she demanded, and shifted her grip on Siyon's sabre, hefting and twisting the blade. Trying to get a feel for it.

Beren winced. "Good luck," he offered, and faded back into the crowd.

Zagiri stared across at Avarair, who was barely moving at all, waiting as though bored, though he lifted an eyebrow at her. Fuck him.

She stepped into the circle.

Across from her, Avarair stepped in as well. As they came closer, Zagiri blinked and nearly stumbled in surprise. Was that *stubble* on his face? And his hair was just a little too long, though he had far to go before he reached the elegant lengths Izmirlian's had attained.

But this was not the prim, precise, perfectly trimmed Avarair Hisarani she'd encountered previously.

She remembered Balian at the post-Ball funerals, saying, *Since the Ball, he's been strange. Prickly. Distracted.*

He'd said more. About Rowyani, and how he'd treat Avarair if push came to shove. Zagiri glanced up at the Council seats, where Rowyani was watching, arms folded forbiddingly over his chest.

"You don't have to do what he says," she told Avarair. "We all get to decide who we are. What being azatani means."

He rolled his eyes, sneer stretching his mouth as he said, "I'm sure *you* think it's—"

Then he leapt back.

Zagiri had known, from the first twitch of his face, that her words would get her nowhere. So she lunged forward, sabre held loose and low, to slash at his knees.

She knew she'd missed even as she swung. This blade was heavier than either of hers, and she'd misjudged the length. Avarair danced back, but he barely needed to bother. Still, it had shut him up, and Zagiri hefted the sabre, settling it more comfortably in her palm.

He glared at her. She grinned at him. "We here to talk or fight?"

Which might have been a mistake. He came at her then, in a blistering string of feints and darts and strikes that had Zagiri giving ground, working desperately to get out of the way, and to turn aside those attacks she couldn't avoid. After a frantic disengage she spun away, circling wide around the edge of their dueling space.

Avarair let her go, his eyes tracking her. Eyes so much like his brother Izmirlian, and yet in this moment, watching her this steadily, seeing far too much, also like his brother Balian.

Zagiri was all too aware that he likely saw everything she was realising. That the heaviness of Siyon's blade was already starting to tell in her wrist, in her elbow, in her shoulder. That the binding up of her *other* arm was tipping her balance just a little bit off.

That she was going to lose.

Despair coiled choking around her throat. She wanted to deny it. She wanted to insist—they'd done so much! They'd brought the whole *city* together, Avenues and barons and everyone in between. They'd managed it in half the time and scrambling desperately. Surely, after all of that, she couldn't simply lose. The world owed them more.

But if the world worked like that, Lusal Hisarani would still be alive.

Zagiri pushed forward again, engaging and, for a moment, pushing Avarair back in his turn. Roars from the crowd mingled with whistles and bravi cries. It should fill her limbs with energy, like an alchemical reaction. But Zagiri just felt it as a weight. All their hope. All their expectation. And she was going to let them down.

She wondered if this was how Siyon had felt, when the earth rattled beneath him.

"Don't worry," Avarair said with a little smirk. "We can make it look good, for the show."

"Fuck you," Zagiri snarled, and kicked at his knee. Dirty fighting, even on the tiles, but he skipped back smooth enough. "Your brother told me, you know, your family's nasty little secret." That got a twitch of an eyebrow, even as he lunged in again, an attack she barely evaded. But the words kept coming anyway. "Telmut Hisarani *didn't* win the duel."

Avarair's mouth thinned, and he brushed aside her next attack with scant regard. "We still defeated the Duke. That is the truth that matters."

"And even if I lose here," Zagiri said, breath starting to come rough in her throat, "you will still be defeated. You think I'll be the only challenger? Everyone's seen how it's done now. I've showed them. Mezin Velo showed them. *Siyon* Velo showed them. We're all coming for you. I'm just one of many."

She shrugged out of her sling—*ow*—to lift her off hand, beckoning like a bravi for a little audience appreciation. All for the show.

Avarair's glance flickered to the stands as the crowd *screamed*, and they—

No, wait. They were *really* screaming.

All around them, the azatani noticed too, huddling together, looking around. Looking *up*.

And one of them shrieked: "The Sorcerer!"

Avarair fell back, blade still held low and ready even as he scanned the top of the hippodrome wall. A sensible place to look. But Zagiri followed her instinct, and the glint of bronze at the edge of her vision, and looked straight up into the sky.

He loomed above them, the Alchemist himself, in his purple coat. Tall as the crag and shimmering bronze, faint as though he was painted on the blue sky.

Siyon had come, after all.

The Alchemist arose, Siyon climbing out of the depths, setting his foot in the midst of his city and straightening up to stand tall.

Oh shit. *Really* tall.

The city fell away below him. Trees tickled faintly at his ankles. The clock tower in the square might have come up to his knee. He was awash in power, swelled up with it, seeing the world in a glittering clarity even as it spread out around him. He could see *so far* from up here. Bezim seemed almost insignificant, spread around him like an unfortunate puddle. Over the marshes to the north, far along the coast, there was the distant smudge of another city—it could only be Revarr. The wide sweep of the ocean covered the eastern horizon, and the chop and bite of cliffs down to the south, spray rising from the distant headland where the coast cut back to the west. The hills to the west of the city, rolling on until they tipped into the gentler territory of old Lyraea, or the harsher reaches of the edges of the Khanates.

So much *world*. Siyon had never seen even this much of it.

It was amazing. It was his. Not to own, but to keep. To explore and cherish and protect.

But not alone.

He turned again to the eternity of the ocean, that he knew, without sight, did *not* go forever; he could feel the tickle of land on the other side, the New Republic in all its patchwork complexity lurking beyond the horizon. But above that horizon, just the tiniest black speck at the moment...

She came. Siyon could feel—both her coming, and the wind rushing around her arrow-like flight, the ocean spray against her belly, the tip of her wings dipping into the waves. She came enraged, at the city, and at *him*, at his ongoing, determined choice of these people who had betrayed them both.

The wind billowed around Siyon, dragging up the faint screams of distant fighting gulls.

No, wait. Those *weren't* gulls.

He blinked, and looked down. Down and down, Bezim spread out like a patchwork below him. The big oval of the parklands, with the rubble of the Palace in the centre. The cut of the river, and the white span of the Swanneck, incandescent with sun and Mundane power both. The sweep of the Boulevard, punctuated by the Scarp, but continuing regardless, out to the gleam of the Observatory's dome.

And the little double-hand cup of the old hippodrome, throbbing with the energy of the city's concentration, bright with faces turned his way, sharp with attention fixed on him.

The Sorcerer.

Nearly. The Alchemist. The Power. The avatar of the Mundane itself.

Siyon Velo.

He came closer—perhaps lowered himself, perhaps shrank, perhaps just bent over. None of the usual words seemed to apply, like this.

He focused on the old hippodrome, in any case, and the crowd there, in the stands and in the arena, pushed back from a drawn circle that crackled with burnished energy—with intent, with ritual purpose, with meaning given to it by everyone present. Two little figures in the centre, staggering apart, each with the glint of a blade in their fists.

A duel. Quite the duel, in this place, in front of all these people. A duel of *significance*.

And that…that was Zagiri. Siyon recognised her less by sight than by feel. The bright spark of her, so determined to burn.

The other he recognised as well. So similar to a familiar and beloved soul (Izmirlian, in the corner of his mind, just out of reach, just gone from the room with his scent remaining) but twisted tighter. Tangled in knots of his own making. Straining against his constraints without knowing how to get free.

Siyon reached out—and hesitated.

His hand was enormous. He could span the entire hippodrome with his thumb on one wall, littlest finger on the other. Each finger was as wide as the chariots that had run here, more than a century ago.

Humans were so tiny in comparison. So delicate. Such creatures of intricate nuance.

Turtle eggs on the beach, easily crushed and destroyed.

They were all looking at him, eyes wide, mouths open, noise and noise and *noise*. Not all of it screaming—they were laughing, they were cheering, they were jubilant and terrified and everything in between. They *were*, all the time, so full of energy and life.

They were looking at him, as though he could solve all their problems. As though he'd ever *solved* any, rather than making new ones. Because he was just a person as well, flawed and trying. Because he was too much more.

He *couldn't* solve their problems, with a touch too large to come close to the details.

They didn't need *him*. They had everything they needed to solve their own problems, far better than he ever could.

Siyon pulled back his hand and straightened again. Until his hair brushed sizzling at the underside of the dome he'd drawn over the city, like the stretched-taut skin of some blanket he was hiding beneath, thin as a bubble and just as beautiful. Energy crackled around him, swirling and eddying and gusting.

So much of it, boiling and fuming and churning over Bezim.

So much more than Bezim needed, or was comfortable with. Time to set it all free.

Siyon looked east again, and here she came, the dragon winging low over the sea, fast as second thoughts, sharpened by intent. She shone like a polished bronze mirror beneath the sun, her anger ready to burn.

They dare—

"They don't," Siyon murmured—and maybe it was just between them, or maybe it rumbled like thunder across the sky. He couldn't tell, like this. "They're afraid. They're only human. But they can do better."

Centuries, she snarled, ferocious wing beats raising spray behind her, catching the sun, giving a rainbow halo to her sparkling black scales. *They have had centuries to do better.*

"It's not like building a wall," Siyon pointed out. "Or maybe it is. It needs maintaining. Rebuilding when it crumbles. But they always *can* be better. They just need to choose. Let them choose."

You choose them, she snarled. *You always choose them!*

"I do," Siyon murmured. "But I also choose us."

He breathed in—or at least he *pulled* in, sucking up everything that the city and the people within it could be—the bravi and the merchants and the students and the workers and *everyone*; bright and bold, kind and cunning, grasping and generous, intricate as a puzzle. See. This is us.

This too is wondrous.

A roar—in his mind and in his ears. The dragon came shooting over the city, wings flaring now, as though maybe she wanted to stop after all. But she was moving too fast, a massive body of black scaled bulk, wings wide as night, her parchment-pale eyes with their star-shaped pupils—

And Siyon standing there, large as the city, like a shield between her and it.

She smashed into Siyon—*through* Siyon, like a punch to the chest knocking all the wind out of him, like a ballista bolt launched through his soul.

He exploded into billowing power.

CHAPTER 28

From the edge of the drawn duelling circle on the hippodrome floor, where she'd elbowed her way in a hurry, Anahid gaped with everyone else. Siyon loomed massive and burnished, tilting down over the hippodrome to lay his hand over them, like some second sky, like a blessing, like a protection.

The stands were in pandemonium. People screamed and shoved, laughed and raised their hands. "The Sorcerer!" someone shouted, and that felt not quite right, even though he was wearing the purple coat, flickering in and out of visibility behind the roiling bronze sheen that passed over him like scudding clouds.

The dark spot that was Laxmi was reassuringly unmoving, still in the place they'd agreed she'd stand. Solid—they could all use a little of that solidity right now. They needed to know what this was. They needed to be nudged in the right direction.

Anahid waved—one hand, then both, and despaired of being seen at all. Gritting her teeth, she pulled free her headscarf—pins tugging at her hair and pinging away into the crowd—until she could lift it and wave the black-beaded length of it above the azatani.

Outrageous. Scandalous. Unthinkable.

Enough to get Laxmi's attention.

That distant figure unfurled, darting into the crowd. Anahid lost her in the tumult, but caught sight of other black-clad figures, wriggling through the chaos, stopping to gesture and shout.

The chant rose from that section of the stands, drifting up on a stamp of feet. "Velo! Velo! Velo!"

It spread, trickling through the stands, picking up more and more voices. Not everyone—there was a low, seething undercurrent of shouting and jeering and disagreement—but the uniformity of the chant bubbled up through the rest of the noise. "Velo! Velo!"

Anahid's heart beat with it; she lifted her head and laughed, though there were tears in her eyes. Pride, for Siyon, for Laxmi, for all of them.

How could the Council deny *this*?

Above them, Siyon straightened, a massive illusion over the city again. As the crowd chanted, he lifted his hand, like a ward or a pause, pointing out to sea. His lips moved, but the words were faint down here, over the ongoing chant. Anahid could only make out fragments. "...can do better," she caught, and then, "...Let them choose."

Was he talking to *them*? Or was there something else?

Anahid started to turn, looking toward the eastern sky, when a fast-moving shadow flashed overhead. Someone screamed: "Dragon!"

And it was. The massive bulk of the dragon, every black scale glittering in the sun as she streaked in from over the sea. Not a mystery in darkness, this time, but here with full daylight glinting off the curved barbs of her wings and the talons on her massive, grasping feet.

She was terrifyingly beautiful.

Shadow trailed in her wake, enclosing the entire hippodrome in darkness as she—

Plunged through Siyon, in a wild explosion of burnished sparks.

The noise hit them then, a thunderclap as loud as a giant's hands beside Anahid's head. She cried out, hunching over with her hands over her ears—too little, too late. Her head was ringing, her vision a shattering of black and bronze, dancing aside with each frantic blink.

The whole hippodrome tottered in shocked silence.

Until a voice bellowed, big and bold: "He saved us! The Sorcerer is protecting us from the dragon."

Shouting and shoving, people running for the exits, but others standing firm and pointing to the sky. The dragon wheeled, unsteady and apparently disoriented, beyond that thin film of bronze that still lingered, like a curtain drawn over the sky.

Like the shell of Siyon's benediction.

The chant rose again, blooming out of every corner of the stands: "Velo! Velo! Velo!" Until the entire place shook with it, voices ringing off the stones, hands clapping and feet stamping, making a thunder of acclaim.

Movement within the duelling circle pulled Anahid's attention back; she turned with her headscarf still dangling loose, and her hair blowing into her eyes. Both Avarair and Zagiri had staggered apart at Siyon's appearance, gaping at the sky like everyone else.

Now Avarair shook his head, like he was ridding himself of some unwelcome thought. Or like he was denying it entirely. He lifted his gaze, eyes clear and determined.

And he lifted his blade.

"Zagiri!" Anahid shrieked, moving forward with her scarf in one fist. *Damn* the rules of the duelling circle, she'd tackle Avarair Hisarani herself before she let him cut down her distracted sister.

But even as Zagiri whirled around, dragging her sabre point up with a visible effort—even as Anahid's toe broke the line of the circle—Avarair tilted his sabre aside and beckoned with his off hand.

"Strike me," he called, words barely reaching Anahid's ears under the chanting from the stands. He stepped forward, and Zagiri fell back, confusion blooming on her face. "Don't you see!" Avarair's jaw set, his shoulders braced, his face sharp with clarity. "He's *right*."

The azatani near Anahid crowded in closer, returning their attention to the interrupted duel. Avarair scanned their faces, as more people crowded in behind Anahid, pressing her over the edge of the circle. She wasn't sure it mattered anymore.

Whatever this was, it was no longer a duel. Everyone seemed to sense it. The chant in the crowd rolled on, but those closest to the arena were nudging at one another and craning to see.

Anahid caught sight of Nihath, across the circle, up on tiptoe to see. She waved at him, with her scarf-wrapped hand, and cupped the other around her ear. He looked confused for a moment, until she wiggled her fingers, and then he brightened. His brow creased and his face glazed over in that expression he'd always worn, when he was engaged with the planes and with alchemy and not *at all* with whatever was going on with Anahid and their lives together.

For once, it didn't enrage her.

He twisted his hands, tossed them up, and suddenly Avarair's voice leapt loud into the hippodrome air.

"—so much more in the world! We didn't understand. *I* didn't. We wanted to be able to grasp it all and hold it steady. We *wanted* to set limits. We wanted to bind the city with control and with fear." Avarair's mouth twisted; he looked venomously up to the tiers of the Council seating. "We wanted *more* to be impossible. But it isn't. They were right. *He* was right!"

He pointed at the sky, where Siyon had been, so undeniably enormous and strange.

"I'm sorry, Izmir," Avarair whispered, and even that sighed out over the whole hippodrome.

Then he lifted his sabre over his head and called: "Bezim! This is *enough*. The challenger is right: We can do better!" He lifted his other hand as well, both of them over his head, visible to all as he tipped the blade into his empty palm. Turned it. Pulled.

The crowd hissed, as though they all felt the pain of the cut across their own palms. As though their blood had been drawn as well.

Avarair turned back to Zagiri, threw his bloody blade down on the sand, and showed his red hand. Like a challenge or a demand. "I yield," he said, voice ringing from the stands.

And he smiled.

While the crowd exploded, in thunder and cheering. The bravi were on their feet along the wall of the hippodrome, brandishing their own blades and screaming their mottos.

Even the azatani around Anahid were applauding, while she pushed forward, across the circle to where Zagiri wavered on her feet, staring agape at Avarair.

"Are you all right?" Anahid demanded, grabbing at Zagiri's shoulders, and then letting go in a hurry at her sister's wince. "You *idiot*," she snapped, breathless with relief. "What were you thinking? Where has your sling gone? Here." She tied a hurried knot in her own headscarf.

"Ana." Zagiri dropped the sabre clattering onto the sand to lift a hand to Anahid's shoulder, fingers digging in. "What just happened? Did we— Have we *won*?"

Anahid didn't know. She didn't know what winning even *looked* like, in this roiling chaos, in this wild celebration, in this mess of a city.

But even as she opened her mouth to say so, another voice cut across the cacophony. "Bezim!"

They whirled around, Zagiri still hanging on to Anahid grimly. Up on the balcony, Azata Filosani was standing in the registrar's place, holding the other woman at arm's length as she made use of the amplification charms. "Bezim!" she called again, and the chant died down in the stands, making more room for her. For what she had to say.

This was no time for elegant speeches. "What say you?" Filosani demanded. "Is this city ours? Is it *all of ours*?"

The joyous roar of the crowd rattled Anahid's teeth in her skull. She found herself laughing with it, pulling Zagiri closer.

On the balcony, Filosani stepped aside, yielding to the disgruntled registrar with a gracious gesture. The registrar stomped back into her place, and lifted her own voice. "*Council* of Bezim," she said with huffy emphasis. "What say *you* to the proposal raised by Councillor Kurlani, that membership be widened beyond the azatani? Who votes in favour?"

The crowd quietened, but didn't settle, as full of the menace of storms as the sea in late spring. Anahid's heart still beat wildly—with fear and exhilaration and the possibility.

Surely there was only one way they could answer.

But still relief flooded her, weakening her knees, as hands raised across the ranks of councillors. Not all—of course not all. But so many. More than she'd expected.

Enough.

"We've done it," Zagiri whispered beside her, as though she couldn't believe it. "Ana, we've *done it*."

And she burst into tears.

Anahid pulled her close and held her carefully. The azatani were shouting all around them, some in outrage and others in bright jubilation. The crowd screamed wildly. The noise thundered like the beating heart of the city.

Over her sister's shaking head, Anahid looked at the sky, still sheened from Siyon's benediction. There, black as a raven, was the dragon, wings flaring wide as she swooped in to perch atop the crag over the city.

Where something gleamed brightly bronze.

Siyon floated in the wash of Mundane energy. It lulled him deeply and slowly, soothing and salving, pulling him back together after he'd—

What?

He'd been at the old hippodrome, *over* the city. So many people there, but even among all the churn and spark of Bezim, Siyon had recognised individuals. The dancing flame of Daruj among the crowd, casting his light. The twisting spark of Mayar, up atop the walls, flickering a merry pattern. The bold brightness of Laxmi, still tinged with the Abyss, smoldering steady as a coal.

And down in the arena, there was Anahid, with her cards and her coins and her knife-blade patience clutched tight. There was Zagiri, pacing the sand like a tiger with sabre in hand—a rebel blade, a just blade, a levelling blade.

Pacing like a what?

A tiger, affirmed a corner of his mind, and with the word came an enormous orange-and-black striped cat, prowling through jungle like a Dockside alley bruiser, shoulders rolling, impatience writ in every twitch.

It was a wondrous sight. But not enough to distract Siyon entirely.

You, he said, to that corner of his mind.

He'd been over the city, when he'd been shattered into mist by *her*.

A sense of shifting, the rustle of wings and scales, the scrape of claws against stone all around him. *I regret that*, the dragon informed him. *It was more difficult to arrest my momentum than I had anticipated, in the fervour of my anger.*

Siyon laughed—couldn't help it, boiling up inside him. And the laughter put him back together, knitting him back into reality. Breath pulled into actual lungs, mirth shaking solid ribs, his throat scratching with it, and that meant he had a body, lying on stone and aching. It meant he had eyes that he could force open.

The dragon made a second sky over him, constellations of sparkling black scales and the splayed canvas of spread wings. Sun glinted off the barbs at the joints of her wings and the horns atop the head she tilted down to consider him. She was *beautiful*, in the daylight, in her full glory. With her long neck twisted, Siyon could see the ruff of spikes around her head, sheened in midnight blue and deep blood-red and the green of the deepest sea. Her parchment-pale eyes had a burnished sheen to the star-shaped pupils.

Why are you so attached to humanity? This insistence on physical form is tiresome and unnecessary.

Laughter still tickled around Siyon's chest. "Says the one swanning around like *this*." He gestured weakly up at her, but he also wasn't letting her off the hook on this one: "Are you saying you're *sorry*?"

As the dragon huffed, Siyon turned his head, slowly and creakily, vision swimming. But he could make out enough, sparkling new in the sunshine. He knew those rocks, this delicate scoop at the top of the world. He was lying atop the crag.

He rolled onto his side, climbing laboriously onto hands and knees. Actually, apart from feeling like he was learning to use his body again from first principles, he didn't hurt as much as he probably deserved, waking up on hard stone. He grabbed at the nearest outcropping of rock and used it to pull himself up to standing.

Beyond, the edge of the crag fell away, and there was Bezim, tipping down from university hill, flowing around the parkland, swooping down to leap the river chasm, spilling into the bay. The streets glittered with power and danced with sparks. The hippodrome still burned like a cauldron, brewing a future.

My city, Siyon thought, and knew it at once for . . . not a lie, but also not a truth.

Siyon Velo belonged to the city, but the city couldn't belong to him. He had too much sway already. No one person should carry so much weight in these streets.

And the Power of the Mundane could not belong to one city alone.

The breeze blew cold and clear and refreshing into his face as Siyon tilted to look up. The bronze dome still curved over the city. The boundary he had drawn around the familiar.

He looked back to the dragon, hunkered down over the top of the crag. "*You* just fly through it like it's not there."

She blinked at him. *You could as well, if you wanted.*

Bitterness caught at the back of Siyon's mouth. "What, that easy?"

She considered that, crouching down lower, tucking in her wings. *I did not say it was easy.*

Siyon looked down at the city that had raised him, that was everything he had ever known, and heard again his mother's sharp voice. *Seems the nudge helped you along.*

Rather embarrassing, that he'd done all this, come all this way, and he still needed someone else to point the way. Still needed the dragon to come back for him, making anew the offer he'd already, in his knee-jerk panic, rejected.

To fly together, out into the world.

But leaving behind everything he'd ever known was more daunting than Izmirlian had made it look.

A sound reached Siyon's ears from the city below: a heavy *clunk*, with a faint twanging echo. A moment later, a ballista bolt went sizzling overhead, arcing across the blue sky and falling away down toward the steep hills on the other side of the river. It came nowhere near the dragon, hunched down carefully atop the crag.

That was *why* she was curled up like this.

"Shit." Siyon scrambled around until he could see over the edge, to the ballista emplacements atop the city wall. One crew furiously working winches, hefting a new spear-like bolt. The other crew members were turning their ballista, pointing it up at the crag. "*Shit*," Siyon repeated, ducking down again. "How long have they been doing *that*?"

While he'd been unconscious, putting himself back together, she'd been here, waiting under fire. Curled up over him. Protecting him.

It was as clear a sign as Siyon could have asked for; so obvious that he couldn't help a huff of sharp laughter. "This is no place for us."

The people of Bezim *were* afraid. It *was* understandable. But that didn't mean their lashing out would hurt any less.

Siyon took a breath. Let it out. "Going away doesn't mean not coming back, right?"

The dragon didn't answer. She didn't have to. She was living proof that you *could* come back, but that the world you returned to would never be the one you left. Not really.

Then again, *you* wouldn't be the same either. Hadn't Siyon felt it himself, on the streets of Dockside? Maybe you couldn't outgrow a place until you had the room to do so.

"All right," Siyon said. "All right. Let's go."

The dragon turned an eye on him but needed no further prompting. She shifted, getting her feet more firmly beneath her, talons gripping deep into the rock. Her wings flared out again, held ready. The shadows she cast solidified somehow, deep as the darkness of the caves beneath the city. The very tilt of her neck, ruff spikes glinting colour, was expectant.

She was so much bigger, so much realer, than she'd ever seemed in his visions and dreams. So much bigger *here* than out in the wilderness.

Another twang sounded, and the ballista bolt scraped past the edge of the crag, clattering off the rocks. It shocked Siyon into motion, hurrying along her side, to where she'd cocked a foreleg. Before he could think himself out of it, he *climbed up the dragon*. He had to jump to grab at one of the curved spikes on her shoulder, scrambling at her flank to get up onto her back, settling uncomfortably between the knobs of her spine.

When she straightened, he slipped, bumping down between her shoulders, where he grabbed at the spikes at the base of her wings to hold himself steady. There was a little hollow here, when she flared her wings out, almost sheltered by the massive bunch of her muscles. Siyon could kneel here, and hold on, and peer over the sweep of her wing.

The view was terrifying. He was so high. He was *on a dragon*. She bunched her muscles beneath him, all power and promise, ready to launch.

"I'm sorry," Siyon called. "That it's taken me so long."

Amusement hummed through the body beneath him. *Barely a blink.*

And he supposed, to her, it was. Siyon could feel her satisfaction that he was here now. That they could launch together upon their next adventure, whatever it may be.

Her wings spread, barbed and massive.

Siyon swallowed. "I'm also frightened," he admitted.

The amusement this time was sharper, brighter, and yet warm and enveloping; it wrapped around him like a bronzed blanket. *Of course you are; you're not a fool.*

He barked a laugh. "Could you tell that to some—"

She took off, pushing up in a violent rush, and words fell away from him.

One leap up into the sky, one massive beat of her wings pushing them higher as Siyon's stomach dropped away behind. She clawed at the air, and for a moment it felt as ungainly and unnatural as flying with Laxmi had.

Then the wind caught in her wings, and they were gliding, shooting away from the crag, swooping down over the city again. The last time Siyon might lay eyes on it, and he felt a pang—less for the city, and more for the people he was leaving behind. He would miss them. He wished he could take them with him. He wondered if Izmirlian had felt this way too.

The dragon tilted her wings, and they were flying straight for the edge of the city, the bronze bubble rising in front of them, coming at them too fast for Siyon to raise a hand, to sharpen his intent, to even think—

It popped around them like a laundry bubble chased by a curious child, hanging just as scintillating in the air for a moment, all rainbow sparks and the echo of absence.

Something shattered in Siyon—something safe and known, that had reassured him without his even being aware of it.

But he knew this sensation. He'd felt it before, hauling himself out of the river on the lower city side, with everything he'd known left behind.

Siyon had made his life—made him*self*—anew then. Found so much more than he'd imagined.

As Bezim fell away behind them, Siyon turned his eyes forward to the horizon ahead. And they flew like an arrow, like a little paper boat on a wave of burnished power, flooding out into the world.

Toward all the possibilities that awaited.

CHAPTER 29

The celebration had long since boiled over from the old hippo-drome. As the sun settled low on the horizon, Anahid walked slowly through streets that felt as fizzing and sticky as djinnwine, bub-bling with jubilation. She'd left her headscarf behind, securing Zagi-ri's injured arm again, and no one mistook her for an azata or felt the need to moderate their behaviour. Half the city seemed inclined to swagger and boast as though *they* had called challenge for Bezim's future, down on the sands of the arena.

But that was the power of what Zagiri had done. She *had* stood for all of them. She'd called their challenge. They'd all faced down the Council, and won when it gave ground.

When *Avarair* gave ground. After years of doing her best to not give the eldest Hisarani son a second thought, Anahid found herself wondering what would become of Avarair now. He had thoroughly scuttled his career with the Pragmatics. Not that it mattered to her. After the possibilities opened up by today's events, there would be more than enough jostling and rearranging with the District and the barons; Anahid wouldn't have any time to pay attention to the Avenues.

Nothing was decided, of course. Not in a single day. It might be months of argument over every single detail before the scope of the new Council seats was determined, let alone any selection processes for who would occupy those seats. The election for prefect would still need to be held, though surely Buni Filosani's role in the victory today had tipped expectations firmly in her favour. The barons, Anahid suspected, would be pleased with how things had gone.

Every step firmed the ground beneath Anahid's feet. Solidified the arrangements she'd made in the District, turning a hasty and desperate tangle into a proper weaving. The longer they settled together, the harder it would be to tease them apart again. A new agreement between the barons and the city would be negotiated, and it would be sealed with some manner of Council involvement. Each step would drag all of them closer and closer to respectability. Perhaps not Mama Badrosani, nor even her sons, but one day they'd be barons no longer. They'd govern, rather than threaten. Conversations over tea, rather than the knife.

Anahid had won, even if there was much more to do. It might just take the rest of the city longer to realise and make their peace with it.

But now the sun was setting, and the District would be opening soon. She had a House to manage.

She turned her steps downhill, squeezing between knots of celebration and merry-making. That last flash of fear—when the dragon had swooped down off the crag and winged across the city—seemed to have been entirely forgotten.

Not by Anahid. Not the sharp stab of primal unease that had hunched her shoulders and sent her into a crouch. Not the melancholy that had settled over her as the dragon flew away, dwindling into the distance.

She looked again now, along the wide street that ran to the southwest. As though she might still be able to see the black speck of the dragon on the sunset-stained horizon. As though she'd come back *again*, with the city's ballistas still pointed at the sky.

Anahid might never see such glory again, as a dragon soaring over the city. Of course, with everything that Siyon had reawoken, she was quite sure there'd be plenty of new wonders.

What there wouldn't be was Siyon.

Somehow she'd known, watching the dragon fly, that Siyon went as well. There had been no sight of him in the dragon's awful claws, nor in those narrow, lizard-like jaws, but then again, was Siyon still so tangible as to be carried? Had he *become* the dragon? Could Anahid even comprehend what he might be capable of? She'd barely comprehended the way he'd loomed over the hippodrome, massive in apparition, his hand extended as though in blessing.

Or, perhaps, farewell.

He might not be quite human anymore, but he was still her friend. Strange to think that Anahid had only known him for half a year. He'd changed her life. Or, perhaps more accurately, she'd changed her life, with his support.

This was *an* end, but not *the* end. Anahid had lived before Siyon, and she'd live even better for having known him.

Anahid smiled, standing there at the intersection, with the crowds singing and laughing and dancing and drinking all around her. "Maybe we'll meet again," she said beneath the hubbub.

"Who?" a man asked, just behind her.

Anahid whirled around, and Vartan Xhanari took a step back, an apologetic wince on his face and his hands raised.

He looked surprisingly well, for the last few days of chaos, in which—Anahid knew from Zagiri—he had been working nearly as hard as she had been, out on the streets at all hours, keeping them as close to order as had been feasible. Vartan wasn't wearing grey, but rather that red shirt that had always suited him so well, beneath a plain brown coat. His hair had grown out a little, enough to show that it lay flat against his skull as no azatani's did. But it suited him, as did the shadow of a beard that was growing in along his cheek and jaw.

His wince twisted into a self-deprecating half-smile. "Not me, obviously."

He said it lightly, but Anahid thought he had, actually, hoped she'd been thinking of him, as he'd approached her in the midst of all this levity. Anahid felt a little bad about that; it was not really his fault that she'd scarcely thought of him at all in the last half-season.

"You look well," she said, only the truth. "Zagiri mentioned you had cast aside your badge." And Anahid had scarcely believed it.

He tugged his coat unnecessarily straight and smiled faintly. It was a handsome expression on him. It always had been. "I thought there were things that were right and true, unquestionably. Having to question all of them was...uncomfortable."

But he hadn't flinched from it. He'd confronted them and reached a decision, be it ever so drastic. Anahid couldn't say she was surprised. That was the sort of man he was. He'd been unafraid to stalk his duty through the Avenues. He'd been unafraid to dig into the business of the barons. Of course he'd walk away from the inquisitors, if that seemed right.

"I don't want to intrude," he added, "but when I saw you, I thought...I just wanted to...wish you well."

Anahid tipped her head to one side, considering him. Of course he knew what she had wrought—he might be the only member of the Special Crisis Task Force actually paying attention to what was happening in the baronies. And now he was wishing her well?

Fleetingly, Anahid wondered what Laxmi would make of him; she'd probably delight in getting her fingers at every one of his ticklish points. With a smile blooming, Anahid found herself saying, "Are you waiting for me to offer you a new job?"

Worth it, for the widening of his eyes, for the sudden if brief flush in his cheeks, for the straightening of his already upright posture. "I hardly think that—" he began stiffly, and then seemed to realise: "You're teasing."

Rather more that she'd been testing the table to confirm her suspicions about the cards in his hand. "I was. I'm sorry, Vartan. If you wanted to save me from this life, you're much too late."

His mouth twitched; she'd called him out. But to his credit, he inclined his head. "I think I always was."

He'd said to her once that it would be a very foolish person who underestimated her. And while Vartan Xhanari was many things, he was not a fool.

"But," Anahid said lightly, "I do hope you'll be keeping me on my toes." At his confused glance, she smiled. "Come, in the Bezim that will be remade from tomorrow onward, there will be a need for the administration and enforcement of the new laws. Are you telling me you're going to leave that to others?" She lifted an eyebrow. "After how that worked out this time?"

He considered her with an expression that others may have termed stony, but Anahid knew him better. Could see the faint wry tug at the corner of his mouth, and the flicker of interest in his eyes. "I won't do as you ask, you know."

"You never did," Anahid pointed out. And now, after everything, she could smile about that, bitter but also sweet. The past had now passed. And the future...

This future might be fun. Anahid caught herself, in the act of squashing down that thought, that impulse that flickered wicked as a flame. She kept it, instead, tucked away in a corner, even as she nodded her farewell and turned away from Vartan Xhanari.

The sun had set, and the gloaming stretched over a city burnished and glowing with the brightness of its own celebration. Musicians played on the corner of Sailmaker's Row, and the usually quiet street was thronging with lines of people dancing a merry jig. Bravi sat on the windowsills of the street-level apartments, and those on the floor above as well, beating time against their sabre sheaths as they tossed a flagon of rakia from one window to the next. A wild line of children ran past Anahid, each holding aloft a stick with a glittering pixie skink clutching tight, trailing sparks and motes of magic.

Tomorrow, the work of making the city anew would begin in earnest, but few of those crowding the streets tonight would be involved. The spectacle, though...that, they understood. And that deserved all their prodigious capacity to celebrate.

The Flower district was already crowded, the streets and arcades so thronged that it would have been difficult for anyone to find space to make trouble, had they been so inclined. There would be work to be done here, as well. Anahid's federation was neither so strong nor so large as she'd prefer, but it *would* be. It would work for them all, and take disputes from a business of knives to that of tea and talk. She was going to make sure of it.

409

But that also was work for tomorrow.

Tonight, she ducked and skirted her way through the crowds, until she reached Sable House.

The big black doors were open, and lights glittered in the star jasmine spilling from the window boxes. Lejman himself was at the door, and he greeted Anahid with a faint tip of his head. "Mistress. I hear things went well today."

That was one way of putting it. "Time will tell," Anahid replied. "But I am very hopeful indeed."

The main gaming floor was just as crowded as the streets, and noisy with the clatter of the lottery wheel, the clack of tiles, the cries of the winners and losers at the carrick table. The dining hall was rowdy with toasts to anyone and everything. As Anahid passed, empty glasses hit the table, bottles sloshed their refills, and someone shouted: "To the Sorcerer!"

"The Sorcerer!" they all cheered.

And in the rear yard, a crowd was already gathering, thick and merry, with a barker working them up further, calling for those willing to take on the Harpy—surely there was someone who thought he was man enough!

The Harpy in question waited just inside the rear door, smirking as she bounced on her toes, shaking out shoulders that had been well-oiled beneath her leather armour. She smirked wider than ever to see Anahid and lifted a hand to beckon arrogantly.

Anahid shook her head, staying out of reach. "You'll get me dirty," she said, just to see Laxmi's smirk widen. "But when you're done with your business, come up to the office. I've some interesting things to tell you."

"Have you?" Laxmi considered her, eyes hot as molten honey, and grinned. "Am I going to get to have fun?"

Anahid thought about Vartan Xhanari, about the city that was going to be built, about all the work that was still to be done, in pulling all the baronies grudgingly toward stability. She could feel her own mouth tugging into a smile probably closer to a smirk. "Oh yes," she said. "I think we both are."

When Laxmi grinned, all teeth and delight, Anahid felt the echo of it in her heart.

As the sunset bell rang, the last of the golden sunlight trickled away from the top of the hippodrome wall like the last members of the crowd were draining from the stands. It wasn't empty yet, but it had long ago proven too confined to hold the crowd's reaction to all of the day's events. They'd flooded out into the city, taking the news and the possibilities with them.

Part of Zagiri still felt ebullient about it, held aloft and bobbing by all the things that *could* be, like an empty bottle on the sea.

The rest of her, frankly, was exhausted. Her shoulder ached, even bound tight with Anahid's headscarf, and her body twinged like it was her first week running with Bracken all over again. She felt like that empty bottle, hollowed out of purpose now that all the things she'd been driven by were out of her hands and underway.

Yet she was still here.

The arena floor was scuffed and littered with rubbish—bottles and food skewers, lost headscarves and shoes, a discarded coat and a torn length of skirt. The flotsam left behind by the tide of people who had swamped it in the wake of the Council's momentous membership decision. The bravi had led the wave, of course, leaping down from their perches, sweeping among the azatani, catching Zagiri up to hold her aloft. They'd chanted—not her bladename, which wasn't *hers* any longer, nor any tribe's words, but something new: *Our blade.*

Even now, with the sun barely sinking on the day's events, Zagiri could hear someone lingering in the stands, fiddling with an oud and trying out ways of turning phrases to commemoration. The curve of the stadium carried the sound easily, when there was no crowd to soak it up and drown it out. *The Blade of Bezim*, he'd sung, more than once.

Zagiri wasn't sure if that meant her, or Avarair, or both. Wasn't sure how she felt about any of it.

She sat here, on the edge of the balcony of the noble stands, almost where the registrar had stood to announce their impossible victory.

Legs dangling over the edge, good elbow and chin resting on the lower railing of the balcony, waiting for it to feel more real, less a dream. The jubilation all around her, the handshakes, the curious azatani with their political questions pulled aside by wild bravi insisting they dance.

They'd all gone now, drifting away to celebrate properly, or to make plans. Zagiri wasn't so naive—not anymore—as to think everyone was equally happy about how things had turned out. She hadn't been so caught up in celebrating that she'd missed Rowyani storming out, with a good dozen councillors around him. She didn't think they would simply *stop*.

Maybe that's why she felt so hollow. This *was* a victory. But it was also the beginning of so many new struggles. There would *always* be something to fight. But Siyon was right. They *could* do better. They could choose to be better.

They just had to keep choosing.

"What are you still doing here?" a sharp voice asked.

It made Zagiri smile. She tilted back, twisting until she could see Jaleh Kurit, one demanding hand on her hip and a smile of her own on her lips. "What are *you* still doing here?"

Jaleh came over to lean against the railing next to Zagiri. "Trying to see if I can find any trace of Siyon, actually. That last pass from the dragon seems to have . . . well, I don't know. He'd had us modulating the flow of planar energy, which *had* been strong but volatile, but now it's all smooth as a becalmed sea. I guess he finally figured it out." She sighed, eyes on the sky. "Mayar says he's gone."

Gone fell heavily; Zagiri curled around it, like a body blow. "I don't want him gone." She realised even with the words on her lips how ridiculous it sounded.

Jaleh snorted, but she didn't say any of the things she could have. *That's not our decision, is it?* Or even, *Then you should have tried harder to make this a city he could stay in.* Instead, she sighed, still looking at the sky, streaked with fire and blood slowly fading toward bruise and black. "Better than the alternative."

The alternative. Siyon *here*. Here in a city with a government that had already tried to kill him once. Where he'd always be tangled up in everything, the first port of call for blame and entreaties both. A walking distraction for a city that needed to stand up and solve its own problems.

Much as Zagiri hated it, she had a point. She dragged in a breath, scraping together some sort of perspective.

But as she opened her mouth, Jaleh cut in. "I swear, if you say something fucking maudlin like *We'll always have him in our hearts* I am going to push you off this bloody balcony."

It startled a great gulping hiccup of laughter out of Zagiri. "You could *try!*" she shot back, and her voice rang from the empty stands; the oud fell briefly silent. Zagiri blinked, feeling strangely new-woken. Herself, again.

"Oh good, you are actually alive." Jaleh nudged at Zagiri with her toe. "Go and get some rest. There's so much more still to do. But talk to this one first; I don't think he's waiting for me."

As Jaleh walked away, Zagiri twisted around again. Up in the seats of the old noble stand, where the newly commenced Council had been sitting, there was indeed a young man waiting, so quiet she hadn't even noticed until now.

Balian tipped her a very polite nod, perfectly pitched for the younger child of a first-tier family to the younger child of another.

Zagiri clambered somewhat creakily to her feet, a far cry from the easy roll she should have been able to manage, but it *had* been a long day. Her shoulder twinged with the effort, and Zagiri resigned herself to being scolded by a healer when her mother inevitably dragged her back to have it checked yet *again* tomorrow morning. Or possibly, from the sounds of the city outside, tomorrow afternoon.

The shadow deepened over the noble stand, but there were faint pearlescent strips of light running along the base of the seats, some last remnant of pre-Sundering alchemical work. They painted Balian in pale stripes from odd angles. He was a mystery, like this.

He often had been. And yet he knew *her* so well.

"I feel like that could have gone worse," Zagiri said.

One corner of his mouth twitched up, or maybe that was just a shift in the lights. "No one died this time," he pointed out, and that was definitely a wince of grief passing over his face, a match for Zagiri's flinch. "I don't mean—"

"No," Zagiri interrupted. "It's fine. Not—*fine*, but…" She shook her head. "It will always have happened. It will always be my fault. I can't make it right. And maybe we will get Bezim to the point where turning myself in will matter. Will get *everyone* who deserves it. But until then, I don't want to forget. I need to remember the price of my mistakes and choices."

Balian just watched her for long moments. The oud player started up again, with the rippling notes of a popular opera aria. Zagiri couldn't remember what opera it was from, but even she knew the tune; something about the desire to wake up as another person.

Zagiri understood wanting to leave behind your own problems, but she'd worked hard to become who she was, thank you very much.

With a faint smile, Balian said, "The price could be steep. From the number of people I've heard speaking about you, they're going to insist on you being a part of this new Council."

He laughed at the face she pulled; such a warm sound Zagiri couldn't help the tug of her own smile. But she still hated the idea. She didn't want to tuck neatly into the system. Every time she'd tried, she'd made a mess of things. She wasn't going to climb over that mess to reach what everyone thought she should want.

He'd started her thinking now. "How is this even going to work?" Zagiri wondered out loud. "A councillor for the bravi? What, all of them? How could they not favour one tribe over the rest?"

Balian shrugged. "That's just one of the things we're going to have to figure out. And probably *keep* figuring out, for the next ten years or more. If being better were easy, after all, you wouldn't have had to beat the city into doing it."

It was true. It was exhausting. It was—just faintly, at the edges of everything else—exhilarating.

Balian smiled. "You are looking forward to it, after all."

He knew her so well.

Zagiri cleared her throat. "And what about you? Back on the trade routes, or are you the face of the next Hisarani generation in Bezim, now that I've kicked your brother's arse?"

He lifted one haughty eyebrow and suddenly looked very much the brother to both Avarair and Izmirlian. "Excuse me? My brother *yielded* to you." But he was smirking as he said it. He added: "I don't know what I do now. There's still so much of the world to see, and yet how am I ever going to best Izmir's explorations? And if I stay here in Bezim, what can I possibly make for myself that won't be overshadowed by the way Avair's name will appear in the history books."

She couldn't believe what she was hearing. "And that's all that matters, is it? Being the biggest and best and most remembered?"

It was only when he smiled up at her, where she'd taken a step closer to loom over him, that Zagiri realised he was baiting her. "What else is there?" he asked.

That was a serious question. She answered it as one. "Making a difference. Making azatani mean what you want it to mean. Choosing who *you* are."

A choice that she might keep making, every day of the rest of her life. That could have felt exhausting, but instead, it seemed a terrible relief.

Balian rose from his chair, the stripes of light falling away from his face, leaving both of them in thick blue shadow. "It occurs to me," he said quietly, beneath the distant song of a celebrating city, and the yearning melody of the oud, "that we've never been properly introduced."

He smiled—that pleasant and genial smile of his, but it was tinged with sadness now, and with fatigue. He held out a hand, in the narrow space between them. "Good evening to you," he said. "I am Balian of the Hisaranis."

The most proper of introductions, like he'd never given before.

Zagiri cleared her throat and set her hand in his to shake. A meeting of equals, children of the first tier. "Zagiri of the Savanis," she replied, and the next polite formula sprang readily to her lips. "Are you undertaking significant endeavours in the coming season?"

His lips quirked, just a little twitch she might never have noticed, when she'd *really* first met him. But she knew him now, at least a little. He still hadn't let go of her hand. "One or two things, yes," he said, bland as politeness. "There's a lot that could still go wrong."

That was putting it very mildly. And yet there was also so much that could still go very right. So much *more* they could do, than had been possible before now.

"Perhaps I can help with that," Zagiri said, matching her tone to his. "It so happens that I have extensive experience in things going wrong."

EPILOGUE

Forests were the most amazing thing Siyon had ever seen. He was used to trees by themselves, in twos or threes, artistic little clumps like larger flowers than would fit in a vase. This was . . . *more*.

So many trees, spilling down the side of one hill and racing up the next, a rippling carpet of whispering green, fluttering and rustling beneath the downdraft from the dragon's wings. And *bright green*, not the deep glossy green of the wintering pines of Bezim, but the thick, sap-drenched green of late summer.

They'd flown so far from everything he knew.

The dragon huffed beneath Siyon's knees and tilted her wings to bring them lower, as though sensing Siyon's fascinated delight—and she almost certainly could, in the same way that Siyon knew she was amused at his wide-eyed naivety, but also simmering with something like pride, for this world she'd flown for centuries, and could now show to him.

They were still growing accustomed to what they were and how they fit together, but some things just *worked*.

The upper branches of the trees tossed and swayed in the wind of the dragon's passage, frothing up like whitecaps on the ocean. And yet not at all like the ocean—the forest looked more like the quilt Siyon had slept beneath in Anahid's house, mounding and flowing in fluffy humps. It looked thick and soft and—

Curiosity and temptation abruptly overwhelmed him; Siyon rolled sideways from the hollow between the dragon's wings, slipped over her ribs, and plummeted.

Wind whisked around him. Siyon whooped—at the thrill, at the world speeding past, at the sudden cramp of panic. He'd thought of the dragon's flight as being low—and for her, it was. But for him, this was still *so high*.

He fell, curling too late into a protective ball, as he crashed into the first layer of foliage. It *wasn't* soft, of course. It was leaves and twigs, whipping and scratching against his skin. It was thicker branches, snapping against his side. It was—

Energy, brightly bronze, congealing on his skin, stretching around him, thick and cushioning. He crashed through the leaf cover, like a caterpillar rolled up in a cocoon of burnished power, bouncing off branches with a dull sensation of impact like the distant memory of a bruise. With each crash and ricochet, he slowed a little, until finally he came to an abrupt halt, wedged in the fork of two massive branches.

Silence descended around him like the last of the falling leaves, as though the forest had been shocked by his sudden entrance.

Siyon started laughing. Breathlessly but helplessly, with his ribs creaking and power leaking away around him, soaking into the branches, dancing away with the leaves. Clear blue sky above him, just starting to fade toward the beginnings of sunset, fringed with leaves on their high branches, waving as madly as though they couldn't believe what had just happened.

He wished Daruj were here, to have leapt with him, to be shaking his head and shouting at Siyon's stupidity or luck or both. He wished Zagiri were here, to compare their falls. He wished for Anahid and Mayar and even Jaleh.

He wished for Bezim. For everything he'd known. For the comfort of the familiar.

It was as sharp and piercing as a ballista bolt. But it flew just as swiftly, through him and away.

The wish for Izmirlian lingered. A softer, more entangled want. Siyon wished Izmirlian were here, yes, but he also missed words on a page. He had his satchel—somehow pulled from memory and thin air the first time he reached for it absently—but it was empty of journals. One evening on a distant beach, awash in the bloody sunset, overcome with wonder, Siyon had tried carving a message with a stick into the smooth black sand. But in the crystal-pale dawn that had followed, his words were still alone and lonely.

The strangest thing was that Izmirlian *felt* closer than ever. So many times Siyon had caught himself turning to comment over his shoulder, sure there would be someone to hear his thoughts.

Perhaps it was just Siyon imagining himself closer to Izmirlian, having taken his own leap into the unknown.

Izmirlian hadn't even appeared in his dreams since Siyon left Bezim. As though the memory were contained in the city. Or as though the dragon drowned him out.

Siyon could feel her, even now—banking into a turn and circling back, grumbling all the way, but the tight knot of her feelings was a complicated bundle, grumpy and amused and proud as the parent of an audacious child. By the time she came back, her shadow sweeping over the forest, Siyon had just about managed to haul himself up to sitting on one of the branches. Climbing trees, it turned out, was entirely different from climbing a building, which didn't flex or sway or have inconvenient twigs sticking out of it just where Siyon wanted to put his hands that then broke off when he tried to use them to pull himself up.

The dragon hovered, a far more ungainly maneuver than the ospreys and gulls made it look; her wings clawed and gulped at the sky, and her talons spread uneasily, like those of an agitated cat.

What was that for? she demanded.

Siyon grinned up at her, turning his good humour and the still-bubbling thrill of his fall on her like an opera spotlight. "Fun."

She huffed, an acrid gust setting the remaining leaves to fluttering. *Now what?*

"Come on in, the water's fine," Siyon called up, just for the faint tickle of her confusion, even as she sorted through all the memories and feelings and context that came with the words in Siyon's mind.

It was a strange way to communicate, this. But they were growing used to it. Growing accustomed to each other.

The dragon stretched her neck, tilting her head in that way she used to look around. *I assume you are still squeamish about travelling by night?*

Siyon shuddered at the memory of that first night, clinging to the spines on the dragon's back with freezing fingers as the blackness whistled past his face, impenetrable and eternal. Her secondhand sight had been no comfort at all.

A little scratching gurgle reached Siyon's ears from above; she was *giggling.*

Very little about this whole business had been quite what he'd expected.

We'll stay here, then. She clawed at the air, tilting off to one side. There was a clearing over there—he knew, from her—where she could land in relative comfort.

"Wait!" Siyon called as she slipped out of his field of vision, behind the trees that all looked the same. "How do I find you?"

This way, she sniggered in his mind, and she was right; he could feel where she was. Could have walked to her in the blackest night or the deepest cavern. Already had.

It took a lot more time than he'd thought it would for Siyon to clamber down—well, mostly *fall* down—from the tree. He limped and battered his way through the forest to the clearing the dragon had found. In one way, he'd been correct: The forest *was* thick as an azatani eiderdown, not just trees but smaller trees and shrubbery and tangling vines and roots downright eager to grab hold of stumbling feet.

When he came staggering into the clearing, knocking one last enterprising branch out of his face, the dragon turned her long snout toward him. Her eyes were as pale as the moon just starting to rise over the trees.

It was probably quite a large clearing, when it didn't have a dragon coiled around it, crushing the eager young saplings and filling the evening air with the green scent of sap and broken wood. She growled out a breath and shifted to tilt one shoulder toward him, with his satchel twisted around one of her spines. It was only then that Siyon realised his stomach was knotted with hunger.

She eyed him sidelong with her star-shaped pupils as he unbuckled the satchel, rummaging in the meagre stores therein. "I know," Siyon said aloud, pulling out a strip of cured meat whose provenance he hadn't asked too closely about; the trading settlement where he'd picked it up had been far too nervous about the presence of the dragon for him to feel comfortable sticking around too long. "I know this isn't necessary. I'm working on it."

It *wasn't* necessary, not eating and, he suspected, not really sleeping either. It was only in retrospect that Siyon realised he hadn't done either in the days that had passed between his execution and his flight from Bezim, and if that had made him feel at all weird, it had been lost in all the *other* weirdnesses. But they were difficult habits to break, his body still tangled up in memories and expectations.

Siyon clambered over the dragon's resting forearm, avoiding the spine at the point of her elbow—or what sort of *seemed* like her elbow, if you didn't think too hard about what was going on with her entire construction. He settled into the little nook between her inner arm and the soft, tiny scales of the side of her neck.

She twitched, like she always did; it was ticklish, this spot, and only on display when she was relaxed like this. Usually, her ruff of spines protected the area. If Siyon lay his head against her scaled skin, he could feel the warmth beneath the air-chilled scales, and hear the thundering multi-rhythmed flow of her blood.

It was only then, as he relaxed against her, chewing at the meat, that he remembered: "Didn't we pass a town, earlier? On the edge of the forest? Should we be lingering?"

Villages were one thing; small enough to present no threat, and usually willing to be flexible for a little trade or novelty. Towns were different. Towns were enough people together for them to start pooling their courage and their fear, until it became a problem.

Siyon wasn't sure they *could* be killed, not with all the power of the Mundane running through the world around them. He'd just fallen off a dragon into a forest and not even been injured. But there was no point being an idiot about things.

Dark, the dragon pointed out, slow and sleepy, and yet the word came with all the connotations and extrapolations she wrapped around it—that Siyon wasn't the only human who preferred not to be out in the unknown world at night, and especially if they'd been *seen* flying past the town, the people inside would likely take the night to work up their courage before they came out to find such a fell and awful beast.

They'd be safe, for tonight, and that was enough. They had centuries, perhaps. They were taking it one day at a time. Every day a discovery.

Siyon lay back against the dragon's neck as she went to sleep, or at least slipped into a sort of doze where her consciousness spread out, wide and intangible as the very power of the Mundane itself. Part of Siyon went with her, fine as mist and just as hard to grasp. The sensation of it settled inside him, a comfort like home.

Almost like. This wasn't *quite* right. He could feel it. In the slow rumble of the dragon beside him, in the warm wash of the power around him, there was still a gap. Something wanting.

Siyon had felt this before and not known what it was, how to get it, where to start looking. But tonight, as though the wild rush of his fall into the forest had scrubbed him clean, Siyon felt a thread of connection. Something that might always have been there, just lost under too much other noise.

He turned aside from his first impulse. He didn't *reach*, didn't stretch out, didn't go looking *elsewhere*. This was carried with him; the whole of the Mundane was carried with him. He could just...tip sideways, like he had off the dragon's back—

"Well, *finally*."

Siyon gasped, because he *knew* that voice; had heard it in his mind so often with inken words beneath his fingers, longing to hear it with his ears.

He gasped, and the air of the forest didn't catch in his lungs, and the rustle of the leaves wasn't clouding his hearing, and the feel of the dragon around him was still there, but *there* was different now.

Siyon opened his eyes, not here, and not nowhere, but *somewhere else*. There was a faint greyish light, and a distant murmur of other voices, and muted colours shifting at the edges of his vision. Siyon had no attention to spare for any of it.

Izmirlian stepped closer, all Siyon could see, like his eyes were parched and now drinking their fill. He looked just the same—clear brown eyes filled with joy, and his hair loose and just a little too long, and a knowing smirk twisting that clever mouth.

"I thought we'd never find a way," Izmirlian murmured, and his fingers twined between Siyon's, gripping tight. "I thought I was going to lose you so many times."

Siyon blinked, and he was still here—*Izmirlian* was still here—and everything was gaining more clarity around him, as though every moment he spent here poured more energy into it, sharpening the edges with burnished Mundanity. He could still feel the dragon, in his mind and against his back. That was real; *this* was also real.

We know about you and the impossible.

But his best and brightest impossibility had always been Izmirlian Hisarani.

Siyon pulled Izmirlian closer, almost terrified to touch and yet unable to resist. Izmirlian's cheek bunched in a smile beneath Siyon's fingertips. He no longer smelled of sandalwood and orange blossom, much as his journals hadn't, removed from their usual environment, taken on new adventures. Now his skin smelled sharp and strange, like mist and alchemy and other things Siyon couldn't find words to explain.

"I have so much to show you," Izmirlian murmured, lips barely a whisper away from Siyon's own. "I never thought I'd be able to. I never thought there'd be a chance. And yet...I never stopped hoping."

Siyon had thought this a weakness. Had thought he needed to let go to move forward. As though he didn't carry with him everyone and everywhere and everything he had ever known. As though Izmirlian—in memory or in person or whatever strange possibility this was—hadn't carried him as well, even as he leapt joyously into the next discovery.

Siyon trailed fingers up Izmirlian's neck, pushed them into his hair. As he had, so few times. As he'd imagined, so many more. His fingers snagged against a tangle, and that was the final perfection; a note of utter reality.

He tugged Izmirlian forward, into a kiss. *That* was real too, with an ungainly bump of noses until they settled together, lips parting, breath sighing, Izmirlian's teeth catching a moment in Siyon's lip.

He could do that again, and again. He could fall dizzy into forever. But Siyon pulled back a little, breathing hard from just one kiss. "What is this?" he asked, holding on tight. "What are we doing here?"

Izmirlian smiled. "Whatever we want."

His smile was different—brighter now, without that edge of bitter sarcasm. Still sharp, but now gleaming with a new promise, unfettered by disappointments. *He'd* changed, as much as Siyon had. He was a revelation all his own.

Like a forest, spread out beneath Siyon. Like curiosity and temptation. Like centuries of discovery and worlds at their fingertips.

With a laugh, and Izmirlian in his arms, Siyon leapt.

ACKNOWLEDGMENTS

This book was written on the traditional and unceded lands of the Wurundjeri Woi Wurrung of the Kulin nation.

What a dream come true to be here, at the end of my first published fantasy trilogy. Bright and bratty teenage Dee absolutely knew she'd be here one day; older and wiser Dee understood just how unlikely it was. A lot of luck and help got me here, and I'm so grateful.

I've been lucky in my parents, who encouraged me to read (even when it got in the way of family holidays) and play with language.

I've been lucky in my husband, Anthony, who's always cleared space for me to write, even when our lives were cluttered and tangled and this outcome seemed an impossible dream. (And who's been patient and helpful as I messed up first chemistry and then law.)

I've been so lucky in my wonderful agent, Kurestin Armada, who never stopped believing in Siyon, Anahid, and Zagiri. We're so far from where we started; what a journey!

I've been amazingly lucky to work with the entire Orbit team, both in the US and the UK, but especially with Nivia Evans and now with Tiana Coven, whose insight and enthusiasm have energised me beyond words.

I was extremely lucky to have a cover artist like Stephanie Hess and a map artist (and bravi model!) like Sámhlaoch Swords.

And I have been very, very lucky to reach readers whose enjoyment of the Burnished City has been absolutely uplifting. Your delight, your shouting, your thoughtful reviews, and your excessive punctuation have kept me warm in the cold and twisty places of trying to make this an ending worthy of your eyes. You are the Zagiri and Anahid to my Siyon; I couldn't have done this without you. Thank you so much for coming with me!

extras

orbit

orbit-books.co.uk

about the author

Davinia Evans was born in the tropics and raised on British comedy. With a lifelong fantasy-reading habit and an honors thesis in political strategy, it was perhaps inevitable that she turn to a life of crafting stories full of sneaky ratbags tangling with magic. She lives in Melbourne, Australia, with two humans (one large and one small), a neurotic cat, and a cellar full of craft beer. Find her online at viscerate.com.

Find out more about Davinia Evans and other Orbit authors by registering for the free monthly newsletter at orbit-books.co.uk.

if you enjoyed

REBEL BLADE

look out for

THE LAST HOUR BETWEEN WORLDS
The Echo Archives: Book One

by

Melissa Caruso

Kembral Thorne is spending a few precious hours away from her newborn, and she's determined to enjoy herself at the year-turning ball. But when the guests start dropping dead, Kem has no choice but to get to work. She's a member of the Guild of Hounds, after all, and she can't help picking up the scent of trouble. Especially when her professional and personal nemesis, notorious cat burglar Rika Nonesuch, is also on the prowl.

At the heart of the mayhem is a mysterious clock that sends the ballroom down into strange and otherworldly new layers of reality every time it chimes. As the party plunges through increasingly dangerous versions of their city, Kem will have to rely on her wits — and Rika — to unravel the mystery before catastrophe is unleashed on their world.

REST WHEN YOU CAN

It's easy to fall into the wrong world.

It happens most often to children. Their grip on reality is loose to begin with, and when their imaginations wander, sometimes body and soul will follow. I've seen it happen. One minute the kid is there, playing in the dirt and whispering to themselves, and the next they've slipped down into an Echo. You have a tiny window, maybe five seconds, where they go a little transparent around the edges; if you spot it in time and you're fast, you can catch them. Otherwise someone like me has to go in after them, and that's dangerous work.

Adults can fall between worlds, too, though it's rarer. If you stumble into a spot where the Veil is frayed or torn, you may suddenly find that all the familiar things around you have gone strange and wonderful. Since Echoes are confusing, you might not be sure when it happened or how to get back.

Echo retrievals were always my favorite part of the job. In my years as a Hound, I'd rescued dozens of lost kids and a good handful of adults. I was the only active guild member with a perfect success record. When I brought them back home through the Veil between worlds, they all got this same dazed look at first—as if wandering through bizarre reflections of reality had changed them, and it seemed impossible that the world they'd left behind was still the same.

I felt a bit like that now. Two months at home with a newborn wasn't *quite* like falling into another world, but I'd had almost as little contact with my old life. Being out in public at a party surrounded by people felt strange as a half-remembered dream.

I haunted the buffet like a ghost of myself, stuffing candy-sweet grapes into my mouth more out of nervous reflex than hunger. I only had a few hours of freedom, so I had to make them count—but blood on the Moon, I'd forgotten how to talk to people.

It would be easier if Marjorie's year-turning party wasn't so... stuffy. Dona Marjorie Swift was on the Council of Elders, and her social peers packed the ballroom: the solid, serious merchants and bankers of the class that ruled the great city-state of Acantis, dressed in elegant tailed jackets or pale puffy gowns, all of them striving to impress. One of their pocket handkerchiefs probably cost more than my entire outfit, even counting my Damn Good Boots (a precious find, knee high in soft leather, practical *and* stylish). This was the first time I'd been able to squeeze back into them after my feet had swelled up so much while I was pregnant.

I searched the room for familiar faces, but it was hard to pick them out from the sea of muted colors. You'd think everyone would dress more festively to greet the New Year, but it was still the Sickle Moon for a few more hours, and that meant sober restraint was fashionable— so, drab colors and under-seasoned food. Not that I could complain; I'd been eating odd scavenged scraps since the baby came, with no time to cook or go to the market. I could hope Marjorie would break out more interesting fare after midnight. Some of the more fashion-able partygoers would have brought a sparkling white Snow Moon gown to slip into when the year turned, or a jacket that reversed to flash silver and crystal in the lamplight. I might get about one hour of a livelier party before I had to go home.

Still. It was a party, and I was here. Without the baby. Which felt more than a little like magic.

I'd hoped to see some of my friends from the Hounds, but the one Hound I glimpsed was Pearson, who only talked to me when he had a mission to assign. There were a few members of other guilds around; they might be my best bet. The guilds didn't care how much money you had or what quarter of the city you hailed from, only what you could do. I spotted a couple of Butterflies—a well-known actor in a silky cape talking to a friend who defied stodgy Sickle Moon fashion with his vivid iridescent eye makeup—and a vaguely familiar shaggy-haired youth with some kind of guild tattoo on their hand, maybe a Raven.

And...shit. There was Rika.

She'd cut her black hair along her jawline, but I'd recognize her anywhere. I'd seen that wiry back disappearing through windows or over walls too often. Been too late to stop those slender fingers from plucking some priceless object from its protections one time too many. Her gown was all smoke and silver, draping around her like she'd only just formed in this layer of reality from one of the Deep Echoes.

Rika was no Hound, sworn to guard and protect and seek and find. She was a Cat, light and nimble, velvet and hidden steel, and she was trouble.

She'd been chatting with an older woman in a violet gown, but she broke off, rubbed her arms, and glanced around as if she felt someone watching. Before I could look away, her grey eyes caught mine across half the ballroom.

Once she might have slipped me a wink or a wicked smile—but it was the first time we'd seen each other since the Echo Key affair. The usually mischievous bow of her lips flattened, and she turned back to her conversation.

The slice of cheese I'd just grabbed crumbled in my fingers. I wasn't ready for this. Not now, when I was a sleepless mess of under-baked feelings. There was too much I'd been trying not to think about before I went on leave to take care of Emmi, and Rika was at the thick of it.

Why was she here? Rika would never come to a party this rarefied for fun. She must be on business. And that meant she was here to spy, or to steal something, or maybe even to kill someone, though I'd never heard of her doing blood work. I had to tell Pearson. I had to figure out what she was up to. I had to—

No. I was on leave.

I'll take Emmi, my sister had said. *Go to the party. You need to get out of the house. But I'd better not hear about you doing a lick of work, or I swear to the Moon I'll put hot pepper powder in all your tea.*

I was here to have fun. To talk to people. Right.

It would be nice if I had any idea how to do that anymore. Socializing was a mysterious activity that Past Kem had done, irrelevant to Present Kem, who primarily existed to make milk and desperate soothing noises. Sure, a few of my friends from the Hounds had come by in the first week or two to meet the baby, some of them bringing gifts of varying appropriateness (my old mentor, Almarah, had been excessively pleased to give Emmi her first dagger, never mind that it'd be years before she could use it), but after that . . . well, it had been pretty lonely.

Apparently my sister had been right when she said I needed to get out of the house. It was unfair; no one that bossy should be right so much of the time.

I nibbled my cheese and wished I could drink. But my sister said the wine would get into my milk and be bad for Emmi, so that was out. I'd have to remember how to make words *and* say them to people all on my own.

"Kem. Hey, Kem. Didn't expect to see you here."

It was Pearson. He had a rumpled, worried look, all stubble and shadows. There was only one thing that ever meant.

"I'm not working." I gave it a bit of emphasis in case he'd forgotten. "I'm allowed to go to parties."

"Right, right." He laughed, as if I'd made a joke, and took a sip from his wineglass. "Listen, do you want a drink? Can I get you something?"

"Can't," I said shortly. "Nursing."

He blinked at me like some sad owl, and I relented a bit. "How are the Hounds doing?"

Pearson leaped on the opening. "It's not the same without you. We've got lots of good people, everyone's great, but nobody like you."

I grunted. "No one who can blink step, you mean."

"Well, yes, but also not much experience on hand at the moment. A lot of our best are on assignment outside the city." He licked his lips. "So, you know, I was wondering—"

"Did you see me on the active roster, Pearson? No. Because I have a baby, remember? Small, potato-shaped human."

"Right, of course, of course." He said it in the vague way you might acknowledge the existence of hippogriffs, or some other animal found in distant lands you'd only seen in woodcuts. "Motherhood. Splendid. Only we've run into something that looks like it might be big—just hints, but maybe some kind of power game stirring in the Deep Echoes—and we've got no one available with much Echo experience, so of course I thought of you." He flashed a tentative smile.

I gave him a flat stare. "It can't be urgent, or you wouldn't be at a party."

"Probably not, no," he agreed quickly. "So you could look into it in your spare time."

"My spare time." I rubbed my forehead. "You're not a father, are you."

"No, no." He seemed alarmed at the thought. "A bit damp, babies. And loud, I'm told. Not really my area of expertise."

"All right then, let me explain to you in four small words." I raised four fingers and then folded them down, one after another. "I. Am. On. *Leave*."

He sighed, and his shoulders drooped. "Can't blame me for trying."

"I suppose not." I lowered my voice. "Did you know that Rika Nonesuch is here?"

"Really?" He was good enough not to peer around openly, but his eyes darted about the room. "She's bound to be up to no good."

I shouldn't ask. It was too much like work. But I couldn't help myself. "Any idea what she might be after?"

Pearson scratched his chin thoughtfully. "Could be looking to rob Dona Swift. Or to spy on the other City Elders—I think there are three of them here. Or she could be after the clock."

"Clock?"

He tipped his head toward the far end of the ballroom. "This supposed antique grandfather clock Dona Swift bought off a sketchy dealer. You only have to look at it to know it's not from *this* layer of reality. Could be a good fake, but I'd bet cold money it's from an Echo."

"That's just what we need." I shook my head. "Well, good luck. I'm not going to go finding things out on purpose, because I'm not working, but if I hear anything useful, I'll let you know."

Pearson nodded. "Thanks. Can't wait to have you back, Kem."

I grunted noncommittally as he moved off. There was no sense letting him know how comments like that currently plunged me into a whole inner crisis. Of course I wanted to go back to work; I missed the Hounds, missed seeing my friends, missed the excitement of a challenging mission and the satisfaction of a job done well. Stars, I missed just getting to walk around the city without a fussy baby strapped to me. But I also couldn't imagine leaving Emmi. I hadn't been away from her for an hour and it already felt *weird* to have my arms empty, as if part of my body were missing. I missed her funny little face, her wide wondering eyes, her tiny grasping fingers.

At the same time, damn. *Damn.* I could do what I wanted, and nobody was depending on me for every single little thing. I was just myself again, existing only for myself, for these few hours at least. I felt light and giddy, as if someone had untied heavy weights from my arms and legs.

Now, if only I knew what to *do* with all this freedom.

Dona Marjorie swept toward me with the inevitable momentum and grace of a galleon in full sail. Acres of suitably subdued forest-green skirts puffed around her, sleeves and bodice trimmed with modest ivory lace; emeralds winked with a splash of cheeky color in the tower of elaborately coiled and woven braids of her iron-grey hair. Her round brown cheeks beamed, dark eyes sparkling. She always seemed so genuinely happy to see me, and I never could tell for sure if that was because I'd saved her son's life or because she was just an absolutely delightful sugar puff who loved everyone. Probably both.

"Signa Kembral!" She threw her arms wide; I accepted her hug, a little embarrassed, as her voluminous skirts enfolded me. "I'm so glad you came. How's little Emmelaine? Is she sleeping?"

"No," I said, letting two months of despair come through a bit. "Not so you'd notice."

Marjorie shook her head. "Oh dear. Do you want me to send someone over to take her for a while so you can rest?"

"She screams like she's on fire every time I leave the room, and I doubt I could sleep through that, but thanks for the offer."

"Well, you just relax and enjoy the party, then." She patted my arm, then dropped her voice nearly to a whisper. "I'm glad you're here tonight. Just in case."

"What does *that* mean?"

Marjorie laughed, lifting her painted nails to her lips as if I'd made a slightly off-color joke. "Oh, you know, politics always get a little intense at the year-turning, that's all. Everyone's all fired up to charge out the gate with new legislation and new alliances as soon as it turns from a Sickle Moon to a Snow Moon, and the knives are out. It's good to have level heads like yours around. Don't you worry about it—focus on having a lovely night!"

My smile slipped from my face as she moved on to greet her next guest, her voice rising in welcome. *Great.* My first time in public in two months, and I'd picked a night when Dona Marjorie expected "politics" to get so wild my skills might be needed—and I doubted it was because she wanted a third at tiles. Maybe I should have worn my swords.

Suddenly a low, harsh, brassy music jarred the ballroom. It shook deep into my bones, reverberating in my teeth, seeming to come from the air itself. Just a handful of notes, each a deep *bong* like a punch to the stomach—and then silence.

A hush fell over the gathering, the kind that comes when a large number of people all hold their breath at once.

The clock. That had been the simple melody the city bells played before tolling the hour; it must be the grandfather clock Pearson had mentioned. He wasn't kidding about it being from an Echo, with a chime like that.

The whole party waited, but no hour rang. The room's other and more mundane clock, a marble antique on the mantel, still showed about ten minutes shy of nine o'clock in the evening.

A smattering of nervous laughter rose up, like a handful of pigeons taking flight to the ballroom's high ceiling. The murmur of conversation swelled back into its usual busy clamor, everyone no doubt telling one another *Oh, it's just the clock.*

I resisted the urge to go look at it. That would be too much like work. If it were dangerous, I'd feel obliged to do something about it; if it presented a puzzle, I couldn't resist trying to solve it. No, I absolutely should not cross the ballroom, weaving between partygoers with one muttered *Excuse me* after another, waving away a servant offering a tray of drinks, nudging an errant chair aside with a swish of my peacock-tail scarlet coat. The last thing I wanted to do was lurk around waiting for the crowd drawn by its disconcerting chime to dissipate, giving me a clear view of it at last. And under no circumstances should I approach it so close that my breath misted on its glass face, staring at it in fascination.

Fine. *Fine.*

I could see what Pearson had meant. The basic shape of it was dignified enough, a grandfather clock with a cabinet of shining dark wood, its round face gleaming. But the carvings surrounding the face were twisted and phantasmagorical, with staring eyes and strange creatures climbing and writhing up into a spiked crown. Each number was in a different style and size, some of them crazily elaborate or tilted off-kilter. The three hands formed wickedly sharp spears of shining steel that patrolled the numbers menacingly, threatening them with impalement.

A single fine crack marred the face, running from top to bottom, starting at the number twelve and snaking down like a bolt of lightning. Iridescent colors showed in the silvery ribbon of broken edge embedded in the glass. I reached out, curious, and ran a finger down its length to see if I could feel it.

The glass felt slick and unbroken. But I pulled away a bloody finger.

I cursed and sucked it. *That was stupid, Kem.* What did I think would happen, petting broken glass?

"Well, well. If it isn't Kembral Thorne, in the flesh."

That was the last voice I wanted to hear right now. She'd come up behind me without making a sound, and it was too late to escape.

I forced myself to turn slowly, as if I wasn't surprised, to face my nemesis, Rika Nonesuch.

STAY ALERT FOR DANGER

My traitor pulse flared up, but I squelched the old anticipation before it could flare to life. We were not going to have some duel of wits and spend all evening trading flirty quips as we attempted to outmaneuver each other. That was over.

"Rika." Her bare name was the closest I could come to a cordial greeting, after what she'd done to me.

"Here I thought you'd retired from polite society." Her grey eyes traveled up and down the length of me, as if to assess my current condition, or perhaps my fashion sense.

I was already feeling a bit defensive about both. I'd done my share of recovery over the years—knife wounds, the deeper scars of Echo magic, you name it—but having your abdominal muscles stretched out and your innards squashed for months on end left its own kind of marks, never mind childbirth itself. And I'd discovered to my chagrin when I tried to get dressed for the party that nothing quite fit the same way now that Emmi had deconstructed and rearranged my whole body. I knew damned well I should be in somber Sickle Moon colors like everyone else, but my scarlet Blood Moon overdress had fit best—more of a coat, really, with split peacock-tail skirts going to just below the knee in front and trailing nearly to my ankles in back—so that was what I was wearing. The neckline was, ah, *different* with my milk come in, however, and suddenly I was very conscious of it.

"Not retired," I said curtly. "You're not so lucky."

"That's right. You'll never retire. You're probably back on the job already. Up to anything dangerous tonight?"

Her tone was too bright, its false surface ease covering an intensity beneath. A faint flush touched her cheeks, as if from drink or dancing, and one tendril of dark hair hung artfully awry—but I hadn't seen her dancing, and there was no drink in her hand. What was she up to?

None of my damned business, that's what. Rika Nonesuch was not my problem tonight.

"No. I'm on leave."

"Your idea of a good time on a day off is to investigate some creepy Echo relic?" She shook her head. "You really know how to relax."

It was too like what she'd said right before the star diamond incident. *You need to learn how to relax. How to stop being a Hound for half an hour.* I'd trusted her, like an utter fool. Heat flushed up my neck.

"The last time you told me that, I woke up under a pile of garbage in a tenement cellar."

"Truth comes in a variety of astonishing guises."

I had no patience for her games tonight. "Why are you here, Rika?"

She executed a delicate shrug that set complex shadows to playing across her collarbones. "Do you always know why you do things?"

"Yes."

"Of course you do." She laughed, and there was an odd, bitter edge to it. "I don't know what fever came over me, thinking I should come talk to you, but it's past now. I suppose I should see a physicker if symptoms recur."

I'd been avoiding her gaze, but at that note of hurt I couldn't help a quick glance to see whether it was real.

Our eyes locked together with an almost audible *click*. Tension bracketed hers, grey irises shining with some silent electric message.

If I let myself fall into them, I could read it—the same way we'd once had a whole unspoken conversation across a room in little twists of expression at a boring political event we were both working.

It was so close. Whatever we'd once had, whatever heady combination of rivalry and teasing chemistry and *connection*, it was right there, prickly and alive and waiting just below the brittle surface of hostility, like water rushing beneath a skin of clear ice. I could pretend nothing had happened and slip into our old patterns; I could say something wry and warm and give her a little half-suppressed smile and hope things would somehow snap back to what they once were.

But I was flustered and grouchy and tired, and not ready to forgive her, and feelings were delicate things I no longer understood how to mend.

I covered the tightness in my throat with a scowl. "Fine. Don't tell me. But whatever job brings you here tonight, you'd better not do anything against Dona Marjorie."

"You always assume the worst of me, don't you." Her lips moved, but it wasn't really a smile.

"Hounds always prepare for the worst." I should have stopped there, but my anger at everything she'd thrown away between us surged up and spilled bitterly out of my mouth. "You should know that, after the Echo Key affair."

Rika's face went flat as a slammed door. *Whoops.* That might have crossed a line.

Cats weren't supposed to be caught. That was, in fact, the entire point of the Cats. Sometimes they helped the downtrodden secure justice they couldn't find within the law; mostly the city's elite hired them for steep fees to sabotage, steal from, or spy on one another—all the sort of tasks they didn't want sticking to their reputations, like mud on a fine silk cravat.

This meant Hounds and Cats had more of a direct rivalry than any of the other guilds. It was often a Hound's job to stop a Cat from fulfilling her mission, but as a professional courtesy it was pretty common to do so without actually *catching* her. Especially if they had a long history of doing each other small, thoughtful favors when they weren't striving to thwart each other—like returning a glove the Cat had dropped fleeing a burglary scene, or picking a lock so that a tired Hound on duty could get out of the rain. Or leaving each other little teasing notes if they were working the same building, or rescuing each other from annoying people at parties. In short, if they were friends.

Which, after the star diamond incident, we most certainly were not. So there was no reason I should feel a sudden rush of guilt, no matter *how* her face looked.

"I see." Rika's voice went sharp, losing all its usual silky richness. "That's how you're going to play this? Fine. I won't coddle you anymore."

She turned on her heel and stalked off.

I'd never once felt *coddled* in the presence of Rika Nonesuch. Either I'd scored enough points in our new enmity that she was taking the gloves off, or I'd been an asshole for no good reason and should go back home, curl up in a ball, and give up on talking to people ever again. By the sinking feeling in my stomach, I had an awful suspicion as to which it was.

A great shattering crash splintered my thoughts to pieces.

I jumped and reached for my knife. But it was just a drunken guest who'd staggered into one of Dona Marjorie's staff, knocking over a whole tray of glasses. I let out a relieved breath as the inebriated tailcoat apologized with slurred speech, trying to help the poor man—Carter, his name was; I recognized his curling mustache—while he waved the young guest off with far more patience and grace than I could have managed.

My nerves still jangled. Between this and my reaction to an innocent clock chime, I might be a little on edge tonight.

Time to prove that I *did* know how to relax, damn it. I scanned the room in desperation, looking for a friendly face.

A sea of conversation lapped at my ears, nearly all of it in the drawling, refined cadence of old money Hillside or the clipped precision of new money Tower district, which only made me feel more out of place. Laughter rose up above the crowd with the loose, uncontrolled ring of inebriation—everyone sure was drinking like it was a Wine Moon tonight. There had to be *someone* else in that crowd who I knew and liked. Someone uncomplicated and easy to talk to, who wouldn't leave me feeling like a mess of wet knots.

My eyes snagged on Dona Harking, talking to Marjorie over by the wine table. Ugh. He was the opposite of uncomplicated, all venomous elegance and a sparkling veneer of charm. Given what I knew about him—and the worse things I suspected—the only way I ever wanted to talk to the bastard was if it would get me the evidence I needed to land him in prison.

Pearson had made me back off from Harking. *You got the kids back, Kem*, he'd sad. *You did what your client hired you to do; you're not a city investigator. The job is done. Let it go.*

I was no good at letting things go.

Harking's gaze wandered and caught mine across the ballroom. He flashed me his classic wry smile and lifted his glass; I forced a small return nod. It was never a bad idea to maintain a certain level of politeness with City Elders, no matter what you thought of them.

The nod must have encouraged him, because now he was heading in my direction. It was far too late to act like I hadn't noticed and drift away. Every muscle in my abdomen tightened. *Here we go.*

"Signa Thorne," Harking greeted me. "I must say, I'm surprised to see you here."

"That's me," I said through a false smile. "Full of surprises."

He did me the courtesy of a chuckle. "Is this your plan for retirement, then? Attending parties with the city's elite?"

"I'm a bit young to retire." I couldn't keep an edge out of my voice. Leave it to Harking to discover something that annoyed me even more than Pearson assuming I'd come right back to work: assuming I was done with work now that I was a parent.

"So you're staying in the business, then?" His dark eyes glittered, assessing. "Teaching, perhaps? I'm sure there are many who would line up at the chance to learn to blink step."

It wasn't an unreasonable question. A lot of Hounds switched to teaching when they had kids, and to be honest I was considering it. But Harking's tone of breezy assumption made my jaw tighten.

"No, I'm going to keep working in the field." I threw it back at him with far more confidence than I possessed, out of sheer spite.

His lids dropped until his eyes were gleaming slits. "A pity."

"Oh? Because I'll uncover all your sketchy secrets?"

"Not at all." His tone was lazy, unconcerned. "Because a field Hound's work is dangerous, and it'd be such a shame if something happened to you, with your daughter so young."

The bastard was threatening me. He must know or guess how close I'd come to uncovering his crimes, and here he was, standing bold as daylight in Marjorie's ballroom and threatening me, because he was a City Elder and could get away with it. And he *dared* bring in Emmi.

I showed him my teeth. "I'm not worried, Dona Harking. I'm exceptionally hard to kill."

"So I've heard." He swirled the wine in his glass. "Nonetheless, Signa Thorne, a dog with pups ought to be careful where she sticks her nose."

"And a City Elder ought to know better than to try to intimidate a Hound. The guilds protect their own."

"My dear Signa Thorne, whyever would you think I was trying to intimidate you?" There was nothing innocent in the cynical grooves of his face. "It was merely an observation. I'm sure you'd never *dream* of overstepping your guild charter and meddling in city politics, so it's hardly relevant to your situation. Is it?"

And that was the crux of the thing. I couldn't go after him without a client; the balance of power between the guilds and the League Cities was too delicate, governed very precisely by intricate charters. You didn't mess with that. And the city would never investigate him so long as he remained rich and powerful enough to prevent it from doing so.

"Of course not," I ground out. "How nice of you to spontaneously express concern for my hypothetical welfare."

"Good, good. I'm so glad you're sensible enough to know your limits." Harking lifted his glass half an inch in a perfunctory salute. "If you'll excuse me, Signa Thorne, I should give my regards to my fellow Elders."

I glared holes into his back. Oh, I was *not* up to dealing with Acantis politics tonight. I itched to pick up my cold leads from the Redgrave Academy job and follow them right to the heart of all his nasty secrets, but even if I *had* a client, it'd be a while yet before I could go back to work. If I could bring myself to leave Emmi in someone else's care and go back at all.

I was thinking about work again. I rubbed my forehead. *Fun, Kembral. You're here to have fun.* There had to be *one* enjoyable conversation somewhere at this party.

And there she was, water in the social desert: Jaycel Morningray. Poet, duelist, socialite, occasional public nuisance, and an old friend from Southside. She was holding forth to a rapt audience as usual, wineglass in hand, with a loose confidence suggesting that said glass was neither her first nor her last of the evening. I started in her direction; Jaycel was an endless fountain of gossip and witty commentary, and she knew me well enough to understand when I wasn't in the mood to talk. I could let the wonderful sound of adult human words wash over me without any pressure to make them myself.

As I navigated the crowded ballroom toward her, a skittering motion caught my eye.

Something small ran under a table—a mouse? No, it had seemed... *shiny.* I paused, my brow bunching into furrows. Surely I'd imagined that sparkling iridescence, a trick of my tired eyes.

Unease prickled the back of my neck. I reached for the white damask tablecloth.

"Kembral darling!"

Jaycel had spotted me and was sauntering toward me. I straightened with a grin.

She was in fine form, flaunting an intricately embroidered dueling cape that hung dramatically from one shoulder, a gorgeous swept-hilt rapier riding at a cocky angle on her hip. Her short dark curls tumbled around her face in a careless way that seemed to come naturally to Jaycel but that many in the Acantis social circuit spent hours of artifice trying to emulate. There was nothing false in her broad smile at the sight of me, and gratitude surged in my heart at the welcoming sparkle in her eyes.

We'd grown up together in Southside, two kids running around the neighborhood. Mostly she got us into trouble, and I got us out of it, though occasionally we swapped.

"Jaycel. Stars, it's good to see you."

"Look at you!" She clasped both my shoulders, theatrical as always, gazing at me as if I were some precious family heirloom returned at last after being lost for three decades at sea. "You look good. Tired, but good."

"I am *so tired*," I admitted, with probably too much passion.

"Bah! We won't let it slow you down. I'm making it my *mission* tonight to find someone scrumptious to dance with you."

Wait, no. "What?"

She threw an arm around my shoulder, gesturing expansively with her wineglass. "It's a challenge! I know you're choosy, and the pickings tonight are slim, my friend." She shook her head. "But we can do this. *Together.*"

"Are you teasing me? I honestly can't tell."

"No, no, I'm deadly serious, darling. Now, let's see—you're a waxing Cloud Moon, right? A seeker of truth! Too bad Dona Swift has almost thirty years on you; she's a half Compass Moon, the journey and the homecoming both, which would be a perfect match. Ooh, if you're looking to make a salacious mistake—"

"When have I ever done anything salacious in my *life*?"

"—there's Dona Harking." Jaycel bit her lip. "I am deeply bothered by how relentlessly attractive he is."

"*Harking?*" That sent my eyebrows crawling up my forehead. "The man is morally bankrupt."

"Of course he is. That's half the draw." She shook her head. "Oh, I can't explain it to you. It's just—those piercing eyes. That sardonic smile. That *ass*." Her fingers flexed. "Plus, he's great in bed."

"*What?!*"

"Oh, relax. It's not like I married him. Sometimes it's not about personality. Well, for the rest of us, anyway—I suppose it always is for you." She let out an aggravated sigh. "I still can't believe you wound up with *Beryl Cascarion*, of all people, who is a walking set of abdominal muscles with a bit of scruff. You *say* you're not attracted to people that way—"

"I'm not."

"But the man has *no virtues whatsoever* aside from being easy on the eyes. Please don't tell me you fell in love with his mind."

She was drunk, I reminded myself. She was drunk, and not trying to be cruel. "Look, he can be really charming. He made me laugh, he made me feel like I was important to him, he made a fuss over me. It felt nice. I was a fool, all right?"

Jaycel clapped my shoulder. "You're not the first person to make a fool of yourself over Beryl Cascarion, and you won't be the last. At least it wasn't Harking, right?"

"I'm going to have nightmares, Jaycel."

"Oh, if you think *he's* a bad idea, wait until you see my date for tonight! And anyway, you're one to talk about questionable choices, given you're gawking at Rika Nonesuch."

"I'm not gawking." I jerked my eyes back to Jaycel from a certain silver-gowned figure I hadn't even realized they'd been resting on.

"Just keep it to looking." She wagged a finger at me. "Waxing Cloud Moon and waning Cloud Moon don't mix. Truth and lies, darling."

"I don't think you have to worry about that. We're not too fond of each other right now."

That might be an understatement. Though honestly, it wasn't like Rika had wound up in the city jail due to the Echo Key affair—I'd checked, not that I felt bad or anything, but her papers were in order and they'd released her to her guild. Nothing close to the shame and discomfort of waking up on a hard floor under a pile of garbage, with a headache like the Moon's own wounds, panicked over whether the drug she'd slipped me would be bad for Emmi. (It wasn't—Rika was too much of a professional not to take that into account—but *still*.) It had taken me days to get the stink out of my Damn Good Boots. And that wasn't even touching the bone-deep embarrassment of knowing she hadn't meant a thing she'd said to me in the café that day.

Jaycel must have heard something in my tone. She gave me a searching look.

"Something happened between you two, didn't it? Are you all right? Do you need me to punch her?"

I sighed and pushed a loose lock back from my face. I'd tried to put my hair up for the party, but Emmi had cried the whole time I worked on it, so it wound up a bit of a honey-colored mess; I'd left a few tendrils down in the weak hope that people would think I'd been going for "artfully disheveled" rather than "panicked rush job."

"I'm fine. You don't need to punch her. I don't want to talk about it. Or my romantic prospects, for that matter." It sounded brusquer than I meant it to, but Jaycel wasn't the type to read too much into tone. "I had a baby, I'm kind of a mess, and I would like a nice, relaxing, low-pressure night out to..." I trailed off. *To remember who I am* sounded overly dramatic, but really, that was more or less what this was about.

An incredulous noise burst out of Jaycel. "Low pressure! And you came *here*?" She flung an arm over my shoulders. "We're Southside girls, Kembral. Look around you. It's all Hillside aristocrats and rich Tower merchants and bankers. You're at the wrong party."

"Maybe," I allowed ruefully. "Why are *you* here, then?"

"To be seen, of course!" Jaycel gestured expansively. "This is a work night for me. Everyone here is a prospective client. I've got to be entertaining. I've got to make a scene. I've got to *perform*."

"That sounds exhausting."

For a moment, she dropped her sparkling public persona and gave me a look that was three parts tired, one part amused. "You have no idea. I wish I'd had the rockheaded stubbornness to stick with the blink step training like you. You'll *always* have value to them. I have to keep dancing like a trained goat or they'll lose interest, and then I'd better hope my family takes me in, or I'm out on the street."

Jaycel had joined Almarah's class of hopeful apprentices at the same time I had, but like most of the kids there, she liked the *idea* of being able to blink step much more than she liked the reality of dedicating fifteen years of her life to learning it. She'd stayed with it for almost a year out of friendship, which was longer than most of the class managed, and she'd kept walking with me to class for months after she'd dropped out.

I shifted uncomfortably. "Blink stepping is only useful if I can still do my job. It's been a while."

"Bah! You'll be fine. Come on—if you want to enjoy yourself, I'm nearly the only one here who can help you. Try one of the crab puffs, and I'll fill you in on all the gossip from the old neighborhood, since you're all fancy living near the guildhouses now."

I let Jaycel's words wash over me as she chattered about a girl we'd known as kids who was running for the Council of Elders, then launched into a story delighting in the current misfortunes of a boy whose eye she'd blacked for calling me names when we were eight (he'd been rude to an old woman who turned out to be an Echo in disguise and gotten cursed). It was beautiful just to bask in her presence.

It wasn't long before she got distracted by the pair of Butterflies I'd seen earlier, coming to talk to her about fight choreography in their new play. I hesitated, not sure whether I felt up to joining them; I knew swordplay, but I didn't know the Butterflies.

Out beyond the tall windows beside me, something moved in the garden.

I snapped my gaze past the glass in time to spot a figure slipping between the bushes with the swift, furtive motions of someone trying not to be seen. It was there and gone so quickly I wasn't sure whether I'd imagined it.

My senses went alert. I moved closer to the windows, eyes fixed on where the figure had disappeared—if it had been there at all. Sometimes when Emmi really, *really* hadn't been sleeping, I saw stuff like that, and I didn't always trust my senses anymore. No sign of it now.

All right. It was probably nothing, but between the skulking figure and the sparkly mouse (or whatever it had been) and the strange clock, this was starting to get weird.

"Kem. Hey, Kem."

Pearson again, startling the daylights out of me. The man didn't know when to give up—but then, he *was* a Hound, even if more the papers-at-a-desk type than the investigations-and-bodyguarding type.

"This had better not be about that job," I warned him.

"No! No. Well, yes, but no." He pushed on stubbornly, ignoring my best skeptical glower. "I was thinking if you won't take the job, maybe I could just *tell* you about it and you could let me know what you think. Like an advisor. That's not work, right?"

That was damned well work and he knew it. Not least because once I heard about the job, I'd want it—and he knew that, too. But I had to be home in four hours to nurse Emmi, and I refused to waste half the party talking about whatever leaking Echo was causing trouble in the city this time.

"This had better not involve a kid or a dog," I muttered.

"If it did, I would have led with that." Pearson started to laugh, then swallowed it with the guilty wince of a man who suspects he's about to be slapped.

He'd deserve it. "The last lost dog job you gave me took me six Echoes down, Pearson. *Six Echoes.*" One Echo down, fine, that was almost like our Prime layer of reality. Two got strange, three downright surreal—and anything past that descended rapidly through creepy and dangerous into pure nightmare.

Pearson nodded. "The deepest any current Hound has gone and returned alive," he said, with a touch of awe that would have been gratifying if he weren't the one who'd fucking sent me there.

"The river was flowing with *spiders* and the walls were dripping blood," I told him. "I had to run from things with *eyes in their teeth*, Pearson."

"You brought the dog back," he pointed out. "You always bring the dog back, even when anyone else would give up. That's why we send you on those things. But no, this is nothing like that. You shouldn't have to go into an Echo at all. I hope."

"You're right," I said, "I won't. Because I'm not taking the job."

Enter the monthly
Orbit sweepstakes at

www.orbitloot.com

With a different prize every month,
from advance copies of books by
your favourite authors to exclusive
merchandise packs,
**we think you'll find something
you love.**